I0819576

COYOTELAND

ALSO BY

VANESSA HUA

Forbidden City

A River of Stars

Deceit and Other Possibilities

COYOTELAND

A Novel

VANESSA HUA

FLATIRON
BOOKS
NEW YORK

This is a work of fiction. All the names, characters, organizations, places, and events portrayed in this work are either products of the author's imagination or used fictitiously.

Printed in the United States of America. For information, address Flatiron Books, 120 Broadway, New York, NY 10271. EU Representative: Macmillan Publishers Ireland Ltd., 1st Floor, The Liffey Trust Centre, 117–126 Sheriff Street Upper, Dublin 1, D01 YC43.

www.flatironbooks.com

Designed by Leah Carlson-Stanisic

Library of Congress Cataloging-in-Publication Data

Names: Hua, Vanessa, author.
Title: Coyoteland : a novel / Vanessa Hua.
Description: First edition. | New York : Flatiron Books, 2026.
Identifiers: LCCN 2025040590 | ISBN 9781250395511 (hardcover) | ISBN 9781250395528 (ebook)
Subjects: LCGFT: Novels | Fiction | Social problem fiction
Classification: LCC PS3608.U2245 C69 2026
LC record available at https://lccn.loc.gov/2025040590

First Edition: 2026

10 9 8 7 6 5 4 3 2 1

To my

BROTHER AND SISTER

Nothing, like something, happens anywhere.

—PHILIP LARKIN

These people go out onto the street, and walk down the street alone. They keep walking, and walk straight out of the city of Omelas, through the beautiful gates . . . They walk ahead into darkness, and they do not come back.

—URSULA K. LE GUIN

COYOTELAND

1

On move-in day, Jin Chang eased the truck around a blind curve. When three bucks and two spotted doe lurched out of the brush, he slammed on the brakes.

"Dad, watch out!" Jane shouted.

"Don't call me Dad." *Dad* sounded too close to *dead*; he preferred *Daddy*.

At fifteen, Jane was long past using such endearments with him, even though he still referred to her as bao bao, little precious. Only in Mandarin, a tongue she never much used these days, did she allow him this tenderness.

The deer were still as statues, posed before a retaining wall covered in ivy. "It's like we're in a zoo!" she said.

"They're wild animals." Jin wondered why they weren't more skittish, what they ate—and what ate them.

As his daughter rolled down the window, the deer bolted, their hooves clattering like high heels. They leaped past a utility pole and down the hill, crashing through the foliage.

Soon, the Changs would learn that hitting a deer was a rite of passage in El Nido. At night, on the dark and winding roads, in the eucalyptus- and oak-studded hills east of Berkeley, the newly licensed always drove too fast—sometimes a little drunk or high, sometimes a lot—trying to make curfew. The drivers felt invincible, glorious, as only someone sixteen and piloting their parents' minivan, Range Rover, or Tesla can be, right up until they locked eyes with a deer made just as bold by the lack of an apex predator. Both parties caught in the proverbial headlights in the eternal moment before impact.

After pulling into the cul-de-sac, Jin backed into the driveway of their new house, which left no room for his wife, who followed in their sedan with their younger daughter, Lily. He got out of the moving truck and motioned for Kai to park in front of the neighbor's house. At the front door, as Jin fished the key from his pocket, footsteps approached—a stocky blond woman who'd rushed out from her car. It must have been an electric vehicle, almost silent as it glided down the street. Their neighbor had been in such a hurry that she'd parked in the driveway, her car door hanging open. Was that . . . a shark fin on the roof?

She was upon them before he could consider the matter further. "Hi! You're parked in front of our mailbox."

He couldn't tell if shrillness was her natural register, or if she'd raised her voice at them.

"I'm Jin."

She froze, as if realizing she'd committed the American sin of failing to introduce herself. "I'm Blair Belle. Welcome to the neighborhood!" She pointed at the curb. "If there's a car parked there, the mailman leaves a note; he threatens to stop delivering our mail."

"I can move the car," Kai interjected.

Jin held his neighbor's gaze. "Does the mail come on Sundays?"

Her smile faded. "You're right, it's Sunday. Life gets so busy, I forget what day it is."

"Sunday. The twenty-fifth," he said. July.

"What *year* it is," Blair said. "We're so glad that a family's moving in! The agent who repped the seller didn't know much about who was coming. Someone from China, that's all."

"From Fremont," Jane said.

Blair pressed on. "The last owners moved to Arizona. But their kids—their grown kids—treated it like a clubhouse while they were getting ready to sell. We worried they were going to turn it into one of those

SuCasa rentals!" She glanced at the girls. "My daughter Quinn's a fantastic babysitter—well, when she has time. Senior year."

"I'm a sophomore," Jane said.

Jin's eldest was tiny and thin, her hair in twin braids, routinely mistaken for being in the sixth grade or younger. Something flickered across Blair's face: embarrassment, and then anger. Even if she herself was only dimly aware of it.

"I'm in the fourth grade," Lily piped up.

Blair fiddled with her necklace. "You'll be going to school with my other daughter, Jordan. And also with . . ." She faltered. "With Sofía."

"Another neighbor?" Jin scanned the cul-de-sac, the tidy homes with pitched roofs, painted cream and gray and tan, bordered by carefully pruned trees and shrubs.

"My nanny's daughter. My . . . babysitter. Housekeeper. I also have a nine-month-old." Blair seemed to struggle with admitting she had live-in help. Americans could be funny that way. Chinese had no qualms about hiring an auntie from the countryside to clean, cook, diaper, and look after the children. The problem, Jin often told his wife, was that Americans wanted to pretend that class didn't exist, that doing so made everyone equal. Billionaires, barefoot and in blue jeans, even though they could blast off to the moon as they would to the Bahamas. Everyone went by their first name, without regard to the title or degree or manners, as if casualness could unseat an emperor. In truth, people knew where they stood economically, no matter if you were communist or capitalist or somewhere in between.

Blair promised to come by with her girls to say hello. After she disappeared into her house, Jin muttered, "She's like a dog pissing on a tree."

"Be careful. She could make trouble for us," Kai said.

"She's more bark than bite." If Blair was the worst they might encounter, then they would be blessed.

"We have to remember not to park there," Kai said.

"She doesn't own the street in front of her house," he said.

Their argument might have continued if he hadn't opened the front door. Walking in, the family fell into a collective hush. The last time they were here, the house had been staged with furniture with the personality of a motel room. Now emptied, its high-ceilinged expanse seemed to stretch to the very edge of the universe.

❁ ❁ ❁

Two days later, Jin studied a hole in the weathered wooden fence, spotted with lichen. The fanfare of their arrival had now dimmed. Sometime after the final inspection, a rotted slat had fallen through. Maybe the wind last night caused it to break off.

The air was nosebleed dry, and fires had ignited in the forests a couple hours north. It was only a matter of time until the smoke drifted down and blotted out the sun. He should give the fence a shake, to check if anything else had come loose, but he didn't want to add another repair to the long list—slow drains, a gurgling toilet, a sinkhole in the front yard—he'd discovered since they moved in, all of which would be necessary to fix before he put the house back on the market.

He'd found the house for Chen, a classmate he'd known since primary school, whose fortunes had wildly diverged from Jin's. They were best friends from childhood, when they'd been close as brothers, sharing what little they had: a steamed bun, a handful of filched plums. Chen, who lived in Beijing, had heard about run-down properties selling for a profit in a matter of months in the United States. He wanted to flip a house—and Jin, in a moment of desperation, volunteered.

Even though Jin was a software engineer, for years he'd combed through online real estate listings, scrutinized county assessor maps and street views, and analyzed comps in a spreadsheet. Looked for notices of estate sales for houses that might soon come on the market. Regimes rose and fell, but land offered stability, success, status. He'd long had his eye on El Nido, and he'd take care of everything, he told Chen, in exchange for a small commission.

The house at 187 Rinconcito had been priced below market, with a motivated seller.

Jin planned to stay in the house through the end of the school year while preparing to flip it, the value almost guaranteed to rise monthly. He could take care of the minor repairs on his own, with the help of how-to videos. New paint, new carpet, new outlets and bathroom fixtures. By the time the house sold, he'd find another in El Nido to rehab.

It was bigger inside than it seemed from the street, an expanse that felt opulent to Jin. Luxurious. In Fremont they'd lived in a one-bedroom apartment; his daughters slept together on the pullout sofa. Here they could spread out, into the living room, master bedroom, kitchen, and wraparound back deck on the first level, and three bedrooms down a steep flight of stairs, along the hillside that sloped into a ravine. The stairs had been the undoing of the previous owners, who'd become too frail to navigate them or to maintain the house, with its old appliances in avocado and goldenrod. Apparently, the couple had to pay for a nursing home after the husband suffered a fall.

Questionable renovations over the years had given it the look of the Winchester Mystery House, that rambling mansion with stairs to nowhere and doors that opened onto brick walls. The curvy acreage—like a snake writhing down the hillside—had made it unsuitable for buyers who may have wanted to raze and replace it.

Now, Chen wanted to get on a call—which was unexpected. After all, didn't he say he was a busy man? And that he trusted no one more than Jin?

Jin reached through the hole, hoping to retrieve the slat, but his fingers brushed the air. He peeked into the neighbor's backyard, at the brick pizza oven, the lemon trees strung with lights, the glimmering pool, and a taupe sectional couch that surrounded the firepit piled high with tempered glass. Such amenities puzzled him. Why go to the trouble of outfitting your luxury home only to forsake the pleasures of air-conditioning? The chickens perplexed him, too. The stink, the noise. A flock clucked by the coop, which resembled a miniature farmhouse, off-white with a black peaked roof. A dog barked from inside the house.

He wondered if the neighbors kept other pets in their menagerie. As he fetched a board leaning against the garage, an orange cat squeezed through the fence and flicked its tail, regarding him.

Though the cat didn't wear a collar, Jin doubted it was a stray; it was too fluffy and well-fed. When he reached for it, it darted away and sat in a patch of sunshine, grooming itself, more at home than Jin felt here. His family was still unpacking, boxes and crumpled newspaper everywhere.

When he propped the board against the fence, a splinter pricked his finger. As he dug it out with a thumbnail, he turned to find Lily watching him.

"What is that?" she asked.

"Don't mess with it," he said.

She peered around him. Nine years old, and she fiddled with remote controls and knobs on every device—just like Jin had, when he'd been a boy. Taking Lily by the shoulders, he steered her away from the fence. "Let's go for a walk."

"Can we go to school? I can show you I know how to get there."

Although the elementary school was only three blocks away, they were reluctant to let Lily walk there by herself. Drivers sped, rolled through stop signs, tailgated, and crossed double yellow lines on the narrow roads.

"You sure?" Jin asked. "Okay."

Next door, the garage opened and Blair emerged, waving. "You settled in yet?"

Yes, Jin said. Her question felt like getting ambushed all over again.

She smiled at Lily. "I'll send Jordan over to say hello!" She mentioned that the fire department had issued pre-citations for potential wildfire hazards. "A few days before you moved in. Maybe you thought it was junk mail."

Jin vaguely recalled something that he'd tossed aside. A pre-citation was not a citation, he'd reasoned, but a warning, so he could put it off.

"My tree guy's coming," Blair explained, "to clear away defensible space. You know what that is?"

He nodded, though he wasn't familiar with the term.

"Low-hanging branches, bushes too close to the curb, that sort of thing. It's to slow down wildfires. When it's super dry and the wind picks up, we have to really keep an eye out." The sky was cloudless, the start of another hot day. She pointed at the sycamore at the end of his driveway, whose branches drooped over the property line. "Looks like they should come down."

Did they have to? Maybe she wanted to improve her view.

"Thanks," he said.

Her mouth dropped open. As he walked away, he almost laughed out loud, thinking of the look on her face! But who made her boss—*queen*—of the cul-de-sac?

She rushed to the sidewalk. "The tree trimmer can take down what's on my side, but you have to thin what's on yours."

"I'll look into it." Petty, he knew. Kai had told him to be more gracious, but Blair was no different from a gorilla thumping its chest: The dominance you established at the beginning defined everything that followed. He clasped Lily's hand and strode off.

* * *

At the kitchen sink, Jane finished rinsing her glass, mortified that her father had been rude to the neighbor lady again. Lately, he'd been so grouchy, snapping at Jane for using too much dish soap, ordering Lily to turn down the volume on her cartoons.

After the mailman pulled up, Jane wandered out, trying to be helpful. Her father usually fetched the mail, hustling out as soon as it arrived. She retrieved a single envelope, from the EDD, marked TIME SENSITIVE MATERIAL. OFFICIAL BUSINESS. PENALTY FOR PRIVATE USE $300. It looked official, but scams often did. Her parents tended to be suspicious, convinced that the world was out to get them. The letter felt flimsy, a single sheet of paper. Probably for the old owners. Then she noticed it was addressed to her father—Jin Chang—and the full name of the agency, in smaller font: EMPLOYMENT DEVELOPMENT DEPARTMENT.

Employment.

Maybe it had something to do with taxes or other government business. She should put the letter on her father's desk or pretend she never saw it, leaving it in the mailbox.

She dropped the letter back in, walked away, but after a few steps spun around and retrieved it on a hunch. Her mother came down the cracked concrete driveway, saying she'd cut up peaches, and did she want a snack?

Jane folded the letter in half and jammed it into the back pocket of her jeans. "Maybe later."

"Very juicy. Very sweet," Kai urged. "Any mail?"

No, Jane said. In the kitchen, she ate a honeyed slice while standing, then another and another until her mother seemed satisfied. She passed Jane a paper napkin.

As Jane wiped her mouth, her mother glanced at her phone. "What does this mean?" She handed it to Jane. An email from work, a dense paragraph filled with jargon.

Her parents relied on her to make sense of American bureaucracy, insurance forms, medical paperwork, and the like, though paradoxically they spoke more languages than her: English, Mandarin, C++, Python, Java . . .

"Rolling out new performance management workflow," Jane read aloud. *360 feedback nomination?* She looked through to the end. "I think . . . it's asking you to ask coworkers who know you well, who can talk about how you're doing." She returned the phone and gestured toward the stack of empty boxes in the corner. "You want me to break these down?"

"It won't fit in the recycling bin," Kai said. "Leave it by the side of the house for now."

Afterward, in her shoebox of a room, Jane returned to her father's letter. She held it up to the lightbulb but couldn't make out what was inside. She traced a finger along its perimeter. She could heat a mug of water in the microwave and perch the envelope over the steam. Or, she could put it back in the mailbox, choosing to believe that her parents could—or should—take care of everything, keeping them housed and fed. Keeping them safe.

Her father had claimed that no one would come looking for Chinese to attack in El Nido. They wouldn't get targeted like the Chinese woman stabbed while walking her dog in a park. Like the Vietnamese father pummeled while pushing his baby in a stroller. Like the Korean elder, kicked down while waiting for a bus, in video after video from security cameras, sickening in the beating but also in the seconds before it happened, when you knew what was coming and they didn't, and in the moments after, when the victims lay heaped on the ground, terribly still.

Jane had vowed to defend her family. She'd picked up a whistle and pepper spray from a swap meet. She'd watched self-defense videos, gripping her keys between her knuckles to gouge out an attacker's eyes and pretending to knee a groin. She'd practiced in the bathroom, the only spot with privacy at their old place. At first, she felt foolish, her back to the mirror, her fist flying through the air meeting no resistance. But with each punch, she'd felt herself grow taller, mightier.

She placed the letter over the mug of hot water for a few minutes, the air dampening with the smell of glue and paper. She slipped a butter knife under the flap to ease it open. A quarter of an inch, half an inch, and then her hand slipped and the envelope tore. With that, she ripped it open and read over the letter, nothing making sense until her eyes fell upon a phrase: "UI Online is a fast, convenient, and secure way to access Unemployment Claim insurance information, certify for existing benefits . . . Failing to sign in a timely manner can jeopardize future payments."

Maybe it was a scam. Hadn't there been something in the news?

Or maybe her father had lost his job.

❁ ❁ ❁

At the intersection, Jin said nothing as Lily turned right instead of left. Hoping, on one hand, that she would correct her path, and on the other that she wouldn't, thereby proving that she couldn't walk to school on her own.

A red Mini Cooper blew past the stop sign, its windows down, music blasting. It was the neighbor's daughter speeding! "You have to watch out. Listen for what's coming," he told Lily. She promised.

At the next stop sign, she pointed at a tiny birdhouse on the back, painted in bright reds and blues. He tapped the side. Sturdily constructed, though it wasn't big enough for a bird.

At the end of the block, they found a dark green one, home to a miniature bear family: papa in a rocking chair, mama at the stove, and the cubs by the fireplace. It had to be the act of a fanciful neighbor. Lily chattered away, in search of more birdhouses, seeming to forget she'd suggested walking to school.

Looking down the block, he did a double take, shading his eyes. The tree towered above the street, at least thirty feet tall, the gold coins of the fruit bright against the glossy dark green leaves. Was it—could it be? Pipa had the look of small nectarines, with the taste of tangy peaches, and they reminded him of childhood, long hot nights spent eating the juiciest fruits, all the pipa and lychee and watermelon that tasted sweeter than anything he'd had since. On their trips back to China, they'd never returned in time for the season.

They were called loquats here, though they weren't grown commercially in the United States. At least, he'd never found them in stores. They were too fragile, easily bruised, and had to be picked at the peak of ripeness.

As they approached the tree, its branches seemed to extend themselves in greeting. He nicked a low-hanging fruit with his thumbnail, peeled the translucent skin, and showed Lily the glistening seeds.

"You want to try it?" he asked.

She shook her head.

Maybe it wasn't pipa, but a poisonous American cousin. He squeezed the flesh, which felt familiar in his fingers, soft yet not mushy. He popped it into his mouth, worried that the taste couldn't match his recollection, that it would make him doubt his memory. The bright flavor was sour and sweet. The juicy pipa slaked his thirst and he reached for another and another, so ripe they came off easily in his hands.

Kai loved pipa, too. Maybe she would see the pipa as an omen of good fortune, of welcome here.

Jin had doubted himself when one tech startup after another had folded, after buying, then losing a home during the recession, after a series of failed investments that left the Changs perpetual renters.

Perhaps it was fortuitous that the latest startup went bust, leaving him available to work for Chen. He had told no one, not even Kai. Why worry his family when he'd find another job soon?

Now he would stuff his pockets, he would return with plastic bags and strip the branches clean, he and Kai would eat and eat . . .

"Dad!" Lily said. "Daddy! Daddy, that's *stealing*."

The accusatory look she gave him made him strangely defiant, as if she'd called 911 on him. His wife's face in hers, dimpled with a sharp chin. Was it stealing if no one else wanted it? If people like his neighbor couldn't see the treasure before them? The homeowners here probably considered such trees ornamental, the fruit a nuisance, fit only for rats, squirrels, possums, and other vermin. Smashed pipa scattered on the street, blown off by last night's wind. A few had fermented in the heat, a jammy rot.

The mail truck rounding the bend startled him. He didn't know if it was coming or going toward their house. He had to intercept the mail, finish unpacking, get started on repairs, and prepare for Chen's call. Instead, he'd quarreled with his neighbor. Instead, he'd been daydreaming.

"Do you know where the school is?" he asked.

Lily bowed her head but didn't answer.

He tugged her arm toward home. He walked too fast and she ran to keep up. "Dad!" she cried. "Daddy!"

He didn't slow down. He didn't turn around. Longing cut through him, sharp enough to steal his breath. His future success had once seemed so ripe for the picking, but as close as his fingers might have come, he could never quite reach it.

2

Days after Ana Rodriguez started working for the Belles, feeding the chickens had become a part of the morning routine: her bosses' youngest daughter, Jordan, would fetch a scoop of pellets from the plastic tub in the pantry. Ana's daughter, Sofía, watching from the in-law unit above the garage, would bolt outside the moment Jordan exited the house.

The girls would meet by the coop. Usually, Ana waited inside for the delivery of the eggs, speckled blue and white and brown, with bright orange yolks, courtesy of Sunny, Moonbeam, Punky, Clucky, and Cosmo.

Wednesday morning, Sofía insisted that Ana come along instead of staying in the kitchen. Ana's left wrist ached, the old bruise faded but tender. Ignoring the throb, she followed Jordan into the backyard, where windblown leaves and twigs were scattered on the ground.

Jordan—who seemed more fish than girl, her bobbed blond hair tinted green as old pennies—walked with a confidence that Ana wished for her own daughter.

When they reached the coop, the door was open, and a few feathers floated in the air. Ana realized that she hadn't heard the chickens clucking this morning. Jordan halted, as if she could tell something was wrong. When Sofía reached the threshold, Ana shouted, "Go back inside!"

"But the chickens . . . We didn't feed them yet!" Sofía said.

Jordan clenched the cup so tightly her knuckles turned white.

"Now," Ana said.

With a nod, Jordan headed to the house, and Sofía returned to their quarters. Holding her breath, Ana poked her head into the coop. Squatting, her eyes adjusting to the dim light, hoping for groggy chickens, their eyes shut and their beaks tucked into the fluff on their necks. Instead, she discovered a mess of entrails and feathers, an eye-watering stink of ammonia and coppery blood that made her want to jump in the pool though she couldn't swim.

By the time Ana returned to the kitchen, Jordan must have told her mother. The girl buried her head into Blair, who rubbed circles on her back.

Ana washed her hands in the hottest water she could stand.

It was the third time the chickens had been massacred, Blair told Ana. "Sometimes they break into the coop. Sometimes . . ." She paused. "We have to make sure the door stays closed."

Jordan pulled away from her mother. "It *was* closed."

The door? The night before, while Ana prepared dinner, she told Sofía to get off the phone, which she'd borrowed to watch videos, and practice dribbling the soccer ball or go look at the chickens instead. Maybe Sofía had left the door to the coop open. Ana's throat tightened. She should explain what happened, take the blame, but what if Blair fired her?

"Do you want to skip practice?" Blair asked Jordan.

No, Jordan said, and left to get ready. Luna, the family's labradoodle, waddled in and lapped water from the bowl.

"I keep telling Sam we should train another Orb on the coop," Blair said. "I work for Orb. But he says there's no point; we're asleep when it comes. And with too many cameras, you get overloaded with notifications."

Ana dried her hands on a dish towel. She no longer believed in God, but made a silent prayer to whoever spared her daughter from getting caught on camera.

During the night, the wind had roared for hours, the branches of the oak trees thrashing and creaking; at one point, she'd woken up from a nightmare that her ex had come after her. Come to collect the rent she owed. She'd moved without telling him, packing after he left for work and their roommates were out, too. Tossed the phone on his calling plan and replaced it, a new number for a new life, where he couldn't find them.

But if the wind had been too loud to hear the shrieks of the chickens, wouldn't it also have been too loud to hear if Julio entered the backyard? Too loud for the Belles to hear her screaming? Maybe she could convince them to install a camera in the side yard.

❁ ❁ ❁

That night before dinner, Blair sorted through the mail, most of it junk, discounts on cleaners and fundraising appeals from the ACLU and the Nature Conservancy. She set aside the offer for another credit card; they were maxing out the limits on their main and backup cards. She'd talk to Sam about getting another.

She started to toss a flyer advertising a meetup for newcomer families. Then she noticed the contact: Nic, whose daughter belonged to a rival swim team, Falling Leaf Country Club, that had dominated every competition. Nic, who was trying to get Jordan thrown out of the summer league's swim finals.

As she studied the flyer, an idea took shape: Maybe the nanny, who'd moved here a week ago with her daughter, could seek intel at the gathering.

She thrust the flyer at Ana. "You should go! The girls can watch Liam."

"Thank you but—no." Ana wiped the counter and swiped at a stain on the white tile backsplash.

Blair insisted. "We'd pay you for your time."

Ana rinsed off the sponge, her shoulders rigid.

Blair would have to explain. "Nic—the organizer—is claiming that Jordan's cheating. At the swim meets."

"Why?" Ana asked.

"Because she wins!" There was more to it, of course. There always was.

Even Jordan's big sister, Quinn—an all-American and high school team captain, who'd been competing since the age of seven and was already verbally committed to Princeton—had never been so driven at that age. Jordan, though: Jordan was a shark. If she stopped moving, she'd die. You'd never guess that she'd been a preemie. She'd been breaking records all season.

Earlier this summer, Blair had reported that Nic's daughter had been sneaking in extra pulls underwater and sometimes using illegal kicks. The other volunteers monitoring the lanes didn't notice or let it slide. But if the girl wanted a future in swimming, she had to follow the rules. Nic found out she'd reported the violation. The poor child had been so rattled, she'd faltered in the next couple meets. And now Nic had retaliated with what amounted to a technicality.

"They want to see her birth certificate to prove her birth date. Like . . . like she's Obama!" Blair leaned against the marble-topped kitchen island. "I've—we've—spoken to the league officials, Jordan will compete in her age bracket as she has all season. But Nic won't stop. She'll try to mess with us on the Mavericks."

Ana cocked her head.

"It's the club team for the best swimmers in the area," Blair said. "Quinn's been on it for years. Tryouts are in a couple weeks. If you go tomorrow, maybe you'll hear Nic say something? Maybe about what she's planning. Or if she's trying to get other parents on her side."

"You want me to spy on her?" Ana asked flatly.

"All you'd have to do is look around. Listen to what she says . . ." Blair trailed off. Yes, she'd asked Ana to spy; yes, she'd put her new employee in an impossible position, in which she couldn't say no unless she wanted to jeopardize her new job and her housing.

An employee who had so far been exemplary, cleaning the messes that her family made. She entrusted the care of her children to Ana. Intimate as family, or almost.

"Forget about it," Blair said. How many times in the last year had she watched yet another viral video of a wild-eyed white woman, lording her privilege? She'd smugly think to herself, Not me, not ever. As she pulled out forks and napkins to set the table, she tried to remember something from *White Fragility*, which she'd listened to as an audiobook at 1.5 speed. "You're from Guatemala?" she blurted. "That's great that Kamala visited. Do you have any family there? Your parents?"

No, Ana said. She straightened the toaster.

Even as Blair wished she'd said nothing, she fought the urge to share that her husband's grandparents had come from Mexico and had run a popular restaurant, Casa Lopez, on the east side of Los Angeles. At the Bellavista—the subdivision Sam was developing at the edge of town—he'd even named two streets after them: Via Paloma and Via Armando. She checked the time. "Sorry to keep you. See you tomorrow."

"Jordan loves to swim," Ana said. A statement, not a question.

"We had her in the pool before she could walk."

"If someone came after my daughter . . ." Ana leveled her gaze at Blair. "I'll go."

"Are you sure?" Blair asked. The forks clinked in her hand.

"This morning, you talked about getting a camera for the coop. How much is it to install one?"

Blair sighed. "I'm trying to make Jordan forget about getting more chickens. We should have gotten rid of the coop when we had a chance!"

While getting dressed for practice, Jordan had sobbed so hard she nearly hyperventilated.

"Sometimes the coyote—or whatever it is—digs under the coop," Blair went on. "We've talked about installing an additional camera trained at the coop."

"A camera could show it coming in," Ana said. "Maybe it's through the side yard?"

"Don't worry: no chickens, no coyote. El Nido's safe, very safe. The police don't have much to do."

Blair chuckled, then caught herself after noticing Ana's worried expression. Where did Ana move from—Oakland? Hayward? Union City? She didn't know what fears kept Ana up at night, and if additional cameras would put her at ease. And she'd agreed to spy on Blair's behalf.

It would cost Blair nothing to grant this request. "I'll write our product manager now," she said. "And get the app installed on your phone."

* * *

The chickens had indeed been attacked by a coyote, a juvenile who'd never before enjoyed the pleasures of the coop. Its fur was the mottled gray and russet brown of autumn leaves, the tip of its tail black, as if dipped in paint. Until last night, this one had mostly eaten plentiful roadkill found in the verdant hills and valleys of El Nido: the leg of a deer, the smashed remains of a squirrel, and the tail end of a garter snake. Carrion.

Let's call him Wily. The residents sheltering in place during the pandemic hit more deer, left more trash that fed more rats, all of which sustained a bigger pack of coyotes over the past year. It had been crowded, competitive, fighting his brothers and sisters to nestle at the center, for the last scraps of flesh, for the fallen fruit.

He'd left his pack in the spring, around the time this year's pups had been born. At one, he'd been overcome by the powerful urge to roam. Like his ancestors, once known as prairie wolves, as song dogs, as tricksters and gods, who emerged from the deserts and high plains. Generations moved west, east, north, south, their way eased by pioneers who killed off predators, chopped down trees, and ranched cattle. When hunted, poisoned, and persecuted, the coyotes scattered and regrouped, their numbers surging a hundredfold.

A couple weeks ago, after encountering the bulldozers at the Bellavista, he'd slunk closer to homes in this neighborhood. Having breached the chicken coop, having acquired a taste for fresh blood and the sweetness of domesticated flesh, Wily raised his ambitions.

3

The next day, Tasha Washington jumped onto the curb, narrowly avoiding an SUV topped by a shark fin. The car barreled past, piloted by a blond lady, the rear window scrawled with what passed for trash talk here: EAT MY BUBBLES.

Tasha knew that the swimmers from the rec clubs—split between El Nido and its neighboring municipality, El Arbol—decked out their minivans and SUVs like parade floats in various aquatic themes: sharks, stingrays, dolphins, gators, marlins, and the like.

People who grew up here set their internal clock to the summer swim season, but Tasha had moved here two years ago, just before the start of her freshman year. Late, by the standards of El Nido, where many kids seemed to have known each other since kindergarten. Since preschool, or maybe in utero.

Because the meets—along with much else—had been canceled during the first summer of the pandemic, when competition resumed, the car decorations were more over-the-top than usual: a mechanized dolphin that appeared to be leaping through waves, flashing LED lights that hung from the bumper, and hubcaps adorned with cartwheeling mascots.

The shark mom accelerated onto the street, cutting off a minivan. Shaking her head, Tasha walked up the steps to the library, and as she entered the sunny atrium, she noticed books piled under the slot for donations.

She'd tell her mother. Dr. Minerva Washington, the medical director at Sunrise Convalescent, liked to get mysteries and romance novels for her patients.

Last year, an early outbreak of the virus at the nursing home where Minerva worked left a dozen residents dead. Every night, Minerva had dropped her clothes straight into the washing machine, then showered and barricaded herself in her room. But she couldn't outrun the virus during the first winter surge. When she'd finally emerged, gaunt and haggard, she'd lost her sense of taste and smell. But at least Tasha and her little brother, Marcus, had been spared.

A leathery woman in tennis whites clutched her purse as she passed by Tasha. A coincidence maybe, but probably not. Tasha headed to the stacks, in search of reference books on local plants. She never saw anyone in the horticulture section at the library; there were books that looked like they hadn't been touched since they'd been shelved. But today she spotted Jacqui there, studying spines—another Black girl, her complexion golden brown compared to Tasha's copper. Her dad was some kind of tech boss and her mom had been a beauty queen.

They'd been in the choir together during Tasha's freshman year. Jacqui, a year ahead, was a soprano who had soloed at the winter concert. She had a voice that could have soared to the highest reaches of a cathedral.

They weren't friends. Jacqui always looked past her in the school hallways. Tasha debated whether she should duck into another stack to avoid Jacqui and wait until she was gone, then decided no. The library was her territory, wasn't it? Then, to Tasha's surprise, Jacqui waved. Tasha was about to wave back when she heard footsteps and realized that Jacqui had been waving to someone *behind* her. Tasha stepped aside so the freckled white girl could pass her. Gwynne? Quinn. In AP Computer Science last year, she'd often logged on to Zoom school from outside, a pool in the background.

Both seniors ignored her, which disappointed Tasha more than she wanted to admit. She hunched her shoulders, wishing she weren't so tall, wishing she could disappear. She fled into the next stack. Seeing them had reminded her that she was about to spend seven hours a day, Monday through Friday, with classmates who remained strangers.

Last spring, when most chose to return in person, cordoned into cohorts, she and her brother had remained on Zoom. They both had asthma, the kind that left them gasping on the floor if they didn't get to their inhalers in time. Their mother had moved them to El Nido in part because of the clean air—not realizing at the time that the stretches of wildfire smoke would start earlier and earlier each year: November, then October, then September, and now late July.

"You found what you were looking for?" Quinn asked.

Tasha peeked through the shelves, unable to resist eavesdropping. She gathered that they were headed to a meeting to brainstorm volunteer projects.

As Jacqui held up the book, Quinn read the title out loud, her tone dubious: "*Starting a Community Garden*."

"It could be fun!" Jacqui protested. "What's your idea?"

"We could adopt Sunrise. Bring cookies and flowers, read to them. Make signs."

"Give it a rest," Jacqui teased. "You don't need to volunteer ever again! You're going to Princeton."

"I still have to do the application! Maybe admissions looks at it and passes."

"That won't happen. Besides, other coaches have been calling, right?"

"They've been calling a lot of people." Quinn ran her fingers along the shelf.

"They're not calling me!"

"It's different for you. . . ." Quinn pulled out a book, studying the cover.

"Different how?" Jacqui asked icily.

Quinn grimaced and slid the book back onto the shelf.

Jacqui broke the silence. "But why Sunrise? I hold my breath when I drive by that place."

"That's exactly why we should do something for them. They're like . . . lepers."

They giggled. To most everyone in El Nido, the nursing home must seem tainted. Yet Tasha's mother dragged herself back there as soon as she could stand again.

"We're late!" Quinn exclaimed.

After they left, Tasha returned to the shelves, even more determined to help her mother. If she looked long enough, hard enough, she'd find a way to return her mother's senses. She brushed her fingers along the spines until stopping on a slim tan volume: *Black Gold*. She'd nearly missed it, squeezed between two thick books. The spine cracked, loud as a gunshot, when she opened it, releasing a sepia-tinted scent.

❁ ❁ ❁

Later that day, when Tasha pulled up the satellite view of the historic walnut trees, she gasped: a gigantic orchard, just over a gentle hill, that wasn't visible from the road that led to the high school. She zoomed in on the photo until it filled the screen of her laptop.

She'd tracked it down, thanks to the library book's hazy black-and-white photos of orchards and hand-drawn maps. She recognized a photo of an intersection, with a familiar view of the hills, and realized that a corner gas station had once housed a walnut-processing plant. She'd been looking for a supply of unripe green walnuts, on the theory that the stickier the scent, the more it might catch on the receptors in her mother's nose. Minerva needed to smell what had been freshly gathered, not concocted in a lab or packaged and processed in a distant factory.

Maybe it was a stupid idea. But she had to try. She closed her laptop and sat back against the couch. Braying laughter erupted from her brother's cracked iPad, yet another gamer narrating his moves. "Turn it down, Marcus!" she said. "Mama's sleeping."

A couple weeks ago, Minerva began pulling overnight shifts at the ER on her days off. She'd entered the lottery for a below-market unit at the new Bellavista subdivision and was saving up for the deposit and down payment. On a doctor's salary, the family qualified. Wealthy elsewhere was middle class in El Nido, and middle class might as well have been poor.

Turning down the volume, Marcus muttered, "Bossy."

Ever since their father died, Tasha had helped look after him. She yanked the tablet from him and stood, holding it above his head, where he couldn't reach it.

"Hey!" he shouted, his arms pinwheeling at her.

She shushed him, but he jumped up, grabbing at the device.

Yawning, their mother came out of her bedroom, dressed in maroon scrubs that somehow looked elegant on her. Regal, because of her height, her posture, and her crown braid.

Tasha followed her into the kitchen and scooped her a bowl of oxtail stew from the Crock-Pot, along with a side of rice. With her mother's appetite annihilated, Tasha had learned how to cook, incorporating what she'd foraged. Blackberries, mint, chickweed. Food was everywhere if you knew where—and how—to look.

At the kitchen table, Minerva dipped a spoonful of rice into the stew. "I had strange dreams. Though I can't remember anything. Just the feeling of it."

"Meat dreams," Tasha said. They laughed. The savory smell had a way of seeping into your sleep, leaving you unsettled. Disturbed. They lived in one of the few apartment buildings in El Nido. Though the three-bedroom was spacious, no one could escape the stew's savory scent. If her mother got the duplex, they'd have more room.

"Was it a good dream? Or a bad one?" Tasha asked.

"I remember stickiness. Like I'd been dipped into a vat of grease."

"You can smell again?" Tasha felt herself rising up and up and up, a pearl diver breaking free of the murk.

Minerva closed her eyes, inhaling deeply. "Something . . . I smell something at the tip of my nose—at the tip of my tongue." She forked a bite of the stew, but after a few chews, she sighed. "Maybe only when I'm sleeping?"

Tasha pushed back the chair. "It needs salt."

Her mother waved her off.

Tasha grabbed an orange from the fruit bowl. Nicking a peel with her thumbnail, she thrust it at her mother. "Can you smell this?" The citrus scent seemed cheerful, fresh and bright.

For a while, Minerva had gone along with the smell training, sniffing strong scents twice a day. You could circumvent the short circuit by thinking about a strong memory associated with the smell. Apple cider at Christmas. The coconut scent of leave-in conditioner. Inhale the stench of an extinguished candle or milk gone foul, to reach the part of your brain that might scream, "Danger!"

Nothing seemed to work. Almost eight months had gone by since her mother had lost her sense of smell. It would come back any day now, Minerva said, and within the year at the latest. That's what the preliminary data indicated.

But what if it didn't? Everyone pretended the pandemic was over, but Minerva couldn't *smell*. Every meal, every day, drained of color. Tasha wanted so much to paint it back in. What if roast chicken forever remained only texture to her mother, a squishy toadstool? What if popcorn only squeaked like Styrofoam?

"We can try tomorrow," Minerva said. "Maybe it's better I don't smell much at work." She set down her fork, most of the bowl untouched. It was clear she ate out of necessity, without pleasure. She got up and filled a water bottle, adding ice cubes that clinked against the metal. "You okay, baby?"

Tasha might have asked the same of her mother, who had circles under her eyes. Her cheeks were hollow from the weight she'd lost.

When Tasha shrugged, Minerva kneaded her thumbs into her shoulders. Tasha inhaled her nutty shea butter scent.

If only she could ease her mother's load. "I saw a flyer at the library."

"Yes . . . ?" Minerva deepened her squeezes.

Tasha exhaled, letting the tightness ease. "A high schooler was charging eighty dollars per hour for math tutoring."

"You always get straight A's."

Tasha twisted around. "*I* want to tutor."

Another flyer had listed a meetup for new families in El Nido. Tasha could introduce herself to newcomers who'd need a dog walker, tutor, or babysitter and set herself apart from the other teenagers advertising their services online.

Her mother pulled away. "I need your help with Marcus."

It wasn't the first time Tasha had asked to get a job, hoping to pitch in, nor the first time Minerva refused. She hugged Tasha from behind. "I'm late."

After she left, Tasha put away her mother's leftovers, wondering how to change her mind. If Tasha landed a gig, her mother wouldn't want her to flake on the responsibility.

Minerva wouldn't like it, though. Tasha bit her lip. This weekend, she'd take her mother to the walnut orchard to lure out her senses. Before then, she could try something else pungent . . . bay leaves? Because she'd used the last of them in the stew, she decided to forage fresh ones from the perimeter of the high school track.

"Let's go," she called to her brother. He'd gone soft in the last year; they both had. In profile, he could have been one of their uncles, his gut pressing against his T-shirt. "Time to touch grass."

At the track, Marcus beelined to the landing pads, left out from high jump practice. He threw himself onto the pads, rolling around as if he'd cleared a sky-high bar. On the other side of the track, two Asian girls did laps.

In the hour before sunset, the light was low and slanting. Dry grass crunched beneath her feet, giving off the scent of sunshine, of hay, as she approached the bay laurel and plucked a handful of leaves. They were scented like menthol, cool as the fog that poured like cream over El Nido's hills.

In the first month of lockdown, she'd stumbled upon the Black Forager, an online influencer who sang silly songs and made pesto out of hairy bitter cress and sorbet from Japanese knotweed. It turned out that preppers weren't all white weirdos who stashed canned butter and built bomb shelters. Tasha's interest might have remained aspirational until she came upon a stand of wild fennel, catching the dark scent of licorice from yards away. She'd been so tired of their apartment, so tired of the same canned and frozen foods from the supermarket, the monotony into infinity. And so, she'd brushed her fingers on the feathery fronds—which looked just like the ones in the video—and then broke one off and sniffed, tentatively, then deeply, its scent spicy and warm as gingerbread, before plucking a handful.

She stuffed a few bay leaves into her electric-blue fanny pack, a gift from her mother. The many zippered compartments held her finds and kept her hands free while foraging. Technically, she should ask for permission to pick here, but she didn't know the property lines and couldn't bring herself to ask. To do so risked getting doors slammed in her face or never opened to her at all.

She checked on Marcus, who crouched down, intent on something on the field. She jogged over. He poked a pill bug, watching it roll into a ball.

"Enough!" she said. "How would you like to get poked over and over?"

When Marcus remained crouching, she poked him in the side. He tumbled on the fake grass at the center of the track, rolling into a ball, then rocked on his back.

Soon after they moved to El Nido, when his second-grade teacher suspected that he might have ADHD, Minerva had wondered aloud to Tasha if there might be another reason he caught his teacher's attention. He was the only Black kid in the class, and one of a handful in the entire school. Young for his grade, too, born weeks before the official cutoff, while other parents held back their children. Some were nearly a year older than him. If he'd been a girl, if he'd been white, would the teacher have viewed him as spirited, instead?

Minerva reluctantly got him diagnosed. They'd noticed he was a klutz, and it turned out that clumsy motor skills, as well as walking on his toes, and double-jointed arms, were correlated with neurodivergence. Meds helped but were no cure. There were studies, she told Tasha, about how the outdoors could ease his inattention and anxiety.

When Tasha reached to help him up, he poked her in the leg. Playing along, she dropped to the ground, tucking in her knees, onto her back. She stretched her arms and legs as far as they could go, like a starfish, then flipped over onto her stomach, getting onto her hands and knees to stretch. She closed her eyes. The field radiated heat from the day.

Something brushed against her calf. Marcus poking her again? Except that it didn't feel like his finger. It was bushy, as if he'd picked up something prickly to poke her with. She ignored him. Then he pinched her.

"Quit it," she said. Something swished on the fake grass, moving away from her.

When she looked up, Marcus now stood a few feet from her, his eyes wide with terror. In the distance, she heard a high thin scream and "Hey, hey, hey! Go away!"

From the corner of her eye, a dark mass came back at her. Panting.

"Run, Marcus!" she shouted.

She tried to get up, to get away, but then needles plunged deep into her leg. Turning, she couldn't believe her eyes: What looked like a scrawny dog had latched onto her left calf. Its eyes an eerie gold. She kicked at it with her other leg, but she couldn't reach it from this angle. It growled and clamped on tighter. Blind with pain, she punched it in the jaw, her fist slamming against what felt like fur and teeth. Her hand wet with saliva or blood. She went woozy, suffocating in its musky wild scent. Footsteps, a whirl, a thud, a whimper, and then she saw nothing.

❁ ❁ ❁

Look big, authorities advised the public afterward. Tasha would be the first but not the last of the people that the coyote would attack in the months that followed, often at dawn or dusk, always those low to the ground: a dishwasher sitting on the curb on his break, a toddler trailing behind his mother.

Look big. Yell, wave your arms, pop open an umbrella, rattle pennies in a soda can, throw something. Look big.

But what if people already thought you were bigger, older, louder, angrier than you actually were? Girls treated like women, boys transformed into men. What if people—in any face-off—might view *you* as the bear, the mountain lion, the coyote? The teenager in braids at the swimming pool in Texas, the family trying to have a barbecue at Lake Merritt, the bird-watcher in Central Park—menaces, all.

And how do you remember to *look big* if you otherwise tried to make yourself invisible in El Nido? If you were invisible, most of the time, until you sharply came into focus.

4

Jane's self-defense training had attuned her to threat, and when the time came, she acted without hesitation, without thinking. When she threw the rock at the coyote's head, it bounded away. She rushed toward the girl sprawled face down. Fuck—the gouge in her calf. Blood had dripped down her leg and onto the grass. Was she breathing?

The girl twitched. She tried to roll over, but stopped, groaning.

"I got you," Jane murmured. Lily bent over, hands on her thighs, retching. "Lily, Lily, it's okay." She turned to the boy. "Is this your sister?"

His eyes were huge, scared. He nodded slowly.

"She'll be okay, I promise," she said, and called 911.

In the ambulance, trying to keep her from going into shock, Jane talked and talked, confiding in her about the envelope she'd opened and her fears about her family's situation.

She hadn't spoken at length to anyone except for her family for more than a year, the four of them confined like astronauts on a voyage to Mars. During lockdown, her only friend, Vivian, had moved to Taiwan; its borders had been closed to most foreigners, but Vivian's family had dual passports. The time difference made it hard to stay in touch. The difference in reality, too. In Taipei, the schools stayed open and rates of infection remained low. It felt like they lived in parallel timelines. The first pandemic summer, Jane told her about a project to teach Asian elders about BLM, young people across the country writing and translating a letter into different languages: *Our silence has a cost and we need to talk about it.* But Vivian seemed to think it was strange and preferred talking about her new school's fashion and sewing clubs.

The day after the attack, Jane sprawled on top of her bed. Her phone buzzed: a text from Tasha, thanking her again.

Jane: anyone would ❤
Tasha: no they would have filmed for ClikClak!

Jane laughed.

Jane: r u feeling okay?

Tasha told her about the rabies vaccine and the side effects, the nausea and headaches. She'd get three more injections over the next two weeks.

Jane: sux sry

Her finger hovered. Another sympathetic heart emoji seemed inadequate, and she wanted to keep the conversation going. She didn't know anyone at Valle Vista, and the first day of school was a little over a week away: Monday, August 9.

She scrolled through the high school's official account, checking out her classmates. She recognized her neighbor, a tall blond, in a photo of the swim team, all the girls pointing their index fingers—#1.

El Nido wasn't like Fremont, but she hadn't realized there were so few Black and Brown students at the high school. Maybe one in every five photos in the grid. East Asians appeared in some photos, one or two at a time except in orchestra or the robotics club, where they dominated. But for all their privilege, they weren't like her. At least in Fremont she'd known what it was like to be in the majority, in a Silicon Valley suburb with a mayor who looked like her parents and a high school with a Chinese American prom queen and Taiwanese American captain of the football team.

Jane: do coyotes come by there a lot?
Tasha: LMAO no
Jane: my first time there
Tasha: welcome!

Tasha was quietly hilarious.

Tasha: in the ambulance u were saying some stuff

Jane sat up, debating how to respond: Play dumb or ghost Tasha? They could pretend she'd never mentioned her family's money problems. And yet, they'd lived through something together. Could the coyote attack bond them like those people who got stuck in an elevator together or climbed into the attic of a flooded home?

Jane: what do u remember
Tasha: something about ur dad

Jane found herself confiding again, explaining she'd never told anyone and she didn't know what to do. She immediately hit Send so she couldn't change her mind. She suspected that Tasha knew more than she let on, and that kindness and discretion made Jane trust her. She exhaled. No matter how Tasha responded, Jane felt relieved.

Tasha: does ur mom know
Jane: idk

Jane didn't like her parents keeping secrets from her, but it seemed worse if her parents kept secrets from each other.

Tasha: know anyone with jobs? friends
parents?
Jane: maybe

Jane wished she knew for certain if he'd lost his job. She could be needlessly worrying. Maybe she should snoop around his desk. Yes, they both agreed.

A few minutes later, Jane pressed her ear against the door to her parents' bedroom. She didn't hear anything and he'd been in there all day. Her phone vibrated with a string of ???? from Tasha. As her mother came down the hallway, Jane dashed toward the stairs.

"Why aren't you in bed?" Kai asked. Short but sharp elbowed; in a crowded Chinatown wet market, she could find gaps, go in sideways, then twist her shoulders and wedge her way through, barking at Jane to follow: *Kuai dian!*

"The doctor said I was fine! Everything's fine," Jane said. Her parents acted as if she might shatter in the slightest breeze. She didn't dare admit that the encounter with the coyote had exhilarated her. The slink of its muscles under its grayish-brown coat had mesmerized her, proof that not everything here had been tamed, mapped, and marked off. Wildness still existed.

"You need to rest," Kai said.

"You and Dad should go on a walk." Jane wanted to search her mother's desk, too. What if they'd both lost their jobs? When she'd been about Lily's age, back when they'd been living in the yellow house, her parents' cell phones would ring and ring, but they never picked up. They had moved to the Fremont apartment after that. Only later did Jane piece together the bankruptcy.

"Take a walk?" Kai pursed her lips. "And get attacked? Are you sure the coyote didn't bite you, too, and make you crazy?"

Kai ushered her down the stairs to her bedroom. The moment the door closed, Jane went to the window, antsy, wondering when she'd get a chance to search her father's desk. She studied the ravine. A part of her wished that she could have traveled back in time to glimpse unending vistas too, unscarred by freeways and high-rises. Silvery sagebrush wafting in the heat. She could have roamed at will like the coyote, beholden to no one, acting as she pleased.

She'd learned about Manifest Destiny, about the violence, genocide, and stolen lands they lived on today, and she didn't harbor any illusions about what kind of life she would have had in the American West; a Chinese girl probably would have been a servant or worked in a brothel.

She pulled open her laptop, curious about the town's history.

El Nido: a nest, a haven. For the Bay Miwok, before the Spanish enslaved them. For the Alta Californian soldiers-turned-cattle-ranchers after Mexico won its independence from Spain.

One of those spreads, Rancho El Nido—an adobe built high on a hill for the tactical advantage—lent the town its name. Ironic: a nest until it wasn't, until you got pitched over the edge and replaced by another kind of bird that sat on the eggs you'd laid.

❁ ❁ ❁

Of all the calamities that might befall their children in America, Jin had never considered the possibility of marauding coyotes. He couldn't have protected their daughters from a threat that seemed about as likely as an alien abduction.

Jane! Jane! How close they'd come to losing her yesterday. His firstborn, his baobei, his treasure! She was the runt of the family—Lily already had the same shoe size as her big sister and would soon surpass her in height. But he'd had no doubt of Jane's courage long before he heard she'd hurled a rock at the coyote's head. Like those bandit-heroes who wrestled tigers, from the legends he used to tell her at bedtime. Her twin braids streaming like a banner.

The other girl would be okay, stitched up and released only a couple hours after Jane. He'd been surprised to hear the girl who'd been bitten was Black; he'd assumed most people who lived in El Nido were white.

"Her mother said to stay hydrated after the rabies shots," Jane said on the drive home from the hospital. "Dad, her mother's a doctor."

By the side of the road, he'd noticed a new sign, BELLAVISTA, in curvy script, advertising a subdivision somewhere in El Nido, with mock-ups of various styles: white colonials, terra-cotta-and-wrought-iron Tuscans, and sleek mid-century moderns. COMING MAY. He almost slammed on his brakes and U-turned, but he had to get Jane home.

New developments were rare in El Nido—exactly why, he didn't know, but he'd made the scarcity a selling point to Chen. By adding to the housing supply, the Bellavista would make it harder for him to flip the house. Even worse: What if it failed to sell for what Chen had paid?

He couldn't let slip these worries. Now, from the bedroom closet where he'd tucked in a desk, Jin logged on to the video call and tried to compose his expression into that of a fortunate, prosperous man. For years, his looks had stayed boyish. His energy, too, remained that of a college student pulling endless all-nighters. He'd been carded at the checkout well into his thirties. During the pandemic, his age had caught up, seemingly overnight. His hair was now streaked gray, his cheeks sagged, and his eyes seemed permanently puffy.

Chen grinned at him through the screen, fifteen hours ahead, a man from the future, but time zone alone couldn't account for how far behind Jin felt by comparison. Chen's high cheekbones were as sharp as when they'd been in college, his hair thick and dark, gelled back along a side part.

Jin smiled in return, a sight so ghastly he wanted to fake technical difficulties and turn off the screen. The bare bulb on the closet ceiling cast a harsh light, but he'd angled the camera so Chen couldn't tell that clothing pressed in from both sides.

When Jin was ten, a stray dog clamped on his cheek until Chen scared it off—one of the many times Chen had come to his aid. And he'd done the same for Chen: found an internship for Chen's nephew and picked up Chen's cousin from the airport and helped her find an apartment, back when Jin had fistfuls of possibilities, prospects that he could share like a feast.

Chen, who'd gotten rich in real estate and construction, remembered to send gifts of fruit and candy to Jin's parents during the Spring Festival.

"How close are the wildfires?" Chen asked now.

"Hundreds of miles away. Not to worry." Jin fingered a pipa pit, which he'd left out to dry on his desk. When he fumbled the pit, it dropped soundlessly onto the carpet.

"How soon can you put the house on the market?" Chen asked.

They'd agreed on selling late next spring, hadn't they? Did Chen need to free up the money now, or was he curious about the strength of the market?

"You have anything in mind?" Jin asked.

"How are the comps doing?"

Jin pondered: Sales surged, but at a minimum, they should wait three months. If he sold the house now, he'd avoid competition from the Bellavista. But then he'd be out of a home—and a job. The repairs wouldn't get finished in time either. He hadn't even started!

A floorboard creaked. Was someone out there? The other bedrooms were downstairs. Muffled by clothes, he didn't think anyone could hear anything they were saying.

Belatedly, Jin realized Chen was asking him a question. He apologized, claiming that Jane had been asking where to find a charger.

Chen chuckled. "When will you go back into the office?"

"Probably not until next year." Jin, in socked feet, curled his toes against the carpet, feeling exposed as a worm drying in the sun. He applied to at least ten jobs a day, but he knew how these things worked; it helped to have someone from the inside put in a good word.

"Work's busy though," he added. "So's the housing market. We could sell now and get a great return, but everything I hear says it'll be better next spring." He sipped from a lukewarm jar of tea, steeped for so long it had turned bitter.

"When?" Chen glanced to the side and held a finger up to someone off-screen.

"April. Maybe May." Jin had to convince Chen to give him more time to sell.

Chen leaned back in his chair. "How *is* El Nido?"

Though Jin had promised updates, he didn't want to alarm Chen by telling him about yesterday's coyote attack. What if it had bitten Jane, like the mongrel that had bitten him?

"It's paradise!" he said, to reassure himself and Chen both. He extolled its natural beauty and proximity to San Francisco (twenty minutes with no traffic), to Napa (an hour), to Lake Tahoe (three hours). The sunny summers and mild winters, large handsome houses and top-ranked schools with surround-sound auditoriums and climbing walls in the gymnasium. A charming downtown with a rose garden, a public library with banks of computers and comfortable study rooms, and an old-fashioned ice cream parlor.

Chen chuckled. "You've already sold me."

"It's an incredible opportunity! This project could be the start. Maybe other investors want to get into real estate here?"

Chen pointed at him. "We think alike! I've already been talking to potential investors."

His friend's confidence in him served as a reminder of Jin's early potential that he hoped might still come to pass, even as he turned forty this year.

He missed his old friend, even though their conversations had become formal and polite over the years, brief updates about weather, family, and work. The business arrangement distanced them even further, the difference in status made plain.

"I wish you could see it," Jin said.

"I've been thinking . . ." As soon as the United States reopened its borders to travelers from China, he could visit. A government official he knew told him the change might go into effect this fall.

Jin's boasts had backfired. He dug his fingernails into fists. "It's a long flight."

"You sleep most of the way."

"But the quarantine . . ." Jin and Kai hadn't yet returned to China because of the two weeks—or more—they'd have to wait in a hotel with their daughters. A friend had applied to visit his mother, dying of cancer, a two-month process that required proof of relationship, proof of imminent death, and other reams of paperwork, only to get stuck in limbo, finally arriving too late to see his mother before she passed away alone in the hospital. Jin had to admit, he'd hoped such restrictions would keep Chen far, far away and reliant on his word.

"I can work from the hotel. Who doesn't need a little time away from their children? Their wife?" Chen grinned. "Besides, it's worth it to get Pfizer."

A vaccination vacation.

The wealthiest topped off their immunity with all the vaccines, in what was known as an MBA: *M*oderna, *B*ioNTech-Pfizer, *A*straZeneca.

"It's already approved for twelve and up," Chen said. "I've heard they don't ask for any documentation when you get your shots." If the timing worked out, the whole family—Chen, his wife, their eight-year-old twin girls—would visit El Nido during the Golden Week holidays, the first week of October.

October! August started this weekend. September, October. He wouldn't have much time to get the house showplace ready. "The news changes every day," Jin warned. American regulators might hold up approval for kids. Even if it became available in the fall, the rollout could get delayed.

As much as Jin wanted his youngest and millions upon millions of children here—*everywhere*—to get the shot, he suddenly, fervently hoped that the vaccines would get delayed until early winter or next spring. He tugged on the collar of his button-down shirt, sweat prickling. He'd turned off the portable fan to take the call, and the closet had become unbearably stuffy. "What if the borders close while you're here?"

Chen laughed. "I don't remember you so cautious! That's good. It shows I can trust my money with you. But we can also trust the officials who know things that we don't."

"Come in February instead, for Lunar New Year," Jin urged. "Turn it into a ski vacation."

Chen said he'd talk it over with his wife. Jin's phone flashed with an incoming call, the handyman he'd been trying to reach all week.

"My assistant will call with the details," Chen said. "For now, how about a video tour?"

The phone stopped buzzing. "Right . . . now?" The house was a mess, packing boxes spilling open in unfurnished rooms.

"Not at this second! For potential investors, put something together, not only a few houses, but all over town. You find a videographer, I'll pay for it. Get a drone!"

Drones: that gimmick with an uncanny whine. A weapon disguised as a toy, scoping out civilian targets. That you heard before you saw, too late to outrun it.

"Show us why it's paradise," Chen said.

After hanging up, Jin slumped in his chair, regretting how much he'd talked up El Nido. A video tour? If only he knew the town better! He checked his email, hoping for a response from a prospective employer. On the corner of the desk, he spotted a flyer for a newcomer gathering that afternoon. Kai said she had meetings back-to-back and Jane needed to rest, but maybe he could get suggestions there. He checked the time. If he left now with Lily, they could make the last part of it.

5

Everyone at the welcome meetup seemed to have a coyote story. In the wake of the attack, Ana could tell how much the dozen parents gathered at Orchard Park wanted to have narrowly averted danger, trying to one-up each other.

"I'm at that track all the time," Raj said. "But I had a call with Singapore yesterday that ran late." If not—he didn't have to say—he could have gotten attacked, too.

More nods from the loose circle, standing in the shade by the picnic table: Everyone could also relate to calls that ran long, and to making clear in a conversation with your neighbors that you were gainfully employed, if vaguely so, with a job important enough to keep you after hours, even if you were currently attired in a moisture-wicking shirt and track pants. The adults were barefaced, but the children wore surgical and cloth masks.

When his golden retriever tugged on its leash, intent on a squirrel, Raj reined him in. "Moose, sit. Sit!"

During introductions, Raj said he'd grown up in El Nido, "went to school in Boston" (which Ana didn't realize was a humblebrag for Harvard), and worked in New York before returning. Ana noticed that Raj and his son—along with her and her daughter—were the only people at the meetup who weren't white.

"A lot of people move back," Nic said to Raj.

He grinned. "Yesterday, I ran into the head cheerleader at the dentist."

"Isn't life high school over and over again?" Nic asked.

The younger kids raced around in the heat, climbing a wooden play structure, squealing as they rode the double-wide metal slide. Beyond lay an expansive lawn, tennis courts, and an abstract metal sculpture, all swoops and hammered steel.

Ella, Nic's daughter, swung by the picnic table, grabbing a handful of organic cheese puffs, next to a pristine tub of hummus and untouched supermarket crudités platter. She yanked down her mask to eat.

From behind, Ella—with her pixie cut, baggy basketball shorts, and loose T-shirt—could have been a boy. Nic and her daughter had the same boisterous sort of energy, the same rangy build.

Ella pulled up her mask. "Let's go to the library," she said to Sofía. "They have a fish tank. Mom, can we go?"

Nic gestured *sure*. Ana gave her permission, even as she scanned the perimeter of the park, on the lookout for her ex.

"Coyotes are harmless," said a woman with startling glacier-blue eyes. Lizzie. "If you leave them alone, they leave you alone. But these attacks are happening more as they move into our habitat."

As *you* move into theirs, Ana thought.

"The news said it was a student from Valle Vista," Nic said. "But didn't give the name. Does anyone know who?"

No one did.

"I hope they catch it," Raj said. "Put that one down and catch the rest. Pump them full of tranquilizers and send them somewhere else, where they can't come back so easily."

"Where?" Nic asked.

"Marin?" he said slyly. He scratched his dog's head. "They could set up patrols around the reservoir."

"Patrols!" Nic tossed her chin. "With all two of El Nido's officers? I doubt they'd see much in the dark."

"But with night-vision goggles . . ." Raj mimed binoculars.

"Like they're the Coast Guard trying to catch drug runners?" Nic asked. "They can't even catch porch pirates!"

Everyone laughed. Ana felt overdressed, out of place in her slacks and button-down shirt, a bank teller at the beach, the only nanny. In her canvas sneakers, she was the shortest and the youngest one, too. Maybe the strongest except for the mother with the sinewy arms in her sleeveless top.

She had been so intent on her job with the Belles, about getting Sofía settled, that she hadn't stopped to consider until now what it meant for her to live in El Nido, too. She had graduated from Oakland Tech, and spoke English and Spanish fluently. And yet, she also understood the mothers in places like El Nido had a language wholly their own, one of endless talk of renovations and vacations. Last night, her boss couldn't comprehend why Ana might not want to socialize with these parents any more than Ana would want to socialize with her.

Nic reached into a tote bag at her feet. "Before I forget!" She handed out flyers. "Info on the Parents' Club and our upcoming fundraisers."

Ana gaped as she read: The minimum suggested donation for each child at Shady Groves was $2,000, which made you a "pearl." Donating more made you a "ruby," "emerald," and so on, all the way to "diamond," for $10,000.

"Cheaper than private school," Nic said.

The minimum suggested donation was almost two-thirds of what Ana made in a month. She had to pay back Julio, pay to renew her papers. And what if you had two or three children enrolled in the school? The Parents' Club wouldn't hold it against you if you couldn't afford to pay. Or would they?

She flipped over the page and discovered a baffling list: Daring Dodgeball. Brats Bash. Hot Vegas Nights. Medieval Times. Kicking It with Kegels. Fire and Ice.

"Those are fundraisers!" Nic explained, seeing her confusion. "Theme parties, to raise money. Some events are for kids, some moms only, others for couples."

A Night at the Zoo. Sofía would love to go. But tickets were $150 per person.

Raj's son came up beside him, rumpled and sweaty from play. "Night at the Zoo," Raj said, as he tousled the son's hair. "How does that sound, buddy?" As the boy bobbed his head, Raj handed him a water bottle, which he dutifully sipped.

"You get to go in the cage of the Komodo dragon!" Nic said.

"What if they bite?" Ana asked. The shade had moved and she edged back in.

Nic didn't seem to hear her question. "One of the parents is on the board. My daughter's crazy for reptiles. Rosy boas are great pets."

The lidless, depthless eyes. The flickering tongue. The silent slither. "What do they eat?" Ana asked.

"Mice. About twice a month." Nic leaned in, as if letting them in on a secret. "I pick them up from the store, but I tell Ella she has to deal with it."

In spite of herself, Ana felt compelled to top this story. "A coyote wiped out the chickens in the backyard."

"When?" Raj asked.

"Two days ago. Sometime in the night, and we discovered it the next morning." Ana had scooped up the remains with a pitchfork. Oh, how she missed the hard surfaces of cities! The concrete and glass and stucco, and the pigeons, rats, and cockroaches, pests on a scale she preferred.

"Just before the attack at the high school, then!" Nic said. "It has to be the same one. What street are you on?"

Her ex wasn't anywhere near, but Ana felt nervous saying the address out loud. "El Rinconcito." All the roads in El Nido had names in Spanish: Los Dedos, Camino del Diablo, Casa Vieja, and El Sueño. She worried that Nic would sniff out where exactly she lived—and whom she worked for.

But Lizzie cut in. "I wanted to ask: I heard that summer swim clubs are a thing here?"

"Yes," Raj and Nic said simultaneously.

Ana listened closely for tidbits to pass on to her boss.

"Get on the wait list now," Nic said. "You can join by next summer. Does your kiddo like to swim?"

Lizzie gestured at her son, navigating the monkey bars. "He loves the water. But which club?"

"There are ten clubs in the league. Most people join the one in their neighborhood," Nic said. "Or they join because they like the coach." She lowered her voice. "And sometimes, the best swimmers get recruited."

"Recruited?" Lizzie sputtered.

"It's ten-year-olds!" Nic said. "They're not getting *cars*. No one's taking them to steak houses! If you're good, really good, your family might get a discount on the membership at the best club. Which usually has a seventy-five-thousand-dollar initiation fee."

Ana gasped. With that kind of money, you could rent an apartment in Fruitvale for years. Pay for an associate's degree, buy a used car, and have money left over.

"That never happened when I was growing up!" Raj said.

"You sure?" Nic asked. A few Olympians got their start in the summer league, swimmers and water polo players. She rattled off a few unfamiliar names, but some parents nodded in recognition. "Some families will pull anything to get ahead."

"How?" Ana ventured. Nic seemed on the verge of gossiping about Jordan.

"Performance-enhancing drugs?" Raj joked.

"You're not far off. . . ." Nic said.

Lizzie interrupted, "What's the big deal though if you don't join one?"

"That's where you meet your neighbors! Other families from the school," Nic said. "You'll see!"

A preschool daredevil clattered by on a scooter, just as a girl leaped off the play structure, landing heavily in the sand.

Nic waved at someone behind her. "You here for the meetup? Welcome!"

It was the Chinese neighbor and his daughter. Ana had waved hello in the cul-de-sac, but they'd never spoken. She got the impression her boss found him peculiar, and he seemed ill at ease here, his movements twitchy. "I'm Jin. This is my daughter Lily."

"What grade are you in, sweetie?" Nic asked.

"Fourth," Lily said proudly, standing tall.

"All the fourth-grade teachers are great," Nic assured her.

"Where does everyone live?" Jin asked. "We're on El Rinconcito."

Nic looked between him and Ana. "You're neighbors, then!"

"Oh, you're the . . ." he started, then stopped when Ana gave him a pleading look. He probably thought she felt self-conscious about being a nanny, but she didn't want Nic to know that she was Blair's nanny.

Nic squinted at him. "I thought I recognized you! I repped the sellers. We met a couple times. Just briefly. Welcome!" She studied Ana. "What house did you move into on Rinconcito? I didn't know another had been sold. Or is it a rental?"

Jin broke in. "So what's fun in El Nido?" His tone sounded a little forced, like he'd rehearsed the question. Maybe he had; maybe like everyone else he'd gotten rusty at making small talk with strangers. Whatever the reason, Ana was grateful for his interruption.

Nic suggested renting paddleboats in a local reservoir or checking out the farmers market. "Tuesdays are concerts in the park; Thursday there's food trucks and movies at sunset."

"What about the Bellavista?" he asked. "What is that?"

"New houses, right?" Raj noted. "Near the high school?"

Ana paid close attention; her bosses were behind the Bellavista.

Nic snorted. "Big houses, all packed together. A disaster waiting to happen."

Disaster?

Raj frowned. "What do you mean?"

Nic gestured at the wildfire haze, but before she could elaborate, her daughter ran toward them, trailed by Sofía. The girl thrust out a dead blue jay, its neck broken, its head tilted at an odd angle.

Ana groaned inside. Another dead bird?

"Drop that now!" Nic barked.

"I want to feed it to Rosie." Ella pulled back her cupped hands.

"It could be sick," Nic said. "It could make Rosie sick, too! Make you sick. Drop it, and go wash your hands."

"It's not sick. It flew into the window of the library." Ella jabbed the bird with her thumb. "It's not stiff yet. It's still warm."

"Now." Nic pointed at the trash.

Ella turned, though not before Lily spotted the dead jay and screamed, and not before Raj's golden retriever jerked the leash from his hand and snatched it from Ella. Moose consumed it in three bites, the bones crunching in its jaws, downy feathers floating in the air.

"Moose!" Raj shouted. Moose licked his chops and wagged his tail, while Nic darted her eyes from her daughter to the other parents. Into the fray, Ana stepped up with a bottle of hand sanitizer that she pumped into the outstretched palms of both girls. Nic directed them to the bathroom, with instructions to wash their hands in hot water for three rounds of "Happy Birthday."

She turned to the parents, open-mouthed in shock, and brightly said, "I brought Popsicles!" She reached into the cooler, waving around a box.

Jin pulled his daughter off to the side to comfort her. Apologizing, Raj dragged away his golden retriever along with his son. Other parents followed, taking a Popsicle to go and thanking Nic.

As Ana stacked paper plates abandoned on the picnic table, Jin joined her, trailed by Lily. "What grade is your daughter in?" he asked.

"Fifth."

"Lily's in fourth," he said. She buried her face in his shoulder. "Are you letting her walk to school?" he asked, stroking her hair. "Lily keeps asking."

"Maybe. Eventually. The girls can go together?"

He seemed relieved. "That would be safer. I can take them sometimes. Or my wife. We both work from home." He paused. "People here drive so fast."

Ana nodded.

"That Mini Cooper . . ." Jin said.

He was obliquely referring to Quinn, but did he really think she'd complain about the bosses' daughter?

When Lily tugged on his arm, ready to go, he told Ana he'd see her around.

After Nic took the plates from her and carried them to the garbage can, Ana picked up fallen bunny-shaped grahams.

A teenager approached, calling out, "Hi! Is the meetup over?"

When Ana confirmed, the teenager sagged for a moment, then gathered herself up. "I'm Tasha. If you ever need help, I can babysit. I watch my brother all the time. We do art, go on hikes, go to the library." He'd just finished the library's summer reading days, she added, and as a reward, he'd get tickets to the Oakland Zoo. "It's a great program."

The zoo. Sofía would love the zoo.

"We have extra tickets," Tasha said. "If you want them."

"Thank you for offering, but she can do the reading."

"The program ends today," Tasha said. "And we have an extra."

They exchanged numbers, Ana promising to swing by later.

Tasha winced, biting her lip.

"What's wrong?" Ana asked.

Tasha gritted her teeth into a smile. "Just a little sore." She pocketed her phone. "Text me anytime, if you ever need a babysitter."

When Ana hesitated, the teenager stiffened. "Never mind."

"I'm a nanny," Ana added quickly. "My boss told me to come today."

"You're a nanny?" Nic had materialized beside them.

The air molecules seemed to rearrange themselves as Nic absorbed the information: Ana wasn't a peer, but the help.

"My daughter's new to the school, too," Ana said. She looked toward the bathroom. What was taking so long?

"You were such a great help today," Nic said. "Good call on the hand sanitizer. Do you . . . ever do childcare on the side? Date nights? We'd love to have your daughter over for a playdate. No charge!" She laughed awkwardly, as though grasping at how to interact with someone both a nanny and the mother of a potential friend for her daughter. "We have an event coming up and none of our regular sitters are available. The teenagers around here get so busy, and then they graduate."

"Tasha babysits." Ana gestured at the teenager, who waved hello.

"I'm vaccinated," Tasha said.

"Sure, sure." Nic thumbed in the teenager's contact info. "You're a lifeguard at Falling Leaf, right? I've seen you."

"Ah, no."

Nic pursed her lips. "You look so familiar though. Are you sure?"

As if Tasha might forget she was actually a lifeguard!

"You at Valle Vista?" Nic asked.

"I'm a junior."

"Did the principal send out anything about the coyote attack?" Nic asked.

"Not yet."

Tasha seemed uneasy. She wore sweatpants though it was close to eighty degrees outside. Was she always cold, or shy about her body?

Nic read the phone number back to Tasha. "I'll text you." With a wave goodbye, the teenager limped to the library, favoring her left leg.

"Who's the family you work for?" Nic asked Ana. "Do they have any kids at Shady Groves?"

Ana stalled. "The baby's name is Liam. Nine months."

Nic's phone buzzed. Apologizing, she walked a few steps away, scrolling and swiping at the screen. She dropped onto a bench with a thump, wrapping her arms around herself.

Ana rushed over. "Are you okay? Dizzy? Do you need water?"

Nic exhaled, then confessed they'd gotten tested for the virus because they were flying to a big family reunion—"first time to see grandparents in more than a year," on Monday, "after the swim finals."

She paused for so long that Ana sensed the bad news before Nic said it: Ella had tested positive. Ana backed away so swiftly she almost tripped.

"Not me," Nic added. "Not my husband."

Ana looked toward the bathroom. Were the girls hanging out inside, in that stuffy enclosed space, stinking of industrial cleanser, particles and droplets of the coronavirus wafting through Ella's mask and through Sofía's, into her nose and mouth? Straight into her darling girl's eyeballs? Ana wanted to run, to throw Sofía onto her hip as if she were a toddler, race home and drop her into a bath with water so scalding her skin would turn bright red. Curse at the virus like a monster under the bed, banish it with bright lights.

Nic sounded faraway. "You should get tested, too, if . . . if you're not . . ."

Not vaccinated. "I am," Ana said stiffly. What if Sofía was infected, and where would they get tested? How would she pay the medical bills? Her daughter, blue faced and bent over. In a hospital bed, the ventilator jammed down her throat like an octopus attacking her. Laid out in a coffin, so terribly still.

"You saw her, she was running around. No symptoms," Nic said. "She's been going to swim team all summer, no cases. A coach at Falling Leaf tested positive in June, but that's it! I would have canceled the meetup if I'd known Ella had it. I never would have scheduled it the day before the championships, but the organizer had an emergency, and next week everyone's gone before school starts."

"What about the other families today?" Ana asked. "Do you have everyone's contact info?"

Nic tensed. Clearly, she was considering her options. If Nic said nothing to the parents at the meetup or to her daughter's teammates, Ana could predict her reasoning: *Ella had been training all summer, and didn't she deserve to compete? And wasn't transmission almost nonexistent outside?* Nic could pretend nothing had happened.

Ana had once worked for someone like Nic, who dug in if told what to do. She would have to take a different tack. "Maybe the test is wrong."

Nic couldn't hide her relief at the idea. "I'll get another test."

"Is Lyra even in the Bay Area yet?" Ana suspected the variant had arrived, but feigning that it *hadn't* would remind Nic that it probably *had*.

The girls burst upon them, giggling. Nic stood. Ella asked for Popsicles, asked if Sofía could come over to see the boa. Sofía wordlessly seemed to plead: It had been so long since she'd had a friend.

Ella sneezed into her mask. Lunging, Ana pushed her daughter apart from Ella.

"What, Mom?" Sofía asked. Her expression surprised, annoyed—and then scared. It wasn't the first time Ana had shoved her daughter out of harm's way.

Nic put an arm around her own daughter.

"I saw a yellow jacket," Ana said. A sneeze, such a little sound, such little droplets caught—mostly but not entirely?—in the mask that covered Ella's nose and mouth.

She'd probably offended Nic. But Ana would have done it again, done much more, to protect her daughter.

6

As soon as Ana explained to her boss that she and Sofía had been exposed to the virus, Blair told them to isolate until after the weekend, after their family left for Maui. It soon became apparent that the girls couldn't stay away from each other. In the backyard, when Jordan went looking for Tigs, their orange tabby, Sofía had run out to join her, Ana in pursuit.

After her boss booked them on leftover points in a hotel, she left a wad of cash in an envelope at the foot of the stairs and texted, Get room service. Get whatever you'd like.

Saturday morning, upon waking at the hotel, Ana felt a tickle in her throat. She was bone-tired, too. The virus? Maybe it was the deteriorating air quality, the chemical whiff of wildfires, burned plastics lofted high above before sinking down here.

They had three nights at the hotel in Emeryville, the fanciest place they'd ever stayed, with a view of the bay. Even though Ana was supposed to house-sit while the Belles were on vacation, her boss told her not to worry; she'd made other arrangements already. Tigs was still missing, but Blair said it wasn't the first time he'd gone wandering.

At the hotel, Ana spent the morning bickering with her daughter—battling over the thermostat, spoiling her appetite with snacks—while also looking for signs of fever, for a cough, anything that indicated a rapidly spreading contagion.

Then her sister called, insisting they come over for lunch in Antioch.

"We're quarantining," Ana said. Sofía curled beside her, watching her favorite spooky show.

"We've all had the virus already!" Carolina said. A month ago.

"Your girls were okay?" Ana leaned against the padded headboard.

"Like a cold," Carolina said, her voice tinny through the speakerphone. Ana rubbed Sofía's back.

Carolina said she and her husband had it worse, even though they were vaccinated. "Like getting run over!" They had recovered, though. Mostly. "So come!"

They were converting the garage into a rental with a hot plate, toaster oven, and compact refrigerator. They had to paint the walls and install a linoleum floor, but Ana and Sofía could stay there while they awaited test results, she said. If they were sick, Carolina could look after them. If they weren't, they could hang out for the week while the Belles were on vacation.

Ana relented.

Soon after Ana had started her new job, she'd contacted her sister for the first time in more than a year. Julio had called her sister a control freak, and Carolina was: So smart, so capable, she could sing, could dance, could change the oil on a car, swap the lock on a door. But sometimes, in Carolina's rush to take care of everyone, she'd empty the dishwasher that Ana loaded (incorrectly, in her opinion) or add salt to the stew Ana made—the minor irritations of a baby sister raised by the older one. Julio had widened the crack between them into a chasm.

Until then, she hadn't known Carolina had moved from Hayward, after buying a fixer-upper. Antioch was about forty-five minutes due east by freeway from El Nido, hotter and drier, on the fringes of the county, on the final stretch of the Delta before it flowed into the bay.

Though Ana worried the conversation at lunch might be as stilted and tense as it had been during their initial call, they picked up as before: squeezing limes for the limonada con soda, mixed tangy the way they both liked it, trying out each other's lipsticks (plum and dark burgundy), and video-calling Adria, their middle sister, living in LA.

Now, after a lunch of velvety homemade tamales (their mother's recipe, the last of a batch from the freezer), Carolina and Ana swayed in a double swing. Their talk turned to Julio.

"He's calling me," Carolina said.

Ana exhaled. "I got rid of my phone on his calling plan."

"He claimed you and Sofía had gone missing, but when I started asking questions, his story kept changing."

Ana pictured him on his cell phone, pacing out on the street, so their roommates couldn't overhear. His fury crackling like a downed wire. Anyone passing by would have crossed the street.

Carolina blocked his number, but then he called from other phones. She blocked those numbers, too. "I'll get a new number this weekend." When she braced her foot, halting the swing without warning, Ana almost fell off.

Carolina asked about the Belles, if there was a good lock on the front door, if there was an alarm, if there were cameras.

Yes, yes, yes, Ana said. She rubbed her hand on the cushion. The sky had a washed-out quality, denim fading to a grimy white, smudged from a second wildfire that burned somewhere to the east.

Sofía hitched her cousin onto her back—Carolina's youngest, born just before the pandemic—for a piggyback ride.

Carolina pushed off again, the swing creaking into motion. "Where do you get your mail? Your credit card bill, the stuff from the bank?"

"It's all online. . . ." Ana tucked her legs, trying to lull herself with the rhythm of the swing.

Wind chimes tinkled on the patio. "What's the address you listed?" Carolina asked. "Did you change it? Is it still his address?"

"In El Nido."

"He can find it online. All that info is for sale." Carolina lifted her chin. "Change it to here."

"Then . . . he'll come here." If she paid what she owed him, would he leave her alone? Maybe she could find a side gig to make more money.

Her niece clapped her hands, popping soap bubbles that Sofía blew through a wand. Chacho, their mutt—a mix of German shepherd, pit bull, and something else—chased and nipped at the bubbles, too.

Carolina touched Ana's arm. "He would have tracked this address down. Eventually." If, when he comes here, she said, she'd turn Chacho on him. "You have to hide the address in El Nido for as long as possible." And if the Belles went out of town again, Ana should stay with Carolina and her family. "It's safer."

* * *

Two years ago, when she started dating Julio, Ana couldn't stop touching the notch at his waist, the groove in his chin, his compact, muscled body. His hands on her curves, at her waist, her back, cupping her butt, heat shimmering between them. He'd also looked after her: packed her lunch, got a new cell phone and put her on his calling plan. He convinced her to sell her car and found a cheaper one for her. When it broke down, he gave her rides to and from work.

Soon, he'd persuaded her to stop hanging out with her friends and family. He alone could take care of her, he said, her and Sofía both. He acted out bedtime stories with Sofía's stuffed animals, and he could be exceedingly kind to strangers, once giving the coat off his back to a homeless man.

Within three months, they'd moved in together. Not long after, he hit her for the first time. Then the second.

Always, he apologized. But still he cuffed her face, still he shoved her against the wall, yanked her hair, and forced her to her knees. Took what he wanted from her when she didn't want to give it.

When she tried to renew DACA, they'd had a big fight. Though they'd been engaged for months, they never set a date.

"You think I'm a liar?" Julio was American born and had grown up in the Mission. He'd scooped up the keys to his truck. "You think I won't marry you? Let's go, go right now to the courthouse." He'd gestured at his paint-spattered jeans, at her sweatpants. "Like this."

When she crumpled, he turned coaxing. "I want it special. Not right now."

She'd let her status lapse. She couldn't scrape together money for the renewal fee, anyway. Yet when the last president had all but ended the program, Julio had been smug. Too late, she realized that he'd wanted to jeopardize her papers. He'd wanted her at his mercy, all this time: the junky car to ensure she couldn't go far, the cell phone so he could keep track of whom she called. He didn't want her to get vaccinated, told her it would mess with her fertility, but she'd gotten the jab without telling him, at a mobile clinic by a church. She hid the side effects from him, muscling through the chills and aches.

After discovering her vaccine card, he'd slammed her head into the wall so hard the plaster had cracked. Days later, after buying a burner phone, she'd called her cousin, asking if she'd heard of any live-in jobs into which she might disappear.

"What about Labor Day?" Carolina now asked. Next month. "You should come here."

"I'm house-sitting." Ana gripped the wicker armrest.

"You don't get it off?"

"I get all the holidays off. They're paying me extra. I'll take all the hours I can get."

"Why?"

Carolina would be furious if she knew that Ana had let her immigration status lapse; Ana didn't like to think about it, either.

"Why are you working Labor Day?"

"For DACA," she muttered.

"DACA? Didn't you renew it?" Carolina halted the swing again. She'd helped Ana with the original application.

She had to get her paperwork extended and renewed every few years. Even with DACA, she remained in limbo, with no option of applying for a green card or citizenship.

Ana traced the toe of her sneakers in the dust.

"Ana," Carolina chided.

Would her sister ever stop treating her as if she were a teenager? "I didn't have the money for the renewal."

"It's expired?" Carolina tucked a loose strand of hair behind her ear.

Ana looked away.

"You could have told me. I would have let you borrow the money." Carolina exhaled. Ana was the only sibling who had papers; Carolina and Adria had crossed over after they turned sixteen, too old to qualify for DACA.

Ana had been five years old, a trip she remembered only in snatches: a blur of bus rides, hard beds, and stiff, stale tortillas. Musky BO and cologne. The blinding-white light and the burning on her feet. A thirst so consuming she'd hallucinated rivers and lakes.

Each of their prospects here had been determined by the age they'd entered the United States, the point at which lawmakers deemed one a child worthy of protection and the other not. Ana had always assumed that Carolina was bossy by biology, by birth order. But maybe this was how her sister found a measure of control in a world that granted her none.

"Julio said he'd call ICE if I didn't tell him where you were," Carolina said.

Ana gasped. "I'll talk to him, I—"

No, Carolina said, wagging her finger. The girls rode by, kicking up clouds of dust—Ana's niece on a tricycle, Sofía on a pink bike. Their American-born children didn't know that their parents lacked permanent legal status.

"I'm saving up." Ana picked at a loose thread dangling from the cushion. "With this job. And side jobs. I'll have enough soon."

"What kind of side jobs?" Carolina prodded.

Her sister tried to be helpful, but Ana wished she'd stop needling her. She listed a few that immediately came to mind, options with flexible schedules: ride-sharing, restaurant delivery, running errands.

"Everything you earn driving goes toward gas," Carolina said. "You barely break even. And what would you do with Sofía? Take her with you? Remember that dad whose children accidentally got kidnapped by carjackers? He was dropping off food and left them in the car, engine running." She stared into the distance. "What about Rafa? Could he help?

Sofía's father. He'd been a chapín, too. By the time Ana had given birth, they'd broken up. He'd moved to Florida for a job. Every so often, he'd send money for Sofía's birthday and on holidays, but work had dried up during the pandemic.

Ana tugged on the sleeve of her drapey shirt, with wide sleeves that reminded her of a kimono. "I got this from the local thrift shop. A lot of clothes there are like new or with tags. Maybe I could sell the best stuff online."

"Seems like a hassle," Carolina said. "You'd always be running to the post office, and people would order things to try them on, but return them."

Ana got up, her back damp. Temperatures would hit triple digits today. She gathered their plates from the patio table, piled with the remnants of their lunch, smeared on crumpled banana leaves. "I'll sell tamales, then," she said, exasperated. Joking, and yet . . .

At her interview with the Belles, she'd brought a gift of tamales wrapped in glossy green leaves. Ana didn't know they had composted them. The family had sworn off pork, off many things, Ana had since learned, with separate diets for each: Paleo for Blair, keto for Sam, vegetarian for Quinn, and pescatarian for Jordan.

Carolina stood. "Tamales? Don't people there prefer . . . Chipotle?"

You could get tamales cheaply and easily at any supermarket, next to the frozen pizzas and lasagnas. And a lot of people like the Belles wouldn't eat them, since the primary ingredient was forbidden: masa, made from ground corn. Blair had told her that corn—technically a grain—could inflame the gut and was fattening, fed to cattle to pack on the pounds.

Silly, but: a tickle of an idea. The people of El Nido had their choice of frozen foods, meal kits, and every kind of restaurant delivery. Ana could offer convenience, plus something else that made her products distinct, for which she could charge a premium. "*Keto* tamales," she said.

Over the next few days, she and Carolina perfected a recipe for tamales made with almond flour instead of masa, along with lard, bacon drippings, and konjac powder to thicken the mixture. The Belles practically lived on almond flour, in addition to yams, coconut oil, bananas, baby spinach, and meat certified organic, humane, and climate positive, as well as an array of powders and ground seeds that made everything seem like a potion.

Blair had given Ana cash to spend on meals while quarantining; instead, she used it to buy supplies—the tomatoes, tomatillos, garlic, red peppers, pasillas, and sambos that now bubbled away for the recado, giving off a savory smell with a hint of char, of sweetness. The kitchen was steamy with the scent that Ana associated with her mother, even as most other memories of her faded. She'd died not long after they arrived in the United States, the cancer sudden, unexpected, and quick. Their father had been felled a year later in a factory accident.

Ana poked a tomato with a fork, checking on the skin. She fished it out and peeled it before putting the tomato back into the pot. The limp skins reminded her of popped balloons.

In deciding how to price them, Carolina suggested doubling, then quadrupling the wholesale cost: $12 per tamale. "If it's too cheap, they'll wonder why it's not cheaper." She set down a spoon with a clatter. "People already think Mexican food should be cheap."

"Not that we're Mexican." Ana pulled the pork off the stove.

"If it's expensive, they think it means the tamales are worth it." Carolina unscrewed a jar of olives, garnishes for the filling. "That *they're* worth it."

That afternoon, when Nic texted to check if Ana and her daughter had fallen sick, if they needed anything, anything at all, she became their very first customer.

7

Meanwhile in Maui, Quinn stole her little sister away to go snorkeling. Just after sunrise, the light was soft and low. It had been forever since they'd done anything together, just the two of them, and she wanted to make sure Jordan was okay. Quinn had noticed that Jordan seemed withdrawn at the swim meet, earbuds firmly planted in. She'd kept to herself on the trip, subdued and quiet at meals.

Jordan seemed her usual self in the water, though. Quinn was relieved that her sister hadn't lost her wonder for the bright yellow tang, butterfly fish, and parrot fish that flitted beneath. Neither had she. It felt like they flew above worlds hidden from the surface. Jordan had a powerful kick, staying under as long as possible.

When Quinn caught sight of a sea turtle in the distance, she tapped Jordan's shoulder, pointed, and they kicked toward it. Both of them were fast, but not as fast as honu. With a single swish of its massive flippers, it glided away as if on jets, with apparently little exertion. After a few more kicks, Quinn gave up and surfaced, spitting out her snorkel and gasping. Jordan popped up, too.

"How long can it stay underwater?" Quinn wondered aloud. A wave splashed her face and she coughed, spitting out salt water.

"Up to five hours," Jordan said.

She had a mind and a memory for the random odd fact that reflected how much else she knew without having to say it. She could probably have rattled off the maximum distance sea turtles could swim, what they ate, and other details she remembered after reading them once. Oh, how Quinn would miss her! By this time next year, she'd be packing for college.

Her skin prickled. She was cold all the time now, even in the warmest water. "Can you imagine holding your breath for that long?"

If it had been up to Jordan, they'd still be racing honu. She was so competitive, always trying to dart ahead when she was a toddler. She wasn't a sore loser—as long as she didn't lose. First to get into the car, first to finish her meal, first to hit the blacktop at recess.

They inserted the mouthpieces and blew out to clear the tubes, then swam back. As they lurched out of the water, their fins clumsy on sand, Quinn checked her tracker: She'd burned two hundred calories.

After they slipped off their fins and headed up the beach, Jordan dragged behind, not racing ahead like usual. Her expression seemed downcast, too.

She nudged Jordan's shoulder. "Hey—you okay?"

Jordan shrugged.

"People are literally the worst. . . ." Although Quinn let the sentence hang, Jordan didn't volunteer anything about the swim finals. "You know I have your back."

The words felt as shallow as a greeting card, but she didn't know what else to say.

Jordan smiled tightly.

Quinn would try again later. Her sister probably missed Tigs. Mom had posted on Neighborz and called the shelter, but he hadn't turned up. Quinn told herself that Tigs was a survivor, apt to return battered and scratched up, but she was also bracing herself. They walked on, the sand cool underfoot. She handed a striped towel to Jordan, before draping one around her own waist.

Her parents came down from the hotel, Liam on her mom's hip. Proof of her parents' sex life had grossed out Quinn, and seeing her mom on bedrest during the pregnancy convinced her she never wanted to have children. It had been fun, though, to have a baby at home during the pandemic—like a puppy, only cuter. And she was glad that he and Jordan would have each other after she left.

"Let's go to the buffet before the line gets too long," Blair said.

Sam obsequiously gestured toward the hotel. "Mademoiselle, perhaps you would like zee crepes?" he said to Quinn, emphasizing *crepes* in a French accent, Pepé Le Pew times a million. He'd used this voice for years, to coax them to dinner, pretending to be a maître d' at a fancy restaurant.

"And for you, zee Froot Loops?" he said to Jordan, who giggled.

"Dad, you aren't supposed to do accents!" Quinn said. But she laughed, too.

"Vat accent?" Sam said. "Vat are you saying?"

"Now you're Dracula?" Quinn asked.

He dropped the accent. "You want to get shave ice this afternoon?" he asked her. Their tradition.

"Yeah." She could let most of it melt.

Jordan was her mother's favorite; Quinn, her father's. He taught her how to swim, to drive, to ski, to juggle. He had so much faith and confidence in her, on the good days—on the best days—she felt like she could fly to the moon or scale Mt. Everest.

Quinn pointed toward the gigantic figure-eight-shaped pool. "I have to swim a slow two thousand before breakfast." (Six hundred calories.)

"Can I come?" Jordan asked.

Quinn wavered. Maybe she could get her to talk if they had more time alone, but she had to get her workout in.

Her stomach growled. Before snorkeling, she and Jordan had each eaten a rice cake with almond butter (one hundred thirty-five calories). After her swim, she planned to eat two hard-boiled eggs, three bites of plain yogurt, a slice of toast, and coffee (two hundred seventy calories). "It won't take long."

* * *

Quinn staggered out of the pool. She'd lagged in the water, but had pushed through. Her head spun and she hung on to the polished metal rail, slick and cold beneath her fingers. She'd had dizzy spells before, a couple times while driving—earlier this summer, she'd hit a deer on a blind curve and totaled the BMW. Her system of logging calories consumed, calories burned, was off-kilter; she had to eat and exercise more precisely from now on.

As she took a few deep breaths, collecting herself, she heard a huge splash. Drops pattered against her leg. She turned to see two boys who'd cannonballed into the pool. They might have been Indian or Pakistani. Jordan had been in a water-gun fight with them yesterday afternoon. They hoisted themselves up, then jumped in again, their arms tight around tucked knees, whooping and screaming with laughter.

From a nearby lounge chair, a white woman in a hot-pink flowered muumuu scowled. A constellation of sunspots spattered her cleavage, the skin thin and crepey.

She tossed back her ashy-blond hair and flagged down a waiter in khaki shorts and Hawaiian shirt, who balanced a tray full of drinks and a fruit plate.

"They're so rowdy! Can you"—she gestured with her hands—*make this go away*.

Karen alert. The boys, oblivious, now started a splashing contest, smacking the water so hard that drops flicked onto the Karen's face. By her expression of horror and outrage, you would have thought they'd urinated on her.

The server—his tawny lion's mane held back by an elastic headband—looked around, probably hoping that he might find their parents. The drinks slid around on the tray. "Let me drop these off. . . ." he said.

"It's the kids pool," Quinn said.

"I was sitting here," the Karen said, but gathered her things.

Quinn grabbed her phone and snapped a photo of the woman stomping off toward the adult pool. She texted it to Jacqui and added, Karen in the wild.

She threw on her cover-up and checked for a response: nothing. The message left unread.

California was three hours ahead, around noon there. Maybe Jacqui didn't have her phone with her.

Or maybe Jacqui was ignoring her. The dumb thing Quinn said in the library hadn't come up again. She should apologize, but didn't know how.

She stared at the unread message. What was she hoping for from Jacqui anyway—affirmation, confirmation? Shouldn't she speak up without being so desperate for praise?

She scrolled through Jacqui's feed and discovered her in a photo with Maddy, posted five minutes ago. They were fooling around at the Valle Vista track, pretending to scream in terror at a phantom coyote. Though officially closed, it had become a popular selfie spot.

Quinn felt a pang. Maddy always tried to get in between her and Jacqui. She imagined what Maddy might say, how creepy it was to take a photo of someone without their permission.

She walked toward the hotel. Last summer, it had gotten a little weird with Jacqui, but they'd patched things up. By a planter bursting with bright red flowers, she checked her texts again—still no reply. She studied the photo of the track, thinking about the coyote attack. Word had gotten out about the victim. Poor Tasha. She searched for Tasha on the socials, scrolling through her photos of wildflowers and mushrooms. Quinn felt bad for not saying hello to her at the library; she hadn't remembered her from class until she read the news. What shitty luck. She DMed her now, swiping through emojis.

8

In middle school, Tasha had been tight with Aisha and Leah. After she moved to El Nido, for a year or so, their group chat lived on. Her friends filled her in on gossip while Tasha shared links to funny local videos: white classmates attempting to floss, their arms and legs flailing. Grandmas in Hawaiian shirts, jamming on ukes under the park gazebo, strumming "Somewhere Over the Rainbow."

So corny. But she also found herself humming the song while foraging. She couldn't explain to her friends how much she loved the quiet here, that her mother and brother did, too, how the oak trees felt like family, like home.

Slowly the chat had tapered off from daily to every other day, to every week, to once in a while.

She'd never really had a chance to make friends in El Nido. She spent the spring of her freshman year online, and the summer after, at the height of the protests against police brutality, dozens of classmates had messaged her: "Sending <3." "Hi." "Hello." "How r u?" She never replied to their DMs. Some, she'd never spoken to, but maybe they went through the yearbook, in search of someone Black.

After reporters interviewed Tasha about the coyote attack, more students at Valle Vista followed her on ClikClak. Apparently, only violence reminded them she existed.

After fluffing the throw pillows and settling into the couch, Tasha checked her ClikClak notifications. The latest, a message from Quinn, from two hours ago:

Quinn: thinking of u ❤❤❤get better soon! what's ur @flashcash? can send Starbucks!

What even. She took a screenshot and sent it to Jane.

Jane: lol, that's my neighbor?!? r u friends?
Tasha: nah
Jane: can she send me $$too?
Tasha: lol

They texted about Jane's dad; she still hadn't uncovered definitive proof that he'd lost his job. Tasha tossed the phone aside. She should check on Marcus, but her limbs felt encased in cement. For the last few days, he'd been afraid to go outside, and he'd hardly moved from the beanbag in his room, granted unlimited screen time. She swirled her glass, ice cubes clinking, and sipped the elderberry spritz, made from the foraged berries that tasted like midnight.

She rubbed her eyes, red and watering, nearly swollen shut from looking at screens all day. She reached for the horticulture book from the library. As she paged through *Black Gold*, a photo caught her eye: a woman in a striped, high-necked dress, her hair in a chignon. Lucinda Stewart.

Something in the curl of her bangs, in the tint of Lucinda's skin, made Tasha wonder if the woman had been passing. She looked like Tasha's aunties from Louisiana—the same high cheekbones and regal nose. The caption noted that Lucinda had urged her husband, Wallace, to cultivate walnuts, after they'd settled here in 1872. The saplings were descended from trees the Franciscan brothers first brought to California. A gracious hostess, Lucinda was known for her large garden—medicinal and ornamental—and for the poems she composed in honor of birthdays and anniversaries.

Tasha flipped through *Black Gold*, hoping to find another shot of

Lucinda, close up or taken from another angle, but only found portraits of bushy-browed, bushy-bearded, stiff-necked founders and landowners. She could have been grasping at nothing; maybe it was no different from when she spotted faces in random patterns: a smile on a clock or knots of wood that resembled eyes, nose, and mouth.

Tasha swung her legs around and gingerly put her feet on the carpet. Her calf throbbed dully, the stitches itchy. Her mother had examined the wound that morning. "It's healing nicely," she'd said. "They did a good job." She couldn't hide her worry, though; since the attack, her cheeks had become even more gaunt.

Every night, Tasha had woken up screaming, the pillow elevating her leg kicked onto the floor and the sheets twisted around her. Her mother had been there each time to soothe her. Though Tasha remembered nothing from her dreams, she'd probably fought the coyote. She didn't blame it for acting according to its nature, even though she never wanted to see or hear one again.

It remained at large. No one had seen it bingeing from the trash cans, overflowing after the swim finals: the chomped ends of hot dogs and gnawed cheese sticks, potato chip crumbs, and apple cores.

When her mother returned from the store, she hovered, offering her a pillow, tea, a massage. "Maybe it's time for a nap?" she asked.

Tasha resisted rolling her eyes. Her mother meant well. Instead, Tasha proposed going to the historic orchard to test out a cure.

Researchers had used essential oils, rose, lemon, eucalyptus, and clove, while showing patients images of the plants, and the results had been promising. Tasha had foraged eucalyptus leaves from a steep stretch of hill above the library. Mint, soft and fuzzy, that massed along the banks of the creek by the elementary school. Prickly pine needles from the playground by the library. Shiny purple camphor berries, gathered from the trees above the tennis courts. Dusky juniper berries from the bushes by the post office.

Unripe walnuts were the most pungent of all, the smell dark and spicy, their husks bright green. Though Tasha had rushed home fragrant specimens, they were already dying—dead—by the time she offered them to Minerva. Maybe you could get a stronger association if you visited where it grew: if you could stroke the petal and press your cheek against the furrowed bark.

As the summer slipped by, the resinous scent of green walnuts might fade in the heat, and she wanted it potent as possible to test on her mother.

"What about Marcus?" Minerva asked.

"Just for an hour?" Tasha asked. "He won't even notice we're gone. Marcus?"

He didn't look up.

"Marcus," Minerva said. "Don't open the door. Don't go outside."

He swiped and jabbed at the screen.

"Marcus, what did I say?" Minerva asked.

"Don't go outside," he mumbled.

"Send a message on the chat if you need anything," she added.

After they got into the car, Tasha guided her mother to the western edge of El Nido. "Slow down," Tasha said as they approached the park. Bushes obscured the turnoff.

"You sure this is a park?" Minerva said.

Tasha pointed at the sign by the mouth of the gravel lot. As they pulled in, she gasped. On the far side of the park, she glimpsed the orchard. Some trees were bent and gnarled as a crone who'd been on her feet all her days; others towered, their branches spreading like the arms of a soloist in a choir, hitting her highest note. Age could do either to you. Some produced hardly anything, but didn't they deserve a rest?

"So now what?" Minerva asked.

"We go in!"

A walnut tree could live more than two hundred years; a human eighty or ninety if they were lucky. Looking at a tree was like time traveling, Tasha thought. When you leaned against the trunk and sat in the shade, you reached toward those who had planted it. And they reached toward you.

Dried grasses poked up between clods of dirt, uneven as a lava field. She stumbled, catching herself on the low branches of a walnut tree. She gripped on to the bough as the stitches pulled taut on her calf muscle. She stifled a moan; she didn't want Minerva, who had gotten ahead of her, to hear. She would order Tasha to get into the car and back to bed.

"Tasha, where are you?" Minerva called out. "Tasha? Tash!"

Her body ached, her stomach curdled from the antibiotics, and her arm was sore from the rabies shot. Her calf throbbed, as if she had another heart in there. She could bear these pains, but it nearly broke Tasha to hear her mother panicked. Minerva was unflappable, by temperament and by profession, and that was how she'd raised Tasha and her brother, too. Tasha would have followed her anywhere.

Caring for El Nido's oldest and sickest should have counted for something cosmically. Couldn't a deity or a force of nature return Minerva's sense of smell?

But Tasha knew no one kept score. "I'm here, Mama." She waved at her mother, who seemed relieved to have her in her sights again.

For years, Tasha's parents had talked about moving to Hawaii or Paris; both of them had lived within twenty miles of home their entire lives, growing up in neighborhoods known as the Black Beverly Hills for their affluence and their views.

Not long before the car accident, her parents had decided on San Francisco. "It's like going abroad without going abroad," Papa had joked.

"For how long?" Tasha had asked.

"A year. Or more, if we like it," her mother said.

Minerva hardly slept in the months after the funeral, bringing Tasha and her brother into the king bed where she could watch over them. Then Tasha's cousin went to a house party—invited by a friend of a friend from her magnet high school—where a teenager was killed. A trombonist, a big brother, an aspiring doctor. The gunman had been aiming for someone else.

When Auntie Di called with the news, Minerva had fallen to her knees, bent over, digging her fingers into the carpet loops. Not long after, she'd applied for the job in the Bay Area. At Sunrise, she'd landed more money, more responsibility. Sometimes you had to leave to prove your worth, she told Tasha. El Nido offered safety, a five-minute commute, clean air, and high-ranking schools; Tasha and Marcus wouldn't have to trek across the city for a magnet or private school.

When they first moved here, they spent their weekends exploring everything within an hour's drive: windswept beaches, briny and bracing; primeval redwoods that exuded—exhaled?—the essence of life.

Now, Tasha plucked a few Ping-Pong-sized walnuts, sticky on her fingers, and stuffed them into her fanny pack. What a rush! Like Eve, wandering Eden, bursting with food that she didn't have to plant or water, prune or weed. Worked by no hand until her fingers had brushed against them.

"You know, this runs in the family." Minerva gestured over the grove and at Tasha. "We have a great-granny—or great-great?—who was a medicine woman, who knew all the healing herbs." She saved the slaver's youngest son from a fever, she added. "But they never freed her."

"Why didn't you tell me?" Tasha imagined the healer kneeling, her fingers nimble and sure. Just like Tasha. Like her mother. What else did this woman pass down to them? Observant, watchful, quick to learn?

"I did, baby. You just didn't remember," Minerva said.

"What was her name?"

"I wish I knew. I've looked, but there isn't much."

The records were murky. The truth had been lost, like so much else taken from them. Still, Tasha held on to this glimmer, what felt like a hidden inheritance.

She couldn't stop thinking about Lucinda Stewart. A lineage not of blood, but of community, of a possibly light and bright woman who might also have loved plants and trees. Lucinda could have come to distant California, a new state of the union, for a new life. Pushed by or pushing away her family. Maybe she herself had never known; maybe one of her foremothers or forefathers had kept the secret from their children.

In trying to track down more information about Lucinda, Tasha had come across an 1870 census of the area, listing the earliest Black settlers: slaves or servants in these valleys, but also two dozen "free colored," who could have worked in the orchards, in the gardens. In the house of someone like Lucinda, or as pit masters, as shoemakers, to make enough money to buy the freedom of their families left behind in the South. She wished she had known this history before; she might have felt less out of place in El Nido.

The sky was hazy again, everything washed in gold like photos from the 1970s in Grandma's albums. The AQI was in the high 140s today, bordering on red. If she spent more than an hour outside, her throat would hurt.

The branches shook as a pair of squirrels raced up to the crown, and something rustled nearby. Tasha froze, then looked for a rock, a brick, a stick, anything she could hurl. Why hadn't she armed herself beforehand? She searched for escape routes in the orchard. How quickly could they get to the road, or back to the car? If she screamed, would anyone at the houses on the ridge hear her?

A deer crept out, startled upon seeing them, and disappeared into the brush. She had to chill. A second attack seemed as likely as getting struck by lightning. Though with the luck her family had, Tasha should dash inside the moment clouds appeared on the horizon.

"You okay, honey?" Minerva asked. "I can't get over seeing deer everywhere!" Looking around, she seemed to take in the orchard's size. "We shouldn't be here."

At ground level, it appeared bigger than in the satellite photo. "There's no fence." Tasha pointed at the waist-high thistles. "No one's been here for months. Maybe for years."

"It's someone's property." Minerva rubbed the nape of her neck. "Even if they're neglecting it."

"No one enforces it. It's open space." Tasha wasn't sure if that was true, and, if so, what access that entailed.

"Not for much longer." Minerva eyed a bulldozer parked at the edge of the orchard. "We don't get squatter's rights."

Shortly before her father died, her parents had explained that if Tasha bought anything at the store, she had to get a receipt and hold it up visibly when she left. She couldn't be sloppy, couldn't wear her pajama bottoms with hoodies and slides out of the house. "You have to dress two notches above everyone else," her father had said. As if she were going to church or a job interview. She couldn't cuss, couldn't, couldn't . . . otherwise people would judge her. "At the park, don't put your hands in your pockets. Don't run if you get stopped by police. Don't move. Tell them your uncle's at the *LA Times*."

They'd judge her anyway. She'd been ten years old, the same age Marcus was now. The following summer, police had murdered more young Black men, Philando and Alton and on and on. Rallies and demonstrations had been all over the news.

During the even bigger BLM protests, she'd finally been old enough to go. "Last summer, you wouldn't let me join any marches," Tasha said.

"The virus," Minerva said.

"You said there are other ways to protest." Tasha gestured around the orchard. "That's what I'm doing." She explained what she'd found online: Trespassing laws originated after the Civil War, targeting freed slaves trying to make a living by selling foods they hunted and foraged. White landowners had tried to put a stop to the practice, and with each leaf and berry and nut she plucked, Tasha joined the resistance.

Her mother murmured, understanding. "Did you ever bring Marcus here?"

"He'd get in the way." Tasha tugged the zipper closed on the fanny pack, bulging with green walnuts.

"Did he come here with you?"

"I already told you, I've never been here," Tasha snapped, then regretted it. "Sorry." She was exhausted. Pretending she was okay took more out of her than she wanted to admit.

"He's getting so tall now. . . ." Minerva sighed.

He resembled their father, baby-faced, with deep dimples and ears that poked out. Tasha took after her mother, both tall and curvy.

Sunlight dappled through the leaves, shadows swaying in the wind. As Tasha held the biggest walnut to Minerva's face, she inhaled deeply from the chartreuse husk. Pressing her hands together, she beamed. "I don't smell anything . . . not exactly. But the shape of it, it's like something emerging from the fog."

Tasha smiled.

"The way you know this land," Minerva said. "You needed space to breathe." Her expression turned wistful.

She was thinking about Papa, Tasha could tell. Sometimes, she wondered if by moving here, Minerva had been making a wish for a parallel universe in which he'd lived. Tasha didn't believe in ghosts. She'd never once felt her father's presence again; he'd never appeared in her dreams, as much as she longed to see him one more time. No magic had stopped the drunk driver who killed him, no magic would bring him back, or the ones her family had lost in the last year: Auntie Louise and Uncle Joe. So many for whom the vaccine had come too late.

She doubted that somewhere in the afterlife her great-great-healer and Lucinda had hatched a plot to bring her here. Yet she couldn't shake the feeling that someone—maybe many—had guided her to this tree, with hands gentle as a breeze.

Rounding the bend, they came upon an empty swath, the walnut trees razed and piled to the side. Tasha moaned from deep within her belly.

Minerva touched her shoulder. "Is it your leg, honey? Do you need to sit down?"

"They were so old."

A sign advertised the Bellavista. The grove would get plowed under for the homes where they hoped to live. "Maybe they'll keep a few trees? To disguise the duplexes?" Minerva asked ruefully.

Tasha kicked up a puff of dust. "They'll keep a few for the view. For the people who buy the biggest houses."

9

Across town, Jin could see what he'd missed in repainting the bathroom: Now dried, the coat looked heavier in some spots, with visible roller marks that arced off in different directions. It looked worse than when he'd started.

Though the window was open, the petrochemical scent made his eyes water and his head swim. He should have waited, but because he'd struggled to hire a handyman, he'd wanted to get started on renovations.

He'd heard that having an address in El Nido led tradesmen to inflate their prices. He'd been prepared to bargain, if only he could get someone to return his calls or emails: No one he found online would respond to his inquiries. After last year's pandemic pause, everyone was renovating and remodeling. He would never have passed up an opportunity to flip the house, but if he'd known, he would have started looking for workers even before they moved.

Dishwashers and refrigerators were back-ordered, too, unavailable for months, and lumber prices had more than doubled. China was very far away, most days, an abstraction but for the supply chain now reminding him that what a factory worker ate for breakfast in Guangzhou, what a dockworker in Hong Kong watched on television, rippled across the globe.

He mentioned nothing to Chen; he didn't want to give him any reason to believe he'd made a bad investment. Jin circled his shoulders, trying to shake off his weariness. Rather than botch more renovations, he should work on Chen's sizzle reel. Kai had had a brilliant idea: Rather than hire a videographer, they could pocket the fee and download and edit together the footage that other agents had commissioned and posted online.

At his computer, he viewed montage after montage, drone footage and soaring music that made you feel like a billionaire arriving by flying car, taking your dominion from on high before you dramatically swooped in.

He adjusted the fan to its highest speed, tucking errant papers under his jar of tea. How could this house ever compare? Especially with brand-new construction. His thoughts returned to the gleaming Bellavista. He searched online. The first link advertised the luxury homes, whose computer renderings made 187 Rinconcito seem dingy and dated. The second link was a news story with the headline NEXT PHASE OF CONTROVERSIAL DEVELOPMENT. As he scrolled down the page, a detail caught his eye: Over the last thirty years, three developers had gone bankrupt trying to build on the old walnut groves. Locals had protested.

In China, a developer with the backing of the government could quickly push any project through, raze neighborhoods for a subway, an Olympic stadium. Here it seemed complaints could snarl a development for years. He clicked on links farther down the list. More about the controversy, gripes about the threat of traffic and pollution from dirt excavated during construction. More about the delays.

At the meetup in the park, the organizer—Nic?—had called the Bellavista "a disaster." She'd implied that a new development would lead to people burning alive in wildfires!

If the current developer failed to reach a key phase by late autumn, its permits would get canceled. Jin picked at a hangnail, an idea taking hold. What if he could somehow delay the project long enough? If the permits expired, the developer might run out of money, might have to postpone the Bellavista until long after Jin finished flipping the house.

Jin was born after the chaos of the Cultural Revolution, but had grown up hearing about the country turned upside down, suspected class traitors paraded through the streets in humiliation. It didn't matter if the accusations were false: The louder the denunciation, the more people piled on.

He could start with an online petition. Jane often forwarded them to him and Kai. He scrolled through his inbox, looking at the subject lines: "Ban Single Use Plastics," "Stop Police Brutality," "Equal Pay Now for Women." He'd never bothered to sign them—why risk exposing yourself?—but plenty of others had.

He'd focus on Nic's argument: that residents wouldn't be able to escape in a wildfire due to heavy traffic on its roads. In late afternoon, he could go to the intersection by the Bellavista construction site and take a photo of clogged traffic. He drummed his fingers. Would that be enough? He pondered how to make the danger more urgent, more real. With a burst of inspiration, he searched for photos of cars burned in wildfires.

He stared at the thumbnails that filled the screen, no less disturbing for their tiny size: abandoned husks of cars and trucks, their exteriors powdery white and silver and black, the insides the melted gray of steering wheels and dashboards. He shuddered, imagining the drivers, their fear and panic when traffic came to a standstill, forced to abandon their cars and flee for their lives.

Anyone who saw the photo would immediately sign the petition.

He clicked on to the website and read through current campaigns, trying to get a feel for what to say. "Stop the Proposed Larchmont Golf Course." "Save Coyote Creek Watershed." "Halt Construction on New Pines."

For every kind of discontent, there seemed to be a petition. What could he name this campaign? Something catchy and to the point. Stop. Save. Halt.

Save El Nido. Not only from the Bellavista, but from any change to what the residents had worked so hard to attain.

Looking over the article again, he noticed a photo of the developer standing by the orchard. Was that his neighbor? The caption listed his name: Sam Belle.

Jin didn't know the man. But his wife . . . Jin relished the thought of cutting her down a bit. Maybe then she wouldn't be such a know-it-all, maybe then she wouldn't butt in.

After weeks of fruitlessly searching for a job, an endless sinking, something now flickered in Jin. He channeled the outrage of the other petitions. "High-risk zone for wildfires . . . threatens not only the safety of its future residents but also puts existing homes at risk . . . irresponsible . . . endangers lives."

He read over the petition with satisfaction, feeling pride in a job well done. A feeling he'd missed in these weeks of limbo. He shuffled through the papers on his desk and found the flyer with Nic's email. If she received the petition, she could sign and send it to dozens of friends, who'd send it to dozens more.

Under "Supporters," the screen seemed as blank and unending as a desert. He gnawed on his thumbnail. No one wanted to be first, or among the first, to sign a petition, even someone like Nic. In Nic's inbox, it would get deleted or quickly forgotten. Or, he could help it along, couldn't he, by making up signatures?

Jin jotted down names, mash-ups of those of former classmates, coworkers, and celebrities. Stephanie Lollar, Tony Hoffman, Robin Portnoy.

Below, the faint sound of music thumped from his daughters' rooms. Down the hallway, something clanked. Kai probably bustled in the kitchen, getting lunch together, braised pork left over from dinner. His family was safe, whole, together. He filled out the individual boxes: first name, last name . . . and email. He left the email blank and tried to click through. He groaned. No. Each name had to be verified with an associated email for the signature to be counted.

But, he realized, you could create as many free email addresses as you wanted. One for each new supporter.

10

A few days later, when the Sunday-night flight from Maui hit turbulence, Blair jolted awake.

While working on a slide deck for tomorrow's meeting, she'd dozed off, her head lolling against the Plexiglas window. A half-moon hung above the dark waters of the Pacific. It had been the family's first trip by plane since the pandemic began, and she realized how much she'd missed working on planes—free from internet distractions, free from her children or her husband knocking at the door, surrounded by the white noise of the jet, that of the womb.

Fantasizing about getting strapped in to work seemed pathetic at best, dystopian at worst. Late-stage capitalism. Yet the pandemic had a way of diminishing the scope of your dreams. She groggily tapped on the keyboard to wake up the laptop and smacked her lips, her tongue a dried-out slug.

She was among the first thirty employees at Orb, which had quadrupled in size on the promise of its extremely small, extremely high-resolution, and extremely cheap cameras that could be easily installed anywhere. *Anywhere!*

The Orb's main competitor, the market leader, performed poorly at night and outdoors; the headlights on cars always washed out the license plate numbers. The Orb's latest prototype, paired with its predictive algorithm, sharpened everything as if under surgical lighting, in crisp color footage. The Orb was also testing out facial recognition: If the consumer uploaded a photo into the system, the doorbell could greet visitors. "Hi, Grandma!" In the future, footage could also get compared to vast databases to assist in an ID and verbal warning. "John Brown, you and your license plate have been recorded!" would scare off porch pirates. Further off, it could seamlessly notify law enforcement during the crime-in-progress. For now, the Orb didn't want to reveal too much to its rivals or tip off civil liberties groups, which would question the technology getting unleashed in their communities.

Some places—well, the wealthier ones—had demanded various kinds of surveillance, some residents chipping in as they might for a memorial bench or paving stone. Critics pointed out that municipalities had spent millions installing security cameras, placed high atop utility poles in notorious intersections. None stemmed crime rates. And often, the purported facial recognition technology had a habit—glitch? Bug? Feature?—of misidentifying dark-skinned people, whose color confounded the cameras.

The Orb would correct all that and more. Their competitors offered individual snatches of a crime-in-progress, but not enough to connect the dots. What set the Orb apart was its ability to go wide *and* deep. How wide? Wide as a coyote's territory. Even in Maui, Blair couldn't stop thinking about the coyote, still at large. To catch the coyote or another roaming threat, you needed a network of Orbs that reached beyond homes.

Trouble was, the Orb was running out of money, in need of another round of investors. In an all-hands email, entitled "Calling All Innovators," the CEO sought "game-changing ideas" for "bold product concepts. Together, let's reimagine our future."

Tomorrow morning, she'd make a pitch for a pilot program, secretly installing the latest prototypes not in private homes but in the decorative birdhouses that dotted the intersections around town. Sam had been leery—"You sure it's legal?"—but suggested intersections closest to the freeway. When she'd joked about planting one by Nic's house, he'd grinned. Without telling him, she added the intersection to the list. Blair didn't know what she would find. Maybe nothing, but she relished the power to spy.

Sam jiggled the baby in the sling, trying to get him back to sleep. Glancing at his texts, he frowned. "The screenshot won't download, but apparently there's an anti-Bellavista petition."

"Is it that guy?" Blair asked. The aptly named Warne, a gadfly who always raised a stink about taxes and new development, complaining how it changed the small-town character of El Nido.

"'Save El Nido.'" Sam set his phone on the tray table.

"You think Nic's involved?" Blair asked. According to the nanny, Nic had trashed the Bellavista at the meetup. Probably getting everyone there riled up.

You weren't supposed to invest your own money in a project, but because of construction-related snafus, they'd sunk their savings into the Bellavista to make payroll and to bridge the financing gap. Any delays would put them in peril.

The bathroom door opened, letting out the stink of urine and disinfectant. She checked on the girls: In the aisle seat, Quinn finished her required summer reading. Jordan, across the aisle, resembled that televangelist's wife from the 1980s: thick coats of mascara turning her lashes spidery, fuchsia and aqua eye shadow up to her brows, streaks of blush dotted with glitter, and foundation thick as a clown's.

Blair had given Jordan money for a T-shirt and other souvenirs, something for the nanny's daughter. By the looks of it, though, Jordan bought out the makeup aisle.

"She came back from the bathroom looking like that," Quinn said.

"When?" Blair asked.

Quinn shrugged. "A few minutes ago."

Blair glared at her husband. "And you didn't say anything?"

"To you? You were asleep," Sam said.

"To her!"

He ducked his head toward Blair's, but she couldn't hear what he said through his mask.

"What?"

He pulled his mask down. "I said, she seemed so excited. I didn't want to make her feel weird."

Now Blair felt guilty. And irritated. Saying nothing made it seem like Sam had given Jordan his okay. For him, swirls and eddies invariably smoothed out. He'd been riding the current all his life. His confidence had attracted her—and still did—but she'd also come to understand it had a whiff of the paternalistic. Did he think Blair was making a big deal out of nothing? *Was* she?

Sometime this year, girls Jordan's age might get their periods, might start getting curves. Jordan, too. Her baby had shot up in the last year, the top of her head reaching Blair's chin in height. She was among the taller girls in her age bracket, which probably made Nic and other parents suspicious.

Jordan had been born seven weeks early, the darkest weeks of Blair's life: her baby so frail, the relentless beep of machines, the snaking tubes and wires in the NICU in Phoenix. Days that blurred into nights, Jordan coming so close to dying more times than Blair could count.

On what would have been her original birth date—June 16—Jordan had been discharged. A fighter, but behind developmentally. Blair got so used to saying her adjusted age—*corrected* age—to strangers and to herself that she insisted they celebrate Jordan's birthday then. Not April 28, a day Blair would forever associate with agony and grief.

However, June 15 was the cutoff date for the summer swim league. Depending on your age on that date, you competed in the younger or older age-group category. Those born shortly after June 15 had *excellent* swim birthdays, since they were among the oldest swimmers in their age group. And that was when Jordan would have been born, if Blair's body hadn't failed her. With an April birthday, Jordan would have been among the youngest in her first years of competition, lost confidence, and never swum again, Blair thought.

And Nic had almost found out.

At the end of the school year, Nic put out a call for baby photos for a collage—a fun class keepsake! Their babies, about to be the big kids at the elementary school. Sam had taken it upon himself to send a photo of Jordan, snapped soon after they'd returned to the Bay Area. Though much smaller than a typical two-month-old in late June, clearly she was not a newborn. That might still have escaped Nic's attention but for the damn metadata: the size of the photo, date taken, dimensions, and so on that popped up when you clicked on photos on your computer and usually ignored.

When Nic went to the summer league with this "proof," Blair had responded by claiming it was a glitch, that the settings had been inaccurate on her phone. She'd provided a dozen photos with metadata she'd modified, and league officials had ruled in her favor.

Now Blair wondered, Did the rumors rattle Jordan? She seemed to shrug them off, but maybe she worried about fitting in.

Sam murmured in her ear, "I already told you what I think: Come clean."

Blair pulled away. "You want everyone to call Jordan a cheater?" The difference in birth dates was only a matter of weeks! It wasn't like those Little Leaguers who faked their ages, those putative tweens who sported mustaches and threw 75 mph fastballs.

"I understood why you did it, at the beginning." Sam stroked the baby's back.

Blair jabbed his arm with her thumb. "*We* did it." She wouldn't let him pin it all on her. In the beginning, the switch had been easy: the preschool and summer swim league accepted whatever date you used to register, no proof necessary. "You should have been more careful!"

He exhaled.

"She'd get stripped of all her records!" she said. "And if we give in, Nic will keep going after Jordan. She'll blow up any little mistake she sees."

The plane began its initial descent, the engines whirring at a different pitch. Soon she'd have to put away her laptop. She yawned to clear her ears. Liam would wake up, and she'd have to nurse him to unplug his ears. At nine months, he nursed less and less, these days mostly for comfort and at bedtime.

What she'd mistaken for perimenopause—the mood swings, the hormonal geysers and droughts, the irregular periods—had been the start of her second trimester. She'd been so scared she'd deliver too early again, going on bedrest in the final month, swelling from preeclampsia, laboring while masked, capped off by an emergency C-section. She sent emails to the Orb's C-suite until they wheeled her into the operating room, and she resumed working before her catheter had been removed. She didn't want them to think she wasn't pulling her weight. Motherhood could derail your career at any moment: If you left early too often, if you missed too many meetings due to a sick kid, management would stop considering you essential.

Over the intercom, the pilot announced turbulence ahead; everyone would have to stay seated until they landed. By the time they disembarked, picked up their car, and drove home, it would be after 11:00 PM, and Blair couldn't wait that long to clean off her daughter's face. She could feel it caking and drying out her skin as if the goop had been smeared on her, too.

Hadn't Quinn been older when she'd gotten interested in makeup? Blair thought she had more time with Jordan before she grew up. She tugged her double masks down for a quick hit of recirculated air, which at the moment seemed as refreshing as a sea breeze. The masks, clammy from hours of exhalation, made her nauseous.

She fumbled for the diaper bag, tucked under the seat in front of her, and pulled out a packet of baby wipes. She passed it to Sam, who held it until she impatiently gestured for him to give it to Quinn, who in turn handed it across the aisle to Jordan.

"Clean it off," Blair said.

"You wear makeup. Quinn, too," Jordan said.

How could Blair explain that once you started, you couldn't stop? You plucked, you shaved, you smoothed, you spackled, nit-picking at yourself until you hid every trace of who you had been.

"I wanted to show you I could do it," Jordan said. "If I could show you, then you'd let me." She stared into her lap.

"You look like you're in synchro," Quinn said matter-of-factly. Synchronized swimmers, glamazons, their smiles bright and blinding, their arms saluting to the beat of pop songs.

Jordan's eyes welled up above her mask.

"Sweetie, we can practice later," Blair said. "But that stuff is bad for your skin. And it can sting if it gets into your eyes. It can get infected."

"School starts tomorrow," Jordan said. Her eyes panicked, pleading: She had no time left to practice.

Didn't Jordan know she was adorable, freckled, with her hair tousled into a Tintin swoop? Blair and Sam exchanged a look. Usually, Jordan wasn't so apprehensive, not like the girls who threw up before meets, scared to lose, scared they might disappoint their parents or their coach.

She used to have a best friend, but during the first year of the pandemic, the other girl had bubbled up with a neighbor. When school resumed in the spring, the girls had been assigned different teachers, different bubbles, different recesses, which didn't mix. Blair dreaded the fifth grade, when girls began to side-eye each other, giggle behind cupped hands or huddle at recess, speaking loudly about their sleepovers and trips to the movies or to Sephora, trips for the chosen few. It would continue through middle school, high school, college—the rest of their lives.

"You're not wearing makeup," Blair said. "You're ten. Wipe it off. Now." Her tone was harsher than she'd intended.

Jordan flung the wipes into the aisle. She used to lose her temper like that when she was younger, but she hadn't had an outburst in years.

"Pick up the wipes," Blair said more gently now.

"Someone could trip," Sam added.

"The captain said we had to keep our seat belts on," Quinn said.

"Well, can you reach it with your foot?" Blair asked.

Quinn tightened the pashmina around her neck and the blanket on her lap, then she shot out her leg, accidentally kicking the wipes down the aisle.

The plane rattled and shook so hard that Blair bit her tongue, and a passenger in the back yelped in surprise. She gripped the armrests, her mouth metallic with blood. She pictured herself punching the tray table, yanking open the emergency door, and screaming into the void. Her periods had spottily returned, with uneven surges in hormones that gave her cramps, and moods she hadn't experienced since she was a teenager. Or did the prolonged pandemic bring on her rage, every time she tried to run through doors that turned out to be walls?

The back-and-forth woke up Liam, who spit out his pacifier, his button nose crinkling. Elsewhere in the cabin, a baby wailed, then another. When she tugged him out of the sling, in a hurry to get him latched on before he added to the ruckus, she knocked over the water bottle on Sam's tray table—a loosely capped bottle that spilled over her keyboard.

"Fuck!" she shouted, loud enough to silence conversation in the rows around her.

She closed her eyes, gritting her teeth, wishing she could rip off her masks, get away from her family, from work, from everyone, from the world.

"Honey?" Sam stroked her arm.

She didn't move, might never be able to move again. Over Liam's crying, she heard fumbling, and when she opened her eyes again, she noticed Sam had passed the laptop to Quinn, who had tented it upside down on her tray table, catching drips on a crumpled cocktail napkin. Futile, probably—Blair would have to stay up until dawn redoing her presentation—but her heart thrummed at how they sprang into action.

Jordan unbuckled her seat belt, got up, grabbed the wipes, and swiped at her face.

"Sweetie—careful," Blair said. "You should get back in your seat." When Liam shrieked, she reached for him, pulling aside her neckline, not bothering with a cover, long past caring if anybody could see. Liam latched on, her breasts tingling with the letdown. Although he gulped with gusto, his eyes closed, whatever calming effect nursing was supposed to have on Blair had long worn off, the gush of oxytocin akin to sparkling water gone flat.

Jordan shook with silent sobs, head bowed, her eyes squeezed shut. Black rivulets of mascara coursed down her cheeks and into her mask. She must be going through more than day-before-school nerves. Did she worry about getting shunned or teased because of the accusations she'd cheated?

Quinn got up to comfort her, murmuring that she should sit down. As Blair lurched to her feet, the seat belt jerked her back. She tugged on the buckle, trying not to dislodge Liam, cradling the back of his head, about to hand him over to her husband when she tripped on the strap of her diaper bag. Although Liam popped off—breast milk spurting onto the back of the seat—she didn't drop him. Sam took the baby, who kicked in his arms, and joined his daughters in the aisle. As Blair tugged her shirt closed, a flight attendant approached, her eyes flashing above her mask, ordering them to return to their seats.

Blair ignored her, wrapping Jordan in a hug, wishing she had a soft fluffy towel or a puffy swim jacket thick enough to warm her under the coldest gaze.

11

On the first day of school, Jane woke to the disorienting sound of rushing water. Was it raining? She rolled onto her side and peeked out the window at the sky, hazy but cloudless. Or was that the wind rustling through the trees? It had been blowing all night again.

Her alarm hadn't gone off, and she was supposed to meet Tasha at the benches in front of the Quad. She rubbed the sleep out of her eyes, splashed her face with water, and skipped the shower, running a brush through her hair. She'd braid it on the walk to school. She dressed in the outfit that Tasha had helped her pick out from the discount department store yesterday. Because Tasha had to stay home to watch her brother, Jane texted her photos from the dressing room: jeans and oversized striped sweater.

In line to check out, she'd picked up a gift for Tasha: a mushroom figurine with a bright red cap, flecked with white specks. She wished they could have gone shopping together, giggling at the random crap for sale: a stool shaped like a stack of bagels, a hot-dog-scented candle, a stuffed gnome with an orange-and-white hat adorned with an autumn leaf. The mushroom held a surprise: It disguised a cheapo nanny cam. Maybe Tasha could use it to film the squirrels she'd said had been getting into the bird feeder.

Jane tugged her sweater straight and ran her hands down the sides of her jeans to get out the wrinkles. She hadn't been back to Valle Vista since the attack, and she felt jittery, her muscles clenched yet strangely slack at the same time. Not that she thought the coyote would return to the track, but she couldn't shake the fear she'd get lost, show up late or to the wrong class. Her freshman year in Fremont had been spent online, until the spring, when her classes went hybrid. Maybe the other sophomores felt like they were starting over as freshmen, too.

She shouldered her backpack and went upstairs. She could tell how proud it made her parents to live here. Her father drove them around, pointing out mansions. From the back deck, her mother admired the view of the mossy ravine, showing it off to Waigong and Waipo. The deer entranced Lily as they grazed on their lawn, their ears and tails twitching, before they bounded off.

In the kitchen, she grabbed a banana and waved goodbye to Lily and her mother, jammed her feet into her white canvas sneakers, and bolted from the house. As Jane reached the curb, Quinn reversed out of her driveway and gunned it out of the cul-de-sac.

Turning, Jane noticed the geyser at the side of the lawn: Hissing, surging, the water emerged crystalline and pure, droplets catching rainbows in the morning sunshine. Like a mountain spring, but instead of flowing into a creek, this one went into the ravine, along the side of their house, and past the window of her bedroom. She dropped her backpack and raced along the flow of water, watching it pool around a flattened pile of moving boxes on the side of the house and a junked hamster cage. (When her friend Vivian moved to Taiwan, she left her elderly hamster in Jane's care, but it had since expired.)

Farther down the ravine, the water had reached the skull of Tigs, whose life had ended between the jaws of the coyote. Wily had been the first to discover the sudden spring, lapping from it a couple hours earlier before he returned to the thick brush where he slept.

The wet dirt smelled like minerals, like the deep dark. Jane ran inside the house, dropping her muddy shoes at the doorstep and calling for her parents. Would the plumbing disaster finally break her father? The last couple nights, she'd heard someone shuffling around upstairs and guessed it was him.

* * *

Jin's insomnia had been triggered by the EDD. The latest unemployment payment hadn't dropped when he'd expected. After he spent hours waiting on the phone, the agency claimed he'd neglected to fill out a form that required his signature. (The details had been in the letter Jane had opened, then discarded.) Their health insurance was also about to expire. A couple more weeks and then they'd have to pay the entire premium. He'd have another job by then, he told himself. An interview, at least. They could have switched to Kai's plan, but then he would have to admit he'd been laid off.

Now, as the geyser shot into the air, Jin considered throwing himself upon it, as if it were a ticking bomb. He pictured the geyser growing in force, a torrent that might sweep the house from its foundation.

Kai took one look and ran back inside. The garage door opened and she emerged with a wrench, and at the water meter, located in a concrete box by the curb, she turned off the valve. She'd acquainted herself with the guts of the house as soon as they'd moved in. She was handy, handier than Jin. He knew if not for the distraction of the move she would probably have noticed he was hiding something from her. She handed him a water bottle before he realized he was thirsty and anticipated which coworker would turn out to be an ally, which a rival.

The geyser stopped. The fix was only temporary, he knew. The girls crowded behind him, all of them staring at the swamp in their yard. "No showers until we get this fixed," Kai said. "And you get one flush on the toilets. Make it count."

Jane took off for school. Back inside, Kai helped Lily finish packing, getting her lunch box from the fridge and filling her water bottle. From the window of the living room, Jin noticed Blair and Ana taking photos of the two girls in front of their house. They each held up a miniature chalkboard. First-day-of-school photos, he realized. In all the commotion, he hadn't snapped one of Jane.

He hurried to the entryway, where Lily slipped on her shoes. "I can print a sign for Lily," he said.

Through a side window, he noticed Blair and Ana rounding the corner with their daughters.

Kai handed the backpack to Lily. "We're late." Kai opened the door.

Shouldn't they commemorate this moment? Lily's first day of school in El Nido! Their new life at last. "I'll drive her," he said.

Lily hitched up her backpack, which used to dwarf her. Now she'd grown into it. "I want to walk."

"We'll take a photo after school," Kai said. "Jane, too."

He and Kai bickered for so long about the photo that eventually Kai announced she'd drive Lily.

❁ ❁ ❁

By the time Kai returned, Jin had left three messages for plumbers recommended on Neighborz. No one had picked up. Kai insisted on asking Blair for a referral.

"We don't want that woman in our affairs," he protested. Not after he'd meddled in theirs.

Save El Nido had caught on. In the comments for the online petition, others had chimed in, worried that the affordable housing would "bring in crime" because its residents—or their associates—would rob houses and sell drugs. Such talk made Jin uneasy, but the campaign needed every supporter.

"The husband builds houses." Kai straightened the sneakers jumbled by the front door. "He must know someone good. Someone who owes him a favor."

Blair had said she knew the seller's agent. Maybe they'd gossiped about the problems plaguing the house. Did the sellers know about the problems, but snuck it past inspectors? Did the real estate agent know, too? Maybe she'd persuaded them not to say anything. Did Blair and Sam troop through during the open house? Who wouldn't? Jin had dragged his family to houses in which they'd had no interest and no chance of buying. He pushed aside the vision of the Belles wandering the halls and finding it lacking, dated and dark compared to the bright, clean lines of their house. He suspected that the Belles—maybe the entire neighborhood—knew that he'd been fooled.

Fooled yet again.

"We don't have their phone number," Jin said.

Kai couldn't hide her irritation. "Just go over!"

He shrugged on his jacket over his T-shirt and sweatpants.

"What's she done to you?" she asked.

"Her dog shit on our lawn!" Jin slid into his sneakers, squashing down the heels.

"You did DNA testing?"

"It's always sniffing around." Jin zipped his jacket. "And her daughter pulls out of the driveway without looking! She's going to hit someone."

When Kai threw up her hands, he grumbled, "I'll go, I'll go." He sidestepped the puddle seeping across the front walk.

He rang their doorbell. Noticing the camera, he ran a hand over his rumpled hair, trying to smooth it down, wishing he'd cleaned up. Wishing he hadn't been so testy now that he needed a favor.

The nanny answered. "It's an emergency," he said apologetically, and explained what had happened.

Inside the house, a dog barked, its tags jingling, its toenails scrabbling against the hardwood. He hoped it wouldn't come running. Ever since he'd been bitten as child, he'd remained on edge around dogs.

"Was your daughter excited for the first day of school?" Jin asked, attempting small talk.

Yes, the nanny said with a faint smile.

"Mine, too."

She left to fetch Blair, who clucked her tongue in sympathy. "We wondered what happened." She recommended a plumber. "Tell him I sent you." She was barefoot, in leggings and a long berry-red sweater. Beside her, he felt like an unmade bed.

Her smile was so friendly he fought the urge to look away. His guilt intensified when she offered the spigot on the side of their house. "Fill up anytime!"

❁ ❁ ❁

The plumber recommended by Blair diagnosed the problem: Tree roots had bored into the pipes that connected the house to the water main. Those twigs, those tendrils that Jin could snap in half? In an odd way, he found it inspiring: a vast underground system that grew slowly but would strangle, would burst whatever stood in its way. The plumber said he'd have to excavate and replace the pipe, and as he ticked off the options, Kai joined them outside.

She brought up the slow drains and gurgling toilet. "Can you fix that, too?"

"Sounds like the roots got into your sewage lines," the plumber said. "We can feed an augur down the pipe, chop up the roots, and flush it out."

"How much just for fixing the connection to the water main?" Jin asked.

Kai shot him a look.

The plumber got into his truck to run the calculations.

"Why don't we get everything done at once?" Kai asked. When her sneakers squished in the mud, she edged away. "If we leave it, he'll just have to come out again. It might be harder to get an appointment next time. And we don't want the sewage line to break before then."

"Chen . . ." he said.

"Chen has to understand it's out of your control. And if he doesn't pay for it, we can. We have to live here until it's flipped. Chen can pay us back then. With interest."

What if the expense made Chen apprehensive about investing in other properties? "Maybe we get a second quote," Jin said, his voice low. He hoped that no one in the cul-de-sac was listening in.

"If we can get anyone else to take a look!"

Jin rubbed the back of his head. "Maybe we leave it for the next owner. Like the last one left it for us."

"They probably didn't know."

"They knew." Jin motioned with his hands, taking in the expanse of the house. "They knew everything." He thought he'd been so clever, when the sellers must have hoped for someone as gullible as him. They'd tricked the home inspector, too, or maybe the man had been sloppy. Jin craned his neck, looking at the crown of the sycamore tree, whose flourishing canopy had once seemed welcoming, a harbinger of better times ahead. It had a mottled tan-and-gray trunk, with leaves crisp and green as greenbacks. The same tree he'd refused to trim when Blair asked.

The plumber returned with his estimate: "Ten thousand dollars."

Stunned, Jin heard his wife—as if from a great distance—asking if that estimate included the sewer lines.

"That's additional, another five thousand dollars," the plumber said.

Jin's heart thudded in his ears and he could barely make out Kai scheduling the plumber, who'd try to start tomorrow, or the day after at the latest. She must know it would empty their savings and take what little they'd set aside for Jane's college tuition.

"Just the water main," Jin interjected.

The plumber said he'd draw up the contract and email it to him. As he walked away, he pointed at the sycamore and said it would probably have to come down; he knew a guy, if Jin wanted a recommendation.

After the plumber drove off, Jin moaned, "They're robbing us." The mud steamed as the sun rose. "But there's nothing left to squeeze."

Kai stared at him. Though he'd been dreading this moment, he could no longer put it off. He wasn't going to land another job anytime soon. He'd lied, not out of love, but out of pride. Not to protect her and the girls, but himself.

His mouth went dry. "SysOps folded." At least he hadn't been fired.

"When?" she asked.

"I'll get a new job soon." Finding work again had been more difficult than he'd anticipated.

"When?"

He swallowed hard. "Recently."

When she tilted her head, probably calculating the dates, he said, "Before we moved."

Fear and fury swept across her face. "You lied to me."

"I . . ." Every time she'd asked about work, he'd said he was busy. And he had been busy—applying for jobs and stirring up controversy around the Bellavista. In addition to the petition, he'd created a website that listed the main arguments against the development and advised how people could contact the Planning Department to complain. He'd also placed a Save El Nido ad in the local weekly.

"I lied to you," he admitted.

She took in the muddy expanse, and when she looked at him again, her eyes brimmed.

Bile rose up the back of his throat. He couldn't tell her about Save El Nido. Not yet, not until she forgave him for this transgression.

He wet his lips. "I can fix this."

"By borrowing money from my parents?"

He winced. Over the years, both sets of parents had invested in his various failed schemes. He'd promised to pay them back, and he had, but not all of it, not yet, not yet. . . . His parents lived on a fifth-floor walk-up, had for years, stubbornly proclaiming it kept them young. But Jin also knew—to his great shame—that his parents couldn't afford to move, not after sinking their savings into his ionic-water sideline.

He and Kai were both only children, and she worried about the distance apart from their elderly parents in China. She'd already put up with so much: the $100,000 racked up in credit card debt. The repossessed car, the foreclosed house. Each time, they'd muddled through, but sometimes he wondered whom she could have become, without him. Without his failure.

When Jin brushed his fingers against her arm, she turned her head away. It had been months since they'd made love—since they'd gone to bed at the same time. He wanted to fall to his knees, to wallow in the mud and beg for her forgiveness.

He looked at the house. On move-in day, Blair had complained about the old neighbors, and her fear that they would turn it into a SuCasa rental.

SuCasa . . . Yes. Yes. The idea came to him now: Despite all the repairs the house needed, it had curbside appeal. And its location in El Nido—rare. Rare, keeping its price high. But also rare for those who might be looking for a place to stay.

He laid out a plan to Kai: "We'll only rent it out on the weekends. For hundreds of dollars a night."

During the second summer of the pandemic, travel had surged. Freed from house arrest, the newly vaccinated had hit the road. According to the news, campgrounds and condo and home rentals were overflowing.

The house took and took and took, and now they should cash in. He tried to lead her back inside.

She shook him off. "Where will we stay? You want us to live out of our car? Like those families parked on El Camino?"

"We'll camp," Jin said. Over the years, the girls had asked to go, but he and Kai had always rejected the idea. Why rent or pay for expensive equipment only to sleep on the ground? To eat over a fire, like a peasant. A caveman. To shit in the woods! The question had recently come up again after Lily read a book set at a sleepaway camp. What a hold camping had on the American imagination! Like the Tooth Fairy and turkey at Thanksgiving, maybe you had to endure camping to assimilate.

"The guests could be sick!" Kai said.

"The virus doesn't last long on surfaces," he reminded her. "I'll wipe everything down."

She looked away.

"You, me, and Jane are vaccinated," he added.

"But not Lily!" She sized up the sycamore from root to crown. If it had been a bully, she would have stared it down. "Ravi asked me a few weeks ago if I knew anyone in QA." Her boss.

"Maybe the position's still available," he said. In the past, they'd discussed the dangers of entrusting their joint livelihood to one employer.

"You think I should recommend a liar to my company?" she spat.

He hunched his shoulders. He deserved it, all of it.

She sighed. "A headhunter emailed me yesterday. About a job in San Jose that pays about ten percent more. But they want us in the office at least three days a week."

From El Nido the commute one way would be an hour and a half, sometimes two hours on the worst days.

"I'll apply," Jin said. "I'll apply right now."

"She emailed me," Kai said pointedly.

"Help me, then." He touched her wrist. "You always know what to do. You see the problems before they happen." Flattering her, but it was true, too.

"We can charge more if we say it's for a deep cleaning," Kai said. "As a precaution for guests. But we do it ourselves. We could have a giant bottle of hand sanitizer at the front door. Open the windows and air out the house. Run bleach wipes over the knobs and switches."

She must pity him, must believe that she had to get involved to prevent total ruin.

She went inside, Jin following. She wheeled around the living room, taking it in.

"We could see if anyone would be interested. It wouldn't take long to put up a listing," Jin said.

"What about the furniture?" Kai gestured at the bare spaces. They'd picked up a couch from a giveaway group—she'd joined as soon as they'd moved here—but they still didn't have a dining room table.

"Something will turn up." Jin swept his arm toward the back deck. "We should get off our screens. Look at the stars." Trees for days, fresh air, and infinite views.

"Get bitten by mosquitos," Kai said. But she'd softened her tone, seeming to warm to the idea. Or at least she was game to try. She was always game to try.

12

For the next two days, Jane and her family made do, using disposable plates and wet wipes, and flushing the toilet with buckets of water they drew from the tap on the side of the neighbors' house.

One night before dinner, she ran into Quinn in the driveway; she seemed confused until Jane explained what had happened.

"Can't you use bottled water?" Quinn asked.

"It's for the bathroom." Jane set down the bucket, water sloshing over the rim.

Quinn wrinkled her nose. "To take a shower? Is that enough?"

Jane's face grew hot. "To flush the toilets."

"You don't have electricity either?" Quinn darted her eyes toward their house. "Do you have flashlights? A generator?"

Jane flexed her hand, sore from the weight of the bucket. Could Quinn tell she hadn't showered since Sunday? The plumbers were coming tomorrow morning. Did Jane really have to explain the mechanics of indoor plumbing? "If you pour enough into the bowl . . . it will flush," Jane said.

Quinn backed away as if Jane were diseased.

* * *

A week later, Ms. Arnold assigned "The Ones Who Walk Away from Omelas" in AP Psych.

The story haunted Tasha. In this utopia, everything was beautiful. No war, no hunger, no pain. The price of perfection? A single child would be locked up. All alone. Starving. Covered in sores.

It was part of a unit on social psychology and group dynamics, repression and desensitization. In class, they took turns reading the story out loud, trading off after each paragraph. Even as her classmates droned, the eerie words washing over Tasha made her feel cozy, like a kid at a library story time. Dust motes danced in a beam of sunlight coming through the window.

"'But I wish I could describe it better. I wish I could convince you,'" Quinn said in her nasally voice, muffled by her blue surgical mask.

She was relieved that Quinn never went out of her way to talk to her, had never reiterated her offer of Starbucks.

"'Omelas sounds in my words like a city in a fairy tale, long ago and far away, once upon a time,'" Quinn continued. "'Perhaps it would be best if you imagined it.'"

Ms. Arnold paused the next reader. "Why do you think the author asks us to imagine a perfect city instead of describing it?" When no one raised their hand, she asked, "Griff?"

"Because she had writer's block?" he joked. Gangly as a scarecrow, Griff was a water polo player whose dark brown hair had turned brittle as straw. His mask had slipped down, exposing his nose.

Ms. Arnold's eyes crinkled above her mask. "Maybe. But why else?" She paced in front of the classroom.

"Because the definition of perfect isn't the same for everyone." Quinn was always one of the first to answer.

Ms. Arnold dipped her chin as if to say *Close, but not quite*.

"Because the town is everywhere," Tasha said. "It's anywhere." She tugged on the straps of her KN95, her ears sore from hours of wearing the mask.

Ms. Arnold held up a finger. "Let's come back to that point after we finish reading it together."

Jane caught Tasha's eye and nodded sympathetically. Even at the start of the school year, Tasha knew what was coming, and what kind of perspective she was supposed to add as the only Black student in this class. Out of twenty-five students, most were white, except for the four

Asians (four and a half, if you included Griff, whose dad was white) and Tasha.

Tasha looked around the room, wondering if and how many of her classmates' parents had signed the Save El Nido petition. She'd scrolled through it last night and shared the link with Jane. Even though the Bellavista would primarily sell multimillion-dollar homes, with a few affordable slots, more than a hundred people so far had signed the petition. In the comments, they called Bellavista a "monstrosity" and a "ghetto" that would "bring down property values" and "didn't conform to community character." Another complaint: Bellavista would "cause a cancer cluster," due to increased tailpipe emissions! Euphemisms, insinuations that meant the same thing: *Stay out.*

She didn't know if they were a vocal minority or representative of the general vibe. And now Ms. Arnold was getting on her nerves. She liked her teacher, who wore cat-eye glasses in various jewel tones with matching cloth face masks and flowy sweaters. But with each paragraph, Tasha dreaded the discussion that would follow. She eyed the clock. Maybe they'd run out of time or get interrupted by a fire alarm.

In the rear of the classroom, a filter whirred by the open windows. Someone jogged by in the hallway, sneakers squeaking. After they finished reading aloud, Ms. Arnold asked, "Who would have walked away?"

Every hand shot up, except for those of Tasha, Quinn, and Jane.

"Why not?" Ms. Arnold asked Quinn.

"Because I wouldn't have abandoned the kid!"

Yes, yes, Quinn's classmates agreed. So righteous, so certain!

"Is this like that King Solomon story?" Maddy twirled the end of her sandy-blond braid. "To figure out who the real mother is?"

"What *does* the child symbolize?" Ms. Arnold asked. "Who?"

Tasha scribbled in her notebook, feeling the weight of her teacher's gaze. She wished her surgical mask covered her entire face.

"Tasha?" Ms. Arnold asked. "Earlier you said the story could be set everywhere?"

The tone of her voice irked Tasha—the excitement, the expectation. The conspiratorial expression on Ms. Arnold's face: *Let's do this!*

Her pen tore through the page. She hated when everyone's heads swiveled toward her when the topic of racism came up. What could she say to avoid the question? She thought of Lucinda, the elegant gardener who'd introduced walnuts here. What would Lucinda do if affronted with an impertinent question? She'd refuse to dignify it with an answer. Or she'd reverse it and make the inquisitor regret asking.

"What do you mean by 'everywhere'?" Ms. Arnold asked.

"Everywhere. At any time," Tasha said with a look, with a tone, that conveyed *right here, right now, in this class.*

Ms. Arnold blinked, taken aback. The others fidgeted in their seats.

After a long silence, Quinn said, "It's about systemic racism."

Jane shot a look at Tasha, then used her hand to shield the side of her face. Her expression prissy, as she silently mouthed the words, imitating Quinn. Jane bobbled her head, as if to signify the emptiness of the buzzwords.

Ms. Arnold pressed her palms together before calling for other examples that the class earnestly delivered: police brutality. Anti-Asian hate. Health inequalities.

Their classmates finger-snapped in agreement and approval. No one mentioned Save El Nido, or anything that slammed the gates against families like Tasha's. *Save* El Nido—from what, from whom?

The bell rang.

❁ ❁ ❁

After school, Tasha led Jane to a blackberry patch along the road, the fruit plump as baby cheeks. Warmed by the sun, wafting their tangy scent. She maneuvered her hand through the blackberry bramble to avoid the thorns and offered a dark jewel to Jane, who popped it into her mouth.

In El Nido, Tasha had convinced herself she preferred being a loner, that she was naturally guarded, steeling herself from things like what went down in AP Psych. Then she'd met Jane, who blasted at everything like a fire hose—with her affections, with her enthusiasm. Being around her had the thrill of a splash zone, even as Tasha risked getting soaked.

The wind had died down, and for now, the skies were blue. Yet she'd read that smoke was on its way again, from a fire somewhere in the Sierra foothills, only 5 percent contained.

"Have you ever thought about selling these?" Jane asked. "They're as big as the ones in Whole Foods."

"You'd pick all day to get a few pounds."

"If I helped you, it would go twice as fast." Jane reached for a blackberry, then winced. A thorn had nicked her finger, a drop of blood welling. She sucked on the wound. Jane bubbled over with ideas, with questions, a propulsive—impulsive?—quality that charmed Tasha. It also made her wary. Jane had hurled herself at a coyote, but did she understand that not every threat would turn tail quickly, or at all?

Tasha gently set the blackberries into a small plastic container. She checked the time on her phone: 4:15 PM. The elementary school let out earlier than the high school, and Tasha had to pick up Marcus from an outdoors class offered by the aftercare program.

Jane pointed at the photo on the lock-screen. "Who is that? Your great-grandma?"

It was the photo of Lucinda. "Sort of." She felt shy, trying to explain.

"She looks intense. Like no one would cross her. Is she from your mom's side, or your dad's?"

Tasha didn't know how to answer. When she'd discovered Lucinda's grove was the future home of the Bellavista, Tasha had been heartbroken. Spooked, too. It felt fated somehow that she'd foraged there, in the final days of the grove's existence.

Sometimes she worried her fascination with Lucinda was born out of wishful thinking, born out of how much she missed her elders in LA. When she'd showed the photo to Minerva, asking if she thought Lucinda might be passing, her mother had murmured, "Maybe. Do you have a photo from a different angle?"

What if Jane doubted it, too? She hesitated, then told her about Lucinda, about her special walnut grove, and her theory about her. "You think it's . . . silly?"

"What's silly?" Jane asked.

"That I saved her to my phone. That sometimes I ask myself, 'What would Lucinda do?'" Tasha blushed, saying it aloud.

Jane ate another blackberry. "No, I get it. . . . Did you know Kai Wright is part Chinese?"

"Really?" Tasha asked. The action hero with the chill vibe.

"His grandma is Chinese Hawaiian. Whenever I see someone famous who might be Asian, I get excited, too. It makes things seem more possible."

She squeezed Jane's arm. Talking to Jane reminded her that anything was possible. If your history was erased or suppressed, you had to imagine it into being.

They foraged in a companionable silence, the minutes falling away. Tasha didn't have to think about Save El Nido or anything except for what was before her: the careful tug, the satisfying pop. She dropped the last handful into the container and wiped her sticky hands on her jeans. She admired her finds. The blackberries were among the best she'd ever foraged, in a microclimate with perfect shade and sunshine and soil and water. Maybe the blackberries had originated in Lucinda's garden, the seeds scattered by birds.

Tasha ate a blackberry, relishing its dark sweetness and the grit of its tiny seeds, the taste of bursting summer abundance. After she snapped the lid shut, they walked toward the elementary school. Jane sidestepped a bag of dog shit tied off and abandoned on the sidewalk. "I forgot to ask. How did it go, babysitting? With the girl whose mom you met in the park?"

Over the weekend, Tasha had babysat Ella.

"When I walk up, there's a package on their porch," Tasha said. "I feel someone staring at me, and then I notice this lady walking her dog filming me. I know not to pick it up. She's watching as I ring the doorbell, probably thinking I'm going to bust a window and break in. When the mom opens the door, I point at the box. Then I turn around and look at the lady, who quickly walks away."

"Was she . . . ?" Jane's expression conspiratorial—giddy, almost—with the assumption that the busybody was the usual someone who summoned their outrage: a Karen.

"Asian," Tasha said. Older, with a perm dyed jet-black and glasses.

Jane grimaced, but maybe she wasn't surprised, either. "I'm sorry."

"You didn't do anything," Tasha said, though she understood Jane's embarrassment, the flip side of feeling like you had to represent your entire race. Their fault seemed like your fault, too.

"I hope she felt stupid," Jane said.

She didn't want to keep reassuring Jane, to perpetually absolve and forgive. "Everything else was fine. Though I caught the kid digging her hands into a package of hamburger meat. Like she was a werewolf."

Jane poked her in the arm. "Aren't you the werewolf?"

Tasha poked back. "A coyote bit me, not a werewolf! I told her if she was hungry, I'd cook it for her. And that she should wash her hands."

"Was she eating it raw? Maybe it was for her dog."

Tasha shrugged. The mom paid generously for the babysitting, probably because she had a weird kid. She'd given Tasha a ride home and had asked about Marcus. "He's such a good reader!" Nic had said, explaining that she had volunteered in his class in the second grade. Pre-pandemic, before everything went online.

The woman was a bit extra, but well-meaning. They always were. And yet, Nic's neighborly goodwill had its limits: She'd also signed the petition for Save El Nido.

Jane peeked at her texts and groaned. "My dad wants me to proofread an ad for the house."

"To sell it?"

"To rent it out. For people on vacation. 'Peaceful retreat!' But who wants to stay in El Nido when you could go to San Francisco?" Jane pocketed her phone. "The repairs must be really expensive."

"Did he say if he lost his job?"

"He must have, if they're doing this! But he and my mom probably don't want us to worry."

They passed a yard sign, cockeyed and in faded rainbow hues. IN THIS HOUSE WE BELIEVE BLACK LIVES MATTER, WOMEN'S RIGHTS ARE HUMAN RIGHTS, NO HUMAN IS ILLEGAL, SCIENCE IS REAL.

In the year since such signs had proliferated across the country, a backlash met every assertion. Sometimes it felt as if only the backlash were real, only the backlash was long-lasting, a return to worse than where you'd started.

Across the street, another sign hung from a mailbox, black cloth, its ends in tatters. "'All are welcome here,'" Tasha read aloud. "'But not too many.'"

Jane gave her a quizzical look.

"I sent you the Save El Nido link," Tasha said.

Jane nodded. "Did you know Quinn's dad is the developer?"

Bellavista. Beautiful view. Belle. The project was named after Quinn Belle's *family*?

That made everything feel worse.

Jane seemed to sense Tasha's gloom and said, "Too bad we can't make the housing prices go down here. People wouldn't be so stuck-up then."

"Like by . . . building an oil refinery?"

Jane shimmied. "Or a strip club."

"An encampment," Tasha deadpanned.

Jane tapped her forearm. "A needle-exchange clinic."

"Drug dealers."

"A grow house." Jane pretended to puff a joint.

She was hilarious and loud in ways that Tasha resisted in herself, a nerdy tree hugger, at her happiest when foraging. Tasha studied the sign again: ALL ARE WELCOME HERE. Mama worked and worked and worked, but for what? And they were just one family trying to get a foothold in El Nido.

Even if you managed to buy, if you were Black, you could still get screwed. Back in the spring, the Tanners—her mother's friends from med school—got their house appraised in Marin. They'd been lowballed, despite the new kitchen and fancy bathroom they'd put in, despite nearby homes selling for $2.5 million. A month ago, they put away their family photos and African art, went for a hike, and had a white friend greet an appraiser from a different company. The new valuation was a half million dollars higher.

Her chest tightened and she took a shallow breath. She couldn't remember if she had her inhaler. She gasped.

Jane touched her elbow. "Hey—"

Tasha couldn't let herself panic. She willed herself to breathe slowly and evenly, focusing on the rise and fall of her chest. One. Two. Three. Four. "Say something funny," she said. "Distract me."

Jane got a faraway look. "Why don't we troll El Nido?"

"Troll?" Tasha asked. The tightness in her chest started to subside.

"We can go *off*. It's a chance to tell the truth about El Nido! People pretend they want different, when really, they want things to stay the way they are. When you found out you were moving here, didn't you look up El Nido online?"

Tasha had come across posts in various internet forums, as well as websites that reviewed cities and neighborhoods, for people seeking advice on where to move. "I warned my mom it was . . . homogenous."

"Like milk," Jane cracked.

"But she said we should try it out." Tasha's backpack slipped off her shoulders and she pulled on the straps. "Like we were foreign exchange students."

"To Denmark?"

"Learn a new language, experience exotic customs," Tasha said with the breathless tone of an advertisement.

"Good schools, good weather, big houses. That's what the reviews said. But . . . not so diverse. Which my parents probably didn't mind. Which my dad probably thought was *good*."

"So, what would we say?" Tasha asked. *We*. Jane had a way of convincing you to play along, despite your reservations.

Up ahead, Tasha noticed a bay nut tree, one of her favorite things to forage. She'd come by with Jane in a few weeks, when the nuts ripened and fell in early fall. "We need footage, too."

"Not the review websites, that's just words and photos," Jane said. "But if it's ClikClak, we could make a video. Add music. A voice-over."

"With the robot voice." Tasha held up her palms, thumbs perpendicular, as if framing a shot of the manicured lawns and three-car garages on the street. "Warning: sundown town."

"How about warning: *woke* sundown town."

Tasha bent over, gasping with laughter. Jane tickled her, making her laugh harder.

She'd missed getting egged on. With Marcus, with her friends in LA, she'd been the responsible one who let herself get tempted. Why not have two desserts instead of splitting one, stay up another hour at a sleepover, or watch the next episode in an endless binge? She needed someone like Jane back in her life.

"Let's do it," Tasha said.

Jane grinned.

* * *

At the elementary school, they plopped onto a picnic bench by the playground. Kids in the aftercare program bounced basketballs and chased each other on the blacktop, the air bright with their chatter.

They had a few minutes before her brother's class ended, and they could come up with something for a real estate website that rated various towns.

"What would Lucinda do?" Jane asked quietly.

It felt like sunshine spreading through Tasha's body to hear her friend invoking Lucinda, too.

"How's this?" Jane asked. "'Beautiful small-town feel. Some racism and very little diversity, but those are pretty much the only problems. The restaurants are nice.'"

"'And not too spicy.'" Tasha put her elbows on the picnic table.

They giggled. "It's like saying, 'El Nido! We're only a little bit racist,'" Jane said.

If anyone had overheard Tasha and Jane trolling, they would have assumed the girls hated it here. That they couldn't wait to escape. But its failings seared precisely because Tasha cared so much for the land. Just like Lucinda once did.

Marcus hurled himself at Tasha. He was growing up, but not so much he'd stop hugging her in public. "You good? You hungry?" she asked him.

Natalia, the after-school instructor, followed close behind, dressed in hiking gear styled with spiked leather cuff bracelets and a tiny stud in her nose. A Goth Chicana studying at Cal, Natalia had taken Marcus under her wing, promising to keep him safe from any coyotes. In the woods that adjoined the school, the kids looked for frogs, dissected dead newts, and climbed trees. On those days, Marcus seemed less wiggly afterward, less anxious, although he immediately wanted to hop back on to his tablet.

"How was he today?" Tasha asked.

"He was so great with the younger kids! Helping them out, helping them see," Natalia said. "That's why I came over; I wanted to text you photos. What's your number?"

As Tasha told her, she noticed her brother's bulging pockets. "What's in there?"

"Plums." He displayed a purple-tinged smile. "For Mama. You want one?"

13

That weekend, the howling coyote woke Blair. It had been particularly active that night, haunting the dreams of dozens of people in El Nido, who stirred and then slept badly.

Blair checked her phone: 3:00 AM. She pulled up the covers, skin prickling with goose bumps, though she was safe and warm behind thick walls. Sam snored beside her, oblivious. If asked, she would have said her fear was primal, atavistic, what kept her ancestors alive, but the coyote also struck at her particular need for order. For control. Even as a child, she'd been driven to measure, to map, to eliminate uncertainty.

Naysayers claimed surveillance cameras made you fear your neighbors, that it broke down social trust, made you think that the stranger walking on your street most certainly had to be your enemy. Nonsense. With the help of the Orb, every customer might protect their families and their homes. Neighbors could share footage with each other as they might once have with a welcome pie. Would-be thieves warded off by the threat of surveillance. The protections of the panopticon, empowering individuals and communities.

Catching criminals, but not the coyote. And that unpredictability, that inability to track danger, shook her to the core.

Tigs! They'd spent hours calling his name and posting flyers around the neighborhood.

Run over, eaten—they'd never know what happened to Tigs, whom they'd called their "feline bodyguard." Patrolling the property, forever bringing tributes of gophers and birds to their doorstep. The hunter, hunted down.

Her chest ached.

They stopped letting Luna loose in the backyard at dawn or dusk, the peak coyote hours. Trying not to picture Tigs's final moments, Blair rolled onto her side. Restless, she checked the anti-Bellavista petition again. She and Sam still hadn't figured out the people behind Save El Nido. She didn't see the Changs; probably they were too new to care.

The husband was strange, but harmless. His wife was more sociable. The other day, when Blair left to walk the dog, and Kai came down the driveway, they admired the sunset together. It had resembled magma, all molten reds and golds. Kai had pulled away and trotted down the block. "I'm almost at ten thousand steps," she'd said, mostly from a treadmill at her desk. While Blair promised to text info about trails nearby, the older daughter wheeled out the garbage bins. Jane, who seemed so responsible, obedient, unloading the groceries and dropping off misdelivered packages. Jane went by the side of the house and returned with a rusty cage that she set on top of the garbage can.

Blair had recognized the cage's dimensions. "Hamster?" Jordan kept one in her room.

"My friend gave me hers when she moved to Taiwan, but it was already pretty old," Jane said.

"She was so dedicated," Kai had called out, still looping around. "When it got sick, she stayed up all night looking after it."

Now as Blair scrolled, she noticed that Nic had signed her name and added a comment, calling for a Zoom meeting. Nic! She was involved in every civic effort in El Nido. And she wasn't alone in her fight to keep the town's status quo.

For all their liberal values, many residents—who once so ardently boasted about the walk score of their fashionable neighborhoods in San Francisco—fought below-market and affordable housing in El Nido, as if it were a medieval city under siege.

She and Sam had hung on for as long as they could in San Francisco, walked to work from their place in North Beach, and enrolled Quinn in a cozy neighborhood day care. Eventually, they joined the exodus, first to a hillier, wealthier enclave of Oakland, before giving in to the pull deeper inland—not a cheek-and-jowl subdivision, but a woodsy town with distinctive houses and good schools. They'd moved to El Nido the year Jordan was born. The diversity was lacking, but they'd vowed to visit the city often. With their various nannies, she and Sam had hoped they might be able to teach their children Spanish, but it never worked out.

El Nido had a reputation for being materialistic and competitive, the children immensely privileged and overscheduled, a reputation it perhaps deserved. But Blair had resented the implication that she harmed her children by living here.

She swiped past a news alert about a fire now climbing over the pass into the Tahoe Basin and checked her email. In the attached report, screeners had reviewed the first batch of footage from the birdhouse cameras, but found no spectacular crimes in progress, no getaway cars careening from robberies—nothing that might help the Orb surpass its rival. She pictured the bored screener in India, in some windowless center, peering at quiet suburban streets, the motion herky-jerky, doubled in speed: an odd job but no odder than that of the radiologists half a world away looking at a blockage in your intestines, the technician watching you swab your nose, or the customer service rep hounding you over your unpaid bills.

She put the phone away, wishing she hadn't fried her brain with the blue light, dreading how tired she'd be at the Mavericks' tryouts in a few hours. The pandemic had fouled up last year's competition season, but in the spring, after Quinn's top finish in the state meet, Coach Ian had called Princeton to put her on the school's radar. After a recruiting visit, the coaches had offered Quinn the last freshman spot.

Every year the Mavericks sent a few swimmers to college on a full or partial ride. By joining the Mavericks, a child might determine if she'd win a gold medal three Olympics in a row, might determine the kind of college she attended, the kind of job she could land upon graduation.

When you signed up for the Mavericks, you signed up for Coach Ian. Quiet and intense, a former marine who kept up with every burpee and plank on the dry-land workouts, but also possessed a quant's analysis of turn velocity and warm-up stroke rate, as well as contacts at the top college programs. He didn't yell, swear, or threaten swimmers either; his hawk-eyed stare was enough to put the youngest swimmers in line.

The tryout was a formality, Coach Ian had all but assured Blair. He'd been tracking Jordan's success for a while. And that was probably why Nic and the other parents cared, because they believed Jordan—who'd crushed the preseason trial session—might diminish the already infinitesimally fractional chances of their daughters competing at an elite level.

You would never recoup the thousands of dollars that you spent each year in club fees, equipment, and travel. God no! You spent the money because your children loved the sport, loved the team and the teamwork, which fostered discipline, focus, and resilience.

But the top schools were harder than ever to get into, even for the children of double-Ivy parents, and swimming gave you an advantage. Only 2 percent of high school athletes received scholarships at the college level—a rate lower than your chances of getting into Harvard, Stanford, and Princeton. You—your child—could take pride in getting a full ride, admitted for athleticism and not because of legacy or need.

Did Quinn's scholarship to Princeton make their family a target? Blair exhaled, trying to still her jangled thoughts. The coyote. The Mavericks. The Bellavista. The Orb. Their credit card debt.

She yearned to talk to Sam. Liam had started sleeping through the night about a month ago, and though the wake-ups had been hell, she missed the coziness of those middle-of-the-night conversations with Sam.

She nudged him, pressing the palm of her hand against his torso, hoping he'd wake up. When he didn't stir, she poked him in the ribs, and he rolled on his side to face her. "What? What time is it?"

"Did you hear the coyote?"

"That's why you woke me up?"

She told him more people had signed the petition.

"You couldn't wait until the morning?" Sam asked, his voice clogged with sleep. "You shouldn't be on your phone anyway." He tugged the duvet over himself. "You always steal the sheets! Don't worry about the petition. It won't go anywhere. But I have a backup plan." To placate protestors, he'd cut the number of below-market units. "That should do it."

Blair hoped so.

"What if I see Nic at the tryouts?" She flipped her pillow onto the cool side.

"You could say, 'Hello'?" Sam pulled her to him and she settled into his arms. "I'll take Jordan."

They'd waited to join the Mavericks not only to avoid Jordan's burning out before she graduated from high school, but also until she could win—and lose—with grace. She could be impatient with her classmates if they were slow to answer a teacher's question. Blurting out the answer, annoyed. It came up during the parent-teacher conferences, but shouldn't such confidence be encouraged, sustained, in a girl?

She ran her fingers along his arm. "I'll go. I just—I just wish she'd leave Jordan alone."

"She will. Coach Ian won't allow it. If she wants her daughter on the team—if she wants Ella picked for relays—she'll shut up."

She wanted to believe him. She inhaled his familiar scent, clean laundry and warm skin. "Would Nic try to look up Jordan's birth certificate?"

"She doesn't know Jordan's full name, does she?" Sam asked.

Jordan went by her middle name; Paloma was her first name, in honor of his abuela.

"Or what county, what state, she was born in?" he added.

Nic would probably assume San Francisco, but Jordan had been born in Phoenix; Blair and Sam had been on a babymoon in Sedona when she'd gone into early labor.

Sam rolled her over onto her stomach and massaged her back, digging his thumbs into her shoulders. She sighed.

"Now can you sleep?" he asked.

Work, though. She sank through the bed, the floor, to the earth's core. Though her company had superior technology, after a spate of bad press, the Orb needed a public relations win. A whistleblower had recently revealed the Orb had been using customer videos to train its algorithms. And it was only a matter of time until regulators discovered a security breach that the Orb had covered up: An employee—since fired—had been caught viewing thousands of hours of bathrooms and bedroom recordings of female customers. Disturbing, but to be expected, typical pains the Orb would outgrow.

Although the CEO sought out new lines of business, the birdhouse cameras had been a bust, she confided. "I promised too much."

"Everyone does. It's sales!" He sat up. "Give me your phone." After she reluctantly handed it over, he turned it off and dropped it onto his dresser. "You can figure it out tomorrow."

Maybe it was already too late. Although she'd worked for struggling startups, she and Sam had never been in such dire financial straits. The Bellavista had sucked them dry. If the Orb went down, so would they.

She fought the urge to reach over him, the missing phone itching like a phantom limb.

As his breathing slowed and deepened, the coyote howled again. No other coyotes yipped in reply. A loner. She pictured its fur silver-tipped in the moonlight, its head tilted in ecstasy. "You hear that?" she asked.

"Birdhouse catch coyote," he murmured.

Gibberish, or maybe there was a logic to it. Maybe the screeners had been looking for the wrong kind of activity; instead, they could review the footage for coyotes. It was so obvious, she berated herself for not coming up with the idea earlier. She'd been too fixated on run-of-the-mill robberies and hit-and-runs. There were probably hours of various coyotes prowling through backyards and cutting across lawns in the midnight hours, lapping from water bowls and going after chickens. Maybe the Orb could pinpoint the culprit, using its prototype facial recognition technology. Tracking down the rogue would be a coup for the company.

* * *

Hours later, after fortifying herself with three cups of coffee, she drove to the aquatic center and dropped off Jordan on the pool deck. Jordan stretched, her arms up, shoulder blades back, quiet but in the zone, with a calm she'd had even as a baby. "If anyone bullies you, if anyone looks at you funny, you tell me," Blair said.

In response, Jordan leaned deeper into her hamstring stretch, seeming to study her toes, which she'd painted mermaid blue, the same shade as the team colors.

Mavericks pride.

As Blair rushed toward the locker room, her bladder bursting from the coffee, Coach Ian flagged her down. "There was a problem with the registration," he said. "The credit card got declined."

Sam must have transferred a balance without telling her onto the household card. She looked from side to side, hoping no one overheard. "There must have been a mix-up," she said. When she promised to pay with another card right away, Coach Ian continued down the pool deck.

At the entrance to the locker room, she heard an argument echoing off the concrete and tile. The voices sounded familiar—Nic and her daughter?—but lockers blocked her view.

"I told you to change at home," Nic said.

Blair rounded the corner and then stopped short, hesitant to interrupt the argument.

Nic dug through the duffel. "And where's your cap? Your goggles?" She let out an exasperated sigh. "I'll be back; I'll tell Coach Ian. For now, you should warm up on the pool deck."

Blair wondered if the girl had emptied out her bag on purpose, in an attempt to skip tryouts. She stepped out from behind the lockers. "Hi! If you need a suit, we packed an extra one. I think she and Jordan are the same size. It's brand-new. Still has the tags." She pulled it from her tote bag. "We have an extra pair of goggles and swim cap, too."

"Thank you, but—" Nic said.

"Sure!" said Ella.

Blair handed over the gear. Ella was fast, though she overreached in her backstroke and breathed a beat too late in her fly. If Blair had to guess, the girl might get asked to take swim clinics for another year rather than join the team.

From the stall, where she finally relieved herself, she overheard Ella complaining, insisting she could get the sunblock on herself, that Nic always got it in her eyes. "Stop! Ow!"

"You have to rub it in." Nic sounded as defeated as Blair often felt, but the solidarity was only momentary. If the situation had been reversed, Blair knew that Nic wouldn't have helped out her daughter.

After Ella changed into the suit, she dashed out of the locker room—goggles and swim cap in hand—Nic calling after her to thank "Ms. Blair."

Blair waved her off. "It's okay. Good luck to both girls." Her tone was friendly, but with a note of challenge, too.

"Ella will need it," Nic said breezily, or did Blair detect a whiff of the self-righteous? She zipped her duffel.

"Ella's a beast," Blair said.

Social etiquette demanded that Nic compliment in turn, but instead, she said nothing. The reek of chlorine, bleach, and mildew grew sharper, stronger in the silence that lengthened between them.

Nic's ponytail had come loose and she tightened the rubber band. Her hair looked greasy and a pimple had erupted on her chin. Maybe she'd had a hard night, too. But Blair couldn't forget, couldn't forgive Nic's campaign against her daughter.

Years ago, Nic had called Ella "a miracle child," conceived after much trying. She'd even quit her marketing job, convinced the stress of it kept her from getting pregnant. Now she staked everything on her.

Well, Jordan was a miracle, too. Blair pictured her baby pushing to the end of the set, everything in her aimed at the wall, white bubbles roiling, splashes thundering around her.

Jordan held nothing back. Neither would Blair. Since Nic had escalated her fight, Blair would respond in kind. "Sorry we missed you at the swim finals!" she said as jauntily as she could manage. "Seems like it was a mild case? First time? You never know with kids."

Nic stared at Blair, her expression stricken. For once, she had nothing to say. She'd told everyone her daughter had pulled out of the finals because of the flu, and not the virus that had halted the world. Let her worry, let her believe that the gossip around El Nido had been about her and her family.

14

A couple days later, while grabbing a snack in the kitchen, Jin invented more names to add to the online petition. The fake ones seemed to have convinced dozens of residents to pile on, and every time he'd refreshed the page, each new supporter triggered a hit of dopamine—an acknowledgment, a reward.

He knew that the campaign was an unhealthy fixation. Even if he succeeded in stymieing the Bellavista, their house would have to compete with other places on the market in the spring.

He popped a savory corn puff into his mouth, from a box of snacks shipped by his parents. Jane's favorite, that you couldn't find here. When the doorbell rang, Jin answered, still clutching the list.

A tree trimmer—in jeans and a dark green T-shirt—asked for permission to pull into his driveway, to get at the branches on the sycamore that straddled their property line with the Belles. "It's the best angle."

"As long as you leave our side alone." A truck was parked at the curb. The wildfire smoke had abated, but the forecast predicted the hottest temperatures yet since they'd moved here.

The trimmer toed his boot on the doorstep. "The tree might look a little strange. Like it's wearing shorts on one side, and a winter coat on your side."

"Will it fall over?" Jin asked.

No, the trimmer said, shifting his weight from one foot to the other.

"Who would pay for it?" Jin asked. "The people next door?"

The trimmer tugged on the brim of his ball cap, apparently used to getting caught in the middle of such disputes. "That's something you'd have to work out with her."

"Then leave it alone." Jin shut the door.

He'd already told Blair he didn't want a tree trimmer, but she probably thought he'd go along with it because she'd referred her plumber.

The other night, when the Belles had guests in their backyard, Jin had peeked over the fence to find the older, silver-haired neighbors he'd seen walking a dachshund. Everyone seemed so relaxed, laughing, sitting at the firepit and drinking wine, while the dogs chased each other. Jin felt left out. Not that he wanted to join while he secretly waged war against them. Not that they had any obligation to invite him and Kai.

But still.

"What are the new neighbors like?" the husband had asked.

Jin didn't hear Blair's reply, but something she said or did set off peals of laughter. He'd hurried into the house. Blair was probably bad-mouthing him to everyone in the cul-de-sac.

Now Kai came up the stairs, asking who'd been at the door.

Workman, he said. "For the neighbors." Every other house seemed to be under renovation, pickup trucks parked around Rinconcito.

She asked about the sheet of paper in his hands.

He folded it in half. "It's nothing." When she reached for it, he reluctantly passed it to her.

She looked over the page. "Who are they?"

"Job leads."

She studied the list. "I don't recognize anyone's names."

"Some of these go back to before we met." The lie came easily. If only everything else in life could be as easy, too!

She raised an eyebrow. He wanted to apologize; he didn't want to deceive her. He wasn't lying about Save El Nido, not exactly, but he wanted the campaign to take hold first. To put a stop to Blair and every inch she attempted to steal out from under them.

Then Kai would understand. After he filled out the petition, he'd clear the browser cache in case she decided to check where he'd been.

* * *

That afternoon, as Jin rolled their garbage can to the curb, he noticed a folded Ping-Pong table in front of his neighbors' house, along with a patio chair missing a leg and a rolled-up carpet.

He hadn't played in years, but he remembered how, with a twist of his wrist, he could send the ball shooting at high speeds into the corners. The table looked dusty, cobwebbed, but otherwise whole. His hands itched to play. As Jin jiggled the frame, hot to the touch from the heat of the day, his neighbor approached, apologizing. "Sorry it's in the street. I can move it."

Jin stepped back. Though the table was bound for the dump, he felt like a raccoon, caught in the trash.

"Jin, right? I'm Sam." He set a crumpled lampshade on the chair.

"It's not in the way," Jin said. If Sam had known that Jin was behind Save El Nido, he wouldn't have been so friendly. His neighbor was wiry in a youthful way, but for his gray stubble.

"We played nonstop during the lockdown," Sam said. "But the girls haven't touched it in months."

Jin squirmed, reminded that this man also had a family to support. But Sam had so much. He'd survive any storm. "It's not broken?"

Sam motioned with his hands. "The surface is scratched up. It also got rained on."

"But everything else . . . ?" Jin's expression must have betrayed his yearning because Sam offered it to him, helping him wheel it up the curb and to the entryway.

Jin stumbled backward, trying to keep up. He couldn't wait to play with his girls, he told Sam.

Sam swiped the back of his hand over his sweaty forehead. "Great!"

Jin thanked him again. After his neighbor loped off, Jin returned to his desk, to check a few notifications from SuCasa. He let out a whoop: Not one, not two, but three people wanted to book the house over Labor Day, only a week and a half from now. August had flown by.

From what he could tell, among those interested were a white couple from Santa Barbara, in town for a family reunion; a Black couple from Los Angeles, moving their son into the college dorms; and an Indian couple from New Jersey, who wanted to check out the area before deciding on a permanent move.

He ran to tell Kai, who was taking a break from programming to install their new dishwasher. Others working from home might run errands or goof off, but not Kai! The dishwasher was used, but new to them from the Buy Nothing group—more stylish, with advanced features, compared to the one that came with the house. Kai had asked the group if anyone might be trying to get rid of a dishwasher, and someone remodeling offered to bring it over in his truck.

Watching her crank the wrench and twirl the screwdriver, he could tell how satisfied she felt, getting at the innards and piecing the dishwasher together. She was so capable, so coolheaded. Probably, she seethed. He'd lied to her; an affair would have wounded her no less. By trying to go it alone, he'd threatened their marriage and their family.

He'd make it up to her. You made your own luck, Jin knew, and yet in Kai, he'd won the lottery.

Next she'd try for a free television, couch, an energy-efficient refrigerator, and whatever else they could install before the first vacationers arrived—items with plenty of utility left in them, but discarded because they were the wrong color or didn't have the latest features.

Around the cul-de-sac, neighbors set out household items, reminding Jin that the trash company was picking up donations; anything unfit for charity would go to the landfill. Couldn't he—he and Kai—cruise around tonight and gather what they needed before the trucks came through? Lamps and rugs, paintings, too. He could search reuse days in other neighborhoods, other cities. It wasn't as if they were digging through the recycling bin, like those scavenging Chinese grannies. He and Kai would tread lightly.

From his first days in grad school, he'd been stunned at what this country trashed. In those days, he'd wired most of his stipend back home and tried to live as cheaply as possible. If the department catered an event, he hauled off the leftovers in Ziplocs. He flicked off the slices of cheese—

whose taste and texture disgusted him, reminding him of jellied snot—and gobbled the rest, supplementing the endless eggs and canned tuna he otherwise ate.

Oh, how Americans loved cheese! He couldn't escape the macaroni and cheese, lasagna, pizza, grilled cheese sandwiches, ice cream, made from the rivers of milk that flowed from the legions of cows. He had longed for meat. At the supermarket, the smell of a rotisserie chicken on a winter's day had once tormented Jin so much that he bought one and devoured it with his bare hands on the bench in a nearby park. He'd all but buried his face in the carcass, steam curling around him. To any passersby, he must have seemed deranged.

Summers had been a revelation, though: People left out baskets of plums, lemons, apples, and zucchinis on their porches. "Take as many as you'd like! More, more!" the people urged if they were home, if they happened to be out in the yard. They gardened for pleasure, got onto their knees, sunshine on their back, their fingers digging into loamy soil, spraying the hissing water hose over their neatly tended beds. They kept beehives in the front yard and planted pollinator pathways down traffic medians.

Over the years, his notion of America remained tied up in overabundance, in giveaways. During the pandemic, he'd missed the tiny cups of coffee at the supermarket, the mini-sausages and roasted red peppers speared with toothpicks, the doll-sized bowls of chili, and the bites of molten lava cakes. Their family didn't often go out to eat, but every time they did, he and Kai grabbed wads of paper napkins, packets of ketchup, salt and pepper, sugar, and mustard, which they stuffed into a kitchen drawer until it was so full they couldn't open it.

His daughters called such behavior "cheap," but why waste what was offered, even if you didn't need it or want it? You might eventually.

If not for the urgency of the upcoming rental, Jin told himself now, his family might have dragged out settling in. Now they could enjoy the house before flipping it.

They'd been right to move. Even before the lockdown, he'd grown restless in Fremont, even if he could hear Mandarin more often than English. Even if the supermarket was stocked with every kind of

Chinese vegetable and sauce. And even if their daughters could enroll in a Mandarin-immersion program. Here, the girls had their own rooms, in a house that signified how far they'd come—and how far they could go. For the first time, they lived among the one percent (though within that percentage point there existed a wide range). El Nido would impress Chen, who probably wanted a house not among Chinese knockoffs, but with "real" Americans—white Americans.

He'd assured Chen that El Nido was exclusive.

In Chinese, 独家. The literal translation: "alone home." Solitary in your splendor. He'd come across the English word *exclusive* often in real estate listings for El Nido and he muttered it out loud now. Until this moment, he'd never considered how it rooted in another word: *exclusion*. The desirability based upon whom you kept out. It didn't matter whom, so long as you remained on the inside.

El Nido's exclusive reputation must have attracted the SuCasa requests.

When he showed Kai, she said, "It's like online dating!" She peered at the screen. "They should bid against each other. Charge more."

Jin laughed. "It's not an auction site." He shared the other good news. "The neighbors gave us their Ping-Pong table, too!"

She lit up, lacing her fingers together and stretching, as though preparing for a match. "Tonight," he promised. She returned to installing the dishwasher.

Was she starting to forgive him? They could order her favorite dishes from the local Chinese restaurant—Chinese American, not Chinese Chinese, but good quality, quantity, and price. He could light that fruity candle and ease out the tightness in her neck and shoulders. Then, they'd reach for each other in the dark.

As a leaf blower blasted outside, he surveyed the living room. The airiest in the house, with floor-to-ceiling windows that overlooked the ravine, that made you feel as if you were in the woods.

Jin had reserved a campsite in the redwoods about an hour south of El Nido. Usually booked a year in advance, but there must have been a last-minute cancelation. The gear had been taken care of, too, borrowed from one of Kai's coworkers. She'd practiced putting together the tent in here, where it remained assembled under the high ceiling.

"Daddy, can I sleep here tonight?" Lily called from the tent. The elementary school let out earlier than the high school, but Jane would be home any minute now.

"Maybe," he said.

She had piled the tent with unfurled sleeping bags to make a nest. She read a book inside there now, under the ruby glow of the walls. Like the stained-glass window of a cathedral. Stretching her arms and legs, she could brush the walls and the roof.

The rental scheme had come together so smoothly, it felt fated. He'd offered a bargain price, netting about $1,000 for the weekend, two nights, three days. Maybe he should have charged more; he could next time, with glowing reviews from their guests. The weather would stay warm through October, wouldn't it? Through early November. Not every weekend, not with Jane's schoolwork, but at least once or twice a month.

Since they'd yet to hang any photos, they didn't have to worry about anonymizing the space. They'd store their clothes and other personal items in the garage, which they'd keep locked and off-limits from the guests. He planned to purchase extra sets of sheets and bedding from the warehouse superstore, as well as $10 bottles of wine, a host gift to foster goodwill and high ratings. They'd empty their cabinets and put any food in the garage, which housed a second fridge left behind by the previous owners.

As he scrolled through the SuCasa requests again, Jane looked over his shoulder. She must have just returned from school.

"Who's that?" She pointed at the profile photo of a Black woman, her curls streaked in silver over a high forehead.

"Someone who wants to book our place when we go camping." He and Kai had agreed they shouldn't mention that he'd lost his job to the girls. Even if Jane suspected, he didn't want to worry her. "There's a few requests."

"What about her?" She tapped the screen.

"I haven't decided." Jin slid the phone into his pocket.

"If you haven't decided, then why not pick her? She looks nice."

"I have to review the details." At her age, he would never have questioned his parents like that. He'd been resigned to—and proud of—a forthright daughter but often he didn't know how to respond.

"They're all offering to pay the same?" she asked.

"Yes." Why was she so insistent?

If any applicants had been Chinese, a man or woman, young or old, he would have picked them. He wasn't naïve: Chinese could cheat Chinese and did so all the time. But he had so little to go on when selecting a renter—their past rating, their profile photo—that a little familiarity edged out a candidate. Everyone did it, not only Chinese people. He'd studied, lived, and worked in this country long enough to understand that, though everyone pretended otherwise.

He wouldn't have been surprised to learn that the oldest neighborhoods, by the country club, had racial covenants that kept out Jewish and nonwhite people for decades—covenants on the books but no longer enforced.

"If they pay the same, you should pick them," Jane insisted. "Because a lot of times, Black people don't get picked, just because they're Black."

"Picked for what?"

"For a lot of things! So why not that family?"

Lily poked her head out of the tent to listen.

Putting his arm around Jane, he tried to usher her away. "They have a son, a freshman in college. What if they have a party?" he asked. He pictured red plastic cups lined up on the Ping-Pong table, like he'd seen in the movies. Maybe that was why the Belles had dumped it, to avoid such potential hassles.

Jane halted. "Why would they have a party?"

Jin knew he sounded irrational—or worse—but that had been the first thought that came to mind. Guilt spasmed in his chest. In grad school in southern Illinois, his landlady had taken a chance on him. He'd been an oddity, but an agreeable one. "I love egg rolls!" she'd said, by way of making conversation.

"She said they're moving him into the dorms," Jin said. "But what if that's a fake story? What if that's not her photo?"

Hypocritical, when he himself had launched a fake campaign. Save El Nido had heightened his suspicions about the world.

"Why would they lie?" Jane asked, louder now. "If they're lying, then everyone else could be, too."

"Why do they need a whole house?" Jin jutted his chin.

"Does it matter? Or only for them?" She called out, "Mom?"

Kai emerged from the kitchen and gave him a warning look: *Drop it.* His hackles raised, doubling down even though he didn't want a fight, this fight. Like pressing on a sore tooth, a shooting pain from the rot within, best left alone.

15

That weekend, when Tasha reached the end of the chapter, she asked her brother if he wanted her to continue. The Great Molasses Flood loomed. Boston, 1919. The steel holding tank leaking, groaning, about to rupture and spill millions of gallons.

Yes, he said.

For years, she'd read to him, but now they usually retreated to their screens instead. Yesterday, at the library, she'd spotted a book they hadn't yet read, from the series that starred kid heroes who lived through the sinking of the *Titanic*, the crash of the *Hindenburg*, and the eruption of Mt. St. Helens. No matter the peril, you knew the main character survived, which had been a comfort early in the pandemic, when death had hovered by.

She had to speak up over the whir of the air filter. As he snuggled against her—sweet faced, all dimples and long lashes—she could see the versions he'd been: the chubby bundle of a newborn; the kindergartner obsessed with trains; this lanky boy who liked to cuddle with his giant squid, Big, but sometimes couldn't fall asleep, too worried about the fate of axolotls and the two lakes where they remained in the wild.

Instead of sleeping in Sunday morning after her night shift, their mother had been on the phone for hours in her room. When Minerva emerged, she announced that she'd found a lead on a job in Los Angeles.

If it worked out, they could move by the end of the year. "Maybe by Halloween!"

In less than two months; it was now the end of August. Tasha stared at her mother. Marcus, too. As the silence stretched on, Minerva's smile faded. "What's wrong?"

"What's the rush?" Tasha squeezed the throw pillow in her lap.

Minerva settled next to her on the couch. "Grandma . . ."

"Is she sick?" Tasha asked.

"No. She's slowing down, though."

Tasha wondered if her mother felt guilty. Auntie Di, who lived a few blocks from Grandma, handled her bills and took her to doctor's appointments.

Back in June, they had returned to Southern California for Grandma's eightieth birthday, the first time they'd seen their family in person in more than a year. Her grandmother had seemed as sharp as ever, throwing back her head when she belly-laughed. Widowed five years ago, she insisted on living alone. But she did seem smaller, shakier, nearly dropping a sloshing pot, which Auntie Di whisked away from her. Tasha missed her family's long hugs, their teasing, even their bickering at the grill. From a shady corner of the yard, she'd plucked wood sorrel and snacked on the lemony leaves—a party trick, but also a skill she was proud to show off. She had twirled a sprig, offering it to anyone who wanted to try, but found no takers.

"I planned to wait until the end of the school year," Minerva said now. "Then a recruiter called me."

"You've been looking?" When the kettle whistled, Tasha made spruce-needle tea, pouring it into mugs. She handed one to her mother.

Minerva sipped, then blew across the mug to cool it off—one she'd made, glazed the iridescent blue of the ocean. She asked Marcus to change out of his red plaid pajamas.

"You always have to be looking," Minerva said. She waited until after he left, then handed her a piece of paper. "From the recycling bin."

Tasha had scribbled ideas on scratch paper before she and Jane had refined another post trolling El Nido. *~~Safe.~~ Very safe ~~but there weren't a lot of minorities like the good ole days~~ like going back in time. Small town tradition!*

She should have been more careful, ripped up the page, buried it at the bottom of the bin! She hesitated. The trolling would give her mother yet another reason to move as soon as possible. "That was for class," she said.

"Class?" Minerva said sharply. "Which class?"

"An assignment in AP Psych."

"Strange assignment," Minerva said, but didn't press further.

How to explain? The posts negging El Nido made it clear that its flaws were built in. People who'd once lived here—or still did—recognized these failings, too. A mutual acknowledgment, a form of communion that felt strangely encouraging. Bonded, banding together, they could have been mighty.

Imagine if each person had realized that they weren't alone. Glimpses of resistance, of *a* resistance that could organize and demand. What could El Nido become if people like that pushed for its transformation? The thought exhausted and exhilarated her.

Lucinda left behind everything she'd known, perhaps because she'd crossed the color line in the years after the Civil War. Even if she hadn't been passing, she must have wanted to reinvent herself, as you could only among strangers.

Nothing would ever change if families like Tasha's stayed away. And anything that mattered seemed impossible at the beginning. Hadn't Lucinda and her laborers reshaped the wilderness, dug up trees and weeds and planted seeds for her garden? According to *Black Gold*, Lucinda's medicinal gardens had supplied an esteemed Oakland Chinatown herbalist—an uncle of her houseboy's—who in turn gave her seeds that flourished in her garden.

Minerva gestured toward Marcus's bedroom. "I'm also worried about him. You have Jane, but he has no friends."

"He didn't back home." Always in his head, making up stories.

"But he'd have his cousins."

"Natalia keeps saying what a big help he is, especially with the younger kids," Tasha said. "I can tell how proud it makes him."

She'd also been telling Tasha about high school internships in environmental science that she could apply to next summer.

"There are outdoor programs in LA," Minerva said.

"But not this one." Tasha sipped the tea, letting the steam bathe her face. It made her eyeballs tingly. Before they moved, her mother had gone on and on about the safety of El Nido. "And what about school? Where would we go?"

Minerva studied her. "I've worried it's . . . hard here."

"We both know what it's like."

Marcus slid onto the couch, leaning his head against their mother's shoulder.

"Where will we live?" Tasha asked.

"Auntie Di said she'll keep an eye out for places nearby," Minerva said. Di, Diana. Grandma had named her daughters after goddesses. "Maybe with Grandma for a while. What do you think, honey?" she asked Marcus.

He said nothing, paging through the book.

Tasha rubbed between his shoulders. He'd tensed up. "What do you do at recess?" she asked. He didn't answer. "Can you go to the library?"

"It's not open." He closed the book.

"What about the garden?" she asked.

"I don't know what days . . ." He stroked his earlobe, a habit when he was anxious or tired.

She turned back to her mother. "What about Sunrise? What about the staff? The patients?"

"I'll hire my replacement. They'll be taken care of."

"What's the new job?" Tasha asked. "Does it pay as much as this one?"

Minerva avoided the question. Instead she wrinkled her nose. "It smells like a tire fire right now!" The winds had shifted this morning, bringing wildfire smoke from afar. She gestured at the balcony, where an oak titmouse darted around the bird feeder.

"You can smell?" Tasha dashed into the kitchen for the tub of dark chocolate peanut butter cups. Her mother's favorite, until the virus turned them into a bland sludge. She flung open the cabinets and found them. She snapped off the lid with a flourish. "Try this."

Minerva popped one into her mouth, letting it melt, sighing, her eyes half lidded with pleasure.

Tasha could have flown up to the crown of a tree. "What does it taste like?" she asked. She inhaled the aroma, toast and chocolate and cream, vivid as Oz, and pictured it flowing through her mother's veins and out her pores.

"Salty, sweet, creamy, nutty," Minerva said. "I could swim around in this. Float on it, all day."

Tasha set the chocolates on the coffee table. "It was the green walnuts!" she said triumphantly. Lucinda's walnuts. She'd never returned to the grove with her mother, but had gone back alone one more time to gather handfuls of what might be the last walnuts from those trees. To save a few that she might plant elsewhere, to continue Lucinda's line.

"It was all the times you trained my nose. All of it mattered." Minerva reached for another chocolate, swirling it on her tongue.

Maybe enough time had passed for Mama to recover on her own. But what if her recovery was tied to this land? Not only hers, but the entire family's? Marcus, the noise in his head quieted after time in the woods. Coming home with rocks veined with quartz, a turkey feather, a twig covered in neon lichen. Tasha, who'd come to see the plants she foraged as her neighbors she checked in on and, in their own way, looked after her, too.

"Shouldn't we wait to see if we get into the Bellavista?" Tasha asked.

"If it ever gets built." Minerva tapped on a Save El Nido ad in the paper left on the coffee table.

Tasha scooted to the edge of the couch. "We could be first in line." The lottery winners would get announced by mid-October. Within five days, they'd have to get their paperwork in order: a mortgage loan preapproval letter, copies of Minerva's federal income tax returns, pay stubs, and bank statements. "If we get in, you can still change your mind."

❁ ❁ ❁

The following afternoon, Blair tore open yet another offer for a credit card. A backup to the backup to the backup, it would be their fourth. They'd paid off the minimum balance on the family credit card, but she still owed Ana her paycheck. Though she wished she could have paid on time, at least Ana and her daughter had a place to live.

The espresso machine hummed and gurgled. Mondays were always frantic. She'd worked through lunch and only now had time to take a break. Usually in the week before Labor Day, the Orb's younger employees would have been heading to Burning Man—all libertarianism, glitter, and silver cowboy hats to celebrate the end of summer. But the festival had been canceled for the second year in a row because of the pandemic.

The wildfire haze that returned yesterday added to the sense of doom.

All day, she'd been messaging coworkers about the ominous signs of cost cutting: a just-announced hiring freeze. When she tried to pay for a "lunch and learn" event—arranging meal delivery to participants working from home—the company card had been declined.

At home, their expenses grew, too. The more you earned, the more you spent: the swim clinics, the trips to the Aulani, their three cars. Four, if you counted the BMW Quinn crashed into the deer earlier this summer. She could've died! (Apparently, deer were the deadliest animal in America, killing more people than bears, alligators, sharks, and rattlesnakes.) The bumper could've been repaired, but Quinn had been so shaken they replaced it with a Mini Cooper the following week.

As she filled her mug, Blair heard a familiar sound: *thock, thock, thock*. Didn't Sam dump the Ping-Pong table on junk day? When she peeked into the backyard, she realized that the sound came from next door, where the Changs had set one up on their back deck. Blue, like theirs had been, with neon-green paddles, too. *Was* it theirs? Unbelievable.

She rushed to Sam's office. During the lockdown, they'd spent more time together than they had in years. Lunch after lunch after lunch; her work husband, her husband, which didn't quite translate. A work husband appealed and excited because he theoretically was an intimate separate from the one to whom you'd made a lifelong vow. At least they hadn't come to despise each other. Which, upon reflection, seemed a low bar for marital satisfaction.

He explained he'd given their neighbors the Ping-Pong table.

"It's noisy." Blair didn't know why she felt so irritated. Over the years, she'd given—and received—plenty: cribs, strollers, baby and kid clothes, and toys, the circle of giving that felt virtuous, neighborly, and environmentally responsible. "Why didn't you tell me?"

"I forgot!" His eyes drifted back to the screen.

"You should have checked with me." Though she hated being taken by surprise, he hadn't intended to keep it secret. Just like it wasn't a secret that she'd trained an Orb on Nic's house. She could, she should mention it right now—it was no big deal, right? Just another intersection under review. "I feel bad giving them our junk," she lied. "Isn't it scratched up?"

Sam shrugged. "He said he could fix it. That his wife could. It's like my grandparents."

"The hoarders?" Blair rubbed her lower back, tight from sitting.

"Total immigrant mentality: They saved everything in case they might be able to use it." Sam glanced at a photo of his grandparents outside the family restaurant, long closed. "Sometimes they could. They parked an old Mustang in their driveway for years. Flat tires, broken gasket. My abuelo and my tío rebuilt it and gave it to me for my sixteenth birthday." He smiled at the memory.

Didn't he realize you had to set boundaries, especially with next-door neighbors? Blair frowned.

"You want me to take it back?" Sam asked.

Of course not, but he was too trusting. "No."

When his computer pinged, he started typing. She stared at the back of Sam's head. He had to work—and so did she!—but she felt deflated, dismissed.

As she retreated, doubt crept in: What was it about Jin that bugged her? The tiff over parking, the disagreement over the tree trimmer? Stressed out by work, her patience vaporized? Would she react the same way if the Millers, the neighbors on the other side, took it? The Millers wouldn't want their junk.

It wasn't because Jin was Chinese!

She was friends with Ming, from college, back when he lived down the hallway. They'd vetted each other's boyfriends. She'd donated to the Stop Asian Hate campaign. When she'd seen that poll about how three-quarters of white Americans had no close nonwhite friends, she'd privately taken pride in her own circle. Maybe not at work now or in El Nido, but if she expanded the definition to include friends from college, from her first job, from her years in San Francisco, then her life hadn't taken a Stepford turn.

And wasn't their family Hispanic? Latino. Latinx? Sam's grandparents were from Mexico, Paloma and Armando Lopez, whose daughter Cathy, pale as candlelight, had married a man practically see-through. Hence Sam—*Samuél*—was pastier than Blair in winter, but he could tan deeply and never burned and had a Roman nose and thick wavy hair that she envied.

No, she concluded, it had been her mistake, to let the Changs use the spigot. Next thing you knew, Jin would poke around their garage, asking if they were getting rid of anything. He'd eye the furniture in their backyard. She wouldn't let him take advantage of their generosity again.

16

Three weeks later, not long after Jane returned home from school, the doorbell rang. It was Mrs. Belle, explaining that they were leaving for the weekend for a swim meet. Their dog was at the kennel, but someone needed to administer the twice-a-day antibiotics to Jordan's hamster, Domino, for a respiratory infection.

She spoke in a rush, twisting her wedding ring on her finger, as she ticked off the responsibilities: feed him pellets, refill his water dish, and spot-clean his bedding. The usual pet-sitter had canceled because of a family emergency. Ana wasn't available either.

Mrs. Belle exhaled. "Domino's getting old, and we've been trying to prepare Jordan. But we're hoping he might rally. The emergency vet's number is on the fridge. Are you interested? I can pay thirty dollars a day. Forty, since it's so last-minute."

She seemed so desperate, Jane agreed on the spot.

Her father wasn't happy with the arrangement when she mentioned it at dinner. "You should be studying, not picking up after their little rat!" he said, jabbing his chopsticks in the air. By then, the neighbors were gone.

* * *

The next morning, when Jane tried to squirt the antibiotics into Domino's mouth, the hamster squirmed out of her grasp. She stroked Domino's head, trying to soothe him. "Easy now. There you go." His fur was fluffy, his scent musky. With his black-and-white coat, twitchy pink nose, and alert little ears, Domino was cute as a storybook, but more ornery than her friend's hamster.

Domino twisted and nipped her finger, blood welling up. She rushed to the bathroom and washed off her finger with soap and hot water until the cut stopped bleeding, wrapped it in a wad of toilet paper, and applied pressure. When she returned to the cage, she realized she'd left the door open, and now Domino was missing. She warily poked her finger into his bedding, in case he was hiding, but he wasn't there.

It had only been a minute. What if he slipped into the walls or a heating vent or chewed on an electrical cord? What if he got outside? Crushed under the wheel of a car, gulped up by a coyote?

"Domino?" she called out. Did he recognize his own name? She listened for squealing and squeaking. She darted from room to room, her panic rising, shining the light on her phone under the bed, behind the curtains, inside the closets. She swiped at a dark shape that turned out to be a dust bunny.

The minutes ticked by and when she checked her phone, she realized she'd been searching for more than a half hour. She sank onto the rug, trying to get a hamster's-eye view, the terrifying voids and dizzying skyscrapers. Maybe she could leave pellets piled by his cage, or in a trail along the hallway. Should she call Mrs. Belle? She'd have to admit she'd lost him.

Then she heard rustling. She slowly pushed open the door to a room she hadn't yet explored, big enough to cartwheel in, every inch covered in medals and trophies. It must be Quinn's room. Tiptoeing in, she kept listening. Under the bed? The desk? The walk-in closet. She flipped the light switch and discovered Domino burrowing into a balled-up pair of jeans.

Using the jeans as a makeshift sling, she lifted him up, raced back to the cage, set him in, and latched it. She checked it twice to make sure it stayed shut. She closed her eyes and exhaled. She needed a moment before she tried giving him antibiotics again.

Trembling, she texted Tasha.

Jane: my life just FLASHED before my eyes
Tasha: u okay?
Jane: call?

When Tasha gave her a thumbs-up, Jane started a video call. She tried to tell the story, but started laughing instead. It was all so ridiculous! She held the camera to the cage so Tasha could see Domino.

"Be good," Tasha chided, which made Jane laugh harder. Domino nibbled on his pellets, whiskers twitching.

"I'm lucky," Jane said. "The house is so big, Domino totally could have disappeared."

She offered to take Tasha on a tour, panning the camera around the bedrooms: Jordan's room, with its rainbow mural, medals, and trophies; a nursery with a Noah's Ark theme; and a master bedroom with a fireplace you could walk around, and the bathroom with its deep double sinks, double showerheads, and an enormous soaking tub under a skylight. An orchid arched in the windowsill.

"Look at this spa-like atmosphere," Jane narrated in a snooty tone. "A sanctuary in your home!"

"A total teardown," Tasha replied, which cracked Jane up.

"A dump. But with so much potential!"

In a home office, she swiveled the camera, taking in the succulent in the windowsill, a whiteboard, a poster on an easel, a mahogany desk with leather accents and three monitors.

"Hold up," Tasha said. "Can you zoom in on the poster?"

It was for the Bellavista.

"You think there's anything about the housing lottery?" Jane propped up the camera, settled into the mesh chair, and paged through printouts piled on the desk.

"Don't!" Tasha said, but Jane was already reading something about parking spaces. Something about trees. And another slashed with strikethroughs, arguing that the number of affordable units at Bellavista should be cut in half, from ten to five, due to environmental concerns, community concerns, blah-blah-blah legalese to justify why the developer could renege on its commitments.

Tasha gasped. "They're cutting it in half?"

"I . . ." Jane didn't know what to say. "I'm sorry."

"The city hasn't said a thing," Tasha said bitterly. Looking away, she told Jane she had to go.

Jane knew how much the Washingtons had held out the hope that the housing lottery might help them set down roots in El Nido. Now everyone who entered had even less of a chance. She felt so helpless, but maybe they could still have a little fun. She stood up. "Wait! I didn't show you Quinn's room yet. . . ."

A smile flickered. "Anything interesting?"

Jane hurried down the hallway, stopping by Jordan's room to fetch the jeans that she had to put away. As Domino groomed himself, licking his paws and smoothing his fur, she jiggled the latch of the cage to confirm it was secure. At the threshold of Quinn's room, she dramatically flung open the door. "Her majesty's chambers," she said, and panned the camera around the room: the color palette the blue and white of Chinese porcelain, a queen-sized bed piled high with pillows, fairy lights strung on the walls, medals galore, a huge autographed poster of a swimmer diving off a block, a rolled-up yoga mat, kettlebell, and resistance band.

"Did you jump on her bed?" Tasha joked.

"In a sec. I'll dump the jeans back in her closet first." She swept the camera over a heap of flip-flops, grimy slip-on suede and sheepskin booties, and a rainbow array of puffy sneakers on the floor, racks and stacks of jeans, T-shirts, sweats, swimsuits, and hoodies. It smelled like cedar and chlorine in here.

Jane squatted down, trying to arrange the folds of the jeans. When she stood up, she bumped her head against a shelf piled with stuffies. Out fell a slim red diary.

Rubbing the back of her head, she exited the closet and sat on the rug. She flipped through the diary before turning back to the first page, dating to May of last year. She didn't notice a stray blond hair slip out as she studied some kind of log, page upon page with a vertical line down the middle: "one carrot," "seven almonds," and "half a banana" on one side, and on the other, lists by hours and type of exercises, swimming and running and weight lifting. At the bottom of the ledger, in block letters in black ink, there was a comparison of calories burned and consumed. Hearts on the days the numbers matched, zeroed out, and a black spiral when more had been consumed than burned. Another annotation . . . for when she pooped?

It wasn't like coming across nudes of Quinn; it was like looking straight into the girl's brain. No—it felt like they'd been *in* her brain, her body, her spiraling misery, her thoughts that circled and crowded and consumed every waking minute.

"You think Quinn's okay?" Jane asked. She wished she didn't know, wished she'd never snooped. It felt like she'd witnessed Quinn edging out onto a frozen lake, cracks spiderwebbing with each step. A snap, a splash, and she'd sink.

"Maybe her coach told her to do it," Tasha said.

Some days included what looked like diary entries. May 20, 2020. "'I don't know what to do about Maddy,'" Jane read aloud. "'She's such a snake. A sneak. A fake.'" She looked up. "I thought they were tight?"

Tasha frowned. "You should put it back."

"'I should feel sorry for her because she lives in the ghetto. But so does Amelia, and she's not toxic,'" Jane continued. "There's a ghetto in El Nido? Don't the houses sell for millions?"

Tasha gestured off to the side. "That's the part of town by the freeway. The neighborhood where we live. By our apartment building."

As much as Jane pitied Quinn, she was also starting to realize how much her neighbor annoyed her.

Tasha walked toward the kitchen, the camera angle jiggling, and poured a glass of water. "She's just repeating what she heard from her parents."

Jane studied the next page. "There's a bunch of names? 'Patty Jones. Becky Chambers. Amy Chambers. Becky Smith. Becky White.' Becky White is circled? Are they also at Valle Vista?"

"I don't think so. . . ." Tasha returned to the couch.

Jane flipped to another list that she read aloud: "'BeckysCozyCorner, BeckysSunshineLife, BeckysMerryMoments, BeckysHappyFamily.'"

Tasha tilted her head. "Repeat the last one?"

"'BeckysHappyFamily.'"

Tasha told her she'd call her back. While waiting, Jane returned to Domino to administer the antibiotic. Tuckered out, the hamster didn't fight her this time.

Tasha texted a link: Check out BeckysHappyFamily.

Jane sat on the edge of the bed. The bio proclaimed, "Becky White, pro-life, mommy of four. My dog is black," and featured a photo of a woman with a blond shoulder-length bob, sprayed into submission, rigid as a helmet. Her smile uptight, showing slightly too much of her gums. Jane scrolled through the various captions on the feed: "Live. Laugh. Love," "ALL LIVES MATTER." "As Fine as Wine" and "Deport Them All."

Jane: WTF
Tasha: Quinn pretending to be a Karen

Tasha started a video call to explain. At the height of the BLM protests, a few girls at Valle Vista tried to out-Karen the Karens online, role-playing the women who called the cops on Black people for selling water on a sidewalk stand or grilling in the park.

She texted a few examples that Jane toggled back and forth on: Simultaneously subversive and self-righteous, the accounts featured photos of flapping American flags, glistening glasses of white wine, and big families in matching outfits. Gingham shirts and rolled-up jeans, white shirts and khakis, standing on a beach or sitting on a dock.

Becky White hadn't posted since Thanksgiving: a photo of a burnished turkey. No doubt, Quinn had become busy, bored, and stopped posting, like so many of her classmates for whom BLM had been a passing internet trend.

Jane had to put the diary back. Returning to Quinn's room, she tucked it onto the shelf of the closet. In a few hours, it would slide, then slip off.

"Why bother?" she asked. She suspected that Quinn and her friends thought they were being edgy, outrageous, fighting racism one meme at a time. Maybe they felt in on the joke, or an associated guilt. They wanted to make it clear: *I'm* nothing like that.

Or maybe they were used to trying on any identity they wanted, whether it was dressing up in a kimono or sari for Halloween or in the service of cultural warfare.

Whatever. Nothing they did would really change anything. And maybe such pranks were worse than doing nothing. At least when you were oblivious, you could blame your ignorance. What did it mean when you knew that you benefited and still did nothing much more than skirmishing online, than offering FlashCash as a form of racial reparations?

* * *

Later that week, Ana discovered magnesium powder spilled on the kitchen counter, from the tub marked CALM. She wiped it up before anyone discovered the mess and tossed the empty tin of blackberry-lavender sleepytime edibles.

When she'd cleaned houses, she'd learned how to help her clients keep secrets from each other, and from themselves. If they didn't see the crumpled candy wrappers, the snacking never happened. If their clothes ended up in the hamper or hung up in the closet, and the upended tubes of lipstick and creams returned to their sentry positions, then they didn't have to remember their frantic self-doubt as they rushed to get ready. And when she offered her anxious clients the respite of tightly tucked, fresh sheets, of a window thrown open, they came to associate her with a well-ordered life.

Her boss had been working long hours, the light on past midnight in her home office. Ana was waiting on her paycheck again—late, the second time since she'd started working for the Belles. Blair blamed the bank and said she'd get it fixed. Ana wondered if something else was going on. She had saved almost enough for DACA; then the renewal would take at least six to twelve months to process. She'd make more keto tamales to try to cover the rest of the filing fee. The tamales had gained a small but devoted following after Nic had introduced Ana to a dozen families, who in turn introduced her to a dozen more.

Ana cooked batches at Carolina's, spending the weekends there. Families typically ordered at least four or five tamales, priced $12 each. So far, she'd pulled in close to $500, and spent about $125 on ingredients.

After fixing her papers, she could pay back Julio. Then she could save for college for Sofía. For herself. An associate degree, to become a nurse in the NICU. She could start those babies on the rest of their lives.

Or maybe the tamales would take off. More customers, a stand at the farmers market, T-shirts and tote bags for fans. She was dreaming bigger than she had in years. Not only bigger, but *longer*, beyond each day, each week.

In the living room, she folded up the soft muslin blanket she'd been using to play peekaboo, while Liam rummaged through a box of toys, the fancy rubber giraffe squeaking under his hand. Soon, she'd take him out for a walk in the stroller. He was turning one later this fall and seemed close to walking, cruising along the beige couch at every opportunity.

If she timed their departure, she could go by Shady Groves during recess. Even if she didn't spot Sofía through the chain-link fence, she liked thinking her daughter was part of the laughter and shouting.

She strapped Liam into the stroller. He smelled like fresh diapers, like tender care. By the mouth of the cul-de-sac, she looked both ways and crossed the street. At the sound of an engine, Ana turned. A white minivan glided by, piloted by a dark-haired woman in sunglasses. Not Julio, but she fought off the urge to sink down, to hide. She wanted to believe he'd given up looking for her, but he could stew. Whenever she let her guard down, he knocked her flat.

But she couldn't cower as though he were always a few steps behind her.

From a block away, a bell rang. Recess. She pushed the stroller to the chain-link fence that bordered the playground. Liam was wide-eyed, alert, taking in the scenery, gnawing on a teething ring. "Jordan's here, Sofía's here! Can you see them?" she cooed.

There she was! Sofía ran across the blacktop, arms pumping, swishing her long brown ponytail, her bright-eyed little squirrel.

Before the pandemic, Sofía had top marks, with dreams of becoming a veterinarian. But for more than a year, when Oakland schools had been closed, they perched on curbs outside the library and other hot spots, trying to get on to the shaky Wi-Fi on a laptop borrowed from the district. Sometimes they only managed to log on halfway through class; sometimes not at all. Sofía couldn't keep up with the assignments, with the schedule and learning apps changing by the week, by the day. She had fallen so far behind that she would have repeated the fourth grade if the teacher had not wearily advanced her and her classmates.

Outside rush hour, the drive from Oakland was theoretically only twenty minutes by freeway, but coming here, Ana felt like they'd broken through the earth's atmosphere for a trip to the moon.

The first time Ana had visited Shady Groves—with its neat rows of desks, well-stocked bookshelves, and garden out front, its raised beds of fattening gourds, caged tomatoes under the steady drip of irrigation—she'd nearly wept. She'd hoped that under such care and attention, her daughter would thrive like that, too.

Sofía should always have had this happiness. Her headaches and stomachaches—which used to overwhelm her—had disappeared. Ana should have left Julio a long, long time ago. She gripped the chain links, the guilt swamping her like a sneaker wave.

Like an angel, like an apparition, Nic appeared in the distance. She strode over, waving hello.

As Ana tried to compose herself, Nic touched her shoulder. "Are you okay?"

Her eyes stung. Ana couldn't remember the last time anyone had asked her that question. "I'm fine," she said shakily. She couldn't break down in front of Nic.

Nic glanced at Liam, who'd fallen asleep in the stroller. "You work for Blair."

Ana wondered how long she'd known. "I'm fine. We're fine."

"How far is your car?"

"We walked here."

"I'm driving you home," Nic insisted. "Or wherever you need to go."

Ana tightened her grip on the stroller. "But the car seat . . ."

"Let me walk with you, then."

"That's okay," Ana said as firmly as she could.

Nic glanced toward the front office. "I just came out of a meeting with Bill. The principal," she clarified. He complained that the fifth graders were among the "worst behaved" in his career. The latest offense? Running from lunch to their classrooms, rather than walking in an orderly manner. "He's retiring early. Doesn't he realize the kiddos went through a lot, too?"

Even here, Ana realized, which she found oddly reassuring.

"We all did," Nic said. "It's not easy, moving somewhere new. But everyone's so involved. Everyone cares."

Ana wanted to believe her, if not for herself, then at least for Sofía. Talking to Nic made her realize that she had to seize every opportunity here. Even though she owed Julio $1,000 in rent, she'd sign Sofía up for classes at the local wildlife rescue. Expensive, but Ana wanted to give her daughter the enrichment that the other children had in abundance.

For too long, Ana had been a bonsai, pruned and twisted and stunted. Now she could reach into the light again.

* * *

When the front door slammed, Blair assumed that Ana had just returned from a walk with Liam. He'd go down soon for his late-morning nap. Maybe she'd go by to give him a cuddle. But when a new email arrived, she got distracted by the latest birdhouse Orb footage.

She gaped at the screen: Nic's daughter fed a coyote what looked like chunks of hamburger, straight out of her hands. The coyote wagged its tail.

From this distance, she couldn't make out the expression on Ella's face, but her body language couldn't have been more at ease. She wondered if Ella had been setting out meat for weeks in the grove of pine trees, first to lure the coyote and then inching closer and closer. Ella sat cross-legged, her arm outstretched, as if playing with a labradoodle in the park. The coyote's eyes glowed, like it had been possessed by demons, before it finished eating and bounded off.

The Orb that surveilled Nic's house had a wide view, not only the front but also the rear, the backyard that edged onto the open space. According to the screeners, the girl had fed the coyote at least three times, at twilight every other day or so in the last week. How long had this been going on? Maybe habituation had triggered the coyote, turning it into El Nido's Most Wanted. DNA testing, saliva swabbed from the bites, had linked numerous attacks.

She pictured Ella luring the coyote: whistling as it padded down the street, then tossing a fistful of raw meat. The coyote catching the scent and circling back to feed. Maybe its fear of people had ebbed so much when it came across the teenager at the track, the coyote decided she might well be prey. She should tell Nic before the coyote turned on Ella, but then Blair would have to explain why an Orb had surveilled her, surveilled a number of intersections in El Nido without legal sign-off.

If Nic hadn't meddled with the Belles, she could have paid closer attention to home, to the wolf—or rather, the coyote—at the door. Blair could tell her boss; he'd see at once that such footage would go viral. Animal video + kid video would break the internet as much as any Kardashian. On Neighborz, every other post railed against coyotes or mountain lions stalking their pets. In El Nido, surveillance had its appeal. Many people outfitted their properties with home security cameras and video doorbells that would have been the envy of Checkpoint Charlie. To boost sales of the Orb, the footage would have to go beyond David Attenborough; it had to help authorities nab the coyote.

She'd wait a few more days to tell anyone, at least until she'd collected more footage. In the meantime, she'd request the installation of an additional dozen Orbs across El Nido. She'd tell the CEO that the data would be of interest not only to authorities, the general public, but wildlife biologists, too—emerging markets that the company could propose selling into, thereby attracting potential investors.

When Luna ambled in, Blair scratched her head before shooing her out and shutting the door. She heard footsteps and cooing, probably Ana carrying Liam up for his nap.

During the early months of the pandemic, the neighborhoods had been all but overrun by herds of deer who'd lost their skittishness. Battalions of Bambis feasted on the expensively landscaped tender shoots and lapped from sprinklers that flowed into the gutters. A pair had been spotted chasing after a mangy coyote, all three running at full tilt.

Farther down the valley, feral swine big as miniature ponies came from the hills, digging up yards and chasing hikers. Lured into traps bristling with cameras and motion detectors, shot dead in the night.

On the Peninsula, flocks of crows marauded across towns, shitting on alfresco diners, on their gleaming Teslas and McLarens. Local officials blasted boom boxes and aimed lasers to scare them off.

More and more of Sam's projects ended up in these transition zones at the edge of the wilderness, including the Bellavista. The setting, with its abundance of nature, was a key selling point, and though he'd planned on more affordable housing, ultimately he'd been forced to cut a few units to pacify Save El Nido.

Blair rewound the clip and watched it again. Ella seemed to bond with the coyote, in no clear and present danger. Maybe feeding the coyote prevented, rather than caused, the attacks in El Nido. If sated, wouldn't the coyote avoid going after people or, at least, with less frequency? By waiting, Blair might save a pet or two—Tigs, oh, Tigs!—and ward off further confrontations. Soon, she convinced herself that her reasons for keeping quiet about the coyote—far from being self-serving—were selfless.

17

Something smelled in Quinn's room. At first, it was musty, probably because she'd been gone all weekend. She opened the windows to air everything out. A couple days later, when the smell persisted, she looked under the bed for a forgotten plate, for moldy orange peels or soured milk in a cereal bowl. She cleared out a few mugs and turned on the air filter stashed in the corner, running it day and night.

Quinn didn't have much time or energy to investigate further. The cleaners would come next week. Her packed schedule for senior year wasn't a surprise, but she hadn't foreseen the persistent letdown. A hangover, without any tipsy fun. Seniors didn't typically feel this way, she guessed, but nothing had been usual in the suspended animation of the last year. Forgetting how to talk, to dress, to be. These past weeks felt like she'd undergone a freakish growth spurt, her bones and skin humming. Tripping over her own feet. Even Jacqui—who had the poise and cool of a tightrope walker crossing between skyscrapers—got flustered at lunch, on the brink of tears, when she couldn't zip her backpack closed.

She lit a candle and spritzed citrus perfume, but the mystery scent returned and sharpened, everywhere and nowhere, as if it were inside the walls. She sniffed her armpits, wondering if the vinegar smell originated there. She dumped her workout gear into the hamper and ran a load.

Maybe she imagined the smell, her mind playing tricks on her, a part of the wooziness that was coming more often now. Thankfully, it was never in the pool, at the practices held six days a week. Twice-a-days, three times a week. Friday morning, she slumped on the toilet seat in the locker room, trying not to pass out. So far, no one had noticed. Not Coach Ian. Not her parents or her sister or her friends.

That night, she looked for her old diary, to compare the data to what she now tracked on her phone. When she went into her closet, she wrinkled her nose. The smell was in here, too. When she reached behind her stuffed panda and owl where she'd hid the diary, her hand only met air.

Trembling, she pushed them aside. She shook the hangers, swept off the shelves, tees and shirts and leggings jumbled on the floor. She tried to remember when she'd last seen the diary. Sometime last year? Maybe she forgot about hiding it elsewhere. She had become so spacey and scattered that she'd searched online to see if teenagers could get Alzheimer's.

She kneeled, riffling through the pile, and discovered the diary. It must have fallen off the shelf. After she stumbled out of the closet and cracked it open, the neat rows of data calmed her like nothing else could.

During Zoom school, Quinn had grown self-conscious staring at herself, every imperfection staring back at her. The pimples on her chin. Her wide-set eyes like those of a hammerhead shark. Her scraggly hair. She'd started the diary in the earliest days of the pandemic, doodling until it became something more. Without practice, without routine, without Coach Ian and her team, she felt her outline dissolve. Everything she believed bold and permanent as a Sharpie had faded away. The entries, line by line, day by day, filled her in again.

She itched her back, skin dry from the chlorine. Her mother poked her head into the room, asking if she wanted to join Friday family-movie night.

Quinn nudged the closet door shut, hoping her mother wouldn't notice the mess. "I want to get started on a paper. I'll come down as soon as I can," she promised.

"It's Friday," her mother said, in a tone so disappointed that Quinn reconsidered. For the first time, she noticed her mom's limp hair, greasy and unwashed, and a yellow stain on the sleeve of her shirt. When Quinn told her, she smiled wanly, thanking her for pointing it out.

After she left, Quinn went into the closet to pick up the mess. She retched at the acrid smell coating her mouth, her tongue. Tossing her clothes around must have uncovered the source of the reek. Dark brown droppings dotted the corner. Mice? Her stomach churned and she dug a fist into her mouth, trying not to heave. If only Tigs had been around to hunt them down. She'd have to wash everything in here; luckily, she'd been living out of her suitcase since she'd returned so at least those outfits had been spared. She looked closer. There was a stain on the cedar floor and the baseboard had been gnawed upon. She spotted familiar tufts of silky black and white hair: Domino? He was a bit of an escape artist, but when? Not in the last few days, though the longer the urine remained soaked in, the more pungent it became.

When Luna wandered in, Quinn retreated from the closet. She reached down to pet Luna, stroking her curls. A car pulled into the driveway next door. She went to the window in time to see the garage door slide closed. Until then, she'd forgotten about the pet-sitter, Jane. Maybe Domino had gotten loose over the weekend.

She checked the center of the diary, where she'd tucked a strand of hair to catch anyone spying. It was no longer there.

She pictured Jane scrambling around the house, ducking, kneeling, crawling. Maybe the hair had fallen out when the diary tumbled from the shelf. Or had Jane discovered the diary and read what Quinn had written about her routine? About Maddy, Jacqui, her parents? She paged through the diary and cringed at an entry: *I wish Jacqui would back me up. Just once.*

If her craziness got out, her parents would put her in a psych ward. It could threaten everything she'd worked for.

Downstairs in the kitchen, a microwave dinged, and a moment later, the smell of buttery popcorn wafted through the house. She'd had enough to eat today, but the smell made her want to grab the bowl and tip everything in (four hundred twenty-five calories).

She should go to the gym, lift weights, and run on the treadmill, pound every upsetting thought out of her head.

She looked around her room. Did Jane do anything else in here? Try on her clothes, rummage through her drawers like a stalker? It was no different from if Jane had taken a dump in her closet.

Peering out the window again, she noticed the Orb trained onto the side gate. Every time her parents received an alert on their phones, you would've thought they'd discovered the house burned down. The footage from their front door wasn't exciting: delivery people, salesmen, and the occasional neighbor.

Maybe something more interesting would turn up from the cameras inside.

❂ ❂ ❂

Out along the coast, in a campground tucked among the redwoods, Jin willed the bars on his phone to appear. He rubbed his thumb across the greasy screen, trying to summon the genie. They'd arrived after dark, and between setting up the tent, making dinner, and building a fire, he hadn't checked his phone until after washing the dishes.

As the girls toasted marshmallows, he broke the news to Kai, who stood a couple meters away from the campfire.

"Why did you book us somewhere with no service?" Kai asked.

Jin protested that he hadn't known.

Maybe it was on purpose, Kai conceded. Americans liked to "unplug."

"We could go back. . . ." He rubbed his arms against the evening chill and inched toward the fire.

"Where would we stay? The house is rented out!" The light flickered across her face.

The first "guests" left the house cleaner than when they'd arrived. When Kai wavered about continuing, he persuaded her after he installed a doorbell camera and doubled the rental price. He could tell she hoped that no one would book at that price, and then, when the reservation came through, she couldn't pass up the money; she'd wire it to her parents, whose refrigerator and stove had conked out.

He volunteered to spend the night in the car—solo—somewhere with cell service. "Maybe that supermarket?"

"Then we'll be stranded here," Kai said. Earlier, she'd pointed out that the campground was only half full. She tugged down her knit cap.

"Maybe it'll be okay. Maybe they'll be like the first guests we had. They're on a writing retreat." Two women and a man. White, as far as he could tell.

"Writers!" Kai scoffed. She tucked her hands into the pockets of her fleece. "Did you recognize their names?"

No, Jin said. He let his roasting stick get too close and the marshmallow that had toasted golden went up in flames, the air smoky with burned sugar.

After tucking his family in, Jin drove a half hour on the winding roads to get service. The moment his phone pinged in the cup holder, he searched for the nearest pullout. He came in too fast, tires skidding in the dirt. He slammed on the brakes, jolting against the seat belt, and checked for messages. None from their guests, and the security footage indicated no activity at the front door.

He also checked on Save El Nido. After reading a news story about antidevelopment campaigns, he'd experimented with a new tactic: proposing that the land become a protected habitat for a rare species of salamander. Dozens had chimed in with their support. He marveled at the care lavished on such a slimy little creature; in China, the government flooded ancient villages and displaced more than a million peasants whose ancestors had called the Three Gorges home.

He rolled down the window. The air tasted sharp with salt. The stars above the coast, so numinous, numerous he felt dizzy.

Starting the ignition and shifting the car into gear took all the strength he had left in him. Exhausted on the drive back, he blasted the radio.

At the tent, he got in as quietly as he could, trying not to wake his family. He got onto his knees, crawling to his sleeping bag. He fumbled for the opening and wiggled in. Kai was so still, she was probably awake. He willed her to understand that everything would be okay. At least Chen had put off his visit. Regulators had not yet approved vaccinations for children, maybe not until November or December.

A rock or root dug into his back, and though he edged against the side of the tent, he couldn't escape. An owl hooted. What else lurked out there? He wondered if he should fetch the knife on the picnic table to defend his family. Soon, he fell into a dreamless sleep.

❁ ❁ ❁

Not long after sunrise, Jin woke up dry mouthed, sunk deep into his sleeping bag. Birds twittered frantically as he stumbled outside, wincing from the cold. He reached for the torn plastic bag in the wet grass; something had feasted on the marshmallows they'd left out. The damp earth smelled like new beginnings. He drove to the same spot: again, no messages, no activity detected through the front door. He rubbed his eyes, hoping that the rest of the weekend would be uneventful. He'd surprise his family with breakfast. He popped open the tube of biscuit dough, a celebratory sound. After punching a hole with his thumb, he'd fry rings of the dough on the camping stove and toss them in a paper bag with cinnamon and sugar, another recipe Lily had insisted upon that had become a tradition. Pillowy and not too sweet, not like those gooey buns slathered in frosting that made his teeth ache.

After breakfast, Jin urged his family to climb a nearby peak. He had a hunch it would have signal. They labored up the switchbacks, stands of redwoods giving way to pine trees, the air syrupy with sap, warmed in the sunshine. Every time someone suggested turning around, he forged ahead, desperate to check his phone.

When they reached the top, he backed away from the edge. Heights made him queasy, a fear of falling paired with the inexplicable pull of the void. To become one with it, to become nothing. While his family took in the Pacific and the rolling hills below, he searched for new messages—none—and also the doorbell camera, which had detected the guests leaving, dressed in running gear. He showed the footage to Kai. Sunlight glinted off the screen, which she shaded with her hand. "I thought they were writers?" she asked.

"They need a break," Jin said.

"A break . . . from sitting?" She handed the phone to Jin, her smile open and girlish.

They agreed the guests didn't seem like they'd cause trouble.

"Hello! Hello! Hello!" Lily hooted, and the hills shouted back. *Hello! Hello! Hello!*

❁ ❁ ❁

Jane settled against the sun-warmed rock. Her parents were all giggly, but weren't they weirded out by strangers sleeping in their beds? Her room didn't feel like hers anymore, not with the decor practically dug out of the trash. They were lucky no one had called the cops on them! One of the rugs had a rusty stain that made her wonder if they'd poached it from a crime scene. Her father agreed to dump it, but not the white wicker papasan chair or the hammered-bronze vase that now adorned her bookshelf.

And she had so much homework: a paper due on Monday and an Algebra II / Pre-calc math test on Wednesday. Though she'd brought her laptop and textbooks along, she couldn't study much until they returned home tomorrow. Then she'd have to help clean, washing endless loads of laundry, vacuuming, and scrubbing the toilets and showers. She hoped they wouldn't go camping again anytime soon.

The only consolation: At least she'd avoid running into Quinn. She felt uneasy around her; she knew too much about Quinn and Quinn knew nothing at all about her. Jane shouldn't have read her diary, shouldn't judge anyone from the depths of lockdown, but in the moment, it felt like getting back at the Belles for slashing the affordable housing. She'd also been trying to cheer up Tasha, trying to impress her, too—daring to be daring—but she'd gone too far.

She fingered a crevice that split the length of the boulder. Her father's decision not to book the Black family a few weeks ago gnawed at her. She'd tried not to sound as if she were lecturing him, but he'd bristled anyway. Her mother hadn't stopped him. Yet how many times had Jane also said nothing when her parents were racist . . . racial? Checked the locks on the car door at the intersection if a Black man waited at the light. Wondered aloud why the shoeless Black woman slumped at the bus stop didn't find a job and claimed that homeless didn't exist in China (neither did "the gays").

She'd been too embarrassed to tell Tasha what happened.

Didn't her parents remember what she'd told them, how Asians kept getting pitted against Black people? During the BLM protests, her parents had grumbled about the traffic shutdowns. The other night over dinner, when she mentioned Grace Lee Boggs and Yuri Kochiyama—activists from the 1960s, who'd gotten their start before her parents had been born—her father had fixated on their ethnicity.

"Is Yuri the Japanese?" her father had asked, then shoveled in a bite of mapo tofu.

"Yuri is Japanese *American*," she'd said.

The government had rounded up Yuri and other Japanese Americans during World War II, trapping them behind barbed wire. Later on, Yuri moved to Harlem with her husband and children, where she became an activist and a friend of Malcolm X. When he bled to death from a gunshot wound, Yuri had cradled his head in her lap.

"Grace is Chinese *American*." Jane served herself another scoop of rice. For decades, Grace and her husband, James, a Black autoworker and activist, had marched and protested, fighting for civil rights. "Both Yuri and Grace were born here, but their parents were immigrants. Like our family."

"Not the same," he'd said, waving his chopsticks at her.

Their examples had inspired Jane—proof that Asian Americans weren't all newcomers, that they'd been here already, standing up for others. And that she could, too. If you followed the news, you might never realize that Asian Americans had fought *for* affirmative action, fought *against* police brutality. When you defended people getting screwed, they'd defend you.

The people who spoke loudly and impatiently to her parents, certain they didn't understand English . . . who asked Jane where she was *really* from . . . the police who pulled over any Black man in a hoodie while responding to reports of a robbery . . . couldn't her parents understand it was all related to the same failure to differentiate them? All look same, all act same, all are same.

Now she plucked a yellow flower by her feet, rolling the stem between her fingers. There were other weeds, serrated leaves and prickly balls and wispy white flowers. Tasha could have helped identify them. She'd shown her the apps that helped you pinpoint birds by recording a snippet of song, pinpoint plants by snapping a photo. After you knew a thing's name, the world felt simultaneously smaller and bigger. Sharper, not blurry.

She wished Tasha could have come along. She'd asked, but Tasha couldn't go. Because her mother worked weekends, she had to look after Marcus. Jane had never met anyone like Tasha: serious, smart, but funny, too. Tasha sounded like a grown-up, unlike Jane, whose voice sometimes seemed as high-pitched as her little sister's. In an apocalypse, she'd follow Tasha anywhere; left alone, Jane would get impatient, hungry, and gobble the first poisoned berries she found.

They'd privately roasted Quinn for abandoning her online persona. Not that Becky White accomplished anything. Now Jane found herself sympathetic: It was hard to keep up the fight. How did Yuri Kochiyama and Grace Lee Boggs carry on? She tossed a pebble over the edge and watched it sail away until it disappeared. As if she'd dropped a penny down a well, she wished she might become as brave and bold as them.

18

After swim practice, Quinn borrowed her mom's phone, claiming hers had died and she needed to look something up. She wanted to comb through the Orb footage. She'd seen her mother swiping the Orb app; hopefully Quinn could figure out how. Though it was a sunny afternoon, a metal chill from the bleachers seeped through her swim parka. The outdoor pool felt like ice: her teeth chattering, her body livid with goose bumps. She'd gotten out a few minutes early, ungainly as a penguin wobbling onto land, and told Coach Ian she wasn't feeling well but promised she'd swim twice as hard tomorrow.

Quinn swiped through the menu, which listed when the Orb detected motion, and checked recordings from last weekend. It recorded a man placing a door hanger. A woman who left a business card. Finally Jane, who looked pale and warped in the fish-eye lens.

Her mother tracked Jordan in the water, in an outside lane, where waves from the other swimmers bumped hard into her, and she struggled to maintain her rhythm. Quinn didn't have much time with the phone before her mother would get suspicious. She switched through the indoor cameras, the one mounted above the hall closet trained on the front door, one in the living room, and another in the kitchen. Jane passed through with a bottle of antibiotics and a syringe.

"Quinn?" her mother asked.

Quinn startled, nearly dropping the phone. She turned it face down in her lap. "What?"

"I asked if you'd heard anything."

Coach Ian, pacing the sidelines, called out, "Keep your head down, Sullivan! Swim taller, Belle!"

"About what?" Quinn asked.

Her mother sighed. "About Jordan."

A whistle blew. "At the top!" Coach Ian shouted, sending off the next set of swimmers from the wall.

Quinn hadn't seen Nic and her daughter at practice; she'd heard that Ella had strained the tendons in her shoulder. At first, Nic had dismissed the soreness as "growing pains"; she didn't want Ella to lose the feel of the water. What might have been an injury Ella could have iced and rested for forty-eight hours now put her at risk of missing the rest of the season.

"Does she seem okay to you?" Blair asked, her voice ragged with exhaustion.

Why was her mother so tired? Didn't she go to bed after dinner last night? Quinn rubbed the edge of the phone. She should have been paying more attention, should have been watching out for her sister.

Her mother held out her hand. "Are you almost finished?"

Quinn hunched over the phone. She didn't see any sign of Jane chasing Domino through the house. There weren't any cameras by the bedrooms, though, and Domino could have run around up there.

What if she dusted the diary for fingerprints?

Like she even knew how!

She couldn't accuse Jane point-blank. If she was wrong, she'd seemed unhinged.

* * *

That night, coming back from the gym (weights, two hundred twenty calories), Quinn lowered the window on her car. The neighbors' house echoed electronica and blinked colored lights in dark red, indigo, and emerald. She could hear but not see people talking, probably on the back deck, from which drifted the skunky smell of marijuana.

She parked in the driveway. Upstairs, she discovered Liam bawling in her mother's arms. His room overlooked the Changs' back deck, and even with the white noise cranked on high, he'd woken up.

"Did you call the neighbors?" Quinn asked, almost shouting to be heard.

"It goes straight to voicemail!" Blair shushed in Liam's ear, circling her hips. Yesterday, she'd seen them loading their car, she said. Maybe they were out of town.

Quinn wanted to plug her ears with her fingers. "Do you want me to ring the doorbell?"

"Dad's already tried." The police had been by, but the music turned up again.

"You called the police? It only escalates the situation."

Blair rolled her eyes. Other neighbors had called, too, she said. "This isn't a hotel district! SuCasa has a ban on parties, but it's useless."

As Liam flailed his arms, wailing, she rushed out of the room. "I'm trying the dryer," she called out. The sound of the tumble dry might soothe him.

Quinn pulled aside the curtain and peered at the guests smoking and drinking. Jordan padded into the room. "The sound feels like . . . it's coming out my nose."

Quinn laughed. "It'll stop soon."

"How do you know?"

"Mom and Dad are trying to shut it down." She dropped the curtain.

"What if they can't?" Jordan asked, her voice thick.

Was she actually asking about something else? "Did something happen at practice?"

No, Jordan said.

"Are you sure?" Quinn asked.

Yes, Jordan said.

Taking her by the shoulders, Quinn steered her to her room. It really did feel like the music came out her nose!

She hoped her sister never found out about her compulsions. So much of what Jordan liked had followed Quinn's lead. She returned to the nursery and looked out the window. What if she crashed the party? Walked right in, skirted the people dancing in the living room and drinking in the kitchen, and went through Jane's room, the way Jane had gone through hers. It wouldn't take long. She'd be back home before her parents noticed. She leaned onto the windowsill. Though loud, the party didn't seem big enough for her to hide in the crowd. And what if the police showed up again, busting the party while she was there?

Maybe she didn't have to go tonight. If these people could rent the Changs' house, so could she.

❁ ❁ ❁

Though Wily no longer remembered curling against his mother and littermates in the den, a yearning remained. He traveled between the packs that spanned the area's rolling hills and wide valleys, the walnut grove and the bulldozers, the curving streets and cul-de-sacs, the creek that flowed into the reservoir from where he drank.

Though he'd come across the markings and scat of other coyotes, he'd yet to find a new pack to join and he didn't know how to start his own. He was as attractive to potential mates as he'd ever been: strong, his coat sleek, his vision sharper, the difference between well-fed and near starving. Even though the girl's scent and stealthy movements—like a raccoon—put him on edge, he couldn't pass up what she offered: tender morsels like the venison chewed and regurgitated that he ate as a pup.

In early autumn, the nights were longer and colder, too. He felt compelled to cross the busy two-lane roads that the alphas shied away from, that marked the edge of their territory, and see what was beyond: the oak leaves rustling beneath his paws. The savory scent pouring out from a smoker. And now the storm above him, that came from a house.

In the ravine, he discovered a pile of ribs he feasted upon. A guest had knocked a paper plate over the banister. The marinade would curdle in his stomach, leaving him listless and ill-tempered. Tomorrow, he would nip at a five-year-old boy in the park, retreating only after the nanny hurled a bike helmet at him.

The music above him swelled. As a pup, he cowered in a thunderstorm, confused by the noise, never knowing when the first or last clap would arrive, but these vibrations were sustained and contained, the party rumbling through him. Would the sound, the sensation, return after tonight? Squatting, he staked his claim.

19

Late Sunday morning, as soon as they reentered cell service, Jin's phone pinged. As he reached for it, he crossed the double yellow line. The narrow road curved along the cliffs that dropped steeply to the Pacific.

"Be careful!" Kai cried. "Let me check."

Notifications exploded like popcorn on the verge of scorching.

"What is it?" Jane asked from the back seat. "Is it bad?"

After checking messages—from the Belles, from the guests—after reading posts on Neighborz and reviewing the security footage, he and Kai figured out that the trio of guests had been joined last night by a dozen or so of their friends. What they didn't know: Ayahuasca led to severe gastrointestinal distress and an epic toilet clog, fouling the plumbing recently repaired.

The neighbors might simply have been annoyed—again—but for the disoriented guest who shambled onto the back deck. After bumping into the Ping-Pong table, she tumbled over the railing. No one inside heard her screaming. The Belles had called 911.

Police arrived to break up the party, and an ambulance had taken the injured woman away. The Neighborz post—"Really loud, obnoxious rave going on in the valley tonight"—had over a hundred comments.

As Jin pulled onto Rinconcito, Kai glowered beside him. She and the girls waited in the car while he unlocked the front door. He investigated:

the guests had pushed aside the furniture, left dirty cups and plates around the house, the reek of body odor so thick it seemed smeared on the walls, and a horrific mess in the master bathroom: vomit on the floor, and shit spattered all over the toilet bowl and lid. Jin gagged.

He hoped that any damage to the home would be minor. The damage to his marriage, though—that might be irreparable.

❁ ❁ ❁

A few blocks away, Kai ducked into the open house.

She didn't have a destination in mind when she took off with the girls, but if she'd spent any longer with him, she would have screamed. At her husband, but also at herself for failing to forestall a disaster. He'd been so selfish, chasing after his latest surefire dream. But wasn't she the bigger fool? Pride blinded her, not pride in him, but in herself, because she believed her smarts, her abilities, could make up for his failings. Each mistake expanding into a destruction so total it ate stars.

For once, let him clean the mess! She and the girls were dressed for camping, in dusty sneakers and T-shirts, their hair gathered into ponytails. The real estate agent, in a fitted sheath dress, strode toward them, introducing herself. "I'm Nic. Let me know if you have any questions!"

Glossy flyers fanned out on the kitchen counter, as well as bottles of water and a tray of chocolate chip cookies. Fresh baked, tinging the air with brown sugar and vanilla. "Let me know if you'd like a personal tour or if you'd rather look around yourself."

"Just looking," Kai said. The girls had already deserted her.

Neither she nor Nic recognized each other from the open house for 187 Rinconcito; Kai had only stopped in briefly before dealing with a work emergency.

To the agent, Kai must seem like a lookie-loo, a mainlander with a suitcase of cash who wanted to buy into the school district. She had the snaggle teeth that marked her as foreign—the overbite of someone who didn't have a middle-class American childhood.

The agent resembled the many Kai had encountered over the years, all gleaming smiles and aggressive eye contact.

Nic extolled the town's "semirural" charm, a term often used to describe El Nido. It had puzzled Kai at first. Not the country, not the suburbs. In time, she had come to suspect it had something to do with the abundant deer and flocks of wild turkeys with their guttural gobble gobbles. And perhaps it was a mark of distinction: El Nido wasn't a cookie-cutter subdivision like the kind that sprawled farther south and to the east.

"Anything in particular you're looking for? Anything you don't like?" Nic asked.

Kai pointed at an alcove off the kitchen. "This seems a little small." Though she had no intention—and no means—to buy, she enjoyed playing the part of an imperious shopper. Especially now, with their claim to El Nido in danger.

"It's a dual-purpose space," Nic said. "A second living room and a bonus office."

Apparently, this agent could turn every flaw into a selling point. Just like Jin.

How handsome he'd been when they'd met! That square jaw, the whorls of thick black hair. Straight-backed, earnest, and sincere. Her parents had been delighted when she told them she'd gotten engaged. Chinese, an engineer—she'd be well taken care of, her father said, which had irritated her. Hadn't she also landed an engineering fellowship to attend graduate school, hadn't she also secured a job in Silicon Valley? She could provide for the family, for them, too. What her parents didn't understand about Jin—what few did—was that as quiet, methodical, and measured as he might seem, he could dare like a gambler, putting everything on the red or black and letting the roulette wheel spin.

He'd suppressed those inclinations until he kept getting passed over for promotions, denied raises, viewed as a team player but never a leader. Never as a visionary, all of which compelled him to strike out on his own.

At first, he dreamed, she executed. With work, with their girls. Against her better judgment, against her every instinct, she'd gone along with this latest scheme, with its liquid pull, gravitational as the moon on the tides. Not because she believed that their success was guaranteed, but because she wanted to see if they could return to conspiring. If they couldn't, they were finished.

She'd reluctantly gone along on his treasure hunt and had found herself getting competitive, spotting what they might use—*There, there!*—up until a homeowner stepped out to walk her dog. Kai, putting a lamp into the back seat, wanted to dive into the car and peel out. The woman's look of pity made her want to explain that they weren't paupers.

Exhaustion sank in and Kai fought the urge to lie on the couch, to sprawl onto the carpet where she might sleep and sleep for days.

Nic mentioned she had a few upcoming listings. "Would you like to sign up for the mailing list?" She pointed at the clipboard on the counter.

"How's the market in El Nido?" Kai asked.

"There's a lot of pent-up demand."

Did Kai detect the slightest hitch in her voice? Although Sunday morning should have been busy, no one else had passed through the open house. The refreshments seemed untouched but for Lily, who'd wandered into the kitchen and nabbed a cookie. "Careful of the crumbs," Kai chided.

When Jane reappeared, Kai thanked the agent and left. On the sidewalk, she asked, "What did you think of the house?"

"I liked the cookies." Lily wiped her mouth with the back of her hand.

They started walking. "Besides that?" Kai asked. Bees buzzed above a rosemary bush that gave off a dusty, resinous scent.

"What were you talking to the agent about?" Jane asked.

"Nothing. She didn't seem to know much." Kai hoped the agent hadn't exaggerated the health of the housing market.

"Her flyer said she was 'five stars on Yip!'" Jane said with mock admiration.

"All those reviews are fake," Kai said. "Written by friends. Or paid for."

She'd put off the inevitable long enough. Time to go home and face the havoc from the party. Or . . . they could hit the open houses first and check if they attracted more prospective buyers. At the intersection that usually bristled with open-house signs, there were only three listings. She studied the addresses.

She didn't know her way around El Nido yet. During the lockdown, she used to take early-morning walks in Fremont. Too dangerous, Jin had argued, but she persisted. Once, after she'd forgotten her phone and disappeared for more than an hour, he'd driven around looking for her, convinced he'd find her stabbed, punched, and crumpled on the sidewalk. Instead, she'd beaten him home.

She never told her family that the farther she walked, the farther she wanted to go, to the horizon, past it. She got a tracker and competed with a few coworkers. Her resting heart rate plummeted and her hours of sleep grew. The years fell away, and she returned to being the girl who could kick around the shuttlecock for hours, the undisputed champion of her neighborhood. A girl who danced on air, circling the globe.

Now Kai bounced on the balls of her feet and charged ahead.

20

In late morning, Jin got off the phone with police, who detailed what had happened and told him they'd come by later to take a statement. He paced across the living room, examining the wreckage. A bottle of kombucha had spilled, leaving another stain on the carpet. As he waited for his family's return, he gathered the cleaning supplies from underneath the kitchen sink, snapped on rubber gloves, and got to work in the master bathroom. The reek! An overturned outhouse on the hottest day of the year. He put on an N95 to block out the fumes, but the smell of his own breath, the bleach, and the shit seeping in made him retch.

He staggered onto the deck, gasping for fresh air. He spit over the railing, then hunched over, resting his hands on his thighs. He tore the gloves off his sweaty hands and backed away from the railing, which probably wasn't up to code. Cups and bottles cluttered the Ping-Pong table.

He supposed they were lucky. The renters hadn't broken any windows. And the woman who fell could have cracked open her head, but police said she'd been so floppy from the drugs that she'd only had the wind knocked out of her; the pile of pine needles had cushioned her landing. If she'd fallen a few inches to either side, though, onto jagged rocks . . .

His scheme was foolish and only Kai's love for him—for their family—had kept it going for as long as it had. Or maybe it wasn't love, but obligation, that of the capable around those who were not, who mopped up messes or averted them. She'd gone along, not for him but for their daughters, to provide for them now and through college.

He sniffed, smelling smoke. Someone barbecuing, or carried aloft from a distant fire? Nothing close by, he decided. It would be a disaster if Chen's investment burned down.

The silence of the empty house was almost too much to bear. He couldn't remember the last time he was alone. In Fremont, someone in his family had always been banging, bumping, clanging around the apartment: his wife firing up the kitchen exhaust fan, Lily throwing open the cabinets in search of a snack, Jane jumping along to a workout video. Even when they were still—reading, watching a lesson online, typing at the laptop—sometimes he swore he could hear them breathing through his noise-canceling headphones. Loud as a swarm of bees descending upon him. Wasn't that marriage, wasn't that parenting: Someone always breathing in your ear?

With no one mooring him right now, he could have floated into the sky, slipped free from gravity, from debt, from responsibility. Hurtled at light speed across a universe always expanding.

He opened the SuCasa app to delete it and noticed another request, someone claiming that she wanted a quiet getaway in a couple weeks.

Lies.

He trashed the request and shoved the phone into his pocket. He should finish cleaning, and when Kai returned, he'd beg for forgiveness. Tell her that he would call Chen and reveal everything—well, some of it. Not that he'd been renting it out, but that the house needed major repairs. They could sell it as is, potentially at a loss, or Chen could pour in more money to finish the renovations. And Jin would pull the plug on Save El Nido.

His phone blared: Chen calling, which startled him so much he almost dropped the phone. Had Jin called him by mistake? It was the middle of the night in China, and he hoped he hadn't woken Chen up. But—no. Maybe Chen had contacted him by accident, sleepily hit the wrong button. Or maybe he'd discovered what happened at the property.

The phone blared again.

When Jin picked up, at first he didn't understand. Chen repeated himself until Jin grasped that his mother had collapsed. Ma awaited tests in the hospital. Ba had been trying to reach him—and Kai—for the past few hours, but the calls never went through. Then he called Chen, asking for help.

Jin sank into an Adirondack chair. Ma! He hadn't seen her in three years. He pictured his parents in the hospital, cold, alone, and scared. Monitors beeping, mocking in their insistence.

"How did he . . . sound?" Jin gripped the armrest.

"Tired but okay," Chen assured.

"Did you talk to her?"

"She was asleep."

Was his friend trying to shield Jin from the gravity of Ma's illness?

"I'll make sure she gets the best of everything," Chen added.

Jin sat up. "Send the bill to me."

No, Chen said. He'd take care of it.

Jin couldn't pass up his friend's charity. "You'll tell me if I need to come home?"

"She'll outlive us all!" Chen paused. "Why didn't their calls go through? Is there an outage where you are? How close are you to the wildfires?"

Here was the opening, the shift in conversation in which Jin might come clean. But he heard himself saying that the wildfires were hundreds of miles away, not to worry. They'd camped in the redwoods—spectacular. Jin could take him there.

"We don't need to talk business now. Later, later," Chen said.

After they hung up, the brush twitched—a coyote, *the* coyote? A parade of bulky wild turkeys wandered out instead, the birdbrains the coyote should have gone after. The natural order had gone off, and he wouldn't have been surprised if it fell dark at noon. The world had been knocked askew: skies in the Bay Area that turned orange as Mars; floods in Germany that washed away villages; a heat dome over Portland that buckled roads and melted power cables; red algae blooms that killed off thousands of fish around the bay; seeming anomalies that weren't.

In a few hours, Ma would wake up and he'd call her then. The doorbell rang. The police already? He rushed through the house and swung open the front door.

"You just got back?" Blair asked. Her eyes were bloodshot, the skin beneath puffy and dark.

Yes, he said.

"So you know what happened last night." When she peered over his shoulder, he widened his stance to block her view of the mess.

"Yes, I heard. I'm sorry. Very sorry."

"Is that girl going to be okay?"

Yes, he said. "She's very lucky."

"You are, too. She could have died!"

He didn't disagree yet he didn't like having it pointed out to him. And as for luck, this woman seemed to have no idea how much she possessed. "It won't happen again."

"How will you make sure?" Blair asked.

He wondered when Kai and the girls would return. He was sorry, truly sorry—he knew he'd wronged the Belles, his family, and the neighborhood—but what else did she want from him? To get on his knees?

"You'll stop renting it out?" she asked.

He chafed at her aggressive tone. "That's what you want?" He folded his arms across his chest. If it were up to her, his house would get bulldozed and turned into a nature preserve.

She pivoted and gestured around Rinconcito. "It's not just me. This is a quiet street."

"Quiet? Your daughter drives like a maniac!"

Blair ignored his accusation. "The parking, the parties . . . It's too much. And all these strangers, every weekend."

"You want to protect and preserve the character and charm?"

She nodded, giving no sign she'd detected his sarcasm.

"I understand." He bowed humbly. To make her go away, he agreed to take the posting down. "Thanks for coming by."

❁ ❁ ❁

Blair had indeed detected her neighbor's scorn, and something else, too. The phrase "protect and preserve the character and charm"—with its catchy alliteration—featured prominently on the Save El Nido website.

At her desk, when she checked the online petition, she didn't see Jin or his wife. She lingered on Nic's name. She'd become a leader of Save El Nido. She wondered why Nic cared about the Bellavista. Maybe she worried that the development would drive housing prices down because of the additional inventory.

Nic might also believe the affordable housing tarnished what she and others in the community had worked so hard to attain. She and her husband—both the first in their families to attend college—had scrapped and scraped their way up, and Blair had gathered that Nic had never lost the fear that you were one paycheck, one accident, away from disaster. You had to be vigilant when it came to your children and your home.

Nic used to post "Bad Nanny Alerts" on Neighborz about the caregiver who'd been on her phone the entire time, the one in the black ball cap and pink leggings, or another in jeans and bedazzled sweatshirt who gave the toddler what looked like blue Gatorade. Gatorade!

Blair leaned back in her chair. She would bide her time, holding on to the footage of Ella feeding the coyote; Nic would hate for it to go public. She tidied her mess of a desk: scribbled printouts, two dirty coffee mugs, and a half-empty can of seltzer. She wished she could talk to Sam about their neighbor, but he was on a long bike ride and wouldn't return until later this afternoon.

Last night, as the party raged, she'd harped on the Ping-Pong table. "You never should have given it to them! They probably listed it as an amenity!"

He'd promised to call a contact in El Nido's Planning Department and to talk to the Changs, but Blair couldn't trust that he wouldn't give the neighbors something else. *Need a car? A couch? Here you go!*

Even at the height of the party, he'd been sympathetic. "They must really need the money," he'd said. And Jin had seemed beaten down when she'd gone by just now, sweaty and bedraggled.

Sam wouldn't be so softhearted if she discovered a connection between the Changs and Save El Nido. *Protect and preserve. Character and charm.* Was the phrase only a coincidence, something Jin had read in the paper?

She punched the URL into the WHOIS directory, hoping to find contact information, but it only listed the domain registrar, a company whose name she didn't recognize. She took off her reading glasses and pinched between her eyes. What was she looking for again? Fogginess descended, her thoughts thick and soft and blank, the edges a blur.

She blinked until it came back to her. A quick search, and she discovered the website was registered with one of the biggest service providers in China. *China?*

Though she couldn't prove it, she wondered if Jin was behind Save El Nido. That kind of hostility seemed next-level, though, an effort monumental and mind-boggling.

But hadn't this nonsense started around the time that the Changs moved in? She wondered what else might be brewing online. Poking around, she discovered posts across several forums criticizing the town. Nothing she hadn't heard, nothing that she didn't acknowledge as sort of, sometimes true—of *other* people. Nothing that journalists hadn't gleefully chronicled about El Nido over the years: squabbles over leaf blowers, a dustup over swim fees at a country club. The school district siccing a private investigator on a Mexican nanny, trying to kick her out for residency fraud.

The posts made her cringe: "If you want to live in a bubble, then you will fit right in!"

"Entitled. The adults whine worse than their children if they don't get what they want. Toxic."

"If you are not rich and white you will be belittled. Don't work here. The people here act like you should bow down to them or that they own you."

She studied the dates: The oldest entries were years old, but the newest ones were time-stamped in August and September. "More Karen's here than anywhere I have ever lived!"

She felt pummeled in two different directions: by those who condemned El Nido, and those who condemned any changes.

She wanted to rush downstairs and ring the Changs' doorbell again. Repeat those words—*protect and preserve, character and charm*—and see if he'd flinch. She'd keep investigating. But since he had made trouble for her family, she'd do the same to him.

❁ ❁ ❁

An hour and a half later, on the back deck of the house, Jin placed a video call to his parents. Almost 9:00 PM in California, noon China local time. His parents, after checking out of the hospital, had returned home. He asked if they needed additional help, if the girl who worked every other day might come daily for a while.

"I'll pay for it," he said.

"A hassle." As always, Ba held the phone too close, offering a view of his nostrils.

Ma looked over his shoulder. "Waste of money." Her face was drawn, her features sharper. A sign of the underlying illness?

"What about the herbalist?" Jin asked.

"Stopped by on the way home." Now the camera trained on Ba's forehead and the ceiling.

"I'm supposed to steep and drink it twice a day," Ma's disembodied voice said. "It's boiling now. Stinky!" Feisty as ever, but her voice sounded weak. She grabbed the phone and squinted at Jin. "You look tired. Your eyes so puffy, wah!"

"When's your next appointment?" Jin asked.

"The medicine is ready." Ma handed the phone to Ba.

Jin wanted to ask them more about what the doctor said, about the next step in her treatment.

"Hao le, bye-bye," his father said, and hung up. Cagey, hiding something; Jin knew they didn't want to worry him.

Only by seeing them in person would he truly understand how they'd aged: a slowness in their step, a hesitation in their thinking not apparent on their calls.

He messaged Chen, asking about Ma's prognosis. The moon cast a wan light over the ravine. He settled into the Adirondack, a sturdy Buy Nothing find.

Through the sliding glass door, he noticed Lily curled next to Kai on the couch, the blue light of the television flashing onto their faces. Robots battled each other, gladiator-style.

While he'd cleaned the house, she'd toured open houses with the girls. She'd returned with suspicions that the housing market had cooled.

"It'll pick up in the spring," he'd said with more confidence than he felt. "No one wants to move their kids right now."

While he waited for a response, his phone flashed with an email alert: someone replying to a mass thread about a neighborhood picnic, days of discussion so far about plates, condiments, brownies, tables, chairs. He ignored it.

Getting chilled, hairs raised on his arms, Jin was about to go inside when Chen texted his reply: Jin's mother was suffering from dizzy spells, a weakness in her legs, and ringing ears that doctors hadn't yet cured.

He pictured Ma in the dank stairwell, getting woozy, losing her balance and her body tumbling down.

They didn't tell me! he texted.

Chen: My mom was hit by a bus. Didn't say anything until the next day!

Chen mentioned an apartment in one of his buildings, only a few years old, with an elevator. He'd already spoken to Jin's parents, and they seemed open to moving there. He'd charge them what they paid now in rent.

Jin asked if they could get on a video call.

Chen: Later. In a meeting
Jin: It's too much
Chen: You'd do the same

Chen promised to call soon.

Ma was okay, would be okay, Jin told himself. A breeze rose, ruffling his hair. As old as he felt some days, at least he had a full head of hair, brushing against his ears and the nape of his neck. He searched the darkness of the woods. He'd never explored what probably stretched for less than half a mile, but felt secluded. If he listened hard enough, long enough, those bandit tales he'd read as a kid would come to life: rebels hiding out there, emerging to defend teahouse girls and steal from the rich.

Growing up, Jin had always been the first to answer a teacher's question, first to ask one, too. First to quip among his friends, and at dinner with his parents. "A little emperor should watch his tongue!" his mother had scolded. First to proclaim he'd go to America, and the first of his friends to do so.

On his flight to America, somewhere over the Pacific, maybe above the international date line or perhaps the moment he walked down the Jetway in San Francisco, his transformation had already begun. In the terminal, he'd halted at the view: the heavens a boundless blue compared to the smoggy skies of his hometown. Then a man on a cell phone had bumped into him. Jin stumbled, knocking over his roller bag. The man didn't stop, didn't apologize; he gave no indication that he'd seen Jin, and the sensation of invisibility only grew the longer he stayed in America.

His conversations with his classmates never progressed into anything that resembled friendship. Jin seemed a different person altogether in English than he was in Mandarin. He couldn't keep up with the jokes, couldn't *tell* the jokes. It wasn't a matter of fluency, though, or his accent. Even if he'd spoken like a posh Englishman, he felt out of sync, like a poorly dubbed movie, which led to awkward silences, stilted explanations, inadvertent offenses.

Instead of completing his PhD, he left the program after getting his master's and took a quality-compliance software job in California, where he met and married Kai. They'd started a family soon after, late by Chinese standards, but early by those of Silicon Valley, where he'd never met so many practically geriatric parents. Green cards followed and, eventually, US citizenship.

In a couple years, Jane would leave for college, unless—as he secretly hoped—she lived at home while attending Cal. They'd been a trio for almost six years, before Lily came along, and though he loved his youngest fiercely, he sometimes missed the days that preceded her. They'd bought their first house when Jane was in preschool, but by the time Lily arrived, it had been foreclosed. The decade since had been a struggle; still, he and Kai would find a way.

The patio door slid open and Kai came out, holding up her cell phone. "Did you see this?"

In the email he'd ignored, a neighbor warned about a coyote she'd spotted in her backyard. "Lock your doors!" Then she'd chimed in about putting a stop to SuCasa.

Looking over the email, he concluded what Kai had, too: The neighbor had replied to this thread by accident, inadvertently including Jin and Kai. The neighbors must have a separate thread in which they discussed how to prevent the Changs from renting out their place again.

Jin fumed. The Belles were building a huge development—that they'd named after themselves!—but wouldn't let anyone else profit off El Nido's prestige. He couldn't let the neighbors bully them like that.

"She said we were lucky," Jin said.

"We were." Kai sat in the Adirondack beside his.

He gestured at the Belles' house. "People like them, they're born lucky. But people like us, we make our own luck."

He retrieved the request from the SuCasa app. A Becky White had booked it for one night, in a couple weeks, for $500. He scrutinized the photo, her message, which was polite and grammatical, friendly and open: nothing to hide. He showed it to Kai. "We should accept the reservation. Before the town blocks it completely."

"No more." She muttered a proverb: *Spin a cocoon to bind yourself.* "I won't let you get us caught up again."

The mistake, he argued, was failing to stand guard. "Next time I'll park around the corner, monitor the app all night, and return at the first sign of trouble." The soreness from sleeping in the car would be worth it. He could earn enough to cover the repairs they'd already made, the repairs to come.

Crazy, Kai said. "We're trying to fix up the house!"

He'd talked to his parents, he said. "They said they didn't need extra help."

"They never let us help."

"They let Chen," he said, his voice breaking.

"He's nearby," Kai said gently, which only intensified his guilt. He'd abandoned them!

Ma was sicker than she let on, according to Chen. "I can't let Chen pay for all of it," he said.

Kai put her hand on his. He hadn't convinced her yet, but he might. She could be traditional when it came to marriage. Sometimes, he wondered if tradition might have been all that kept her from leaving him.

21

The next day at school, when Jacqui stood up, Quinn blinked in surprise. "Where are you going?"

"I told you, the career center," Jacqui said. "But you haven't listened to anything I've been saying."

Quinn protested, but she hadn't really been paying attention. She hugged her legs, tucked into her chest. "I'm a little distracted."

Jacqui gestured around Senior Lawn. "We all are. But we aren't ignoring our friends."

Quinn couldn't deny it. Maddy, sitting a few feet away, peered over, as if sensing an argument brewing.

Quinn got to her feet, her legs numb from sitting, her neon-pink leg warmers damp from the grass. Monday was the first day of Spirit Week: 80s Flashback.

Jacqui folded her paper plate over the remains of her cheese pizza. In an aqua jacket with padded shoulders and matching eyeliner, her hair in a high asymmetrical ponytail, she resembled the slashes of an abstract painting.

The savory smell of the pizza (two hundred fifty calories) made Quinn nauseated and hungry at the same time. Her mouth watered. She couldn't give in, though. At practice before school, her swimsuit felt tighter, tight as a sausage casing, cutting into the tops of her thighs.

"Did you turn in your application yet?" Jacqui asked.

"Last week."

"Then you're in!" Jacqui tossed her plate into the trash.

Not if the coaches knew the truth about Quinn: She was worthless, weak. Never exercised long enough, never ate clean enough.

When she'd been a kid, younger than Jordan, she hadn't dreamed of becoming a swimmer. She wanted to become a mascot like Lou Seal or Stomper the Elephant. To wear gigantic fuzzy costumes, moonwalk, and pratfall anonymously. Instead, she wound up in a sport in which she couldn't have been more exposed.

"What about you?" Quinn pushed up the sleeves of the off-the-shoulder sweater that she'd borrowed from her mother. "Are you done with applying?"

Jacqui wanted to go to NYU, to double major in music and business. Almost immediately, Quinn stopped listening. It took her a moment to realize that Jacqui had gone quiet.

"Sorry, I . . ." Quinn said.

"Forget it." Jacqui turned to leave. "You've been acting so weird." She shot a glance at Maddy.

"You're a lock at NYU," Quinn said.

Jacqui bit her lip. "You really think so?" She didn't usually need—or want—reassurance.

Quinn swept her arm up. "You're *literally* stacked with talent." She ticked off accomplishments. "You were the lead in the school musical. President of the French Club. Varsity tennis. All that volunteering. And your stats! We scored the same on the SATs."

Jacqui lifted her chin. "Higher."

Okay—true, on the second try. By thirty or forty points or something like that. But wasn't bringing it up kind of rude? Submitting scores were optional this year, anyway.

Jacqui studied Quinn. "I was thinking of applying to Princeton, too. My cousin was talking it up. It looks like Hogwarts!" She made a face. "It is in *New Jersey*, and not New York, but close enough."

Was Jacqui messing with her? She'd never mentioned applying there. Quinn felt queasy all over again. "Isn't NYU better for music?"

"Obviously." Jacqui shrugged. "But I want to keep my options open."

She was applying to Quinn's dream school—on a whim?

"I guess."

Jacqui frowned.

"Yes, I mean yes, it would be great if we both got in!" Quinn hoped that her enthusiasm didn't sound fake. What if the university only admitted one student from Valle Vista? She pictured Jacqui, in a classic camel-hair coat, passing through Blair Arch, traipsing past piles of autumn leaves. "Someone with your stats, your background, you'll get in everywhere."

"My 'background'?" Jacqui asked, her eyes hard. "Growing up in El Nido?"

Maddy smirked.

"The consultant said that . . ." Quinn faltered.

"Let me guess, the consultant said schools take a lot of things into consideration: Like legacies? Like athletes who get in with lower scores?"

Quinn winced. If only Jacqui knew what was bothering her; Quinn would have to explain. She took Jacqui's elbow and led her away from Senior Lawn.

By the garden, dotted with ratty sunflowers and spiky weeds, Jacqui asked, "What is it?"

Quinn spilled about her suspicions, and the missing strand of hair in her diary.

"You really think she read it? Maybe she took photos, too."

Quinn hadn't considered the possibility that Jane could have photographed the entries and post them online. She drew a shallow breath, feeling squeezed. Anything digital, she could probably deny, calling it a fake. But it made her crazy, knowing Jane went through her things.

The whole family was so foul, the dad giving Quinn the evil eye whenever she drove by, their chaotic SuCasa parties, their busted toilets.

"What's in it, anyway?" Jacqui asked. "You talking shit?"

"No!" If Jacqui ever discovered what was in her diary . . . Quinn had cringed, rereading it, whining about Maddy and her "jokes" that were jabs, and how Jacqui never defended her.

Quinn toed a crack in the walkway. "It's a training log."

As much as she wanted to keep her compulsions a secret, she felt guilty for never telling Jacqui. But Jacqui held out, held back on her, too. She had friends she'd never introduced to Quinn, from a service organization in Oakland. Black friends. Quinn had looked it up; by invitation only, it sort of sounded like a sorority.

"When I thought about her going through my stuff, I—I booked their house on SuCasa." Several times, Quinn had been on the verge of canceling the reservation.

"You rented their *house*?"

Quinn flushed.

"How?" Jacqui asked. "Don't you have to be eighteen? And upload an ID?"

"I used Becky White's."

Jacqui frowned.

Quinn's gleam of pride dimmed by Jacqui's obvious annoyance that she'd brought up the subject of Becky White again.

* * *

Last summer, that lady in Central Park had called police on a Black birdwatcher. Accused him of threatening her life after he asked her to leash her dog. It was the very same day that police murdered George Floyd in Minneapolis by kneeling on his neck. It had opened Quinn's eyes. She was ashamed to admit that, until then, she hadn't thought much about how Black people, surveilled and harassed in public spaces, could end up dead.

She tried to educate herself; from what she'd read, she wasn't supposed to burden her Black friends with questions. Like everyone else, Quinn shared and reshared inspiring quotes and protest art. *Justice for George*, his head wreathed in flowers. The ethereal portrait of Breonna in the flowy aquamarine dress. The activism didn't feel like much, because it wasn't. At least her parents had donated to the ACLU. . . .

Then she noticed the fake accounts designed to bait—and then mock—entitled white women, the kind who wanted to speak to the manager, who called the cops on Black people for every little thing, the ones who'd been nicknamed #PermitPatty, #BBQBecky, #KarensGoneWild.

She'd invented her own persona, Becky White, aka BeckysHappy-Family.

She combed social media, looking for Karens popping off: "My son was a straight A student, president of the Latin club, and Boy Scout Eagle Award. And he didn't get into any colleges!! It's ridiculous. Giving spots to unqualified minorities," a mom from Ohio wrote.

"Colleges lowering their standards," Quinn had commented as BeckysHappyFamily.

"Exactly. It's reverse discrimination," someone else chimed in on the thread.

The comments went back and forth until BeckysHappyFamily slipped in an extreme view: "Bring back segregation!" With increasing desperation and confusion, the real Karens tried to reason with the fake. "I didn't mean it THAT way," one wrote.

But sometimes, the Karens would get tricked into agreeing, walking into the trap Quinn set. She regretted posting the nastiest comments, but it had to be done. Real Karens spouted off far worse, with their real names and photos!

She modeled herself after her Grammie Marilyn—her mother's mother in La Jolla—who complained about rioters who'd turned every city into a hellscape, about "illegals" flooding the border. Didn't Grammie realize her son-in-law was half Mexican, that her grandchildren were a quarter? At least she wasn't QAnon. Quinn had tried to speak up to Grammie, but nothing had been as satisfying as embarrassing stand-ins online.

Once, when Quinn showed off a Becky White post, Maddy and Jacqui had exchanged a scornful look, almost too swiftly for her to notice. Like they'd been texting about it, behind Quinn's back. She'd thought Jacqui would find it hilarious. That she'd approve.

She never confronted Jacqui about it, but for a couple weeks they each left their messages unread for longer and longer stretches. On Jacqui's birthday, Quinn sent her flowers and a rose-gold karaoke mic, gifts that thawed relations between them.

For Quinn's birthday, Amelia—another faux Karen, another Karen foe—had purchased a fake ID as a gag gift. A forty-five-year-old woman from New Jersey. "I showed it to you, don't you remember?" Quinn now reminded Jacqui. "That's what I uploaded to SuCasa."

Jacqui pursed her lips. "How much is it per night to rent?"

"I have Christmas and birthday money." Quinn tugged on her sleeves, drawing them over her hands.

Jacqui stretched, cupping an elbow across her body, then the other. "For how long?"

"One night." Quinn shivered. She wanted to get back into the sun.

"When?"

"The Saturday after next." The same day that her parents would attend a school fundraiser, a boat dance, departing from a dock in Oakland, she said. "They're gone until eleven."

"Why don't you ask her?"

"Ask her?" Quinn sputtered. "What if she didn't read it? It's already weird with her parents."

"We can go by her and see how she reacts." Jacqui looked up and down the hallways, as if pondering which direction to try first. Wind gusted, scattering leaves and crumpled wrappers. A pack of boys went by, dribbling a basketball and wafting musky body spray. "Let's try the Quad."

Quinn trailed along, buoyed by her friend's plan. Jacqui in charge was a Jacqui who cared. They slowed down as they approached Jane, who sat cross-legged in the grass, gesticulating, her face twisted in disgust. "It was so gross, I almost puked!"

"But it's cleaned up now?" Tasha asked.

They must be talking about the aftermath of the SuCasa party.

Neither one had dressed for Spirit Week. The sort who grinded away, Quinn guessed. No fun. Tasha had never responded to her DM. For that, Quinn had been grateful; she shouldn't have offered FlashCash to someone she barely knew.

As Jane spoke, she seemed to notice them, standing a few feet away. She fell silent. Maybe she didn't want them to hear about her family's woes. Or maybe she was hiding something.

Jacqui propped her foot on the planter, reaching down to tie her high-top sneaker. "So someone searched your room?" she said in what amounted to a stage whisper.

Jane went rigid, staring straight ahead. Tasha sipped from her water bottle with a studied casualness.

"Maybe your sister?" Jacqui dusted off her hands, her jelly bracelets sliding down her arm. "Your mom?"

Quinn tugged the wrists of her fingerless lace gloves. "It was someone who left a smell. Someone who smelled like a rat."

Jacqui arched an eyebrow, getting into the role, the kind of performance that had won her the lead.

Jane looked even more stricken, her shoulders drawn up as if someone had dropped snow down her back.

"Someone with boundary issues," Jacqui said. "It's an invasion of privacy."

Quinn nodded. "Total invasion. Invaders."

When Jane's expression hardened, the back of Quinn's neck prickled.

"You ever noticed how whenever there's a group of three friends, it always falls apart?" Jane asked, loud as an actress projecting to the last row of an auditorium.

Tasha brushed crumbs from her lap. "Like how?"

"Two 'friends' ganging up on the other one." Jane, gesturing with her hands, still didn't look at Quinn. "Dragging them, talking behind their back."

Quinn went clammy. If she tried to walk, she'd fall.

Tasha rested her chin on her steepled hands. "Three always turns into two against one?"

"But maybe the one left behind deserves it," Jane said. Only then did she lock eyes with Quinn.

Quinn took off, Jacqui close behind her. When Quinn rounded the corner, she halted, panting.

"You okay?" Jacqui asked.

Quinn wrapped her arms around herself. It wasn't true, it wasn't true. Or was it? She'd brought it upon herself; she shouldn't have taunted Jane.

Quinn had to remember: Jane had wronged her, not the other way around.

"Was that something from the diary?" Jacqui asked.

"It was about some girls on the team," Quinn blurted. She swiped at her eyes with the back of her hand. If she said anything more, she'd start bawling.

"She read it, then. Since she went through your stuff, you should go through *hers*." Jacqui linked arms with Quinn. They could have been eight years old again, running in from recess. She should have confided in Jacqui from the beginning.

They walked back toward Senior Lawn. "What if the family locks everything up? What if there's nothing of hers in the room?" Quinn asked. "Renting the house will feel like . . . overkill." Like breaking open a bank vault to discover it empty. Traveling at interstellar speeds and landing on a barren planet.

They passed the student wellness center. BE KIND and YOU'RE NOT ALONE posters hung in the windows.

The idea seemed to come upon them at the same time.

"I could . . ." Quinn said.

"You could have a party," Jacqui finished.

They gazed over Senior Lawn, where their friends lazed under the shade of three redwood trees, their trunks so massive that it took two people holding hands to get all the way around.

The warning bell rang. Five minutes before class started.

Quinn had known these kids all her life, and now it was coming to an end. It had been so long since they'd been to a party! Last year had been a disaster, and they'd never get that time back again. And it would be safer than drinking at a turnout in the hills.

But what if the neighbors called the cops?

"Okay, not a party," Jacqui said, as if sensing her reluctance. "But a few friends. A year from now, we'll all be somewhere else. We can wear masks. Keep the windows open. Everyone's so stressed."

On that point, Quinn couldn't agree more. She shuddered, a rubber band about to snap, stretched to its limit, and past it. A girls' night could smooth things over between her and Jacqui.

Jacqui said she'd take care of everything. The drinks, the snacks, the music. "All you have to do is open the door."

* * *

Within days, word got out about the party: spread from text to text, DM to DM, until people were openly discussing it in the hallways, in the locker rooms, in class. No invitation was more freely and liberally issued than one that wasn't yours to give.

22

In a note marked *URGENT* in all caps, the CFO questioned a slide Blair had built. He'd also texted her phone and via the office messaging app. Tomorrow morning, the CEO would present to investors—ones that the company needed to survive the next eighteen months.

Yet Blair couldn't stop thinking about Jin. What a surly man! She felt sorry for his wife. Save El Nido . . . China, China. What was the connection to China? It was like one of those grid logic puzzles in which you crossed off possibilities and pieced together clues. She felt wired, wide-eyed, after her fifth shot of espresso. She'd crash later, but right now she could move so fast it felt like the rest of the world stood still. Typing so quickly, it sounded like teeth chattering.

Under the search terms *El Nido + China*, up popped a list of local Chinese restaurants, and a link to a Mandarin after-school program. She'd have to get more specific: *El Nido + real estate + China*. She clicked on a website in Chinese and, with the help of the browser's crude translation, discovered a video captioned "Golden Opportunity."

From on high, every house seemed majestic. The Tuscan estates (charming but not so different from an Olive Garden); the Cape Cods (charming but not so different from a Red Lobster); or the concrete boxes (striking, like a Bond villain's lair). She recognized the art deco movie theater marquee, Main Street, and a clip from the Fourth of July parade, before returning to empty, sunlit houses.

Then, there—her house. She rewound the video and watched it again. It was only a few seconds, but there was no mistaking it. The leaves on the sycamore tree hadn't changed color yet, the foliage untrimmed on both sides, so the footage was from sometime before the last couple weeks, this year or another.

Her mouth tasted sour. "Sam. Sam!" He didn't answer. When she poked her head into his office, he didn't turn around, presenting on a video call. She ducked out of sight. In the kitchen, she cracked a can of seltzer, but at the first sip, she felt like she might vomit, the fizz swarming in her throat. She needed fresh air and sunshine.

Outside, she stood in the middle of the street. A bright autumn day, the smoke cleared. Someone in a car, or on foot, had filmed their house from this very spot. Creeped out, she spun around the cul-de-sac.

She studied the Changs' house. The buyer had paid too much. Good bones but run-down. Just look at the fence between their houses, where a slat had fallen through. Much of the wood in that section had rotted, covered in lichen. A strong wind, a hard push, and it would come down.

Jin had acted on behalf of a buyer who was in China, but in what capacity: Caretakers? Tenants to an absentee landlord? And how did it fit in with Save El Nido and, now, this video?

When she caught sight of the sycamore, she winced. Once stately, it now had the look of Jekyll and Hyde. She went inside. Could the Changs be behind the video? What if Jin—and whomever he represented—were making a play for El Nido? The mysterious investor might seek the downfall of the Bellavista because the development interfered with his plans.

She felt herself teetering into conspiracy territory, drawing strings across maps, connecting pushpins. She was onto something, though!

Or maybe she was alone too much in her head. As she returned to her office, she wondered, What if Save El Nido wasn't a grassroots campaign? What if it was fake?

Astroturf. The Orb had been considering this strategy—named after the fake grass in sports fields—to combat local grassroots opposition. Last week, in the introductory meeting, the consultant had gone over different possibilities: hiring actors to attend city council meetings; paying people to flood government officials with emails and phone calls; and pretending to be supporters online.

According to the consultant, campaigns took on a life of their own, as the unsuspecting joined what seemed like a crowd. "If you don't keep up with this, then you're left behind," he said. Trim in a puffer vest, though he was sitting inside. He clicked onto the next slide, which detailed "sock puppets," fake online personas created to stir up divisions.

"Like the Russians?" she'd exclaimed. She'd glanced around at the little heads in the little boxes. Why wasn't anyone else speaking up?

She wasn't opposed to a creative interpretation of regulations. You could build a billion-dollar company in the gray zone; innovation flourished in the in-between. Flood the sidewalks with electric scooters, skirt the regulations and taxes around lodging and taxis, and install cameras everywhere. But this approach had seemed drastic. More than that: It seemed to portend the future of the Orb and the depths into which the company might sink. Secretly installing additional cameras benefited her neighbors; astroturfing only rewarded the Orb.

Now she wondered, What about the Save El Nido petition? Were any of the signatures fake? At her desk, she hovered her hands over the keyboard before she chose a name from the petition and searched for more information. She turned up an address on Corte Royal—a local. Another person had been quoted in the weekly, and another name popped up in a listing of Parents' Club officers at one of the elementary schools. But the next two—Tony Hoffman, Robin Portnoy—didn't seem to have any connection to El Nido. Maybe they'd scrubbed that information from the internet for privacy reasons.

Or maybe they didn't exist.

And how did SuCasa fit into this scheme? Perhaps the owner didn't know about it; perhaps it was a side hustle for Jin. She checked the listing. Though he'd promised to take it down, it was still up. The Saturday after next had been blocked off—which possibly meant it had been booked, or else the Changs didn't want to rent it out that night. A week and a half from now.

Sam knocked on the doorframe. "You needed something?"

She took off her reading glasses to look at him. Her theory about Save

El Nido, still coming together, was too outlandish to share. "Saying hello. How's your day going?"

Sam didn't return her smile. "The city called. They just issued a stop-work order!" Something technical, he explained, that the city now seemed to interpret differently from his attorneys. "We're talking later." He rubbed between his eyes.

"For how long?" she asked. Long enough for the permit to expire? She felt trapped, cornered, hunted down. The project had already been beset by cost overruns, labor shortages, and supply-chain issues.

"What if you cut more units?" Blair asked.

"We can't cut any more affordable ones and we need the others for the project to pencil out."

"Was it because of the petition?"

"It probably didn't help. Probably 'fanned the flames,'" he said. "With all the panic about wildfires."

Fuck. Fuck Save El Nido.

She couldn't yet prove if Jin was behind the campaign and if it related to his listing on SuCasa. But if the house had indeed been rented out, Blair would train an Orb—or two or more—on it to document what happened and finally end the parties.

* * *

That night, Blair spooned Jordan, relishing her warmth, her weight. Jordan tucked her feet in between Blair's legs. Blair scratched her back in slow circles, the way Jordan liked, inhaling the sweet scent of her shampoo, then gave her daughter one more big squeeze.

Her hand brushed against Jordan's ribs—had they always protruded this much?—but when her fingers probed, Jordan wiggled free. She yawned and wiggled away: goodbye.

Jordan might be going through a growth spurt; maybe she'd been training so hard with the Mavericks that she needed more protein. "Why don't you eat eggs anymore at breakfast?" Blair asked. Glow-in-the-dark, stick-on stars illuminated the ceiling.

"I don't like the ones from the store," Jordan said. "They don't taste like anything. They're rubbery, too."

"Ana could make them another way. Soft boiled, over easy?"

"The ones you buy could have been laid two months ago!"

Every time Jordan had asked about replacement hens, Blair had vaguely promised, *Maybe after the next meet*. Weren't Luna and Domino enough for now? Tigs . . . ! They didn't want to get chickens only to leave them again for the weekend, and the fall had been busy with swim meets. Blair preferred to raze the coop. If the fates of the previous flock foreshadowed what was to come, the next ones were all but sentenced to death upon arrival.

But if the fresh eggs, speckled blue and white, with their bright sunshine yolks, whetted Jordan's appetite . . .

Blair promised to call Hen Haven tomorrow, to inquire about their supply of rescue chickens. They went over chicken names, debating whether they could recycle the old ones. "They'd never know," Blair said.

"Chickens are smarter than you think." Jordan ran her fingers along the arms of her threadbare panda. Domino's cage gently rattled as he climbed the sides.

"How about Peppers? Poppy? Sharpie?" Blair asked. "Should we ask Sofía?"

Silence. Blair wondered if the girls had been getting along, if Sofía resented how much time her mother spent caring for another family.

"I already asked," Jordan said. "She said she couldn't think of any."

"There's no rush." Maybe Sofía had been traumatized by the slaughter and wanted nothing to do with chickens.

Blair should take the girls out for ice cream sometime.

Not long after, she pulled herself out of bed. Some nights, she was so tired she almost fell asleep beside Jordan, but if she dropped off for only a few minutes, she'd have insomnia.

In bed, after Blair propped herself up against the pillows, Sam reached over, rubbing the back of her neck. She leaned into his touch. She crept her hand onto his thigh and brushed her fingers against his crotch. Then, remembering the real estate reel, she grabbed her phone. She hadn't fully hashed out her theory, but he might have ideas.

"You want to watch something?" Sam got up to lock the door. "Maybe turn the sound off," he said over his shoulder.

"It's not that kind of video." As she explained what she'd uncovered, Sam took her phone and studied the screen.

"Chinese investors are interested in El Nido?" He sipped from a glass of water.

"It's a total invasion of privacy." Why wasn't Sam leaping out of bed, tracking down the culprit?

"Did you check the exterior footage?" He ran his fingers through his hair; it was getting long again, but Blair preferred it that way, even shot through with gray.

"There's nothing," she said.

"Too bad. You could have tracked them through the birdhouses. Whatever happened with the birdhouses? Did the cameras get the rogue coyote? Now *that* I'd want to see."

Blair still hadn't told him about Ella feeding the coyote. The power of watching creatures who didn't know they were being watched had been irresistible.

The more she watched, the more she became convinced that something troubled Ella. Maybe when she'd missed the summer swim finals, Ella had realized how little she cared. Maybe swimming felt like a job to her now, but she didn't know how to tell her mother. Her giddy delight at the feedings contrasted with how quiet and withdrawn she now seemed at practices.

The longer Blair put off telling Sam, the more daunting it became. She pushed the thought away. "I'm trying to find out more about the company that's promoting the sizzle reel," she said. "Looks like an outfit in Beijing."

"We could use investors like that." Sam sighed. "Especially if the stop-work order goes on indefinitely."

Why couldn't he understand the threat it posed? "Investors who are trying to destroy you?" she sputtered.

"That's kind of a leap, isn't it?"

Maybe she was grasping at nothing, or maybe a Chinese real estate developer wanted to corner the market here. "The Save El Nido domain is from China." On a Chinese service provider. As she spoke, she realized how far-fetched the evidence sounded. How . . . racist.

Seeing her distress, Sam squeezed her shoulder. "It's a lot, isn't it?"

His attempt to comfort her only made her feel worse. His unflappability in the face of a crisis. He handed back the phone. "Maybe Save El Nido got a good deal on the website. Maybe they got a cheap designer in China who handled the registration."

"And the video?" She thumbed the side of the phone like a worry stone.

"Real estate investors are always looking. Their research could have turned up El Nido." He yawned, his eyes drooping.

"But—our house?"

"Odd. But everyone's always filming everything, right? Those cars driving around, filming for street-view maps. Random people taking videos, snapping photos of anything they think is cute, or strange or whatever."

Their house did have excellent curb appeal. . . .

"Then they post it and someone grabs it." He yawned again. "It could be a coincidence."

She'd prove it wasn't. Until then, they might turn this discovery to their advantage.

Why not attract potential Chinese investors to join the Bellavista? As investors, as homebuyers. The creator of the sizzle reel could not match Sam's expertise here, she said. "If they're interested, you have to show them how much more El Nido has to offer," she said. "You can make them feel at home."

"We don't know who they are." Sam turned off the light on his bedside table and slid under the covers. He tuned her out, like her father always did with her mother, murmuring, his thoughts elsewhere.

She'd try gentle persuasion. She stroked his cheek. "You won't have to go to them," she said softly. "They've already been sniffing around. If you—if we—welcome them to the Bellavista, they'll come running."

23

While Tasha zipped up her backpack, she overheard Maddy talking about the theme of the party: Big Pimpin'.

The Y2K classic from Jay-Z had been trending on ClikClak—"We be big pimpin', spendin' cheese"—evoking sunshine and the carefree time before 9/11, before smartphones and social media.

"Pimps and hoes," Maddy said to Griff. "*Everyone's* dressing up."

He grinned. "The girls, you mean."

Maddy punched him in the arm. "The women." She cocked back her cowboy hat.

The conversation left Tasha unsettled. As she and Jane headed toward the Quad, Tasha asked, "Did you hear that?"

"I didn't know what she meant," Jane said.

Tasha searched the hashtag on her phone and showed it to Jane: ClikClak videos of swaggering attendees in #Pimp #Pimpcostume massive fake-fur coats, leopard fedoras, gold chains, low-cut tops, and #Hoe #Hoedown sequined short dresses, and lace stockings. In one clip, a white woman with waist-length blond hair waggled her hips, her buttocks stuffed with padding. Dollar bills were tossed into the air like confetti.

"This is so . . ." Jane paused. "No one will get dressed up."

A group of girls walked by in cowboy boots, straw hats, knotted plaid shirts, and denim booty shorts. "You sure?" Tasha asked.

"People here love costumes," her mother had dryly noted. "Not just on Halloween." It was their right to cosplay anyone, anytime, anywhere, but if you were Black or Brown, people questioned your existence in Middle-earth or in a galaxy far, far away. Minerva had been telling Tasha what had happened at a school fundraiser, a casino night. A would-be showgirl in a glittery headdress attempted to hand her a dirty napkin, mistaking Minerva's black pantsuit for a server's uniform.

For Spirit Week, Tasha hadn't bothered with any costumes, and neither had Jane. Still, if Tasha had felt as if she were a part of Valle Vista, she might have joined in. More than half of their classmates had gotten into the spirit: neon for 80s Day, muumuus and kukui necklaces for Hawaii Day, black and maroon for School Colors Day, and rakish bandannas and hoop earrings for Pirate Day. *Pirate Day?* Halloween wasn't until the end of the month, but maybe the kind of person who got decked out for Spirit Day grew up looking for any chance to get dressed up for a party.

They sat at the corner of the lawn, where their classmates sprawled in circles every few feet. It was a relief to be outside after hours of masking in class. Tasha slid off her sandals, digging her toes into the grass. She scrolled through more examples of partygoers who seemed to have no qualms. A few were Black; most were white.

"No one is going to dress like *that*," Jane insisted.

"I've seen it in Halloween stores." Cheap suits in jewel tones and leopard print, fedoras, and gold-topped canes. Tasha pulled up the "Big Pimpin'" video, which featured a gigantic white yacht cutting through the water, dancing Black women in bikinis, and Black men adorned in gold chains, two-fisting forties.

Tasha pictured her classmates dolled up in imitation. If Black icons could dress like that, so could they. *So fun!* A modern-day minstrel show, even if they didn't swab black shoe polish onto their faces.

Jane offered grapes to Tasha before popping one into her mouth. "Even if they don't think it's messed up, people won't be able to find a costume in time. People won't bother."

Tasha set her phone on top of her backpack. "Maybe not everyone. A few though. A party gives them an excuse to do something they aren't supposed to." A taboo wasn't a taboo if your friends did it, too. Like those teenagers she'd read about, who'd privately posted racist memes, trying to top each other, racking up transgressions like points in a video game.

As she dug into her leftover pasta salad, she had another thought. "Maybe some of them will do it to make fun of people who do things like that." Like Quinn's alter ego. "Remember Becky White?"

"They're being ironic . . . not racist?" Jane asked.

"That's what they intend. But that's not how it seems. Not how it *is*." Tasha bit into a squishy mozzarella ball. "When is it? Where is it?"

"Not this Saturday but the one after," Jane said. "We're camping that weekend." Another SuCasa rental.

In the aftermath of the last party, her parents argued for hours on the back deck. They spoke in Mandarin, she said, so she didn't understand everything, but she recognized that they were talking about Nai Nai, who was out of the hospital but needed extra care and follow-up visits with doctors. Eventually, her mother agreed to rent the house out again to cover those costs.

"What if the party's at your house?" Tasha joked.

"Don't jinx me!" Jane opened the SuCasa app on her phone. "I can check."

"You know your dad's log-in info?"

"He keeps his passwords on a sheet of paper in the top drawer of his desk." Jane leaned in and lowered her voice. "LilyJane8888." Swiping through the reservation, she yelped in surprise. "It says . . . Becky White reserved it."

"Becky White?"

"Quinn!" they exclaimed at the same time.

A few days ago, on 80s Day, they'd had that run-in. In the moment, Tasha had tried to remain calm, but cowered a little inside. When Quinn had insinuated the Changs were *invaders*, Jane had fired back.

Quinn couldn't prove anything, though, they'd decided.

Tasha pulled up Quinn's Becky White profile and compared it side by side with the SuCasa headshot: a match. A blond woman, with thinly tweezed brows, a toothy grin, and bobbed hair.

"I don't get it, though," Jane said. "Won't she get busted by her parents?"

Tasha finished the pasta and stuffed the empty jar into her lunch box. "Maybe they'll be out of town." She wondered how Quinn had paid for the rental. Her family must be loaded.

A Frisbee arced over their heads and Griff jogged past, apologizing. "My bad!" Across the lawn, girls attempted to dance in unison, botching the steps and collapsing into giggles.

Jane popped the lid back onto the tub, the label for whipped butter faded on the plastic. "And Jacqui . . . Why wouldn't she tell them the theme is effed up?"

"Because she grew up with them," Tasha said. "Because they're her friends. Because she's tired of being the one who's 'supposed' to tell them."

Because Jacqui, for all her seeming steel, could get scared, too.

Neither of them realized that Maddy had secretly proposed the theme to mess with Quinn. And that Jacqui—increasingly fed up with Quinn—had gone along.

In the high blue dome of the sky, a hawk levitated, riding the thermals, on the hunt for its next meal.

"Why wouldn't she rent it somewhere else that isn't next door?" Jane asked.

"Because it's *your* house." Tasha shredded a blade of grass.

"I should have kept my mouth shut! The house will get trashed."

Tasha imagined the havoc in the aftermath of the party, the spills and stains. Her classmates as blithe, as destructive, as toddlers. And yet . . . "What if you let them?"

"Let them?" Jane asked.

Their roles had been reversed. Usually, Jane came up with a fanciful scheme, and Tasha served as the voice of reason. "Let's say you get your dad to cancel," Tasha said. What a thrill, Jane must feel, each time she plunged headlong. "He'll probably rent it out again. And sooner or later, it'll blow up again. But this time, we'd make it count."

Count for every person who'd felt as hurt, as frustrated, as angry.

Tasha looked around the lawn, but no one was close enough to hear. "We set up nanny cams all over the house." She panned her hand through the air. As she pictured the eye of an all-seeing camera, her inherent restraint kicked in. "Never mind. It's your house. Your room."

"Not really." Jane shrugged. "It doesn't feel that way. We don't have any pictures up. Most of the furniture is from Buy Nothing. Or picked up from the curb! We're basically living out of our suitcases."

The warning bell rang.

"But your parents are trying to sell it," Tasha said. Even though Jane's hesitation was giving way, she shouldn't encourage her.

"They'll keep the security deposit, then. Use it to remodel." Jane laughed, wiggling her fingers like a maniacal magnate. "It couldn't be any worse than the *ayahuasca* party! And neighbors will call the police before it gets out of hand."

"The chaos, though . . ." Tasha regretted that she'd brought up the idea, but also felt excited. Scared, too.

But Jane had already moved past any fear. She uncapped her lip balm and reapplied. "If people have nothing to hide, they shouldn't care. But if they eff up the house, if they show up in blackface, we have proof."

"And then we put it online," Tasha said.

The only thing worse than being a racist was getting *called* a racist—and going viral. She'd read about high school students who got caught saying the N-word while driving around with friends, at parties, singing along to songs. In videos they sent friends, in videos their friends filmed. After the students got canceled, colleges yanked their admissions and took away scholarships.

Their trolling, though cathartic, had ultimately been inconsequential. People anywhere maintained the status quo, even when you held up a mirror. But you couldn't ignore the problems if your children starred front and center, if they gleefully embraced such a sexist and bigoted theme.

Getting the receipts on their classmates would serve as retribution for anyone who'd been screwed, boxed into shitty jobs, shitty schools, shitty housing. For Lucinda's walnut trees, chopped down and carted off. Retribution not for any single incident but for the accumulation, like ash in a wildfire that slowly then all at once stole your breath. An ash indifferent to your pain, that you hid from, that you hoped might get carried away on the wind. Always, the ash would keep coming.

But at least she and Jane wouldn't go down gently.

* * *

The next day, with their house-sitting and babysitting money, they picked up nanny cams from the discount retailer, disguised as a pair of dice or

Lego blocks. Even though it was a basic model, without internet access, Tasha thought the sound and clarity were creepily sharp.

They scoped out the best spots everywhere attendees might congregate at the house: in the kitchen (on top of the refrigerator) and in the living room (tucked into the plastic monstera).

Every time they hesitated, debating whether they should go through with the plan, the theme of the party made them fume all over again. (Not *one* person questioned it?)

Though Tasha also had a morbid curiosity about how inappropriately her classmates might interpret the theme.

She paired her phone with the stereo in the living room, playing "Big Pimpin'." The flute sample was so dope, hypnotic as a snake charmer. You just couldn't listen to the lyrics too closely.

Drawn by the music, Lily peeked into the living room. "What is that?" She pointed at the camera.

They'd have to find a better hiding place.

"Science project," Jane said.

Lily beelined toward the plant. "But the plant's fake."

Jane pocketed the camera before Lily got to it.

Lily held out her hand. "Can I see it?"

"We're not supposed to let anyone touch it," Jane said, then relented. "Don't break it though!"

Lily held it up to her eye. "Cool!" When she shook it, trying to make it rattle, Jane took it back.

Their parents were out running errands. "You want to go to the library?" Jane asked. "I'll take you, if you just let us finish the assignment." After promising, Lily disappeared into her room.

They moved the camera to the bookshelf, then hid one out on the deck, nestled in another fake potted plant, aimed at the Ping-Pong table.

Jane held up the paddles. "Want to play?"

Tasha served, and they settled into an easy back-and-forth. They didn't keep score, rallying for as long as possible instead.

"What if someone finds a camera?" Jane asked.

Tasha let the ball bounce into her hand. She tilted her head toward the Belles. "What if they hear?" she asked in a half whisper.

"I don't think anyone's home. I noticed Quinn leaving this morning with her sister, and the parents biked off with the baby like an hour ago." Jane lunged for the ball, but missed. It bounced on the deck before she corralled it with her foot. "Lily spotted the camera immediately. Won't people be pissed if they find one?"

"They'll just turn it around or block the lens. They're not supposed to be there. SuCasa doesn't allow parties, so they can't complain!"

"If my parents find out I knew about the party . . ." Jane flung out her arm to return a corner shot.

"Your parents won't find out." Tasha thwacked the ball. "Neighbors will call the cops and break it up before anything happens."

"Someone went over the railing last time!"

"Then it can't happen again," Tasha said.

The Ping-Pong ball sailed high into the air before bouncing off the edge of the table. "Sorry!" As Jane scrambled after it, Tasha peered at the Belles' house, which seemed even bigger from the outside, compared to what she'd seen in Jane's video chat. It was strange to think that Mr. Belle—who could determine her family's fate in the housing lottery—lived next door.

"What's he like? The dad," Tasha asked.

Jane set her paddle down, tucking the ball into the handle. "I dunno, friendly? He waves when he's walking the dog. On the weekends, I noticed they leave early in the morning—like, before the sun's up—and are gone all day. Sometimes he's driving off with a bike or surfboard strapped to the car."

"Loves the outdoors." That was the argument he was making, wasn't it, to cut the affordable units at the Bellavista? The view.

But the project itself seemed in doubt.

The local paper had published an article about a stop-work order. Mr. Belle vowed to fight, but Tasha wondered if it would take years to get settled, long after her family left El Nido.

Which reminded her: She had to go to the farmers market to buy a sourdough loaf for her mother before the stall closed.

Lily opened the sliding glass door. "You said you were doing homework!"

"You can't play Ping-Pong with three people," Jane said. "Come on, let's go. I'll take you to the library. We'll walk over with Tasha."

❁ ❁ ❁

The kettle corn stand made everything smell like a carnival. At the next stall, where Tasha munched on a slice of Asian pear, a bearded redhead tried to hand her a clipboard for a petition. "Care about the future of El Nido?" he asked.

"I can't vote yet." In big block letters, the petition urged "SAVE THE SALAMANDERS!" and called on the city to halt construction on the Bellavista and redo its flawed environmental-impact study. "Construction would irreversibly damage this habitat, leading to loss of biodiversity. We must prioritize preserving these delicate ecosystems rather than sacrificing them for short-term gains."

Someone called her name: Nic, the mom who'd hired her to babysit. "Tasha! I was going to text you. Are you free on Saturday?"

Shaking her head, Tasha handed the clipboard to the canvasser, who moved on.

"Ah, that's too bad. Is your mom going to the Fire and Ice party, too?" Nic asked.

No, Tasha said. Fire and Ice? Maybe it was a school fundraiser party.

"Do you know anyone else who could babysit?" Nic had a clipboard, too. She dropped a crumpled bill into the guitar case of a strumming folk singer.

Promising to ask around, Tasha went looking for Jane, who poked at leathery red pomegranates. She'd already dropped Lily off at the library. Then she seemed to spot something—or someone—behind Tasha. "Quinn's parents," Jane said in a hushed voice.

The mom looked like an older Quinn, but wider, softer. Beyond their sturdy build and blond hair, both mother and daughter had the same intense vibe, charismatic yet also a little unnerving. Did they ever blink? The mom, who'd strapped the baby to her chest, carried a canvas tote, kale and a baguette poking out of the top as she ordered from the dim sum vendor.

The father was tall and hawk-nosed, with longish dark hair, those fancy slip-on sneakers, the ones with knit patterns like sound waves. And maybe . . . something else going on? Half Asian, or half Latino, a racial ambiguity that had faded in his daughter?

As Tasha and Jane inched toward them, Mr. Belle tugged the clipboard from Nic. He held a half-eaten apple in his other hand.

Tasha sensed the bad blood between the families: business rivals, star-crossed lovers? An altercation on the soccer field or in the parking lot of Trader Joe's?

Nic jabbed her finger at him. "What's the harm in evaluating the environmental impact?"

Jane stepped up. "What about the harm to families in the housing lottery?"

"What was that?" Mr. Belle asked. Laughter burst from the nearby playground.

Jane gave a little wave—"Hi, Mr. Belle!"—and he waved in acknowledgment. "I said, the housing lottery. For the Bellavista."

Nic retrieved the clipboard.

"Bellavista has a vital below-market component." He ran with Jane's argument, emphasizing Bellavista's greater public good. He invoked the housing crisis, how the units would go toward deserving souls priced out of El Nido.

Nic interrupted, "There's availability nearby, just over the hill, that isn't salamander habitat."

"You mean Oakland?" Tasha asked. Oakland: the city that loomed large in the imagination of El Nidans, that locus of car break-ins, hulking apartment buildings, and other urban ills.

Nic nodded, apparently not realizing that Tasha was being sarcastic.

But Mr. Belle seemed to acknowledge the assist. "Oakland has its own housing it has to build. Every city, every town, has to. That's the law."

He pointed at the firehouse across the street, where a truck was getting soaped up in the driveway. "First responders and schoolteachers should be able to live in the communities where they work."

Salamanders versus hardworking families. A crass exchange, Tasha knew, but maybe this conversation would spur him to restore the units he'd slashed and maybe add a few more.

"Where'd you hear about it?" he asked Jane. "Your parents?"

"From the paper," Jane said.

"I wish my kids read the paper!" he said jovially, but the tone sounded forced. His wife joined him, shifting the tote bag from one shoulder to the other.

Nic walked off.

"You ever ask who's behind this committee?" Mr. Belle called after her.

Nic turned around, almost knocking over a stack of wart-studded gourds.

"You don't know, do you?" he asked. His stance was wide as a wrestler's.

She clutched the clipboard to her chest.

"You ever look up the names on the petition?" Mr. Belle asked.

"You wonder who might be using you?" Mrs. Belle asked. "Outsiders." She glanced at Jane, only for a moment, but it felt significant.

What in the hell?

"Check the Save El Nido website, ask where it's from," Mrs. Belle said, her voice high and strained. "But you might have to ask in *Chinese*."

24

Days later, Blair unveiled the Bellavista's website redesign.

The outburst at the farmers market hadn't been their finest hour, but she'd been trying to fend off Nic. In her eagerness to prove that she in fact welcomed the Chinese, she commissioned a new website. A rush job that cost extra. In the prototype, the landing page was red and its font gold, colors of fortune and abundance. The new phone number: a string of lucky eights. After researching what might appeal to Chinese buyers, she'd also rewritten the marketing copy, emphasizing how the Bellavista backed up against a hill (feng shui) and its proximity to the Golden Gate Bridge (world-famous) and how El Nido was home to players from the Golden State Warriors and the Giants (prestige).

Sam rolled a chair to her desk. "You don't think it looks cheesy? Like a casino?"

She pictured the billboards along 101 and 880, the same red-and-gold color scheme, and a photo of a smiling Asian woman fanning out twenties. *Pai gow poker, loose slots!*

"It must work." Blair sipped the last dregs of her midafternoon coffee.

In high school, she had been an excellent debater, powered by the force of her will as well as the force of her arguments. She learned to speak authoritatively about matters she knew little about, until eventually she did.

Working twice as hard, studying twice as much only got you so far, and after that, you learned not to break stride.

She asked Sam if he'd figured out a way to tap into immigrant investors, the ones clamoring for green cards. You could get a special visa if you invested close to a million dollars and created at least ten jobs.

"Not yet," Sam said in a tone that indicated *not ever*.

"Millionaires, billionaires, don't need another house, another yacht." She swept her arm like a hostess on a game show showing off the grand prize. "They want freedom, to be able to travel, to live where they want. Maybe not immediately, but it's insurance in case they ever need to leave quickly."

He rubbed his chin, unconvinced.

She gestured at the screen. "You hate it."

He leaned back in his chair. "It might turn off buyers who aren't interested in feng shui."

"Lots of people are into it! Not only Chinese."

"The colors . . ." Sam said.

"Maybe you have a separate web page, with a link that only gets shared in Chinese real estate forums."

To attract some Chinese, but not too many. There was a tipping point, she and Sam had once discussed—above 15 or 20 percent—when a wealthy Asian influx drove white flight, and an enclave became a Cupertino, San Ramon, or San Marino.

Hammering started outside; the Millers were installing solar panels. She got up to close the window.

"You're trying to turn the Bellavista into a honeypot for Chinese investors," Sam said. "While at the same time, you're accusing Save El Nido of being under Chinese control?"

"Me? You agreed!" Blair felt like Cassandra, forever raising the alarm. Shouldn't Sam believe her? He was just so . . . levelheaded. He'd always patronized her, just a little, just enough. When they'd met, a couple years after college, it made her feel as if he were taking care of her. They'd settled into that dynamic for years, for *decades*. Sometimes, she'd pushed back by acting cartoonishly fake mad when she was actually mad. But now that they'd had kids together—now that Quinn was going to college—more and more she resented how he treated her as high-strung, as if her ideas were outlandish.

She picked up the empty mug, weighing its heft. Pictured herself hurling it at the wall. He had no appreciation—no awareness—of everything she did to keep their life running smoothly. She exhaled. She couldn't let herself get angry or teary-eyed. Not if she wanted to persuade him. "You yourself said it was a coincidence, that Save El Nido had nothing to do with these potential Chinese investors," she said evenly. She sat down. "Shouldn't we try to attract Chinese interest? If there is interest?"

He didn't answer. She didn't have to remind him: They were late on their bills, the Bellavista was under threat, and, by extension, the Belles. Sam's lawyers had been negotiating with the city, with his pledge to build fire-resistant roofs, install mesh screens and chimney caps, gutter protection, and double-paned windows, gravel pathways, and stone borders—wildfire safeguards that went far beyond what the law mandated. So far, the stop-work order hadn't been rescinded. The salamanders, with their Day-Glo polka dots and resting smile faces, made everything trickier.

Blair turned up the volume on the website; she'd added theme music, too. "That's a Chinese fiddle." Elegiac and ethereal, conjuring misty mountains unfurling banners of red silk, the heady scent of sandalwood. But was it a touch too far?

"It's great," Sam said while checking his phone.

She could tell that he considered it another of her cute ideas that he'd praise, but hoped would peter out. She wouldn't give up. Maybe some of her punches had gone wild, but with enough blows, at least one would be a knockout.

* * *

That night, when Carolina texted, asking when Ana would come over on Saturday, she fought off her irritation. She was busy catching up on her own chores. Her sister shouldn't assume they didn't have other plans, even if they'd been spending every weekend there, making triple batches of keto tamales on Saturdays and Sundays.

Ocupadas, Ana said.

But Carolina wanted to take them to a pumpkin patch, which had opened for the season, complete with a corn maze, farm animals, and rides. Halloween was three weeks away. Ana waffled. Sofía would love it. She'd see—and want—the candied apples, kettle corn, and saltwater taffy. Ana couldn't afford those treats or the overpriced pumpkins or the rides right now, though. Not on top of the snow-leopard costume Sofía had found online. Blair had been late—again—with her paycheck, some excuse related to her employer. For groceries that week, Ana had shopped in the Belles' pantry and fridge. She'd dipped into her meager savings to buy more ingredients for tamales. She had no leverage though; she couldn't threaten to quit and risk losing their housing and access to the schools.

No, she insisted, they couldn't go. She wouldn't tell Carolina about the problems with her paychecks. Not yet, not until she'd decided what to do.

Her phone rang. She considered sending it to voicemail, but Carolina would worry.

"You heard anything from Julio?" Carolina asked, after Ana answered.

"No." Ana emptied the dish rack. She'd never admit to her sister the sliver of disappointment that he hadn't found her. Maybe he'd decided she wasn't worth his time. "Have you?"

"No," Carolina said. "You should sleep here. It's safer. Your bosses are around all the time during the week, but on weekends, they're out a lot, right?"

"Swim meets." Ana dropped a handful of spoons in the drawer.

"You can't come over?" Carolina prodded.

"My boss needs me," Ana said sharply. She retrieved a stray fork amid the spoons. She peeked at the bedroom, wondering if Sofía was listening in.

"Did you get any powders yet?"

They'd been discussing limited-edition flavors, like bright green matcha, sapphire-blue butterfly pea protein, and midnight squid ink. It had started off as a joke. People loved trying foods that resembled cartoons—especially if the ingredients were also supposed to be healthy. Maybe their tamales would go viral!

"Not yet," Ana said. She was on track to sell $1,000 worth of tamales, doubling her sales from last month.

"Can you come Sunday?"

Next weekend, Ana promised.

It was too complicated to explain the other reason she couldn't go, which sprang from the beef between her boss and Nic.

Yesterday at Mavericks practice, Ana had followed Liam as he cruised along the bottom row of metal bleachers. She loved his curiosity, his exploration, even as it made her job harder. He reminded her of Sofía, at this age.

The facility where Jordan practiced was outdoors, with an Olympic-sized pool, a diving pool, and a lap pool. Even if you weren't in the water, if you weren't competing, the gigantic digital clocks made you aware of time. The seconds slippery, not to be wasted. Overstuffed duffel bags and kicked-off slides littered the pool deck.

Liam reached the end. "Uh-oh!" she said. He tipsily turned around to go in the other direction. She pointed at Jordan in the water, swimming the butterfly, a stroke that looked like you were a dolphin, or that you were trying to drown yourself. "That will be you someday," she told him. She'd never learned how to swim, after she'd nearly drowned in the fourth grade, slipping off an inflatable raft that had drifted from the edge of a pool.

She wiped at the silvery drool hanging from his chin. Teething again. In the bleachers, Sofía read a book. From a couple rows above, Nic waved and then clambered down to join them, each step jolting.

Ana thanked her yet again. After Nic had promoted the tamales, Ana could hardly keep up with the demand, but she didn't like being in anyone's debt. The bill always came due, and Nic made clear then what she wanted in return. "Do you know if Blair's going to the Fire and Ice party?" she asked.

When Liam tripped, Ana had steadied him. He continued, relentless as a killer robot. Nic repeated her question, following alongside her.

Ana didn't look up. "Do you need a babysitter?" Nic was the only parent who bothered to acknowledge her at practice, but couldn't she tell that Ana was busy?

"We're set!" Nic said. "We'd love to see Blair and Sam. There's been a mix-up about . . . about a lot of things, and if we could just get together . . ."

Liam reached the legs of a mother, who cooed at him and moved up one row so that he could get past. At the end of the bleachers, he dropped onto all fours and crawled toward the chain-link fence. There, Ana helped him stand and he gripped the fence, rattling it, to make it jingle.

"Yes, they're going," Ana said.

She should probably warn Blair. Then again, the two women couldn't keep avoiding each other. At the party, Nic and Blair would have it out, once and for all.

* * *

On their walk home from school, Tasha and Jane hashed out the final details. At the intersection, waiting for the light to turn green, Jane fiddled with the drawstrings on her hoodie. "I looked it up. The Save El Nido website was registered in China."

"Whatever, China's huge," Tasha said.

"What if there's something to what she was saying?" Jane's mouth trembled.

"Don't let her get to you!" At the farmers market Mrs. Belle had practically accused the Changs of being commie spies—one more reason to film her daughter dressed up in a racist costume.

They crossed the street.

"You want to call her out online?" Tasha asked. "'Skip the farmers market. Locals love Chinese food but hate Chinese people.'"

Jane laughed. "If Mrs. Belle ever sees it, she'll know it's us."

"Why would she look at real estate reviews? She already lives here."

"IDK. If you're in real estate, wouldn't you keep track? What if we troll the other lady who got into it with them?"

"Nic." A yellow school bus rumbled past. The woman for whom Tasha had babysat, the woman who'd not only signed but circulated the Save El Nido petition at the farmers market.

"She's a real estate agent," Jane said. "I saw her at an open house. What if we neg her, but make it seem like Mrs. Belle wrote it?"

She probably wouldn't see it, probably wouldn't blame Mrs. Belle. But still. "If she does, she could cause more trouble than we ever could."

Tasha pondered how to ensure Nic would see it. "On the petition for Save El Nido? Put it in the comments?"

A squirrel scampered on the trunk of an oak tree, jauntily waving its tail, like the plume on the hat of a musketeer.

Jane grinned. "We can post it to her Yip page!" She searched online and found the reviews, all five stars, calling her "phenomenal," "a rock star."

A rock star who wanted to keep out families like Tasha's.

Tasha gave it a try. "'Hypocrite NIMBY.'"

Jane laughed. "With an exclamation mark. Two. Three! 'Hypocrite NIMBY!!! Killing a dying town,' I'll post it tonight. She. Will. Flip!"

Until now, their trolling had been general, not about anyone specific in El Nido. "Maybe we shouldn't," Tasha said. They could get caught, get sued.

"It's exactly what my neighbor thinks," Jane said. "We're just putting it out there. It's the truth, isn't it?"

Reluctantly, Tasha agreed. They could always take it down.

A mother approached, pushing a stroller with a toddler riding on the running board. "Down, down!" he shouted. He picked up a stick that he waved around. When she told him to get back on, he sat on the sidewalk, thrashing his head. She dropped her tote bag, which toppled over. An orange rolled out and into the gutter.

"Do you need help?" Tasha asked. The mother didn't answer; she seemed too distracted to respond. Embarrassed, too.

They returned to the final hurdle: Saturday night, Jane's mother and sister would be camping; Jane had begged off, claiming she had a term paper due and would crash at Tasha's. Her father planned to stand guard, parked around the corner from the house in a nearby cul-de-sac. The moment he noticed any unusual activity, he'd bust the party.

"Is there a way you could distract him?" Tasha asked. "Can you make up a story that it's an emergency, that you're feeling dizzy? You can tell him you need to go to the hospital."

"I can't. The medical bills. And after all the stuff with my grandma, I don't want to stress him out. . . . Maybe I could say we had a fight and that I want to leave."

"That's not much time, though. And then he'd probably make you wait in the car with him while he monitored the camera."

Halting in front of a bay laurel, Tasha emptied the main compartment of her backpack, setting the binders onto the ground, and scooped up nuts scattered on the sidewalk. Tasha would flick off the mottled purple flesh with her thumbnail, lay the seeds in a pan to dry for two weeks, then roast them in the toaster oven and crack off the shell. They had the taste of cocoa nibs and coffee. "Is there some way we can substitute video filmed on another night, a quiet night, that he'd see instead?" she asked.

"Like a heist movie?" Jane joked.

Thieves, faking the live feed to trick the security guards at a bank or a museum.

Jane swiped on her phone, searching for more information, but nothing turned up. "I could turn off the Wi-Fi. But then he'd rush back to see what was wrong."

Tasha noticed that she'd missed a call from her mother; it never buzzed because she'd accidentally set it to "do not disturb." The solution to their dilemma dawned on her: "What if he never got the alert?"

"You mean if I deleted the app on his phone? Maybe he wouldn't notice at first, but then he'd download it again."

Tasha explained: What if Jane snoozed the motion detection for a few hours? Secretly log into his account and schedule it in advance. During the day, her father would receive notifications as usual. He'd suspect nothing as he packed up for the camping trip. During the party, he wouldn't get any notifications about people coming and going.

"He'll probably drive by a few times, to make sure," Jane said. "How do we keep him away?"

"Tell them it's too dangerous to go camping without him. Without you."

"Dangerous? Because of the coyote?"

It had struck again a few days ago, chomping on the hindquarters of a convenience store clerk squatting in the alley, smoking a cigarette. The fifth victim.

Tasha winced, the scar on her leg throbbing every time she remembered her attack. She wouldn't wish what happened to her on anyone; she also knew that the coyote—if and when apprehended—would die.

Jane apologized for bringing it up. "If anyone's going to scare off a coyote, it's my mom! They aren't going far. My dad found a campsite that's only fifteen minutes away. In the hills. I can say, if there's a problem, he can get back quickly. That he shouldn't sleep in his car. And that he should go to protect my sister."

"So that gets him away from the house." Tasha wiped off her hands, then searched for a how-to video. "Here. Look." If you snoozed motion detection, recording would pause and you wouldn't get any alerts. "You can disable the live view."

"He promised my mom he'd monitor the camera from the campsite."

"He can't stare at it the whole time." Tasha shouldered her backpack, heavy with bay nuts, and tucked her binders under her arm.

"That's why she agreed to put it on SuCasa again." Jane nudged a clump of dirt with her sneakers. "If this goes bad, I don't know what she'll do."

"You should tell them then." Tasha knew how much Jane wanted her parents to succeed in El Nido. Knew what living here meant to Jane, too. The pandemic shrank everything down, she'd said, everything cramped in their apartment. Now she felt like a goldfish freed from its bowl, able to swim every direction.

"If something matters, you have to go all in," Jane now said. "What would Lucinda do?"

"What would Lucinda do?" Tasha echoed. Their rallying cry. Lucinda had turned problems into possibilities.

Jane couldn't distract her father that night. But what if Lily did? Like the toddler with the tangled ringlets, dirt smeared on his cheek, who'd demanded all of his weary mother's attention. Lily, pestering. Lily, fierce like her sister—maybe fiercer.

"You think Lily can help us?" Tasha asked.

They turned toward the elementary school to fetch Marcus.

"Lily?" Jane asked.

"She can keep him busy that night, so that he's not checking his phone so often." Everything hinged on a nine-year-old? It was a lot to ask of Lily, a lot that had to come together perfectly. The plan would fall apart before it began.

On the blacktop, kids raced around with the whirling frenzy of electrons.

"She can't keep a secret, so I can't tell her about the party." Jane said. "I could say it's for him. That he's on his phone too much, and he needs help staying off."

Lily would be proud, excited to be enlisted, eager to prove herself, Tasha suspected. Vigilant, coming up with excuses to take him away from the phone. "Can she keep it up the whole time?" Tasha asked.

"You've seen how she is—relentless! You know what really motivates her? If you tell her no. If I bring up the idea, and then tell her to forget about it, she won't give up. She'll stay on him all night. You tell her something is impossible, she comes back twice as hard."

25

That night, tinder-dry Diablos hissed with menace, leaving everyone in El Nido sleepless, disoriented, perpetually thirsty and on edge. Originating in the deserts above Nevada, roaring down the mountains to drought-parched grasses and trees below. The days hot and dry, the skies a sinister blue. Days in which you stained your favorite shirt, broke your favorite mug, in which your pets went missing. Days in which you found yourself weeping in the shower, irritations flared into arguments, and old grievances tipped into revenge.

* * *

Saturday night, when the first pimp arrived, Quinn slammed the door in his face.

He must have been at the wrong house. She smacked her lips, her mouth dry from the edible. It had kicked in, after an hour of debate among her friends. *Do you feel it? I think I feel it. You're faking it, you always fake it.* Smiling, heavy lidded, they'd sprawled on the couch and the carpet in the living room, listening to a playlist as mellow as their conversation.

The doorbell rang again. This time, the pimp in a furry white coat was joined by a girl in a leopard-print velvet coat and sunglasses—plus three classmates in dresses that barely skimmed their asses. She banged the door shut. Seriously? She was so thirsty, a skunky aftertaste in her mouth, from the edible or from the weather.

She'd heard about a big party somewhere in El Nido. A costume party. Big Pimpin'. "Let's just hang out at the rental," she'd said. It was 10:00 PM now and her parents were due in an hour. The people outside knocked, fists pounding while the doorbell jangled over and over again.

The pimps must have swung by to pick up a friend. Or what if they'd decided to party here instead? Quinn leaned against the wall and then slid onto the carpet. She ran her fingers through the dense loops. If she didn't answer, they'd go away.

Jacqui wandered up. When Quinn tried to explain that they had to hide, they had to turn off the lights, turn off the music, until everyone went away, Jacqui opened the door. By then, the crowd had grown to two dozen on the doorstep, who now swarmed inside. More cars pulled up, circling for parking, the dizzying exhaust wafting in.

Jacqui helped Quinn to her feet. When she tried to shut the door, Jacqui tugged her away. "Leave it."

"Then anyone can get in." Quinn braced herself against the wall, her fingertips brushing against the irregular bumps.

"That's what happens at a party," Jacqui said.

"You knew about this?" Quinn had agreed to a chill hang with the girls, not a giant rager! Her friends let her go on and on about how happy she was to skip the party tonight.

They'd lied to her.

Someone pounded on the door. Jacqui admitted two guys in Afro wigs, sequined dresses, their chests stuffed with athletic socks, the backs half zipped, their basketball shorts peeking from the hems. Hoes. Not because Aidan and Griff were bi or gender fluid or future drag queens, but as the ultimate flex: boys confident that no one would ever mistake them for girls.

At a party pre-pandemic, Quinn had hooked up with Aidan—a slobbery kisser, who'd squeezed her breasts like stress toys—and he still used the same woodsy deodorant that sent her back to the squeaky bed, the musty sweat socks, and the funk of his crotch.

She suspected the costumes had been his idea. Probably, he'd convinced his wingman that they would attract attention from certain girls, who now shrieked and giggled at the sight of them. Who now seemed to consider the slutty outfits an invitation to get handsy, the tables turned.

"Someone's getting lucky," Jacqui said to them. Aidan and Griff simpered and sashayed past, followed by a boy from AP Bio, a red bandanna tied around his head, matching plaid shirt, buttoned only at the collar, with a case of malt liquor on his shoulder. Quinn tugged on her crop top. His girlfriend followed, also outfitted in red plaid and oversized khakis, hoop earrings, darkly outlined lips. Her eyeliner winged, three black teardrops inked in. Something you did to honor the dead. Even in Quinn's altered state, it seemed cruel, funny only if death had never touched you.

Aidan bumped fists with the gangster, then punched him on the shoulder. "*That's* your pimp costume?"

Griff laughed. "Weak."

The gangster waved them off. "Pimps are gangsters, aren't they?"

"Nah."

"But they roll together," the gangster insisted. He slid the case off his shoulder, ripped the cardboard open, offering up the beer. When they cracked the cans open, foam spewed over the rug, the cream color turning grimy, someone's muddy sneaker print tracked in. As they clinked cans, the front door slammed against the wall, blown open by a gust. Quinn had told her friends to come in through the back, but everyone else had been recorded on the doorbell camera.

She pushed the door shut. "It's on camera!" Quinn sputtered.

"But not you. Not us," Jacqui said. Her reassurances grated. As if she wouldn't be freaking out if the situation had been reversed.

Someone switched the music to that hip-hop queen, turning up the volume on the stereo to its maximum. Quinn stormed over, waving her arms, *No, no, no.*

Jacqui handed her a red Solo cup, with a look that said, *Don't be a buzzkill.*

They tapped their cups together, and then Quinn guzzled. She recoiled at the foul taste, grape cough syrup and 7UP. She swirled her tongue, desperate to wash out her mouth, yet she felt compelled to sip again, hoping she might feel bolder, brighter. She'd eaten nothing all day and the edible combined with the booze made her head feel like a balloon, floating above the crowd.

Quinn gestured over the living room. "Who did you invite?"

Jacqui didn't answer.

"What about them?" Quinn pointed at their friends, now upright, now dancing. It had been so long since they'd had this much fun! And she'd made it happen, a realization that filled her with a curious pride.

Jacqui shrugged. Probably, their friends each invited one or two, who in turn invited a million more. Quinn would have done it, too, if she'd been in their position. She had, many times, before . . . in the Before.

In the kitchen, something shattered, setting off cheers. "Party foul!" Aidan shouted.

"I'm so busted," Quinn moaned. What if the cops pulled up right when her parents got home?

"You heard about a party," Jacqui said. "You didn't host it."

The rental would get trashed. Even Jane didn't deserve that! After seeing the shabby interior of the house, Quinn had come to feel sorry for her.

"How do I get them to leave?" she asked Jacqui. Flick the lights on and off, cut the music? They'd tell her to fuck off.

"They'll go when the alcohol runs out," Jacqui said.

A wave of nausea hit Quinn and she bent over, the room spinning.

Jacqui passed her a water bottle, which she drained. "Thanks." The floor steadied beneath her feet, though it seemed tilted, as though the house were sliding into the ravine.

Jacqui hugged a girl in leather booty shorts, complimenting the outfit, before turning back to Quinn. "We'll go out back, to your house. Cops won't find us." Jacqui spoke crisply, as if they'd gone over the plan multiple times.

Sometimes her briskness could clarify like a splash of cold water: advice on the dress that didn't fit, on the toxic friend to ghost. Right now, Quinn felt dissed. She squinted at someone in a crushed-velvet suit, with a white ruffled shirt, and a wig with flowing black locks.

When the Prince knockoff waved at her, she did a double take: a freshman girl who also swam for the Mavericks. Her classmates had gone all in, maybe because they'd been denied Halloween and prom and homecoming in the last year. Here they might pretend the pandemic never happened, that the pandemic wasn't still happening, that the forests weren't on fire, that their brains hadn't time-lapse aged—a flower rotting into black, a loaf of bread caved in with mold.

Quinn set down the empty water bottle and pointed at Prince. "That doesn't bother you?"

Jacqui folded her arms across her chest. "Does it bother you?"

"It's just . . . weird." Quinn traced a finger on the rim of the Solo cup.

"You think it should bother me more than it bothers you?" Jacqui asked, an edge to her voice. "When people dress as rednecks, hillbillies, do you get offended?"

Did she think Quinn was a loser, that she'd grow up to be a Karen—that she acted like one already?

Jacqui stalked off. Maddy intercepted her, their heads bobbing close together. Jacqui was sharp-tongued, sharp-eyed, and kept you hoping you'd remain at her side rather than in her sights. They had no qualms about farting in front of each other, had shared news of their periods, their first kisses, first hookups. And she knew better than to say, "I don't think of you as Black," knew better than to glance at Jacqui in AP U.S. History when the subject fell to slavery and Martin Luther King Jr. and Rosa Parks. They rolled their eyes every time the Black Best Friend™ appeared in a movie or show, sassy yet accommodating. *You go, girl! Slay!*

Quinn also knew that her friend's fierceness, her intensity, was both her superpower and shield. And that the party might actually disturb Jacqui, too, for reasons she didn't want to discuss with Quinn. Not right now, maybe not ever. What Quinn had been trying to say had come out all wrong, but Jacqui might feel that she couldn't call out their classmates. So she got mad at Quinn instead.

Fine. She finished her drink and snatched another from the hands of a girl walking by, draining that one, too. She grabbed a cheetah fedora off the quarterback's head and lifted a gigantic diamond dollar-sign necklace off a lacrosse player. A pink feather boa, a furry cape, gold boots someone had kicked aside, until she'd assembled a costume, too.

Her parents loved to tell this story: When she was a toddler, she'd come across a bag of cotton puffs, stuffed them into her mouth, and dramatically threw back her head to reveal a weird grin. Of her siblings, Quinn had inherited her father's humor. He was also a goof, the *silly daddy*.

When a girl from the pom squad strutted around the room, Quinn fell into line. Her arms and legs were jerky as a marionette's, as she kicked with her right leg, then bringing her left foot beside it. Popping her knees out, bowlegged as a cowboy, before starting all over again. She hadn't felt this free in forever, supple in spirit if not in her limbs.

From the bookshelf, the camera recorded it all.

26

As the music thumped from the party next door, Ana snuggled with the girls on the couch, each leaning against her, Luna curled at their feet. Liam had been out of sorts all day, but she'd managed to get him down upstairs, by setting up the pack-and-play in the walk-in closet and turning on the sound machine.

She glanced at her texts, an order for tamales from one of her regulars, Raj. He also asked if she ever catered. Intrigued, she pictured birthday parties, anniversaries, and baby showers, with trays of tamales piled high.

Yes! she texted.

As the credits rolled, the girls begged for one more episode of that underworld-monster show. "Bedtime," Ana said. When she clicked off the television, they heard the new chickens squawking up a storm. She got up and peered through the sliding glass door into the darkness beyond, lit only by a crescent moon. Cracking it open, she heard rustling and snuffling. She ran, slid in her sock feet on the hardwood floor, scrambling for the flashlight in the kitchen, before dashing outside, waving and shouting, "Hey, hey, hey!" The beam of light was too weak to go beyond a dozen feet. The squawking grew louder in pitch, their terror proof that not every chicken had perished.

The girls pushed behind her: Jordan armed with two metal pot lids, Sofía with a metal spoon and pot that they each clanged—a chaotic clamor, but the wet snuffling did not abate. Even from a distance, the stink made her eyes water. Luna, roused from her nap, barked, but Ana didn't want the dog running at the coyote—what if it had rabies?

She yelled at the girls to go inside and pushed Luna after them. After jamming her feet into her sneakers, she ran to the side of the house and yanked on the garden hose, the rubber gritty and cold. When the hose snagged on the wheel, she tugged until the kink gave way. She wrenched the knob, turning on the water at full blast—hissing and spitting as it coursed through the hose. She sprayed it toward the coop, shouting, "Go away. *Go away!*"

The creature growled, long and low, then scampered into the brush. She exhaled, amped up and exhausted at the same time. Wind thrashed through the trees, roaring like a tidal wave. As the clucking tapered off, she wondered how long it would take for the chickens to fall asleep. She should go by with a flashlight to see what mess it had made and dispose of the remains before it attracted anything else tonight. Or maybe she could leave it for her bosses.

When the girls peeked outside, she told them to get ready for bed.

"But . . ." Jordan said.

Ana steered Jordan away, promising that she'd check on the chickens, then nudged Sofía toward the stairs to their quarters. "I won't be long," she promised.

Taking a deep breath, Ana trudged toward the coop. There, she spied a pile of dirt where the coyote must have dug its way in, and the remains of the chicken that it had dropped when fleeing. The survivors stirred inside, their wings flapping as they settled down. From a few feet away, the branches of the pine tree creaked and groaned like a ship in a storm.

She poked the carcass with the toe of her sneaker. You couldn't blame the coyote; she almost regretted interrupting its dinner. Nor could you blame the chickens, their fate inevitable the moment their ancestors had been domesticated, put their trust wholly in their masters, and lost the ability to fly. No, blame her bosses, for getting chickens yet again, knowing full well they'd be sitting . . . well, chickens.

Laughter, the thump of feet, and the *thock* of Ping-Pong floated over from the neighbors' back deck. She'd messaged her bosses about the party next door, but it had remained unread. She should try calling now and tell them what happened.

When she turned, she ran headlong into Julio.

She'd feared him for so long, heard him in every footstep that came up behind her and felt his hands yanking her hair in every tangle. How long had he been watching her—watching them?

His hair had grown out, scraggly over his ears and the nape of his neck. His arms were still ropy with muscle, and his fists, balled at his sides, were still craggy, heavy.

"I've missed you," he said, his voice husky. The softness that she'd fallen for so many times before now felt like nothing. Like he'd never had a hold over her at all. She could see him for whom he was: small. And she saw herself without him: limitless.

"You need to leave."

How had he found her? The noise of the party must have masked the sound of his truck.

"Can't we talk? Don't you owe me that?" His tone coaxing, but with an edge to it, the teasing that could turn on her in an instant.

"I don't owe you anything."

"You don't have what you owe. That's why you ran, ran like a thief."

"I'll give you everything I have on me and meet you tomorrow with the rest." She'd ask for an advance from the Belles or borrow it from her sister.

Julio looked around. "You like it here? It's so damn dark. It's not safe."

She didn't answer.

"Don't you want to come home?" That coaxing tone again. How had she ever let it sway her? If she tried to run, he'd catch her. Could she convince him to leave the backyard, tell him that they could talk by his truck? Anything to get him away from the girls. But then he might force her in. "You need to leave," she said.

"Why the hurry? Your bosses aren't home. We got time."

"They just texted," she lied. "They're on their way." She hoped they'd get back early. Probably, they would text her to say they were running late. Her hands twitched at her sides; she cursed herself for leaving her phone inside the house. "They'll call the police."

"So let's go. You and Sofía, pack up."

When his fingers closed around her wrist, she wrenched her arm away. "Get out," she spat. Then a bright white flash exploded.

She found herself on the ground, her neck aching and her face numb. He'd punched her face, knocking her down. The ground was muddy from the water she'd sprayed from the hose, soaking her jeans, and the scent of the carcass, of mineral blood and musky entrails, made her retch.

She scooted backward, her legs wobbly. When he kicked her, something crunched inside. She staggered to her feet, her side throbbing. Had he cracked her ribs again? Wincing, she searched for a rock, a brick, anything that she could fight him off with. She hoped desperately that the girls—if they'd seen what happened—had locked the doors and called 911. If she screamed for help, would the neighbors hear? The music was so loud she couldn't move, couldn't think.

"Scream all you want," Julio said. "And then we'll go."

She tried to run, but Julio caught her and spun her around. He shook her until her teeth rattled. She clawed at his face. When she shoved him, he pummeled her, cursing her out. She swayed, and she heard herself crying, begging him to stop. Every time her body twisted, pain stabbed at her left side. He let go, panting, his eyes blank with rage.

A soccer ball whizzed past, just missing Julio's head, and bounced away in the darkness.

Sofía ran toward them, her fist raised. Something glinted in the moonlight—a blade. The paring knife that Ana hid under her pillow, which Sofía must have discovered. She motioned toward Sofía to get back, to get away, but Julio pried the knife from Sofía's hand.

With a swift kick, Ana punted the carcass high and hard enough to send it straight into the sun. Its body wobbled and spun, wings splayed, before it spattered on the side of his head and into his open mouth. Sputtering, he dropped the knife, slipped in the mud and fell to his knees, spat, and heaved.

She shuddered, the cracked rib making it hurt to breathe. She'd caught him off guard, made him want to puke, but he wouldn't stay down for long. She and Sofía slipped around the side of the house, through the gate, and toward the lights next door.

* * *

For weeks, Wily had had no need to venture beyond Ella's backyard for his sustenance, but the meat had stopped appearing. He'd returned there for days, to no avail.

At dusk, he'd hunted for gophers in a nearby field, but out of practice, he'd had no luck. The Diablo winds unsettled him, riffling his fur. After following the dusty scent of chickens, and leaping over the fence, he'd ravenously torn into one. Blood, salty and sweet, pulsing through the flesh. The few mouthfuls made him hungrier than before.

Now he bolted through the woods, the clanging pots ringing in his ears. His eyes stung from the water sprayed at him. He sniffed, trying to pick up the trail of something else he might hunt or scavenge: a withered apple, a smashed rodent, dog kibble, a blown-over trash can.

The wind gusted, carrying delectable scents that tickled his nostrils. He bounded back in the direction from which he'd come.

* * *

Jane elbowed her way through the party, trailed by Tasha. They couldn't stay long; they'd check out the costume parade and then leave. They'd told Marcus, already in bed, that they would return in an hour. They were supposed to be babysitting; Tasha's mother had picked up a night shift at the ER and wouldn't return home until the morning.

The crowd spilled through the living room and onto the back deck, the sliding glass door left open and smeared with handprints. The room a swamp of sweat, body spray, and spilled beer. Jane glanced at the front door. Could Lily really hold her parents at bay at the campsite? She pictured them tucked into the tent, sleeping bags pulled past their heads.

People huddled in the corners, talking and drinking, and three dozen or so grinded against each other. About a third of the attendees had attempted costumes, probably digging through their parents' closets for pirate shirts and velvet bell-bottoms and fuzzy Big Bird jackets. Their interpretation of the theme was as muddled, misguided, and poorly translated as those

signs in English in China. Most partygoers weren't wearing any kind of mask; she and Tasha hid their faces with KN95s.

To her relief, the house wasn't trashed. No windows smashed, no cushions slashed. But she'd been willing to risk everything just like the activists she'd idolized.

A boy approached, in a skintight dress and an Afro wig with a corona wide enough to blot out the sun.

Jane nudged Tasha. Griff, from AP Psych.

He grinned at Tasha and reached toward her double Afro puffs.

No. No!

When Tasha backed away, he gave her a thumbs-up before loping off. Jane wanted to chase after him, grab him by the shoulders, and ask him what he meant by the gesture. If he was saying, *Love the hair*. If he was asking, *We cool?*

Jane should have knocked his hand away. She asked Tasha if she was okay, if she wanted to leave. She followed Tasha's gaze: Jacqui, standing across the room, her expression unreadable. Jacqui turned and stepped onto the back deck. No one realized that she was leaving, that she crept down the stairs and around the side of the house and walked home.

Tasha swiped at the screen on her phone. It wasn't until the music cut out—to a murmur of complaints—and another song started that she realized Tasha had wirelessly paired her phone with the stereo. As the driving beat thumped, people resumed grinding. Tasha shout-sang, Jane joining her. Soon most everyone sang along, stumbling in the moments of the rapid-fire delivery, sinking into the drawn-out phrases.

When they reached the chorus, the words dried up in Jane's mouth: the N-word over and over. Some of her classmates mouthed it or stopped, bobbing their heads to the beat instead, but most continued singing, her neighbor Quinn loudest of all.

Tasha's playlist continued with more tracks, a deranged campfire singalong.

If anyone noticed what the songs had in common, Jane couldn't tell. The more they heard the word, the louder they sang, the less forbidden it became. It drilled into Jane's skull with the piercing whine of power tools.

To her shock, some people were filming themselves, holding their phones high in the air. The volume got turned up, so loud that it rattled the glass patio door and rang in her ears. When she touched Tasha's shoulder, her friend flinched. Her expression seemingly neutral—only her hand betrayed her, gripping her phone as if it were a life preserver.

From the corner of her eye, Jane noticed a commotion, but she couldn't make out what was happening.

"It's the last song," Tasha said hoarsely.

Then the power cut out.

* * *

Moments earlier, a squirrel had scurried along a branch a few blocks away, fleeing the bone-shaking noise of the party, eager to return to its den. As it leaped onto the next tree, the wind sent it awry. The squirrel twisted its body trying to right itself, spreading its legs and flattening its body, its tail a rudder that might have guided it to safety if not for the transformer it landed upon. With a bang, the squirrel went up in flames, knocking out power in a half-mile radius.

From its charred flesh and fur, an errant spark lofted on the wind. Several times, it nearly winked out, but then it landed on an oily pile of rags left beside a garage. The flames crept up the wall, licked at its roof, until the lithium battery in the electric car exploded like a supernova.

27

Blair had almost skipped the school's signature fundraiser. Tired from—well, everything—she told Ana that they wouldn't need her to babysit on Saturday. But Ana had seemed so disappointed—"We were going to have a girls' night. They already picked a movie!"—that Blair changed her mind. She and Sam could use a date night.

The chief appeal of a boat dance: You were on a boat, a motherfuckin' boat! The chief drawback: You were on a boat. After you circled the decks, shimmied on the dance floor—to a pandering mix of 80s and 90s music, *oldies*—oohed and aahed at the view, and downed a cocktail, hours remained until the boat returned to the dock.

In search of the restroom, she left Sam at the bar, chatting with another swim-team dad. She tugged at her shapewear. She usually shied away from touching her jiggly postpartum gut, slashed with a C-section scar, which pushed up to meet her water-balloon breasts. It was humiliating, getting it off to pee, but then she could breathe. She'd always had a spark plug of a body and had prized the power in her thighs, never yearned for twiggy wrists and ankles. Solid yet nimble, never too self-conscious to laugh loudly. She didn't recognize her body now, and the intensity of her shame and frustration stunned her.

Through the hall window, she glimpsed a lifeboat and fantasized about commandeering it, motoring back toward shore, her hair billowing in the briny air. She stopped herself: She had no reason to run away, no reason not to hold her head high.

She hadn't received any updates from Ana. Out on the bay, though, the cell service was spotty and the boat didn't have Wi-Fi. The boat lurched and she braced herself against the wall. Because of the winds, the waves were choppy and whitecapped. Sam, already queasy, had asked for ginger ale at the bar. She never got seasick and neither did her girls, a genetic quirk in which she secretly took pride. A superpower of sorts: Roller coasters? Car trips? Air turbulence? *Bring it on!*

In the stall, as she finished contorting and flushed, someone puked into the only sink. It had been years since she held back the hair of a girlfriend in a dive bar. She'd offer to help, to fetch a bottle of water, to pat her back in that fellowship of the ladies' room.

Blair adjusted her surgical mask. When she emerged from the stall, Nic looked up. Their eyes met in the mirror. Vomit flecked Nic's mouth, her eyes were red as a rat's, and her dress was soaked from where she'd leaned against the sink. Her blue mask lay crumpled up by the faucet. By the looks of it, she'd eaten the sun-dried-tomato, gluten-free penne pasta from the buffet. Blair caught a sour whiff and despite her iron constitution she dry-heaved. As the boat rolled and pitched, Nic leaned over, moaning, and retched again.

"Do you need me to get your husband?" Blair asked.

He was dressed as a fireman, helmet cocked jauntily on his head; Nic, in her red ombre dress, might have been flames.

Nic dabbed at her mouth with a paper towel, her skin sallow under the fluorescent lights. "There's nothing left." Apologizing, she cleaned the mess in the sink.

Muffled bass thumped through the wall. As Blair washed her hands, Nic fumbled for her purse and thrust something in her face: an Orb.

A couple days ago, the Orb had recorded Nic catching her daughter setting out the meat. The camera was too far to pick up what they were saying, but Blair had been riveted. Nic jabbing her finger, Ella jabbing back at her, defiant.

Ella hadn't appeared there again. The coyote returned at dusk for a couple days before it disappeared. Worried that the coyote had been run over, maimed, or had moved on, Blair had been tempted to leave out raw hamburger to lure it. Ella had been feeding it by hand for weeks, so how much harm could it pose? Then she came to her senses.

"Don't you work for them?" Nic held up the Orb, turning it in the light like a jeweler.

"You need a repair?" Blair was impressed. Nic must feel like hell yet she'd pulled herself together to confront her.

Nic lowered her arm, the Orb loosely cupped in her hand. "Why did I find this aimed at my house?"

"Is it your neighbor's?" Blair asked, her palms sweaty but her tone even. "I don't personally know everyone with a system!" She laughed lightly. She had to leave the bathroom before she incriminated herself.

"The birdhouse on the back of the stop sign looked like it had been knocked loose," Nic said.

From the winds? Twigs and pine needles had drifted ankle-deep in the gutter today.

"When I reached up, this fell out. Looks like it had a view of my backyard."

"Maybe the police put it there? They're testing it out?" Blair instantly regretted saying anything. The other cameras would have to be yanked down before Nic asked around.

The door banged open and a woman burst in, barely making it to the stall before she fell to her knees and hurled. She was dressed as the sun, in a yellow felt costume with matching neon-yellow sneakers. A bilious stench rose up, the restroom turning dank as an underground dungeon. The PA crackled, but Blair couldn't make out the announcement. While Nic tended to the barfer—"Lizzie, do you need water?"—Blair peeked into the hallway, where a janitor with a cart clanked by, loaded with a garbage can, bags dribbling sawdust, and a broom. The music had stopped and the engine sounded different now, no longer cruising but throbbing into high gear.

"People . . . are throwing up . . . all over the place." The woman, Lizzie, winced. "Over the side, on the dance floor."

"Food poisoning?" Blair asked. Stuffed into her spandex, she hadn't touched the buffet.

Lizzie shuddered. "Seasickness. High winds. The captain's turning the boat around."

Poor Sam. She should check on him; no doubt, he would be relieved the night had been cut short. Blair offered Lizzie a mint, which she accepted before wobbling out of the restroom. Blair passed the mints to Nic, who sucked on one for a long moment, the mint clacking against her teeth. Nic passed the Orb from hand to hand and Blair fought the urge to knock it away, flush it down the toilet, toss it over the side of the boat.

"Stop harassing us," Blair said.

"Harassing *you*? You're the one slamming *me* online."

Blair recoiled. "What?"

"Don't pretend." Nic tucked the Orb into her purse and pulled out her phone, summoning a screenshot. "I know you wrote this."

Blair read and reread, trying to make sense of it: a one-star review trashing Nic, calling her a hypocrite NIMBY. "Where was this?"

Nic withdrew the phone. "You didn't think I'd see it?"

"Why do you think I wrote it?"

"It was right after you made those accusations at the farmers market!" Nic insisted.

"You're so busy making up stories, you don't see what's happening right in front of you."

Nic narrowed her eyes. "So you were filming us."

"You think I'd have to spy to know Ella's going through something? You can't see it because you don't want to."

Nic seemed shocked—then angry.

The floor tilted at all angles, dropping them into an Escher print. Nic steadied herself on the wall. "How is Paloma?" she said smugly.

Blair's stomach dropped, an elevator snapped free from its cables. She swayed in her heels. How did Nic know Jordan's full name? Paloma Jordan Belle. Jordan could have mentioned it in passing.

Or maybe Nic—riled up because she believed Blair had been trashing her on Yip—had been compelled to resume her campaign against Jordan.

Blair fought the urge to flee.

Nic practically ran Shady Groves, as head of the Parents' Club, and volunteered there every day. She could have convinced the school clerk to share the registration records, including the birth certificate that Blair had slightly altered before uploading, swapping in the June birth date.

That might deter Nic. Or with that information, would she have tried to look up the original birth certificate?

"I've always wondered," Nic said, measured as a cat before it pounces, "is Phoenix hot yet in April?"

❁ ❁ ❁

In the hills, Jin drifted off to sleep in the tent. When his phone pinged, he fumbled in the dark, searching for the pocket of the tent where he'd stowed it. His eyes were sticky because he'd left in his contacts. He hunched over, swiping at the screen to avoid waking up Kai and Lily.

A text from the power company alerted him to an outage: "No estimated restoration time." He sat up. Without electricity, he couldn't monitor who came in and out the front door.

Through the app, he'd watched the guest arrive around 3:00 PM, dragging a roller bag and wearing a big straw hat, sunglasses, and a caftan—coastal grandma chic, if he'd known the term. She hadn't left again.

Though the wind had picked up at sunset, the camping spot was protected, tucked in a grove of oak trees. A tranquil evening but for Lily, who'd demanded his attention nonstop from the time they'd arrived: hiking along a creek, fishing for crawdads with chunks of bologna, pointing at satellites zipping across the horizon, and stargazing.

Lily was still at an age where he could impress her by answering most every question and where she found his silliness—his voices, his jokes—funny. He worried about her. Since the pandemic, she'd turned clingy, anxious if either he or Kai were out for longer than a couple hours to run errands. Every time a siren had gone by, Lily had been convinced they'd died. She wanted to tie pillows to the bumper of the car in case they got into an accident. It could have been worse. In the Fremont apartment complex, a neighbor, a Korean girl, had been taken away in an ambulance, strapped to a gurney. She'd secretly been burning herself with matches. She'd only been twelve! That she was Asian shocked Jin more. Only Americans had problems like that, he'd assumed.

The first time he reached for his phone, Lily told him that he was "addicted." And maybe he was. He'd set his phone to vibrate, waiting for the notifications that never arrived. There was a glitch with the live view, which he had to restart a couple times; he never suspected Jane kept turning it off.

Now he swiped on the doorbell camera app and, as he'd feared, the conked-out Wi-Fi had killed the live view. He needed to get home. He unfurled his jacket, which he'd balled up as a pillow and wiggled out of his sleeping bag. He'd left his sneakers outside. He fumbled for the zipper on the tent, which snagged, fabric caught in its teeth. His fingers felt thick, stiff. He wiggled the zipper, trying to free it as Kai sat up, asking what was wrong. As he explained, a gust rattled the branches above them, the leaves rustling ominously. He suspected that Kai also feared a bough would come crashing down. Maybe they could move the tent away from the trees. "I won't be gone long," Jin said.

"If you go, you can't come back in," Kai reminded him.

He swore softly. The sign on the gate decreed no in-and-outs after the curfew, probably to prevent teenagers from partying here. A dog barked. Earlier, a rottweiler had snapped at Lily, who'd cowered as they'd walked toward the bathroom. The owner—a weather-beaten man in a rusty truck—had viciously cuffed the dog with the back of his hand, but didn't apologize.

"We should all go." Kai put on her glasses.

"Go where?" Lily asked, rubbing her eyes.

Jin hesitated. The guest was probably fast asleep; Becky White might not know the power had gone out until tomorrow morning. "It's nothing."

"Is it Da Jie?" Lily asked. Big sister. Jane. "Is she okay?"

"Go back to sleep," Jin said.

"Did she call?" Lily asked.

He unlocked the screen; she hadn't texted.

"Call Da Jie," Lily said softly.

"What did she say to you?" He knew—he knew!—something was wrong, but Kai had told him not to pry. They were both glad she'd found a friend, a good girl, the daughter of a doctor.

"Mei Mei, we want to know if she's safe," Kai said.

"What did she say to you?" Jin repeated. Cold air drifted into the tent, half zipped open.

"Not to me." Lily wrapped her arms around herself. "She and Tasha were playing Ping-Pong. I opened the window so I could hear. They were talking about a party."

"A party?" Jin asked. "Where? At Tasha's?"

"At . . . our house."

They left everything at the campsite and piled into the car, Jin flooring the accelerator and careening around curves.

Ten minutes later, when the fire truck appeared in the rearview mirror, red and white lights flashing, Jin pulled onto the shoulder. Even with the windows rolled up, he smelled smoke.

He sped after the fire engine, his heart pounding, minutes from home. As the siren blared, he pictured 187 Rinconcito in flames. Set off by faulty wiring, yet another undisclosed problem in this money pit of a house. Teenagers fleeing, but some trapped inside. Jane! Jane! They never should have left her.

The stoplights were out at the intersection. The fire truck slowed, then raced through. Jin followed. When it blew past the cul-de-sac, Jin exhaled. He hadn't realized how tightly wound he'd been. The fire must be nearby.

It was very dark here, the kind that closed in on you, the walls of a coffin lowered into the ground. He slammed on his brakes. In the headlights, a coyote nipped at the buttocks of a man who'd fallen to his knees. He kicked backward until the coyote let go. The man got to his feet and whirled around, staring it down. As the man slowly backed up, it lunged at him again. He flung something silvery at the coyote's head. A knife.

When the coyote drew back, Kai leaned over and honked the horn, the staccato bleats and blasts of an SOS. Lily screamed. As the coyote ran off, the man limped into the darkness.

Jin steered the car into the driveway. "Stay in the car," he ordered Kai and Lily. "Call the police."

As he jogged toward the front door, it burst open and teenagers brushed past him—"Cops, cops are coming!" Inside the doorway, a boy slammed into him, knocking Jin against someone else, who in turn crashed into another attendee: a writhing pit lit up by phone screens.

"Jane? Jane?" Jin shouted. She didn't answer. He had to find her, get her out of here. Whirled and tossed by the crowd, he popped up by the sliding glass door. About a dozen people perched on the deck, talking and tapping at their screens. A few were dressed strangely. When a girl leaned against the railing, he remembered the guest who'd gone over the edge. "Get back!" he screamed. Everyone ignored him. When she didn't budge, he rushed toward her, waving his arms in warning. Everyone ran for the stairs that led into the ravine. The deck might have endured the pounding but for the dry rot, the cobwebby fungus that ate and ate at the wood, but for the searing Diablos that had blustered all day. The beams shook, then crumbled.

28

In the stampede, Ana gripped Sofía's hand, joining a pack of teenagers sprinting toward the fence between the Changs' and the Belles'. As one climbed over, the fence groaned and a section tumbled down. The rest of them charged through. Ana stumbled across the backyard, peering through the inky darkness, hoping Julio wouldn't come at her again. If she could make it to the apartment, she'd push the couch against the door. Call Carolina for help. She clenched her throbbing ribs with her free hand.

All of a sudden, the ground disappeared. Her legs churning, arms flailing as she splashed into the pool. She struggled to get her head above the chilly water, her soaked jeans and sneakers dragging her down.

"Mama? Mama?" Sofía called out. "Help!"

If she could get to the side, she could hang on to the lip, could pull herself out. But she'd lost her sense of direction, up, down, left, or right. Water shot up her nose and she coughed, sinking, flailing, lungs burning. Something bumped against her feet. The bottom of the pool, she faintly realized, as the water thickened into molasses. Into tar. She was going to die like those mastodons who'd been sucked under. Then an arm curved around her chest, tugging hard, and her face popped through the surface. She wheezed and sputtered, trying to catch her breath.

Clinging to the concrete lip, her fingers frozen into claws, she had seconds left of her strength until she slipped under, coughing and coughing until she spewed. People grabbed her arms, pulling her all the way out, her shirt riding up, stomach scraping against the edge. She lay on her side, water pooling around her. "Sofía?" she cried. "Sofía?" Tired, so tired. She could fall asleep here. When a bright light appeared above, she shielded her face with her arm. "Stop shining it in her eyes!" someone shouted, and the light moved away. Sofía called out, "Mama, Mama!" Ana tried to make sense of the ring of dark shapes above her until Tasha squatted beside her. Dripping wet, her hand on her arm, murmuring—wheezing—that help was on the way.

❂ ❂ ❂

It had been a slow night in the ER—an accident with a bagel cutter, a child's high fever, a stomachache—which was fortunate, since they were down a doctor and a nurse. Just after 11:00 PM, the first ambulance radioed ahead: A deck had collapsed in El Nido, about ten minutes away by freeway from the hospital. About a dozen victims en route, teenagers from a party, the shift captain told Minerva. A party! Thank God Tasha was at home with Marcus, thank God Tasha had found a friend in Jane.

From a spot with cell service, she texted, all good? When Tasha didn't respond, she tried not to get nervous. The girls were probably watching a movie. It was the first time Tasha had hosted a sleepover since they'd moved to El Nido. Tasha promised they would both rapid-test before Jane came over. Initially, Minerva had refused since she wasn't going to be home that night. After Tasha explained the situation with Jane's family—and that she needed a place to stay—Minerva relented. She hoped that they might reclaim a bit of the girlhood that the pandemic had interrupted.

Her mouth tasted stale beneath her mask. She needed a mint. She was about to text Tasha again when the first gurney rolled in: not a teenager, but a woman with a black eye and tangled damp hair. A partygoer, too? Paramedics suspected a fractured rib. There would be a lot of X-rays and CT scans that night, and she hoped broken bones and bad sprains would be the worst of it. A few years ago, several Irish students died when the balcony high up on an apartment building in Berkeley had collapsed.

"She's yours," the shift captain said.

Immediately, Minerva recognized the name on the chart: Ana Rodriguez. The mom from El Nido who'd come by for the zoo tickets. She'd dropped off tamales as a thank-you gift—tender and cloudlike, the best she'd ever had.

Ana didn't seem to recognize her; she could have been in shock or maybe she didn't recognize Minerva out of context, in her scrubs, in a mask. She'd apparently fallen into a pool, but her injuries didn't seem consistent with a near drowning.

When Ana tried to sit up, calling for her daughter, Minerva told her to lie down. She poked her head out of the curtain, flagging down Nurse Marigold to ask about Sofía.

"In the waiting room," Nurse Marigold said.

"By herself?" Minerva asked. Sofía was the same age as Marcus; too young to be alone in the waiting room.

"With another girl."

A *girl*? Minerva asked if someone could check on them, offer them a snack, and stash them in an empty exam room. "Your daughter's here," she assured Ana, promising to bring her in as soon as they finished. "What hurts?"

As Ana listed various aches, Minerva noticed debris under her nails—ragged, one half torn off. Did someone assault her, leaving behind traces of skin and blood? If a specimen was collected it could help with prosecuting the perpetrator. But maybe Ana wanted nothing to do with police. Many patients didn't.

When Minerva mentioned the possibility of the rib fracture, Ana murmured, "No treatment then."

Maybe it wasn't the first time she'd injured them.

"You can ice it, take it easy. But no cast," Minerva said, and offered her a painkiller.

"How much is it?" Ana asked through gritted teeth.

Minerva fished a sample from her pocket. "No charge." The room had run out of paper cups. She offered to get one, but Ana dry-swallowed the pills, grimacing.

Minerva chose her next words carefully. "Because a lot of people experience violence by someone close to them, I've been asking every patient a few questions. No one should suffer from abuse. There are things that we can do to help people who are being abused."

Ana shivered in the antiseptic chill.

"Let me get you a blanket." As Minerva tucked it around her, the tension in Ana's face eased. "If you'd rather not talk to me, since our kids go to the same school, I can bring in a colleague."

Ana blinked, but Minerva couldn't tell if she recognized her.

"I can get someone else," Minerva said.

"It's okay."

Med school had drilled it in: By law, doctors had to report suspected DV to authorities, even if the victim didn't consent to it. In practice, it was trickier. How could Minerva "address the risk of retaliation"—as the guidelines put it—with the women who feared for their lives? "Do you feel unsafe with anyone . . . close to you?"

Ana clenched the sheets.

"In the last year, has anyone close to you . . . hit you?" Minerva asked softly. "Threatened you?" It might take another conversation or two before she opened up. If ever. "You must be exhausted. We can get you to X-rays, then get you home." X-rays that could serve as documentation, to build a case against her abuser. "But I'll give you my number."

Nurse Marigold poked her head in, asking if they were ready for visitors. Yes, Minerva said. Sofía burst through the curtain and ran to her mother.

"Is there anyone you want me to call? Anyone who can wait with Sofía while we finish the tests?" Minerva asked Ana.

"My sister . . . I don't have my phone though, and I don't have her number." Ana struggled upright. "The kids . . . !" The kids she nannied. Her bosses should be home by now, she said, but what if they weren't?

Minerva eased her down, murmuring they'd try to find out. Maybe one of the parents here knew how to get in touch. She turned to Sofía. "Who was waiting with you, honey?"

"Jane." Sofía seemed punchy, her curly brown hair tangled in a clump on the back of her head.

Jane? *Tasha's* Jane? It couldn't be. Minerva checked her phone—no texts. She needed to go somewhere with reception.

Jane peeked through the curtain. "I didn't know if I should come in."

Space was tight in the exam room, with a chair for one visitor in the corner.

"Where's Tasha?" Minerva asked.

"At home. With Marcus. Her phone's dead. It stopped working after she jumped in the pool."

"She saved Mama," Sofía interjected. She stared at the squiggly lines on the monitor above her mother's head.

Minerva exhaled, trying to absorb the information. Tasha, her baby!

"You can message her," Jane added. "She can check her messages." On the app with the disappearing photos. "If you have an account. Or you can do it from mine."

It pained Minerva to think that Tasha could have witnessed the attack on Ana. But she also took pride: Tasha, leaping in without hesitation. Tasha, reaching out a helping hand in a million different ways to anyone who needed it.

"Tell her I'm coming home," Minerva said. "As soon as I can." Though she wanted to race out of the hospital, she couldn't abandon Ana or the other patients now sailing into the ER. "I'll check on imaging."

Jane followed her. In the hallway, a flash of leopard print caught Minerva's eye: a boy was wheeled by, wearing a torn topcoat, with a gouge in his arm. Next a girl who'd lost her shoes—her feet slashed with cuts—but somehow remained blinged-out with a gigantic dollar-sign necklace, fake gold and diamonds. Had it been a costume party?

Jane said she could stay with Sofía until the tests were finished. When an alarm rang down the hallway, Jane startled. Minerva tuned out most beeps except for the essential ones; for visitors, the incessant noise had to be unnerving.

"Were you at the party?" Minerva asked. "Were you *both* at the party?"

Yes, Jane said. Her eyes were red rimmed, hollow with exhaustion.

"Did you have anything to drink?" She didn't smell booze on her. She examined Jane's eyes, to see if they were glassy or bloodshot. "Take anything? Did your parents know?"

"They found out." Jane exhaled. "They're—we're—so fucked." She apologized for swearing. "The kids who fell . . . are they going to be okay?" She choked back a sob. "Is anyone going to die?"

Minerva squeezed her arm.

"My mom left a bunch of voicemails, asking where I was, that they would come get me," Jane added. "I texted that I was okay, that I'd call her." She did a double take and Minerva turned, wondering what she'd spotted. There was a security camera, one of the many stationed around the hospital. Was Jane scared of getting recorded? Minerva passed by so often she'd stopped thinking about them. If Marcus noticed security cameras, he always waved and danced.

"The Belles have a door cam," Jane said. "Maybe they have one in the backyard, too, and it recorded what happened."

"Ana's fall?" Minerva nudged her aside to make room for an orderly pushing a cart.

"Before that," Jane said. In the waiting room, Sofía had told her about the attack. "Maybe Ana would want the footage?"

"I can't discuss her with you," Minerva said, but privately, she agreed it could help. That, along with what was collected from under Ana's fingernails. If only she hadn't fallen into the pool. Evidence could have washed away, and what remained could have been contaminated. The mandate to report DV weighed upon Minerva, but Ana's situation was probably complicated. They always were. Ana might want to avoid having anything on record. Maybe she'd had previous run-ins or she feared the authorities could take away her daughter. She didn't want to assume anything about Ana's papers, but a tenuous immigration status could also deter victims from pressing charges.

If that was the case, getting police involved might change everything.

A few months ago, Minerva went for a walk-and-talk with her big sister, both strolling as they caught up over the phone: about Di's son and his after-school job as a library aide, about her husband's promotion, about Grandma and her arthritis—they might try acupuncture—and gossip about the pastor's daughter, whose husband had cheated.

Then Di, an immigration lawyer, told her about a case she was working on, involving an undocumented victim who'd been pistol-whipped and carjacked. The victim had agreed to testify, and in return, she'd petitioned for a special visa that she'd finally received—"There was a huge backlog, five years"—but it would allow her to apply for a green card and, later on, US citizenship. The U visa. "It's to encourage victims to speak up, without the fear of getting deported," Di had explained.

Minerva had waited at a red light. "Do you trust the police?"

Di worked with them routinely. "Sometimes it's the only chance for my clients. The only choice."

"For every crime?" Minerva had stepped into the crosswalk.

Not all, but some of the scariest ones: human trafficking, involuntary servitude, rape, hate crimes, felony assault, and domestic violence, Di said. Crimes in which the perpetrators silenced victims by threatening to get them deported.

"We're getting the word out," Minerva would tell Ana. "If you know of anyone in this situation, who could use this kind of help, they can call me. Anytime."

29

After Ana left for the X-ray, Jane went to the nurses' station to ask for a cup; Sofía was thirsty.

In the hallway, she remembered to call her mother back. Cell service was spotty in here and she'd have to go into the waiting room or outside. Suddenly, she heard her mother calling out, "Jie Jie!"—as if by thinking of her, Jane had summoned Kai.

She ran to her mother, who hugged her so tightly she couldn't breathe. Lily grabbed her from behind and squeezed, too. The night felt like it had gone on forever, but according to the clock, it was only midnight. Jane was about to ask how they'd known she was at the hospital—maybe Tasha's mom had called them?—when Kai asked, "How did you know Baba was here?"

"Dad?" Jane pulled away from Kai. "Did something happen at the campsite?"

"At the house," Kai said. "He was on the deck when it collapsed."

"Is he . . . ? Why was he . . . ?" Jane's voice broke.

Lily buried her face into Jane's back, murmuring it was all her fault, that she shouldn't have said anything. Jane pulled her around and wrapped her into a hug. "It's not, it's not," she said, stroking her hair. Jane, on the other hand, had quite possibly ruined her family, her every fear come to pass, and for what? Footage that she didn't know would turn out, footage they couldn't release if anyone in it . . . If anyone . . . She didn't want to think what might have happened to her classmates. To her father.

After the blackout, she and Tasha had taken off and crossed into the Belles' yard when the shock waves traveled up through her sneakers, a sensation so startling that she bit her tongue. Then the screams began, guttural, pleading. She'd never forget the sound of their screams.

Over Lily's head, she met her mother's eyes.

Her glasses were smudged and her hair rumpled. "He's getting x-rayed now, but probably he broke his leg," Kai said. "Cracked his ribs, too."

Jane could almost feel the suffocating crush. The kicks to his face, to his ribs. Someone landing on his legs, or maybe more than one. "Is he—when can we see him?" She clutched the back of Lily's sweatshirt.

"They don't let people into the X-ray; the room's too small," Kai said.

"He told us to go home." Lily clung to Jane like she'd been shipwrecked.

Jane willed him to emerge from the double doors. Teetering, but on his feet. Whole.

"We can sit with him while he's getting the cast," Kai said.

"Is he . . . ?" Jane shuddered.

Lily yawned, swaying on her feet.

"Can you take her home?" Kai asked. She'd book a rideshare.

"I have to stay with Sofía until Ana's out of the X-ray." She gently pushed Lily toward the exam room, telling her to wait with Sofía.

"Who?" Kai asked.

"The neighbors' nanny. And her daughter."

A South Asian daughter pushed her elderly mother or grandmother in a wheelchair, going over her symptoms with a nurse.

"Police said they'll interview us tomorrow." Kai's eyes sharply appraised Jane. "Do you know who threw the party?"

"No." Jane resisted the urge to look away. "Everyone was talking about it at school." Her voice cracked, her heart beating so fast that she felt breathless. Did her mother notice?

"Why did you go?" Kai snapped.

Jane ducked her head, wishing she and Tasha had had a chance to figure out their cover story. She stared at her muddy sneakers.

A frazzled mom rushed to the nurses' station, asking for Haley, before getting led around the corner.

Kai sighed. "Was it Tasha's idea?" she asked, her tone softer now.

Jane looked up. "What?"

"Baba wondered." For once, her mother seemed sheepish. She'd never before questioned their friendship.

Jane dug the heels of her hands into her eyes, in tears again. This old hate! If her parents had seen, had heard, what went down at the party, even they might understand why she and Tasha had to take such measures. "Don't blame her!"

"Was it the other kids?" Kai gestured toward her classmates getting treated in the side-by-side exam rooms. "You wanted to be like them?"

"You won't believe me, but it was for you and Baba."

"How? What do you mean?"

"We wanted to make sure nothing broke," Jane said weakly.

"You should have told us!" Kai took off her glasses and rubbed them clean with the edge of her polar fleece. She seemed to be mustering herself for the long night ahead, with her force of will that could bend space and time.

"I hoped after another party Dad would stop putting it on SuCasa." An excuse, but also true, Jane now realized, among the reasons they'd gone ahead with their plan.

An orderly in navy scrubs rushed past, his sneakers squeaking on the linoleum.

"Where's Tasha?" Kai asked.

"At home."

"At least we can go home tonight." Kai knuckled the small of her back, probably sore.

Jane prayed the bedrooms weren't trashed like the living room. Kai eyed the partygoers again, seeming to wonder what Jane wondered, too: Were they going to sue? Uncle Chen would be furious, if and when he found out. Of course he'd find out. How else would her parents explain the collapsed deck, which would have to be razed or replaced before the house sold?

Something else nagged at Jane. She wanted to forget the Belles' accusations, but what if they were true? Partly true? "Did Uncle Chen ask Dad to do anything else?" she asked.

"To do what?" Kai asked.

"Dad will sell the house, but did he—does he have anything to do with Save El Nido?" Seeing her mother's confusion, she tried to explain what the Belles had insinuated, because of the domain name registered in China.

"They said *what*?" Kai frowned. "They're blaming China? Blaming us? Why?"

"It's so racist." But what if the Belles weren't lying? What if her father had been behind the website? Didn't he realize any campaign against outsiders could get aimed at their family, too? He didn't know that Tasha's family had entered the housing lottery, but if he had any hand in the campaign, he'd betrayed the Washingtons and the other applicants. Selfish! She'd tried to tell him, tried to warn him about the lies that turned you against everyone else to get ahead. But he didn't listen. "Could you check if there's a charge for it on the credit card?" Jane asked. "Then we'll know."

"Tomorrow." Kai dug her hands into the pockets of her polar fleece. "We'll talk about this tomorrow."

A family headed toward the exit, a mother with a frizzy bun, an unshaven father wearing horn-rimmed glasses, and Prince on crutches, her right ankle wrapped in Ace bandages. Sprained? Banged up, wig gone, her right sleeve torn, the lace ruffle knocked askew, but alive, alive, alive!

"I think I know her," Jane told her mother. She trailed behind them, eavesdropping: "Call Coach . . ." "Jenny's parents . . ." ". . . lucky, too." Though she didn't follow them into the parking lot, the relief rippled off them like heat from an oven. If anyone had died, sunk into a coma, they would have been more somber. Maybe they hadn't heard yet. Or could it be, then, that most—all?—had escaped serious injury? Wishful thinking, she knew. Maybe jinxing the next patient.

She tried video calling, but Tasha didn't pick up. She messaged her, explaining she'd seen Minerva, who'd come home soon. And that Ana seemed okay or, at least, would be. Three dots shimmered in the chat, then nothing. Tasha had typed something that she deleted. She must be exhausted. By the pool, she'd wheezed until the paramedics gave her a rescue inhaler.

Jane scrolled through her socials, where a few of the injured had posted photos of themselves—one from the ambulance, another in the exam room—with emojis that signified they were okay. She exhaled, relieved. But weren't people like that always okay? Almost always. She messaged Tasha with links to the photos.

Already the party felt like a lifetime ago. Her battery was about to die. She went outside for fresh air, a break from her clammy KN95. At the entrance, she spotted a news truck parked on the street, a satellite dish perched on its roof.

As soon as they moved in two and a half months ago, the house had been cursed, falling apart, falling down. In a strange way, her family's short time in El Nido might protect them, she realized. At the request of her parents, she'd looked over the real estate documents; her duties as the American-born eldest daughter often included reading official correspondence. The contract had been dense and difficult to parse, but hadn't there been an inspection clause?

The deck hadn't rotted only under their watch. The old owners must have known and said nothing. The real estate agent, too, with her lies of omission. The inspectors, failing to note the damage and signing off on their reports.

The lights in the parking lot blotted out the night sky, but she strained her eyes, hoping to catch the wink and flash of a shooting star. To make wishes for herself, for Baba, Mama, and her sister. For Tasha and her family.

* * *

Though firefighters fought off the blaze, the lithium battery burned hot and bright. As ash and smoke lofted high into the air, the scent dark and lurid, neighbors turned their hoses onto their roofs, trying to extinguish embers that arced like meteors.

A series of gusts carried a glowing spark up and across the neighborhood, to the future home of the Bellavista, landing on a waist-high pile of grass and weeds. With a snap and crackle, the fire kindled and spread.

30

After coming ashore, Blair texted Ana. When she didn't reply, Blair called. It went straight to voicemail, but she tried not to worry—the network got wonky when the power went out—and they'd be home soon. Blair offered to drive if Sam still felt seasick, but he got behind the wheel.

She kicked off her heels, which pinched her feet. As they passed through the freeway interchange, Sam said, "You were in the bathroom a long time."

Her body clenched. She'd said nothing about her run-in with Nic, but what did he know? "There was a line," Blair said, glad he had his eyes on the road.

"You saw Nic?"

Blair gazed at the glow of the taillights ahead.

She'd talked to him in the bar, Sam said, told him about the birdhouse Orb, but he'd played dumb. "You spied on them!" he said in a tone of equal parts wonder and disgust. "You stalked them."

She snapped her head around so quickly she jerked against the seat belt. "I had to! For Jordan." And now they had footage of Ella feeding the coyote, she explained. "That's why it started attacking people!"

He gave her a sidelong glance. "Shouldn't you tell Nic?"

"Exactly," Blair said. "This way, we can protect Jordan. Threaten to release it if she doesn't back off, if she comes at her again."

Sam burped and pushed his fist into his mouth. Still feeling queasy, she guessed. Queasy and irritable. "Why didn't you tell her already?"

"I needed to make sure it was Ella." The excuse sounded unconvincing, even to her ears. "Do you need water?" She peeked into the back, looking for a water bottle, hoping it might placate him.

She had more than enough footage of the coyote prowling El Nido to share with her CEO, but she'd held back. It wasn't because she wanted to protect the coyote. Sam wouldn't understand, but she'd wanted to see it up close. Just once, as with a movie star or influencer in the flesh, to confirm if they really looked like that, if they really were like that. And in that confirmation, understand that your eyes, your powers of perception, hadn't betrayed you.

Sam tightened his hands on the steering wheel. "You planning to put a camera in our bedroom? In my office, without telling me? Or maybe you already have."

She'd never. He knew that, but wanted to make her feel stupid. Small. They entered the tunnel, the overhead lights strobing in what felt like hyperspeed. "Why is it okay at a random intersection?" Blair asked.

"Because anyone could pass by. This, this is stalking!" He swerved, attempting to pass a car, and then braked hard to avoid slamming into a truck.

She braced her hand on the dashboard, filled with white-hot shame. Then defiance. She'd defend her family any way she could. Easy for Sam to lecture her. If they both sat back, Quinn would never have been bound for Princeton, and Jordan would never have been a rising star. If they both sat back, people like Nic would snatch everything their family had achieved.

Suffocating, Blair turned down the heat, on at full blast. They rode the rest of the way in silence. She dug her fingernails into her palm. If he watched the footage, then he'd understand. But if she couldn't convince him, he'd never trust her again.

When they pulled up to their cul-de-sac, police cars had barricaded the entrance, red and blue lights flashing. Sam rolled down the window, explaining that they were residents. The smell of smoke tickled her nose, the back of her throat. As the officer waved them through, she asked what happened, but he'd already turned away. Blair knew the answer: another party.

The town shouldn't have dawdled. Now authorities would have to put a stop to SuCasa.

Flashlights circled and dipped next door, but she couldn't make out what investigators were looking at. In the distance, generators whirred. They walked past their paring knife; Sam would find it in the morning, covered in dried blood.

In the house, silent and dark, she fought off her rising alarm.

"Hello? Hello? Where are they?" she asked Sam.

She ran ahead of him up the stairs. Did Ana take them somewhere with power? To her sister's? She tripped and landed hard on her knees. Sam helped her up, his hand at her back, shining the light on his phone. "You okay?"

"Hello, hello? Jordan? Ana? Quinn?" She scrambled up the rest of the stairs and shakily rose to her feet, bracing herself against the wall. In the nursery, she discovered the empty crib. Liam, Liam!

"Sam, Liam . . . !" Her breathing turned ragged, the walls pinwheeling around her.

"Here, Mama!" Jordan replied sleepily.

"She's here," Sam called out. "With Quinn."

"Liam's in the closet," Jordan mumbled.

"What, sweetheart?" Sam asked.

"In the closet," she repeated.

Blair dashed into the nursery and eased open the closet door. Shining the light on her phone, she caught sight of his pack-and-play. When he stirred, she held her breath until he stopped shifting. She'd leave him there the rest of the night.

Even before she entered Quinn's room, the stink hit her, boozy fumes so thick they seemed combustible. As her eyes adjusted, she could see that Quinn was spooning her sister. Somehow, they'd fallen asleep despite the rumble of engines and squawk of walkie-talkies outside. The lights from the first responders flashed through the window and against the wall.

As Sam gathered up Jordan, he murmured, "The bed's wet." He shook off the blanket that tangled around her legs. At the foot of the bed, Luna snored, with the gurgle of water bubbling through a pipe.

"Wet?" Spilled liquor? Then Blair smelled it: urine. "Is it Jordan? Luna?"

"No," Sam said. "Her pajamas are damp, but not soaked through. It's Quinn."

Quinn had peed the bed? Over the summer, they started letting her have alcohol, but only if they'd purchased hard seltzers for her and her friends, to ensure no one spiked their drinks. Blair had seen her tipsy, but never this out of it. And where was Ana and her daughter? Ana wouldn't have abandoned the kids, not with Quinn in this state—unless something had happened to her, too.

Quinn groaned.

"You think she drove like this?" Blair asked. The Mini Cooper had been parked in the driveway.

"She got herself home. Or her friends did." Sam sat Jordan upright, then got her to her feet, murmuring she had to go to her room and change her pajamas. She leaned against him as he guided her down the hallway. Domino's wheel rattled, the hamster on the move.

Blair pulled back the covers and touched Quinn's cheek. "Sweetheart. You have to change. You have to drink some water."

Quinn didn't move. Maybe Blair could let her sleep it off? No—she didn't want Quinn stewing in her pee-soaked jeans, getting a rash. She yanked off her jeans and grabbed a towel from the bathroom to cover the wet spot.

As she pulled the blankets over Quinn, she brushed her hand over her daughter's jutting hip bone. Her fingers grazed against her protruding rib cage. She pictured cattle bones in a desiccated river, her imagination magnifying everything in the dark.

She should have noticed. Why hadn't she noticed? She'd been focused on Jordan's weight, when she should have been worrying about Quinn instead. Though she'd seen Quinn countless times in her bathing suit, she'd assumed the spandex made her sleek. Maybe she hadn't studied Quinn closely because—because of a peculiar pain, bittersweet, proud, and shameful: Quinn's taut body reminded Blair of how she herself had once been and would never be again.

Blair had been confident about getting pregnant a second time, but month after month, year after year passed. Then came the shots in her stomach, the pills, the acupuncture, acupressure, the baby aspirin and Chinese herbs, the retrieval, the implantations, six rounds in all.

In those days, Blair had tried to make peace with the fact that they might not have another child. Quinn could be enough, *was* enough. A handful. The moment you looked away, she took off, at the park, at the library. A tiny figure, arms waving from the other side of the field. They'd put her in swimming lessons early in the hopes of exhausting her by bedtime, but she never tired. If Quinn could fly, she'd be one of those birds that flap nonstop between the hemispheres. How fiercely she'd loved Quinn then, a fierceness tinged with fear, with gratitude. Soon she'd fly far, far away.

She'd neglected her firstborn, who'd leave home in less than a year. A car door slammed outside, more investigators arriving on the scene? The side gate swung open.

Sam appeared at the door. "You hear that?"

They went downstairs and through the sliding glass door into the backyard.

"Ana?" Blair called out at the silhouettes. Wind rustled in the oak trees.

"It's us," Ana said.

"Where were you?" Blair asked.

The smoky scent stronger now, coating her tongue.

"We took a taxi from the hospital," Ana said, her voice hoarse.

"The hospital?" Blair asked. "Is it Sofía?" She walked a few steps toward them.

"I'm okay," Sofía said. "But Mama . . ."

"What about the kids?" Ana asked.

"They're okay," Blair assured.

"Do you need a light?" Sam asked. "Help going up the stairs?"

"It's late. I'll explain everything tomorrow." She winced, leaning heavily on Sofía.

When Blair tried to take her elbow, Ana waved her off. "Sorry we woke you up."

Blair backed off. "You need to rest." She gestured toward the in-law unit. "Sam, shine the light on the stairs."

❁ ❁ ❁

As Blair climbed into bed, she couldn't stop thinking about Quinn. What happened to her, to Ana and her daughter? She should have invited them to sleep here, in Jordan's bed. She'd go by in the morning.

There was a knock at the front door.

"What time is it?" she asked. The power still wasn't back on. She shivered; they should add another blanket before going to sleep.

"It could be the police." Sam sat up. "Or the firefighters."

"Now? Can't they wait?" Blair dragged herself out of bed, her feet and her back aching, and her mouth tasted acrid, even after she'd brushed her teeth.

"Or maybe it's Ana," she said. This time, she'd insist they come in. She followed him downstairs, where authorities told them that the walnut grove and Bellavista's partially built model home were in flames.

31

In the morning, Blair nudged a splintered board with her sneaker. "How fast can we get a fence up? Something temporary?" she asked Sam. He'd returned home a few minutes ago, but had been too amped up to go to bed. She'd hardly slept, tossing and turning until Liam awoke.

She hitched him higher on her hip. Without the fence, she felt naked. Worse than that: Without borders, without boundaries, she felt like an amoeba spilling its protoplasm. Anyone could get into the breach. And if she had to look at the Changs—and the Changs could look in on them—she might scream. There was a lot to sort out, but one thing was already clear: Such chaos had never visited their cul-de-sac until the Changs had arrived.

"The whole thing has to get replaced," Sam said before he set off along the perimeter, hobbling, his lower back acting up again.

Blair glanced up at the in-law unit. She hoped Ana and her daughter could rest; she'd check on them a little later. She ventured to the chicken coop, where flies buzzed around a carcass. As the rest of the flock stirred, she surveyed the mess, the stink of insides spilled out. She couldn't tell which one had succumbed to the coyote's jaws, the black feathers that could be Dora, Beaker, or Henrietta. Jordan would be heartbroken.

With the power off, she hadn't been able to review the footage. Liam squirmed, wanting to get down. Just this week, he'd taken his first steps, wobbly but steadier each day. Her baby, now a toddler. He seemed impervious to the morning chill. She set him in the grass a few feet away, but quicker than she anticipated, he was back upon the massacre. "Honey—no!" She kicked it aside, leaving a bloody print on her sneakers, the Italian ones that came pre-scuffed. A limited edition, with silver duct tape on the toes. Liam reached again. Her youngest had the unerring ability to go after exactly what she and Sam hoped he wouldn't notice, wouldn't touch.

She scooped Liam up again and carried him off farther than before. He giggled and walked stiff legged as Frankenstein toward her. She'd have to dispose of the mess, hose everything down before Luna got to it. It was cold out. She blew on her hands and tucked them deep into the pockets of her workout jacket.

As Sam approached, Blair asked, "Can your crew come by?"

"They're out on other jobs." Sam touched a cockeyed fence post that had remained standing.

"They can see right in," she hissed. "What if they rent out the house again, have another party?"

"I doubt they will." The broken deck planks were jumbled like Popsicle sticks.

"The Bellavista . . . is it as bad as the photos look?" Blair asked. He'd texted pictures and videos of a walnut tree, its crown an inferno, of a bulldozer throwing off thick black smoke. In his silence, she understood it was worse. If the wind whipped up again, it could rekindle hot spots and threaten the high school on the other side of the grove.

"Was it arson?" she asked. What if Save El Nido had gone rogue?

"Probably not. There were spot fires all over town."

"Will the insurance cover it?"

"Maybe. But not all of it," he said grimly.

She'd never seen him so defeated, the shadows deep and dark under his eyes. His clothes reeked of smoke, of melted plastic. She felt burned-out, too; one poke and she'd disintegrate.

Liam toddled up and clung to Sam's legs. He tousled Liam's hair.

When Blair tried to pick him up again, he squirmed out of her grasp and wandered off.

Sam exhaled. "There was just enough signal over there to check email. The mortgage autopay didn't go through."

He'd get a cash advance off their latest credit card and move money around, he said. Only a temporary fix. "We have to start considering other options."

Scrap the Bellavista and sell the land, he didn't have to say. Her head throbbed, and her body felt stiff as a plastic doll. Other bills would come due soon: for the cars, for Ana, for the electricity. "When do you think the power will come back on?" she asked.

"The wind downed power lines all over."

The door to Ana's unit swung open. Blair hoped the sound of their voices hadn't woken her. "Do you need anything?" she asked. "We have a French press."

"Liam! Honey!" Ana shouted. Blair turned to see Liam poking at the chicken.

"Dirty, no—no!" Blair dashed over and made him wipe his hands off in the grass. Blood smeared his cheek. "Sorry we woke you, we'll let you rest. Take a sick day tomorrow. Take the whole week, if you need it."

Ana lurched down the stairs.

"I can come up." Blair handed Liam off to her husband, who took him inside. "Did you sprain your ankle?"

Ana kept going, leaning on the banister, each step creaking.

Blair started up the stairs. "Are the stairs too much? Maybe you could stay with your sister until you're better. Is it all one level there?"

Ana waved off the suggestion. "I don't need time off."

Blair was secretly relieved. Or should she insist Ana rest? She might be worried that she'd get fired. "Take tomorrow off."

Ana stood awkwardly in the middle of the stairs until Blair realized that she was in the way. She retreated a few feet back.

"Sofía has school," Ana said.

"I'll walk them. We'll get takeout today. For everyone. We can see how you're feeling tomorrow night. And if you can't pick up Liam or need help with loading the stroller . . . if there's anything heavy . . ."

At the foot of the stairs, Ana swayed, gripping the banister.

"Do you need to sit down?"

Ana shook her head, but then seemed to change her mind and staggered to the outdoor couch. Blair flicked on the firepit, relieved that the gas hadn't gone out, too, and tried not to stare at Ana's black eye, purpling at the edges.

Ana gestured toward the backyard cameras. "I wanted to ask if there was any footage. From last night. My phone died so I can't see the app."

The flames flickered, blue-gold, the air shimmering above the firepit. "Me either," Blair said. "Not with the power out."

"Could it get erased?"

Blair was about to say, *No, of course it's backed up*, but Ana's urgency made her hesitate. She didn't want to promise certainty, in case something had gone wrong.

"I don't know. I'll check as soon as the electricity's on." Blair paused. "What happened?"

"I cracked my ribs."

"Did something happen with the girls? With Luna?"

"My ex. He . . . hurt me. Again." Haltingly, she described the abuse she'd fled.

Blair gaped, shocked by what their self-possessed nanny had endured, and wished Ana had trusted her enough to tell her sooner. No. She'd turned the lens onto herself, something her mother always did in a time of a disaster, natural or man-made: *I'm* heartbroken. *I'm* devastated. *I'm* praying. *I, I, I.* Blair had always promised herself she wouldn't do the same.

She now realized why Ana had requested a camera trained onto the side yard: to protect herself. Sleepless, scared that her ex would come after her.

She couldn't begin to pretend to understand. She'd never come close to that kind of peril. She reached out her arms to hug Ana, then dropped them, feeling self-conscious.

Ana told her about the party, the blackout, the rescue.

"Who's Tasha?" Blair asked.

Ana explained how they knew each other, and that Tasha's mother had been her doctor in the ER. "Dr. Washington."

Small world. Smaller than you ever thought possible—the coincidences and run-ins that could soothe and suffocate in equal measure. And yet the world was also impossibly vast, too, Blair knew. Vast enough to keep the secrets of those who slept beside you.

"Maybe Quinn knows her?" Blair asked. "If she's at Valle Vista, too?"

"Maybe," Ana said. "Like I said, if there's any footage with . . . with him, I need it." Sam joined them on the couch as Ana explained the special visa. "If there's footage . . ."

"That's proof." Blair had enrolled in bystander-intervention training, and a part of her—which she couldn't articulate, couldn't admit—had been disappointed that she'd never had to step in. Yet. Not that she wished for hate crimes, and not that she wanted to play the white savior, but having been trained—having role-played online and answered the quizzes—she was ready. Now an opportunity had presented itself.

Ana looked past her, at Jin, on crutches, standing by the toppled fence, his wife beside them. Blair waved, then wished she'd flipped them off. "Yes?" she said.

"I'm sorry," Jin said.

"You said you'd take it off SuCasa," Blair said.

"It won't happen again," Jin said. When he retreated, Kai shot him a look. He stopped and cleared his throat. "Save El Nido? That's over, too."

Blair tottered to her feet. Was he admitting he'd been behind the campaign? So she hadn't imagined it. So she hadn't been racist.

She didn't feel vindicated though; she felt hollow inside—windblown, desolate. She wondered if Kai had also just discovered the campaign, if she'd told him to confess. They must have no idea the future home of the Bellavista had gone up in flames. If they'd known, he wouldn't have brought it up right now. He limped toward her, crutches scraping in the dirt, apologizing.

"Go away," she said. When Jin kept advancing, *Go back to where you came from* sprang to her lips. She caught herself in time; she didn't mean China. And yet she did. She actively resisted hate, and yet what did it mean when her mind went there?

"Stay back," she shouted. When Ana got to her feet, wincing, Blair motioned for her to sit. "We can hear you from over here. You're behind Save El Nido? You and who else?"

"No one else." Jin winced, shifting his weight on his crutches.

He had to be lying. Blair looked at Kai. "With you?"

Kai shook her head once, an abrupt snap.

Sam stood up. "Or are you working for another real estate developer?" he asked.

Blair felt a burst of relief. She'd sounded the warning so many times and at last Sam believed her.

"Are you manipulating the market?" Sam asked.

"Tell the truth," Blair demanded.

"I'm sorry." Jin hung his head.

"Sorry doesn't cut it," Blair said. "Can you promise no one will come after the Bellavista again?"

Jin let out a long sigh. "How can I promise that?" he asked, his tone aggrieved. "People have been fighting it since before we got here!"

It occurred to Blair that her neighbors were suffering, with a trashed house, a collapsed deck, and an injured leg. They could settle this later, after they'd cooled off, after they'd gotten some sleep. She was about to suggest as much when Luna rushed past, straight at Jin, whose eyes widened in panic. Sam must have left the patio door open.

"She's just playing!" Blair said with false cheer. If Jin got jumpy, it would rile Luna, already skittish from the blackout. Jin wobbled on his crutches, then swiped at Luna, who scampered away.

"Come, Luna!" Blair said. As Luna jumped up onto her hind legs, Blair cupped her hands around her mouth. "Luna—down. Down!"

Sam lunged for Luna, grabbing her by the collar. "Tell me who you're working for."

"No one." Jin gripped the crutches.

"Why? Why'd you do it?" Sam asked. Luna squirmed against him, barking, before she slipped free and raced in circles around them. He touched the small of his back, in evident pain.

"Control your dog," Jin muttered. Something seemed to unleash in him, then. Something he'd been holding back for a while. "You want to know why?" he said bitterly. "Because you're all like that mutt. You think everything is yours."

Sam shoved him in the chest. As Jin toppled, the crutches flying into the air, Ana screamed. Blair had never known Sam to get violent like that, never known him to raise his voice. But Jin had tried to take down the Bellavista, then taunted him and insulted his family.

Lies. And yet. She remembered the online posts negging El Nido that went back for years. How angry, how hurt, how excluded some people felt here. Not only Jin. "Help him up," she croaked.

Sam stood over Jin, his arms limp at his side. Jin groaned.

What if Jin had broken something else? What if he'd landed funny and now he was paralyzed?

"Stop—don't touch him. I'll call 911." Blair darted her eyes around the backyard. Kai had disappeared. She could have run into the house to call an ambulance. And the police.

Oh. Oh! Thankfully, the power was out. Thankfully, no footage existed of Sam assaulting a man with a broken leg. An *Asian* man.

Wriggling like a fish on a hook, Jin rolled on his side, propped himself onto his elbows and then to sitting position. He groaned again, his leg in the cast splayed at an odd angle.

Sam's expression turned contemplative, a look Blair recognized from when he tried to make amends. "Do you need an ice pack?" Sam asked solicitously, as if he hadn't just nailed him. "Can you check if we have any that haven't melted?" he asked Blair.

"I can get it." Ana wobbled onto her feet.

"Don't." Blair motioned for her to sit down. "Sam, get back."

From the side of her house, Kai dragged something that hissed in the dirt. When Sam offered a hand, Jin flinched and scootched helplessly away from him, his expression a rictus of terror.

Blair sprinted over and grabbed Sam's arm. "Enough!" she shouted. "That's enough." From the corner of her eye, she noticed Kai raising her arms, hands clasped together. She and Sam turned at the same time. With a whoosh, lukewarm water blasted them both in the face, the taste rusty as nails. Sputtering, she and Sam staggered back. Kai had turned a garden hose on them, warding them off like the nuisances they were.

32

The outcome seemed inevitable, considering how their conflict began: over property lines. A clash of personalities. In truth, Jin and Blair, both schemers, were more alike than either would recognize or admit, though only one ended up sprawled on the ground.

Neither would connect their battle to what had played out the night before; neither would understand how Tasha and Jane were also engaged in a struggle for territory. The girls would have said their aims were systemic, though. Call it idealistic, call it generational, but the morning after, for the first time, they felt the weariness of their elders.

When Tasha awoke, she could have howled at the world—at the universe—for the ways it fucked over her family. A howl so powerful it could split stars and birth black holes, where space and time, grief and rage, broke down. She'd caused her mother so much worry, even though Minerva already had a lifetime's share.

Her mother slept beside her, Marcus, too; all three had climbed into Minerva's bed. As Tasha held still, trying not to wake them, her thoughts circled around what had happened. The mission, which had seemed so clear before the party, had turned murky.

Most of the time there, she'd acted like an anthropologist, a dispassionate observer of an exotic tribe. That was how she protected herself. Rather than get disgusted or outraged, she leaned into her fascination.

Like a scientist who'd laid out a maze, she'd watched her subjects nosing their way to the cheese.

The subjects had performed as hypothesized. Not until Griff had reached for her hair did she realize how much she'd wanted someone, anyone, to rebel! To dig a hole or climb over the wall, to reject the cheese.

She'd felt someone staring at her and, even before she turned her head, she knew it was Jacqui. She'd discussed it with her mother. If you were among two—or very few—Black people in a room, you had a choice. You could make your way to each other or nod *I see you*. An acknowledgment of the setting they'd found themselves in.

Or you could turn away.

Maybe Jacqui was tired of others assuming that she and Tasha knew each other. Tasha could remind her of things Jacqui would rather not ponder. She might have told herself she could deal with the theme, that the interpretation wouldn't be that bad. She might have been glad that Griff hadn't touched her hair. She could be defensive about her popularity. Or she could have felt like she barely kept her head above water and couldn't extend a hand to Tasha.

Tasha had cued up the playlist, hoping to goad her classmates, yet she'd also held out the hope that they might at last refuse the maze. No, they'd run straight to the end. Even blindfolded, they might have dashed faster and faster each time. By nature or nurture, by reflex or training? Even if scientists conducted the experiment a dozen times—a hundred, a thousand—they'd never know for certain. Maybe the maze determined how the rats behaved. How she did, too. She wasn't a scientist watching from above; wasn't she also in the maze?

Hearing them sing, she'd lit up with an incandescent rage. Sorrow, too. Moments later, the deck had collapsed in what felt like telekinesis.

❁ ❁ ❁

Later that morning, after the electricity kicked on and Blair plugged in her dead phone, she called the Orb technician. When it went to voicemail, she texted and explained that it was an emergency: The birdhouse cameras had to be removed immediately.

Then she checked the Orb footage from their yard. As Ana's beating unspooled across her monitor, Blair turned away, bile flooding her mouth. She breathed deeply until the nausea passed.

The hospital must have taken X-rays. Just look at the extent of her injuries! She pictured investigators studying the silvery images, pictured them knocking on the ex's door, and taking him into custody.

If Blair turned the footage over to the police, Ana's case against him would be airtight.

A thought unbidden, forbidden, popped into her head: It was a story the CEO could spin, could sell, that seemed more promising than that of the rogue coyote.

She was so exhausted that she wanted to rest her head on her desk. She rubbed her temples. Who was behind the party, anyway? Scrolling through the motion alerts, she noticed something from the camera trained on the Changs' back deck, around the time Blair had been getting ready for the boat dance. The party hosts setting up? A woman in a caftan and straw hat and sunglasses took in the view. The caftan looked familiar, like the one her mother had given her, which Blair had stuffed into the back of her closet. Blair gasped. Even from a distance, she could tell it was Quinn.

Blair jumped ahead a couple hours and witnessed Jacqui, Maddy, and a few other friends climbing onto the deck, via the exterior stairs instead of the front door.

If she turned footage of the beating over to the police, she'd probably have to provide the rest of it, she now realized. Authorities could subpoena video from the entire evening, from all cameras, to check for suspicious activity.

They'd see a horde of teenagers running from the party, which would all get entered into the public record. And the incident would most certainly get reported by the media.

Quinn could be liable for the damage, for the injuries. She'd lose her scholarship to Princeton.

In the kitchen, Sam puttered. Now that the power was back on, he was making breakfast: bacon and almond-flour pancakes, the air heavy with grease and clarified butter. Coffee, too. He must be running on fumes; after being up all night, he'd crash soon. She couldn't believe he'd flattened Jin. It seemed Sam couldn't believe it, either.

Maybe now Sam would understand why Blair had trained the camera onto Nic's house. How, in defending your territory, you could get driven to extremes.

After Kai had sprayed them, she dropped the hose and helped Jin to his feet. Both couples stared at each other before retreating. Ana had stumbled up the stairs to her unit, probably traumatized all over again.

Plastic tumbled in the kitchen, presumably Liam stacking and knocking over Tupperware, again and again, his latest fascination. A builder, like his daddy. Sam turned on the *Freakonomics* podcast. Quinn and Jordan were asleep, or maybe Quinn was avoiding her, in the throes of the worst hangover of her life.

Blair clicked ahead. The cameras had detected more activity: Ana's fall into the pool and Tasha jumping in to save her. She paused the video, but didn't recognize her. Didn't Ana say her mother was a doctor? Dr. Washington. The Washingtons. She reached for the stack of Bellavista applicants on the edge of her desk. She'd been reading through them; even though everything was supposed to be confidential, Sam had received copies. The lottery was largely random, but the developer reserved the right to weigh in with applicants who might benefit the project overall. Applicants who exemplified the hardworking families priced out of El Nido—the kind of people who could quell that fake environmental campaign and get the stop-work order reversed.

The Washingtons had stood out: renters, the mother a widowed doctor, with two kids, a teenage daughter and a son in elementary school. She thumbed through the folder, looked over the application, and confirmed that Tasha was the daughter.

When Blair's phone pinged, she set aside the folder. She felt uneasy, like she'd had one too many bites of something she'd craved.

She checked her texts. A Mavericks mom had asked, You okay? Solicitous, but soliciting, too. A reminder of how quickly gossip could and would spread in El Nido. Oh, Ana. Blair wanted to help—pay for therapy for Sofía; hire an immigration attorney; get a restraining order not only to protect Ana but her own kids, too—anything and everything short of releasing the footage.

A shower started down the hallway. Quinn? She would have woken up confused, embarrassed about why she had no pants on, her sheets soaked in urine. Did she remember much from last night? Blair gazed out the window, with its view of the backyard, the gaping fence, and a sliver of Ana's quarters. Could she really deny Ana the footage that might change everything for her? She pressed her fingers against the glass, the coolness offering clarity: *Help her*. Run downstairs, across the backyard, and tell her the good news. Blair would drive her to the police station, stay at her side every step of the way.

The pool was placid, no sign of the near tragedy from last night. She pictured Ana flailing in the water, the teenager jumping in after her. Tasha had saved her, and for that, shouldn't the family get a spot at the Bellavista?

Blair sheepishly recognized that she was acting like those people who buy carbon credits while booking a flight for a weekend trip. Which is to say, attempting to atone while doing exactly as she pleased. Trading one good deed for another, a switch that happened to benefit herself, too. She wavered. There was no reason she couldn't hand over the footage and accept the Washingtons' housing application—no reason but for her daughter now coming down the hallway, her hair wrapped in a towel and bundled into old sweats with a hole in the knee.

Blair poked her head out. "Sweetheart! Quinn. Quinn!"

"Do you have any aspirin?" Quinn squinted at her. Mascara smeared beneath her eyes.

Did Quinn's friends also get hammered last night? Jacqui, Maddy? She'd never seen Quinn so out of it. How could she be so careless? She could've ended up in that heap, her leg broken. Her head cracked open!

Blair led her to the master bedroom, where Quinn slumped on the edge of the bed. After giving her two aspirins, she instructed her to finish the entire glass of water. Quinn complied, though she seemed queasy; she winced after a sip, then forced herself to swallow in three gulps. She burped and smacked her lips. She smelled like a brewery. No—like fruit punch, fermented in the sun.

She tucked in Quinn, which she hadn't done in years, and let her sleep in their bed. In the dim light that filtered through the curtains, she studied Quinn's angular cheekbones. Her sunken eyes. Dehydration, or had she wasted away in plain sight? Not enough calories or too much exercise.

All this time, she thought she'd raised Quinn to be confident and strong. She never said a word about Quinn's weight, never talked about diets. But Quinn could have seen the way Blair winced at photos of herself, how she'd mixed those disgusting pea-protein shakes for lunch.

Maybe Quinn compared her body to those of the other girls in the locker room. Blair had done it at her age: moaning she'd eaten too much, grabbing her thighs, her sides, as if trying to tear them off. The thinner you were, the more you complained about your flaws so that your friends protested, *No!* Her daughter's determination and drive had dazzled Blair, but Quinn had been falling apart.

Blair had brought it upon her daughter. Without knowing, without trying.

She set a garbage can next to the bed, in case Quinn threw up. She didn't realize that Quinn—like scores of attendees last night—had come down with the virus, an outbreak that would emerge a few days from now, ripping through their house, and through Valle Vista's sports teams, resulting in the forfeit of several important games, and the postponement of homecoming and midterms.

Blair sat on the edge of the bed. "Is there a lot going on?" she asked.

Quinn's eyelids fluttered. Blair stroked her damp hair, at the trace of glitter on her forehead. "Can we talk about it?"

Quinn didn't answer, but let out a deep sigh, her breathing heavy and even. She wasn't faking it. Her darling could have been or one or three or five years old again, all her past selves there, just under the surface. She wouldn't let Quinn down again.

Afterward, Blair texted Ana: When the power surged, the cameras got fried.

33

In the wake of the party, Quinn had deleted the SuCasa account and the Becky White email associated with it. Every post on various socials that made any reference to the party also disappeared within twelve hours, before authorities searched online. The cover-up, though not coordinated, was surprisingly complete because no one wanted to get caught during college-application season. Yet the photos, videos, and screenshots lived on, traded or saved.

Of the injured, no one could remember much. Or at least so they claimed, lawyers at their side, when interviewed by police. None of them spoke to the reporters who knocked on their doors. Haley the soccer star had broken her nose in the fall, but it served as an excuse for the rhinoplasty she'd long wanted. Brock the pitcher had a hairline fracture on his left arm—fortunately not his throwing arm. The various sprains, breaks, bruises, and strains healed, bodies resilient as lizards growing back snapped-off tails, spliced planaria sprouting second heads.

The night changed certain lives more than others: Carrie the soccer phenom and Brady the running back started dating. They'd carry on long-distance through college and marry the day after graduation. Chloe the water polo star would become a physical therapist, inspired by the one who'd helped her recover her gait and flexibility.

No one had died, no one had been paralyzed, though Jin, at the bottom of the heap, had sustained the worst injury. For the rest of his life, he'd limp when tired, and his leg, with its metal rod, would set off airport security and ache whenever it was about to rain.

As for Julio, he washed and wrapped his wounds that night: the knife slash on his hand, the coyote bite on his butt cheek. He'd see to Ana later. In the morning, he popped a handful of pain pills and went to work, installing shingles at a new housing development near the Altamont Pass. By nightfall, he shook with fever and chills, feeling worse than that time he'd been jumped in the group home. The next morning in the bathroom, he twisted around to get a look at the bite. Redness streaked down his buttock, his leg. He wobbled to bed, hoping to sleep it off. As the hours went by, a storm brewed in his body.

Wily licked his wounds, the slit to his muzzle, which grew infected, red and raw as a scream. Delirious, he wandered into traffic, cars swerving around him, and into a culvert, where he passed out. Tongue lolling with thirst, body burning until he lurched by a small reservoir that fed a golf course. There, he chanced upon a miracle: a dish of water and scattered kibble, left for a colony of feral cats. Each bite, each slurp, restoring him.

❂ ❂ ❂

A month after the party, in mid-November, Signing Day arrived. A collective exhalation, a collective rejoicing by the scholar-athletes whose futures had never seemed brighter.

Once a ritual reserved for marquee sports—football and basketball—now swimmers, lacrosse and tennis and volleyball players, rowers, golfers, wrestlers, and the like could also bask in the glory. Across the country, high schools hosted ceremonies: classmates cheering as the athletes signed their letters of intent, posed under banners, and in front of a step-and-repeat. A peak moment of high school, of childhood itself.

Football and basketball had their Signing Day in February, though no one from Valle Vista this year was in contention; they weren't, generally, and those were the sports with the big money. Many recruits were young enough to believe that this achievement indicated that the way forward would be smooth or, at least, smoother than the effort they had already expended to get here. By this time next year, more than a few would struggle: failing a class that would dash their premed dreams, drinking and drugging too much, sleeping or eating too little, their sanity fraying when everything by which they'd defined themselves came up short.

Like the volcanic ash in Pompeii, the pandemic had frozen children mid-stride. Fifth graders behaved like third graders; the first graders like preschoolers; and the eighth graders like sixth graders. Everyone at the colleges and universities acted like freshmen, all anxiety and binge drinking.

For now, the two dozen recruits at Valle Vista would celebrate, would savor the certainty that felt like gold. Certainty they'd lacked until then. Certainty that their peers—now applying and agonizing—would not have until next spring. Certainty that those who'd attended the party had escaped any punishment.

For the investigators, the trail had gone cold. Officially, they sought leads into who hosted the party; unofficially, they agreed not to probe further. The families who'd considered suing also backed off. Though they could go after the deep pockets of SuCasa, the silence around who exactly had hosted the party—and the sense that their kids might have been complicit, that teenagers much like theirs could get collared—made the families decide to put the matter behind them.

The party houses had come to an end. Within weeks of the deck collapse, the city council had rushed to pass a version of the ordinance Blair had wanted: requiring booking four nights or more to prevent future party rentals.

Construction had resumed on the Bellavista. After the party, Save El Nido died, the website taken down. Nic, the linchpin of the campaign, had gone quiet. No one had stepped in to take her place, no one who could rally, organize, and fight with her fervor on behalf of the spotted salamander.

Nic and her husband had realized that their daughter's hand feedings might have spurred the coyote on its monthslong rampage. Whoever had filmed Ella knew that, too, prompting Nic to lie low.

The stop-work order had also been rescinded, after the blaze demonstrated that the city could safely contain a future wildfire at that location.

In another happy accident, the fire sped the clearing of the walnut grove and put the project ahead of schedule.

El Nido had been lucky, so very lucky that the fire hadn't spread. It was a reminder to harden your defenses in a burning world.

Behind the scenes, city leaders had decided that the bad publicity around the party could get counteracted with good news: a press release announcing El Nido's visionary plan to address the state's housing crisis.

❁ ❁ ❁

At the school ceremony, held right before lunch, the Valle Vista gymnasium smelled of lemony floor polish, of decades of gummy white bread, of dried sweat and surging hormones. Of volatility, of flight or fight. Distinguished Schools banners hung along the walls, a few faded by the sun, dated from before either Jane or Tasha had been born, as well as banners for various championships.

They sat in the last row of the bleachers. Down below, Quinn signed her contract, flashing her fingers in a V-for-victory sign, smiling above her mask as her teammates chanted her name. If she felt guilty about last month's party and the subsequent destruction of the deck, she didn't show it.

"She's in, you're in," Jane said. Tasha and her family had received a spot at the Bellavista—lucky for once, lucky like who knew when they'd be again. "Have you been thinking we should let it . . . go?" A silver helium balloon had floated to the rafters. "Now that you have a spot in the Bellavista, should the stuff from the party get out?"

"I don't know." Under the terms of the below-market program, the Washingtons had to live in the duplex for at least five years before selling.

"Maybe we delete the footage, then?" Jane asked. "My dad needs to flip the house next spring."

Uncle Chen had wanted to boot her family, until her father—at Jane's urging—had floated the plan of suing the previous owners for failing to disclose issues with the deck and the plumbing. A settlement was getting worked out. Jin would oversee the remodeling, under the eye of surveillance cameras—at the front door, the rear exterior, and the kitchen—that Uncle Chen could monitor at any time.

For now, her father didn't need to worry about sending his parents money. They'd settled into their new place. Nai Nai had recovered, energetic enough to return to line dancing with her friends in the local park.

Quinn's parents left the stands, Mrs. Belle carrying a bouquet of flowers and two shiny gift bags.

Everyone seemed relieved when the fence went back up between their houses. The Belles, who kept a polite distance, would rejoice the moment the for-sale sign appeared. If only Jane had been there to fight back when Mr. Belle attacked! All that training, and she'd been asleep. Her parents didn't want to press charges though.

"Did Ana ever get the footage?" Jane asked.

"I asked my mom, but she said she couldn't discuss it." Tasha lowered her voice. "This morning, her phone was on the kitchen table." Several texts from Ana had flashed on the screen, Tasha said, but she couldn't unlock the phone to read them.

From what she could tell, in the month since the party, Ana and her mother had been texting every so often, she added. "I don't think Ana got the footage. There was a glitch? So she doesn't want to go to the police. When my mom checked her phone, I pretended I didn't see anything. But I could tell she was disappointed when she read the texts."

Jane traced her thumb along the seam on her jeans. "Maybe Ana won't do anything unless she has it."

"If I were her, I wouldn't either. Have you seen her?"

"She walks really slow. It must hurt—a lot." Jane grimaced. "And the other night, I heard a little girl crying. It could have been her daughter." There had to be a way to help them!

"All the cameras broke?" Tasha asked. "The whole night?"

"I thought that was strange, too."

The Belles were now taking selfies, Mrs. Belle seeming to nudge her husband into shooting from a higher angle.

"You think she's lying?" Jane asked. But why? "You think Mrs. Belle is hiding something?" She shifted, her tailbone sore from sitting. The planks were sticky from a spilled soda.

"Or hiding . . . someone?" Tasha asked.

Quinn and the other athletes posed together with coaches and the school principal. Cameras clicked and flashes fired, a photographer from the school paper circling them. The coach fist-bumped the Belles, and the principal pumped hands. Mrs. Belle presented each of them with a gift bag.

Jane searched for Mrs. Belle online—her first name was Blair, Claire?—and came across a bio for a company called the Orb that made surveillance cameras. A VP of marketing. "If it's her company, I call bullshit. The footage can't be lost. It's backed up or their techs could recover it."

"How could she lie to Ana?" Tasha wrapped her arms around herself.

"It's effed up." As Jane puzzled over how they might change Mrs. Belle's mind, her gaze fell on Quinn. Jane gestured at the recruits below; they all seemed so at ease in their track pants, hoodies, and striped slides. "We know where *they're* going." Most of them had been at the party. "We don't have to wait."

They'd planned to release the footage in the spring; neither had realized that student-athletes would get admitted months sooner, in mid-November, as of Signing Day.

Seeing her classmates made Jane squeamish, though. She pressed her knees together. They—and the consequences they'd suffer—weren't abstract. The clips would go viral, she knew with certainty. The fucked-up costumes, the N-word at high decibels performed by these shiny scholar-athletes. El Nido could become a punch line on late-night talk shows. ("Claiming 'at least it wasn't blackface' isn't much of a defense!") The hosts wouldn't be able to resist the hypocrisy, the paradox of what happened in this ostensibly woke bastion of the Bay Area. And the colleges couldn't ignore it, either.

She pictured the rejections from the admissions offices popping up on phones and computers: "We regret to inform . . ." "After an investigation . . ." Weeks of correspondence with the schools would follow, the accused convinced that *something* could be worked out: special classes, a heartfelt essay, a generous donation in the spirit of making amends.

But for one or two, or maybe a few, the reward for those years of toil—of ass-kissing and brownnosing, of demands for accommodations and dispensations, of endless early-morning practices and late-afternoon games, flash cards and cram sessions—would disappear.

Jane tugged the sleeves of her oversized sweatshirt, drawing them over her hands. "It's just . . . so personal." Like a sniper, picking off victims one by one. Quinn in the crosshairs.

Tasha shrugged. "That's always the excuse, though, isn't it? That it's *not* personal. That they have nothing to do with why Black and Brown people get harassed, get killed. It's not their fault, what happens to other people. Even though they feel bad about it."

The bleachers shook as their classmates climbed down and filed out of the gymnasium, the wooden floor vibrating with the shuffle and thump of their feet.

"You remember that story, 'The Ones Who Walk Away from Omelas'?" Tasha asked.

From AP Psych, about a utopia whose existence depended upon a single suffering child. Most residents were horrified, disgusted, but made peace with this trade-off, unwilling to change anything that might threaten their blessings.

"Everyone said they would have walked away." Jane balled her hands inside her sleeves.

"Quinn said the story was about systemic racism," Tasha said. "I've been thinking about what bugged me. Even when the class named 'real-world' examples"—she pulled air quotes with her fingers—"everything was theoretical. Something that happens to other people. But this—this would happen to people like *them*."

How often would she and Tasha have a chance to do that? Maybe never again.

"What does that make us in the story?" Jane asked.

"No one in the story tries to fight the status quo. Those who disagree, leave. But we can't leave. None of us can." Tasha read aloud from the banners displayed below: "'Princeton, USC, UCLA . . .'" She chewed on her lower lip. "But how will exposing them get your neighbor to release the footage of her backyard?"

She had a point. They had the leverage if they threatened to make the party video go viral, not after they'd done so. "Maybe we don't release any of it. Just threaten to," Jane said.

"We can't change the way things are." Tasha stretched out her legs. "But we can change things for Ana. What if . . . What if we send Mrs. Belle an anonymous email with the subject line 'We know what you did.' In the email we can attach a clip of Quinn."

"Blackmail?" Jane asked, the gravity of the idea sinking in.

"Look, *Quinn* booked the house. *Quinn* let it turn into a party," Tasha said. "But we're not doing it to call her out. Not anymore. We're doing it for Ana."

"Ana *and* Sofía." Jane leaned against Tasha, who leaned back. Her friend's lotion—nutty vanilla—always made her feel cozy. The chance of success seemed as slim as with their original plan—slimmer, even—but the only one that Ana and her daughter might have.

The helium balloon had drifted toward the basketball hoop, bobbing above the school's name in block letters and its mascot, a stylized vaquero, with a jaunty neckerchief and cowboy hat. Jane felt herself carried along in those same invisible currents.

"We can say that we'll release it unless she turns over footage from the backyard to the police," Tasha said.

"And that 'concerned residents' want to know what happened that night." Jane started to envision how it might come together. "Mrs. Belle might think it's from one of the parents whose kids attended the party. Or from a neighbor. Or that lady with the petition!" she exclaimed. She looked around to make sure no one had heard.

"I wonder if Nic ever saw the bad review," Tasha said.

When they'd last checked, Yip seemed to have deleted it.

The auditorium had nearly emptied. Custodians arrived to strike down the step-and-repeat, keys jingling at their waist.

"When?" Jane asked. "Tonight?"

Yes, Tasha said.

"And then what?" Jane redid the end of her braid. "Do we give Mrs. Belle a deadline?"

"We can say that she'll have twenty-four hours to respond," Tasha said decisively.

"What if she doesn't?" Jane knotted the rubber band. Goofy, but she felt like an Amazon girding for war.

Tasha tugged on the end of her braid. "Then whatever happens next, it's on her."

Whatever happened next, at least she and Tasha had each other. A rare, precious thing: a friendship that felt lifelong.

34

The next day, as Ana parked at the curb, she checked the new side gate to the backyard—metal, with a lock. It was closed. For the first time, Sofía had stayed in their apartment instead of coming to Mavericks practice. Door locked, with a chair under the knob, she'd finished a Wanted poster for science class (the culprit: shigella. "Dysentery . . . diarrhea!" she'd said, grossed out but giggling). Ana had repeatedly checked the live feed, watching Sofía at work. She seemed safe, but cameras could fail.

From above, Sofía pulled aside the curtains and waved. Ana waved back. She couldn't shake the feeling that by daring to hope she'd jinxed her daughter. She wished she could erase what Sofía had seen. Julio had called Sofía too soft, too emotional. Once, after they'd come across a dead squirrel, acorn clenched in its mouth—its startled expression resembling that of a mafioso shot dead with a meatball, mid-gulp—she'd cried for a week. "He didn't know he was going to die. Maybe he was going home to his family," Sofía had sobbed. Julio had snapped at her, "Grow up!"

And she had. When the time came, she'd gone after him. Ana vowed never to let him—or anyone like him—back in their lives again. She fumbled for her key chain, heavy and jangling as a prison warden's: car fob, house keys, and a tube of pepper spray she'd started carrying.

With the wildfires extinguished for now, the skies were clear but for high clouds that resembled the silver scales of a fish, tipped in pink and red. Geese honked, flying high above in a V formation.

Blair came down the walkway. Ana wondered if her boss wanted to talk privately. All day, Blair had holed up in her office, without taking a break for lunch.

While Jordan hugged her mother, then darted inside, Ana shouldered her purse. Maybe Blair wanted to fire her; she and her husband could have decided it would be easier to put Liam in day care and give him more stimulation now that he was a year old. Free up the apartment over their garage. Leave it open for guests and avoid the possibility of Julio paying another visit.

Ana unbuckled Liam from his car seat and set him onto the sidewalk. Her rib cage ached, though less than before, and she moved slowly. During her recuperation, what she used to cross in five minutes took fifteen. She'd managed, though.

He toddled toward his mother, babbling. "Mama Mama Mama."

Blair's smile verged on constipated, with an uncanny resemblance to Liam's when he strained in his diaper. She hitched him onto her hip and kissed the top of his head. When Liam pulled on her hair, she pried off his fingers.

Ana reached for him. "I'll take him. He likes watching while I'm getting dinner ready." Did she detect the slightest tug of resistance before Blair handed him over? Ana set him onto the lawn, where he sat down hard and yanked on strands of grass.

Blair fidgeted with her cuff bracelet. She seemed distracted. "I have to send a few emails."

She didn't have to explain to Ana, who was paid to care for Liam whether her boss was working or laughing at internet memes. Blair seemed forever conflicted, though, in handing off her son.

"When you're at practice, what do you do with him?" Blair asked. With the toe of her sneaker, she pushed aside gravel scattered on the walkway.

"He's busy. He loves climbing on the bleachers, walking around the pool deck. Peeking in and out of the lockers." Ana eyed him; he'd picked up a prickly seedpod from the sycamore tree.

"Sounds like you never have a chance to sit down!" Blair laughed, but it seemed forced. Did she doubt Ana's ability to do her job? Did another parent mention something?

Ana never saw Nic anymore; her daughter had been pulled out from Mavericks for the rest of the season. An injury that wouldn't heal, she'd overheard. "I can manage," she said.

"I know, I know." That fake laugh again. "We appreciate you so much." Blair pressed her palms together in thanks. "Have you decided what . . . If you're going to . . . What about a restraining order?"

It wasn't the first time Blair had brought it up; she'd offered to pay for the lawyer to file it. Ana doubted it would stop him. Carolina had mentioned the possibility of a GPS tracker, which Ana had then discovered in the wheel well of her car. He must have gone by Carolina's, found Ana's car, and installed it then.

She and Carolina had agreed: If he got served papers, he might get angry and go after her again. Ana heard he'd gotten out of the hospital, but who knew how long that would hold him at bay? It would have been different if she'd had the footage. If she'd trusted that she might get a U visa, she'd go to the police for a chance at a green card.

"We'll pay for the lawyer," Blair said.

The Belles, who'd returned to paying Ana on time, must have fixed their money problems. She didn't know that Blair had begged her parents for a loan, enough to cover expenses until Sam drummed up more financing.

Blair's eyes were pleading. Glistening, close to tears. She cared, she really did, and must have felt guilty about the cameras failing that night.

Ana was annoyed, though. She still couldn't take a deep breath without wincing, and she had to worry about her boss's feelings, too?

"Still thinking about it," Ana said. Thanksgiving, two weeks away, couldn't come fast enough; she needed the break. Her sister in LA would drive up with her family and they'd spend it together at Carolina's.

Liam put the seedpod in his mouth. "Liam! No!" Ana tugged it from his hands, tossing it aside.

"You can trust us." Blair picked up Liam again. "When you're new somewhere, it can be hard to know whom to trust."

As much as Sofía loved the school, this conversation reminded Ana that a nanny only had one real form of job security: if her boss had another baby.

Blair's skittish behavior reminded Ana that she couldn't count on her forever. Eventually, Liam would go to preschool. Eventually, the Belles would move on from her and she'd move on, too. If Ana wanted to build a life for her daughter in El Nido, she'd have to find another way.

As another neighbor pulled into the cul-de-sac, Blair waved. She mentioned a prototype, cameras that could identify Ana's ex and alert police. "We'll be among the first to test it," she said.

Ana wondered if the technology would work, or how often it might mix up one person with another. "How will the cameras know who he is?"

The question seemed to stymie Blair, which didn't give Ana much confidence in the technology; she didn't want to be a test case for the company.

When Liam arched his back, trying to get down, Blair released him and he wandered toward the front door, his Crocs pitter-pattering against the brick walkway.

"We'll upload a photo," Blair said. "If you have a photo."

In fact, Blair had planned to use footage recorded from the night of the party, footage she had to pretend didn't exist. Though she had scrubbed it from the cloud, she saved a copy to her hard drive. Doing so made her feel less guilty. The *possibility* was almost the same as taking action.

❁ ❁ ❁

At dinner, Quinn swiped her tongue at a chunk of BBQ "pulled pork" jackfruit stuck in her molars. She felt bloated, bulging, tight as a tick filled with blood. Her parents watched, encouraging her to take another bite, reminding her that she'd agreed to eat this meal.

"Quinn . . . please," her father said. After her diagnosis, she'd never seen him so shaken. So old.

If she didn't comply, they'd install an Orb in her room. She wasn't allowed to go to the gym until she'd earned back the right—swim practice only, but that could get revoked, too, if she didn't improve. After they'd taken away her scale, her barbells, her yoga mat, her resistance bands, her mother caught her doing sit-ups and crunches at 2:00 AM. Last night, she slept on the floor to stop Quinn from doing it again.

She managed to hide a few morsels in her napkin and to fidget, curling her toes and continuously jiggling her leg, which could burn up to a hundred calories a day.

When she scraped her plate into the trash, her mother cornered her. "Has anyone been talking about the party?" Blair asked. "At school?"

Was that a quaver in her mother's voice? Her familiar false cheer, whenever she was upset. Quinn rinsed her plate, avoiding eye contact. "No." Every time she thought about it—that night and what happened afterward—she wanted to hide. She'd left out a lot of details: As far as she knew, her parents hadn't figured out that she'd rented the house or how she'd acted there. In the month since, her parents had been so consumed with her treatment that they hadn't grilled her. But seeing her classmates at Signing Day could have reminded them to ask.

"Anyone DM you?" Blair nervously rubbed a spot on the kitchen counter.

"How could I check my DMs?" Quinn loaded the plate into the dishwasher. "You changed all the passwords!" The doctors had insisted. "And blocked the apps on my phone."

If her parents ever found out she'd hosted the party, that she'd been screaming the N-word, her only defense—that everyone at the party had been singing along—was flimsy. But that collective guilt possibly kept the party photos and videos from leaking out. For now. As the weeks passed, she'd tried to convince herself it would be okay, that someone else would do something foolish and her classmates would move on. She and Jacqui didn't talk about it; they didn't talk much at all, though they hung out with the same crowd at lunch. When she'd tried to apologize for singing along at the party, Jacqui held up her palm and walked off. Maybe more time had to go by, or maybe they were done.

Yesterday, at Signing Day, she'd acted happy, cocky, but inside . . . If only she could have run, her cartilage grinding to a pulp, or swum until her limbs turned rubbery, shaking with exhaustion.

When Luna sniffed at the patio door, Quinn grabbed her leash from the hook. "I'll walk her."

"I'll go with you," her mother said. The coyote hadn't returned since the night of the party, but after dark, they walked Luna in pairs.

At the edge of Rinconcito, Blair gently but firmly told her to slow down. Quinn had sped, almost power walking, and Luna, sniffing here and there, couldn't keep up.

"Cold out," Blair said. The catch in her voice was still there.

An autumn chill seemed brisk and bright as a blade. The air smelled like woodsmoke and moldering leaves, like disintegration.

"You warm enough?" Blair rubbed Quinn's arm.

Yes, Quinn assured her, although iciness seeped into her bones.

"I got an email," Blair added. "Last night."

Quinn tensed. From the therapist? From the police? From SuCasa?

"There was a video." Blair played it, the sound screechy but clear as if she'd been connected to a mic. "Is that you?"

For a moment, Quinn wanted to lie. Claim it was only someone who resembled her, claim it was a deepfake. But she couldn't lie any longer. Though she couldn't bring herself to speak, she nodded. She twitched with pent-up adrenaline: dammed, pooling and brimming, about to spill over.

"You were drunk," Blair said. Her eyes were wild, scaring Quinn.

Was that the excuse her mother wanted to believe? The way Quinn saw it, the alcohol and edible had worked like truth serum. Uninhibited, she'd revealed who she really was. Luna tugged on the leash and they kept walking.

"Who else got the video?" Quinn asked. Princeton? They'd pull the scholarship. Or maybe it would go viral. Trending across the socials, remixed, commented upon, turned into a meme. A poster child for racists. Had she brought it upon herself? In channeling Becky White, she became one. It would be the first thing anyone would see about her if they searched for her online. Every school, every job, every potential friend or boyfriend, would deny her. She'd have to change her name, move to another country.

Luna lowered her head, sniffing, her toenails clicking on the asphalt.

"Why didn't you tell me?" Blair asked.

There were a lot of things Quinn should have told her mother. Instead, she'd betrayed her.

Now Blair was talking about unconscious bias, how Prince Harry had worn that Nazi uniform and regretted it, how he dressed like that without realizing how hurtful it was, because of the environment he'd grown up in. . . .

Prince Harry? "What does he have to do with anything?" Quinn asked.

"He wasn't"—Blair hushed her voice—"a racist. Just like you aren't. You acted like that because of . . ." She gestured around the street, at the neighborhood Quinn had known all her life, where she'd learned how to ride her bike, where she'd walked to school and to her friends' houses. "You picked up this point of view, this *unconscious* point of view."

Quinn felt a flicker of hope. If it couldn't be helped, well then—she wasn't at fault. But if that was the case, no one was: the Karens she'd mocked online or the Ku Klux Klan. Couldn't you argue they were all products of their society?

Luna squatted next to a cast-iron sign shaped like a dog pooping with the word NO! in bright white paint. Blair led the dog away.

"Does Dad know?" Quinn asked.

She preferred his parents to her mother's—Abuela Cathy and Grandpa Jack, who traveled around in an RV and sent her trinkets from their travels to the Grand Canyon, Las Vegas, and Hearst Castle. And she loved the Lopez family recipe for enchiladas, which her father made on birthdays. Quinn never talked about being part-Mexican, not because she was ashamed, but because she didn't feel she had a right to the identity. She hadn't . . . suffered enough. What a fucked-up metric for authenticity.

She used to think Dad wasn't interested in tradition and culture; he'd taken Latin in high school and studied in Florence in college. With his children, maybe he'd avoided passing down his heritage. Maybe he thought he was protecting them. He'd told her about coworkers, classmates, who'd talked shit about Mexicans in front of him, not realizing that he was half.

What she'd done at the party wasn't the same and yet it sort of was, too. "Does Dad know?" Quinn repeated.

After Luna crouched on the edge of a lawn, Blair cleaned up the deposit, the leash jingling. She knotted off the blue plastic newspaper bag.

"No," she said, and the tone of her voice made Quinn wonder if her mother could be persuaded to say nothing. Or maybe Quinn was fooling herself. Her mother would tell him, and he'd never look at her the same way again. His disappointment—Quinn couldn't bear it.

They'd ended up at Jacqui's house, knobby gourds piled by the front door. Quinn had had countless sleepovers here, perfected her cat eye, binged on movies, and nicked liquor from the cabinet, topping off the rum with water. She missed Jacqui keenly, a grief so deep she couldn't breathe. The light wasn't on in Jacqui's room. Had her mother planned on bringing her here? Had she texted Jacqui to come meet them? If so, Quinn would fling herself into the sun. She couldn't face Jacqui like this, like they'd squabbled on the playground and their mommies needed to intervene.

"I haven't heard you talking about her lately," Blair said.

Quinn looked away, glad that the darkness hid her expression. "We're both busy."

Blair shifted the leash from one hand to the other. "You think she could have sent the email to me?"

Something rustled in the bushes and Luna strained at the leash, eager to explore.

"No!" Quinn said, louder than she'd intended. Was her mother so desperate to prove her innocence, she'd blame Quinn's best friend? Friend. Former friend?

"I noticed she wasn't in the video," Blair said.

"We lost track of each other at the party." Even before the sing-along, Jacqui had ditched her. "Half the senior class was there. . . ."

"She could be jealous. Or maybe she's upset because of . . . because of . . ." Blair trailed off. "It was one of those fake emails."

Anyone at the party could have filmed her. It didn't matter who did it, but rather what had been recorded.

"Was it the neighbors?" Quinn asked. Though they'd been camping that night, they could have planted cameras everywhere.

"I don't think so," Blair said. "I get the feeling they want as little to do with us as we want with them."

Headlights swept over them and a car pulled into the driveway—Jacqui's. Quinn wanted to jump into the bushes, but Jacqui must have seen them.

Jacqui got out. "Quinn?" She carried a canvas shopping bag, potato chips poking out of the top.

"We were walking the dog!" Blair said brightly.

"Luna loony bin!" Jacqui smiled, but everything felt strained, as if they were reading from a script with barely enough light to see by. She slammed the car door and locked it.

"Busy day?" Blair asked. "Just getting home?" Her tone was sympathetic, though she seemed to be probing. But Jacqui didn't hold a grudge, didn't plot revenge; she'd drop you instead.

More headlights approached, from a red Jeep. Quinn had ridden shotgun in it many times, the top and windows down, radio blasting, rattling and jouncing around El Nido as though riding a roller coaster. Maddy and Celia climbed out, and when they spotted Quinn, they seemed taken aback.

Her worst fears had been confirmed: Her friends were hanging out without her. They could have gotten used to her absence when she'd been grounded. Or maybe she served as their scapegoat.

"We're working on a group project," Jacqui said. After awkward goodbyes, Quinn rushed home, so quickly that her mother and Luna fell behind. This time, Blair didn't ask her to slow down. Tears pricked her eyes and she had to get into the shower where she could cry without anyone hearing.

At the foot of the driveway, when her mother caught up to her and rubbed between her shoulder blades, Quinn whimpered, "Jacqui . . ."

"Jacqui knows more, doesn't she?" Blair asked. "Whose party was it?"

Quinn always played innocent before, but after seeing the video, after hearing her mother's excuses—*unconscious bias*—after her friends froze her out, she blurted, "It was me."

"I know."

Quinn stared at Blair. "You knew? How?"

"The Orb."

Quinn glanced at the Changs' house. Through the gauzy drapes, she could see the blue glow of the television flashing along the wall. She'd been thinking about her neighbor. After school, she'd spotted Jane arm in arm with Tasha, their heads bowed, laughing. Everything seemed so easy between them. She must have looked at them with such longing that they noticed her. Quinn had turned on her heel and hurried off.

"They have an Orb?" she asked now.

"We do. Several."

"But how . . . ?"

Blair motioned toward the Changs' backyard. She must have trained a camera there, Quinn realized. She'd known and said nothing; maybe she'd been waiting for Quinn to confess.

Quinn tried to explain how everything had sped up and spun out of her control. She wanted to run away, run all night. "Is there . . . How can I fix this?" she whispered.

Later, she would recognize this moment as the end of her childhood, the end of her belief that you could fix anything. She'd been raised to believe that if you spent enough time, enough effort, enough money, then you could right every wrong. The irrevocable could get reversed. But what you broke, broke you, too, the cracks always there, even if patched up, spackled over, never the same.

"You apologize," Blair said. "Not only with what you say, but with what you do."

"To you and Dad?"

"To the ones hurt most."

It dawned on Quinn then: Her mother wasn't talking to Quinn anymore, but to herself.

When Blair looked up at Ana's apartment, Quinn followed her gaze. A shadow flitted across the curtains. The window must be cracked open, enough to let out the clank of pots and then laughter, Ana's, long and low, Sofía's, high and sweet, that carried far on a cold, clear night.

EPILOGUE

Near twilight, the pups bounded from the den, their snouts poking at Wily's mouth. Yipping, wagging their tails, excited and hungry. He regurgitated the partially digested remains of a rat. He squatted on his haunches, panting, as the pups lapped it up.

It was a rare break in the storms that had downed trees and flooded roads for months. Just as the pandemic behavior veered from one extreme to the other from the first year to the third, so, too, the weather: from a megadrought and forests ablaze to atmospheric rivers and bomb cyclones.

Two yearlings—the survivors of Wily's first litter—napped in the shade. When the runt awoke, she pestered her sister. They leaped onto their hind legs, growling and nipping at each other. Their mother intervened, grooming the runt in swift strokes, with the air of a vexed parent brushing the hair of a fidgeting child. Such gestures kept the runt submissive. Ever since the pups had been weaned, Wily and his mate had hunted and scavenged at all times of the day. Soon, the pups would join, learning how, and by the end of the summer, they'd go out on their own, roaming the hills and valleys around El Nido.

Wily never again ventured close to any human, not after the night of the party. The jagged scar on his muzzle served as a perpetual reminder: The sounds, the lights, the yelling, he could ignore, but he would never again risk the silver slash, the wound that could tear him and his pack apart.

❁ ❁ ❁

The flight from New York had been delayed, and by the time Blair climbed into the rideshare from SFO, it was Friday rush hour. She wouldn't get home until dinnertime. The car reeked of fruity air freshener. She closed her eyes, but was both too exhausted and too wired to doze after a long week.

When she'd turned over the footage to the police, she didn't get fired or publicly stoned. She'd been promoted. With the footage—not only from the backyard, but also from the birdhouses, which recorded Julio Morales blowing through a stop sign and veering into a parked car—police arrested him. That evidence, along with Ana's testimony, led to his conviction.

The CEO at the Orb had seized upon the case as proof that *more* surveillance, not less, would protect the most vulnerable in society. And he'd tapped Blair to lead the charge. In her new role, she'd assembled a team of diverse hires, including a Chinese immigrant who had recently suggested an exciting new market: installing Orbs to track wayward seniors who suffered from dementia and got lost blocks from home.

Even as tech giants laid off thousands, even as crypto crashed and a recession loomed, investors kept funding the Orb.

When Blair turned over the video of Ana's beating, authorities didn't subpoena footage from all the cameras, contrary to her fears. Stalling had worked in her favor; authorities never bothered to view footage that would have nailed Quinn as the host of the party.

They also declined to pursue a case against those who'd crashed through the Belles' backyard. After the property damage at 187 Rinconcito had been settled between the past and present owners, there seemed little public appetite for their prosecution. If the teenagers hadn't been so emblematic of El Nido—in their privilege, in their bright futures—would authorities have given them a pass? If there hadn't been so many varsity athletes and student council members among them? The mayor's daughter? All involved would have liked to think so.

Ever since then, Blair tried to live as someone who'd had a near-death experience: fully, taking nothing for granted. Be the change you want to see in the world! But did she make those diverse hires in case the party footage got released? *Look*, she'd say, *judge us by our deeds.*

As the weeks and months went by, sometimes Blair wondered if she'd squandered this second chance.

It was a question that her eldest daughter also asked herself. Some days, Quinn forgot about the footage from the party, but right now—as she crossed campus at the end of her freshman year—she remembered that she had almost lost her future and still could.

Jordan had questions, too, just now, after coming across a stack of passports on her mother's desk. They were going to Paris in August, and her mother had to get them renewed. She stared at the photo of herself as a tiny kid, against a white backdrop. Her expression solemn, and her hair past her shoulders, longer than she'd worn it in years.

Under *Date of birth / Date de naissance / Fecha de Nacimiento*, it stated April 28. Not June 16—the birthday her family celebrated, the birthday the other parents had doubted.

She didn't want to believe that her parents had lied to her. To Coach Ian. To everyone. Because if they'd lied about something so fundamental, how could she ever trust them again?

❁ ❁ ❁

With the Bellavista and other suburban sprawl encroaching upon the wildlands, more patients arrived at the wildlife rescue and museum: a singed owl, a turtle that had swallowed fishing hooks, and a red-tailed hawk with a fractured leg.

Sofía was a volunteer-in-training on Friday afternoons—taking out reptiles and amphibians for show-and-tell, caring for rabbits and guinea pigs—and her shift was almost over. The complex also housed a playground, where Ana pushed Liam on a swing. He clapped his hands and squealed—such a big boy now!

Ana scanned the park, always on guard. Julio had been jailed for a month, and after his release, the court had ordered a year of weekly counseling and classes. Whether he'd been changed—by the punishment, by his illness—she did not know, but he hadn't bothered her again.

Even though the petition for the U visa had been filed, Ana remained in limbo; because of a backlog, several years would pass before it would get considered. Minerva's sister, Di, had taken her on pro bono, promising to see the case all the way through. Meanwhile, her DACA had been renewed, eternally provisional, but better than nothing.

Blair texted to let her know she'd landed and was on her way home from the airport. A good boss, by all measures, above and beyond in some regards, but Ana remained suspicious that the backyard footage hadn't miraculously been rescued by techs. Blair had it the entire time, she and Carolina had agreed.

She never confronted Blair though. She suspected—correctly—that Blair's guilt over the matter led to an extravagant year-end bonus, plus a used car after Ana's catalytic converter had been stolen.

In the fall, Liam would turn three, and she wondered if the Belles wanted to put him in preschool.

"Soh, Soh!" Liam shouted.

Sofía ran toward them. She chattered about today's patient, a pregnant raccoon the staff had named Mrs. Pickles.

Ana lifted Liam out of the swing, and together they walked back to the car. With Sofía settled in, Ana didn't want to leave El Nido, but she could find another way to stay. According to Dr. Washington, the apartments where they used to live needed a property manager, a job that included a subsidized unit.

Though Ana had considered getting a nursing degree, she decided she couldn't spend the long shifts away from Sofía. Recently, she came across a flyer advertising an incubator for immigrant-women food entrepreneurs. Couldn't she and her sister develop tamales and other dishes to suit every diet?

They could get into a commercial kitchen, expand into markets, and hire workers. Someday, she'd give a chance to women like her.

❋ ❋ ❋

Jin dug the shovel into the soil, wet and heavy from the last round of storms. With nothing but sunshine in the forecast, it was time to plant the loquat seedling. Sweat dripped into his eyes and he swiped at his forehead.

Though his shoulders ached, and a blister formed on his palm, he relished the exertion.

After the house at 187 Rinconcito sold $200,000 over the asking price, they'd moved onto their next property in El Nido to fix and flip, on behalf of Chen and his investors. After months of renovations, this sturdy ranch house was ready to go on the market.

Kai handed him a water bottle. He shifted his weight onto his good leg, resting the one he'd broken, the one that tired easily, that sometimes felt as fragile as a honeycomb. While he sipped, she made quick work of the hole. The angles, the force, came intuitively to her. With a big enough shovel, she could have tunneled to the other side of the world.

After the deck collapse and the tangled negotiations that followed, Chen had recognized her talents and had insisted any future deals had to include her. Ever since Chen had discovered Blair's website aimed at Chinese buyers, he'd turned even more bullish on El Nido.

On Jin's visit home last month—his first time back since before the pandemic—his parents had warned him about going into business with Kai, that arguments over money could ruin their marriage. But they'd never been closer, now that he'd conceded to the particular dynamic of their marriage: Kai in charge.

Together, she and Jin lifted the loquat seedling out of the container and placed it in the hole. Jin tamped down soil around it, the damp earth fragrant with invitation and possibility.

"Hold on." Kai straightened the seedling. "How's that?"

He pictured the trunk growing up and up—fifteen feet, thirty—its branches spreading, shading the house, heavy with golden fruit.

Lily emerged from the house, her eyes gleaming as she picked up the hose. "Can I water it?"

By the time the pipa appeared, he'd long since have sold this house. And the next and the next. By planting a loquat tree at every house they flipped, they would leave a mark on the landscape in ways they never could until now.

In the community, too. Of the multiple bids over asking that came in for 187 Rinconcito, the two highest—equal in size—included buyer love letters: from the Thompsons and the Tsais. Neither letter had mentioned their ethnicity, but he'd searched online and discovered the Thompsons were from Jamaica and the Tsais were from Taiwan.

Before the accident, he might reflexively have picked the Tsais. Jin might have given himself a million reasons but for one on why they deserved it over the Thompsons. For reasons Jane had tried to discuss so many times before. The Tsais would have another shot, he suspected, more so than the Thompsons, who hoped to move in before their first child was born.

In the ambulance, as he'd passed in and out of consciousness, he'd worried if Jane had made it out of the party. Why had she lied to them? She went there for the sake of the family, she'd said, and he and Kai believed her. Jane had ambitions about how the world should and could be. Her intentions had gone awry, but hadn't his as well? She cared so much—too much—but from then on, he'd vowed to do more than listen.

* * *

When the street ended, Tasha, Jane, and Marcus continued into the hills. Only a quarter of the houses of the Bellavista had been completed, and at night the emptiness could be eerie, those freshly paved but empty streets, and the shells of houses, getting built out from within.

In the golden hour, the shadows were long and slanting, the air fresh after the storm. They were on the hunt for miner's lettuce, which Tasha would sauté with garlic and sesame oil. Her mother's boyfriend—preppily cute, in a John Legend kind of way—was coming for dinner, and the greens were a favorite of his. He was a friend of a friend, a bubbly woman Minerva had met a few months ago, who'd started a group for Black families in El Nido and helped revive the BSU at the high school.

After the walnut grove burned and had been plowed under, Tasha had mourned, aching for all the trees and flowers and weeds that disappeared every minute of every day.

And yet, each time she came upon what had endured, she soared.

Marcus spotted a patch of the miner's lettuce first. In the after-school classes, he'd learned to make a game of the outdoors.

"It's too close to the trail," Tasha said.

He wrinkled his nose. "Dog pee."

Jane crossed the spongy meadow and pointed at a patch, with the glee of an explorer reaching the north pole. So much miner's lettuce sprouted from the ground that she could have rolled around in it, gotten on all fours and chewed it like cud. She once considered it nothing but a weed, but now, she couldn't stop seeing it. In foraging, and in life. The kind of sight that wasn't surveillance; the kind of sight that made the invisible glow as if under a black light, that exposed what you'd been taught as incomplete. As a lie. A sight that you had to fight for, every time others discounted, dismissed, and demonized it.

They spread out, gathering fistfuls of tender leaves. Mud squished under Tasha's sneakers, the dampness seeping into her socks. This fall, she'd major in environmental science at Cal, close enough to visit on weekends and keep an eye on her brother. Her mother had to wait until she could sell; maybe they'd stay until Marcus finished high school, or even longer.

Tasha surveyed the ridge, wondering if the esteemed Lucinda Stewart had taken in the same view, a century ago. If she could have predicted the rise of her walnut seedlings and would have cried at their demise. About a dozen trees that had survived the fire dotted the perimeter, the first nubs of future walnuts nestled on their branches. Squirrels would carry off and bury the nuts in the fall, and in the following year, some would germinate. Drought or disease could destroy the seedlings, or maybe one or two would carry on the line.

Sunset now, the magenta and pink of a tropical drink, of a volcano. As they turned back, a yearling howled. A chorus of yips and growls came from her sisters, her brothers, and her parents, the call of the pack also the call of home.

ACKNOWLEDGMENTS

I began writing this novel as the world emerged from the pandemic. When so much remained unknown, my community helped me find my way.

Much gratitude to my agent Margaret Sutherland Brown for your tireless support, encouragement, and wise counsel on our fourth book together. I'm excited for all the books yet to come.

The amazing team at Flatiron included Kara McAndrew, Steve Boldt, Leah Carlson-Stanisic, Eva Diaz, Katherine Minerva, Mary Retta, Sara Thwaite, Emily Walters, and Claire Sullivan, who designed the gorgeous cover. A huge thanks to president Deb Futter, publisher Megan Lynch, associate publisher Malati Chavali, and director of marketing and publicity Marlena Bittner. Special thanks to Nadxeli Nieto, for championing this novel early on. My deepest gratitude goes to Caroline Bleeke and Kukuwa Fraser for their generous, incisive editing and good cheer.

I'm grateful for the vital support provided by the de Groot Foundation and the California Arts Council, and the time, space, and inspiration provided by Writing Between the Vines and the Corporation of Yaddo.

Dear friends who read draft after draft—whole or in part—include Kirstin Chen, Angie Chuang, Camille T. Dungy, Yalitza Ferreras, Ellen

Lee, Dawn MacKeen, Valerie Miner, Toni Mirosevich, Aimee Phan, Patricia Powell, Susan Straight, and Maury Zeff.

Oscar Villalon, editor of *ZYZZYVA*, has looked out for me from the beginning.

Thank you, Kirstin Chen, for the nonstop conversations; Dawn MacKeen and Bridget Quinn, for your daily pep talks; Yalitza Ferreras for your eternal hilarity; Angie Chuang for your warmth and brilliance; and Susan Straight for your mentorship past and present. I'm so glad to be in this writing life with all of you.

Others who fortified and nourished me include Irene Chan, Josué Hurtado, Jason Husgen, Susan Ito, Jessica Carew Kraft, Ryan Kim, Reese Kwon, Mary Ladd, Krys Lee, Lauren Markham, Alex Marzano-Lesnevich, Hannah Michell, Beth Nguyen, Elena Passarello, Alicia Jo Rabins, Ingrid Rojas Contreras, Shanthi Sekaran, the Berthaloneys, the Freedes, the Pak-Stevensons, the Taylors, the Expat Draw Group, the IBC Book Club, the Love Boat Crew, the Sewanee Swim Club, Tom Ward and his lake, and the House of Prime Rib.

Many thanks to Trina, Gloria, Phyllis, and Ah Chat for your tender care of my mother.

Much gratitude to my colleagues and students who educate and exhilarate me at the Warren Wilson College MFA Program for Writers, Saint Mary's College of California, the Sewanee Writers' Conference, Aspen Words, and the Community of Writers. I'm indebted to Blue Flower Arts, working diligently on my behalf, and to the Writers Grotto in San Francisco, which has offered support and friendship over the years. Much love to the libraries and bookstores that have enriched my life immeasurably.

The mothers of the Five Families—Ev Chang, Anu Gomez, Ellen Lee, and Aimee Phan—model how to parent and how to keep up the fight.

My family's love and support uplifts me: my mother, Sylvia, and my late father, Lo-ching; my sister, Inez; my nephew Declan; my brother, Lawrence, and his wife, Carenna; my nephew Jake and niece Sarah; my in-laws, Robert and Patricia Puich; and my sister-in-law, Kristine Puich, and her partner, Jeff Elmassian.

To my twins: The pandemic blew a hole through your childhood, but together we endured. You are endlessly curious about life's biggest questions, and I'm so proud to be your mother.

To my husband, Marc: Your faith and belief in me keeps me going, your hand at my back, urging me on. I love you.

ABOUT THE AUTHOR

Vanessa Hua is the author of the national bestsellers *A River of Stars* and *Forbidden City*, as well as *Deceit and Other Possibilities*, a *New York Times* Editors' Choice. A National Endowment for the Arts Literature Fellow, she has also received a Rona Jaffe Foundation Writers' Award, the Asian Pacific American Award for Literature, a California Arts Council Fellowship, and a Steinbeck Fellowship in Creative Writing, as well as honors from the de Groot Foundation, the Society of Professional Journalists, and the Asian American Journalists Association, among others. She was a finalist for the California Book Award, the Northern California Book Award, and the New American Voices Award. Previously, she was an award-winning columnist for the *San Francisco Chronicle*. She has filed stories from China, Burma, South Korea, Ecuador, and Panama, and her work has appeared in publications including *The New York Times, The Washington Post*, and *The Atlantic*. She teaches at the Warren Wilson College MFA Program for Writers and elsewhere. The daughter of Chinese immigrants, she lives in the San Francisco Bay Area with her family.